POLITE
SOCIETY

POLITE SOCIETY

Mahesh Rao

G. P. Putnam's Sons
New York

PUTNAM
— EST. 1838 —

G. P. PUTNAM'S SONS
Publishers Since 1838
An imprint of Penguin Random House LLC
penguinrandomhouse.com

LIBRARY OF CONGRESS CATALOGING-IN-PUBLICATION DATA
Names: Rao, Mahesh (Fiction writer), author.
Title: Polite society / by Mahesh Rao.
Description: New York : G.P. Putnam's Sons, 2019.
Identifiers: LCCN 2018049553| ISBN 9780525539940 (hardcover) |
ISBN 9780525539964 (epub)
Subjects: | GSAFD: Love stories.
Classification: LCC PR9499.4.R3666 P65 2019 | DDC 813/.6—dc23
LC record available at https://lccn.loc.gov/2018049553
p.   cm.

Printed in the United States of America
1   3   5   7   9   10   8   6   4   2

BOOK DESIGN BY KATY RIEGEL

POLITE
SOCIETY

PART
ONE

CHAPTER ONE

ANIA LAY ON the hardwood floor in her bedroom and grappled with her thoughts. If she were given a choice between saving art or literature for humanity, she decided that she would preserve literature. This seemed only natural, given that she was about to begin her third attempt at a novel. Her bedroom contained a number of Edward Ruscha screen prints, recently transported from the family's art storage facility in Gurgaon. But she would willingly give them up for a lifetime of excellent books.

It was not unusual for Ania to contemplate drastic hypothetical choices in this way. The comforts of her own life meant that she was seldom called upon to discriminate or restrict: in the Khurana household, they usually ordered four of everything. As a result, this kind of grandiose conjecture had always come to her as something of an exertion, but also a thrill.

She sat up and looked at the screen prints, a series of disjointed words poured over a burned-orange sky. They were the most recent constituent in the refurbishment of her bedroom, a process that was as inevitable as the seasons, although far more capricious.

Some unexpected good news would involve the replacement of a chaise longue or a reupholstering of the window seat. A foreign trip often resulted in sudden inspiration and a hasty call to Delhi's most exclusive bed linen suppliers. After she had finished reading *I Know Why the Caged Bird Sings,* Ania had decided that the hand-painted wallpaper on the far wall had to be replaced. Its birdcage motif seemed to exude a cruel symbolism. The only constant in the room was the view from the French doors: the reclaimed Andalusian tiles on the balcony floor, the wrought iron balustrade, the rich dappling of the gulmohar trees, and, in the distance, the hum of cars making their way through the grandeur of Prithviraj Road.

The constant redecoration was no secret, and it was often a delicate matter, having to refuse the eager services of the wives of her fathers' friends, many of whom had set up interior design businesses a few years into their marriages. But the Khuranas were firm believers in setting boundaries when it suited them.

"Your aesthetic is simply wonderful, but we try not to mix business with friendship. It would be terrible to jeopardize such a close relationship," Ania would say.

The wives would say goodbye and walk down the front steps of the Khurana mansion, casting a forlorn look at the gleaming white façade, the many sets of French doors that caught the evening sun, the stone urns that looked as though they had been in place for generations. But by the time they had swept out of the driveway, the balm of Ania's expression of closeness would have soothed their wounded pride. In any case, they retained the hope that evidence of their flawless taste would eventually persuade Ania to change her mind. There were, after all, five Khurana homes around the world to accommodate the wives' ceaseless creativity.

The Ruscha prints were gorgeous, but Ania could live without them. She could live without the mismatched lamps and the antique rosewood desk and the perfectly lit dressing room. But literature was not negotiable. She allowed herself the grace of a few moments to think about her new novel. She had finally settled on a title—*The Enigma of My Effigies*—and, as with her previous attempts, this important decision firmed up her intent and clarified her vision. She was now at the next stage of her creative process. She loved names and planned to spend the next few weeks homing in on the perfect ones for her characters. Ludmila. At the moment, she had a yen for Ludmila.

The trouble, however, was that Delhi was so uninspiring. Although only twenty-five, she felt that she had spent many decades trapped in a fishbowl, circling round to the same views and impressions. Something cold and rigid was holding her back. She had never had any doubts about her ability, having been assured of preternatural success all her life; as always, it was a question of the correct milieu in which to flourish. What her creativity required was a glorious new vista, exposure to dazzling minds, a seductive environment, the silvery glint of olive trees as the sun began to dip. She would have to speak to her father about this new enterprise.

She left the room and walked down the length of the corridor to the other side of the house but found that his study was empty. Behind her, the Khuranas' ancient basset hound, Sigmund, lay on an Isfahani rug at the top of the stairs, occasionally blinking with a great sense of resignation.

"It's all right, Siggy," said Ania as she stepped past him, "the world really isn't as awful as you think."

Sigmund closed his droopy eyes, and they remained shut.

At the foot of the stairs, she could see that the lights were on in the conservatory, its blues and greens reflected in the enormous glass panes, but this room too was empty. She walked down another passage, past the screening room. The door was open, and she could see that a film was still playing with the sound low, Humphrey Bogart's craggy face filling the giant screen. So her father was certainly around somewhere.

She eventually found him in the breakfast room, staring at a plate of gray crackers that looked like dog biscuits.

"Are those for you or for Siggy?" she asked.

"Technically, for me. They're from Sweden. They're supposed to increase one's metabolism."

"They're not the prettiest things in the world, are they?"

Dileep Khurana shook his head and looked at her much in the way that Sigmund had.

"Papa, sit down, I need to talk to you. I need to get away from Delhi."

"Why? Is there something wrong with your air purifier?"

"No, I need to be inspired. I need a real change. So, just hear me out, and please don't look at me like that, it's really not a big thing. There's a writers' residency in Italy, which is absolutely amazing, and it's the one thing that will really get me going in the right direction with my book."

"I see."

"I'm completely serious. It's not a holiday, it's work, it's a challenge, it's *growth*."

Dileep began to look at her with greater conviction.

She put her hand on his arm and lowered her voice.

"But it's obviously horribly competitive. People are judged on sample chapters and that kind of thing, which can be quite unfair for a work in progress. And that's why I need you to do me a tiny favor. There's another way of securing a place. We'd have to pay a fee, but the experience will be invaluable, worth every penny. So let's not worry about that. But I also need a letter of recommendation from someone a bit eminent. So could you please ask Alessandra to ask Clarence Lam? They're best friends."

"Clarence Lam, the Nobel guy?"

"As it happens, yes, he did win it, but please don't say 'Nobel guy,' that sounds so gross; it's 'laureate.' The thing is, I've heard he's so supportive of new talent. And Alessandra will obviously do anything for us, and they are really close. I found out that she stays with him all summer on some island in, well, I can't remember, somewhere. So, you know, I think we can swing this."

"Clarence Lam. I don't know."

"Papa, have you ever been asked to check your privilege?"

"Check my what?"

"Oh never mind, it's this online thing. But that's sort of what I'm doing. Lots of writers can't get into this residency by calling on friends. But since I can, why should I take up one of *their* places? I think asking Clarence Lam to put in a good word would be the right thing to do. It's saving other people a lot of time and trouble."

"Except maybe Clarence Lam."

"He won't write the recommendation himself. He'll have people to do that. He just has to sign it."

"I could ask Alessandra, I suppose. But you're serious about this? The book?"

"I've never been more serious about anything. I promise you. You will not regret this."

She leaned over and planted a kiss on his shoulder.

He looked at her and beamed. And it was a beam: an exceptional, coruscating, pearly smile. Dileep had just returned from another visit to Dr. Wiltshire (a seven-time winner at the Aesthetic Dentistry Awards), one of a series of appointments he had made on Harley Street. Although Dileep's hearing was perfectly satisfactory, now in his mid-fifties, what he heard more than anything else was the tick of time. Ania was an adult, his wife long dead, and romantic liaisons thin on the ground. Where did this leave a man like him? A charismatic man, certainly, who could reel off the names of scores of friends and associates; but the question still had to be asked. Money? Everyone had money, some people had even more than him. Power? He often found himself in a group, all of whose members could have gained access to a senior cabinet minister's office in a matter of hours. Respect? Well, for all of those who had the first two, the third was bound to follow.

Dileep had a terror of obscurity and irrelevance, and the way he had decided to distinguish himself was by his youthfulness and vitality. In among the paunches and bare pates of his peers, he was a rare object. He lifted up his shirt several times a day in the privacy of his office and gazed at the reflection of his flat stomach from three angles. He employed the services of a nutritionist who had once worked with several stars of *The Bold and the Beautiful*. His customized smart mattress sent him regular updates on his sleeping patterns. He went sandboarding in Peru and, more reluctantly, Dubai.

His wardrobe too was kept au courant. He had not abandoned his stiff cuffs, gray cashmere, and handmade brogues, but a series of unexpected elements had been ushered in, often bewildering his housekeeper and amusing his business partners. He had a New York concierge service send him vintage blouson jackets; his jeans were ordered from obscure shops in Tokyo. It was only after a great deal of reflection that he was able to decide that the latest trend for pastel-colored suits was best avoided.

Looming always was a great dark mass, the threat of the day when he would bend and sag and crumple in a heap, when no interventions would be able to help him, when he would be exposed in terminal decline. Dileep was adept, however, at keeping the darkness just out of sight. He had had much practice.

He thrived on the compliments he received but affected a genial nonchalance. When questioned by friends, he was forthcoming about some of his pursuits—those that demonstrated his vigor and daring. But he said nothing of the sensible care and maintenance that he felt would be read as gross vanity. His visits to Harley Street, he felt sure, would be misjudged.

He also felt that his ability to be a man who was essentially modern and energetic brought him closer to his daughter. In an odd sort of way, he had begun to seek her approval, and he was sure it came more easily because it was her natural province in which he now paraded.

Ania kissed her father again, this time on the arm.

"Please don't eat those crispbreads; they really look foul," she said, and returned upstairs.

Dileep broke one into halves and then crumbled it into a mound. He pushed the plate away and continued to sit at the table.

He often replayed conversations with Ania, imagining he could divine his wife's opinions and advice, hearing the gutsy laugh that would emerge when she tried to play for time. She had died when Ania was only a few weeks old—but the circumstances of her death meant that he had never been able to find the strength to talk about her to his daughter. There had only ever been perfunctory references on purely practical matters. He knew he had failed Ania in this respect, but he had been powerless to act differently. His sister never spoke of his wife in his presence nor did his friends. In their dark verandahs and chilly drawing rooms, old scandals were always carefully tended and stoked at a great remove from the principal players.

CHAPTER TWO

THERE WAS ONE in most of the grand houses in Delhi, usually beached somewhere on the upper floors. A maiden aunt, once expected to marry and move out but whose failure to secure the right kind of alliance during her vernal years confirmed her as a permanent, if slightly unwelcome, resident in the family home. Around her, the neighborhood would change—apartment blocks sprouting up over gardens, glass-fronted shopping centers replacing cinemas called Eros or Gaiety, an overpass suddenly visible in the distance—and the aunt would see it all from an upstairs window.

No one could understand how Renu Khurana had joined their number, least of all Renu herself. In her youth there had been occasional mutterings that she was too educated, too tall, too fussy, but no serious doubt had been expressed about her prospects. And yet, the years had gone by: a few unsuitable proposals, a couple of halfhearted affairs, and one broken engagement. These days it would be fashionable for her to say that she had struck out on her own and chosen to break the mold; that her way of life, in effect, was a political statement. But that would have been untrue. In spite of her unexpressed desire for a traditional kind of life—a husband, a family—the flow of men with honorable intentions had waned and then ceased altogether.

The Khurana house had gradually anesthetized her, diminishing any desire for an independent life. Her twenties softened into her thirties, and these crumpled into her forties. She quit her job as a museum curator and tired of her clamorous friends. Instead there were plump cushions, thick carpets, a bountiful supply of true crime paperbacks, and a swirl of cream in the dishes that came up to her on a little trolley. With each passing year her face accommodated more of her father's handsomeness, the eyelids becoming heavier, the jaw sitting a little more squarely.

Every so often her thoughts would spark in a particular direction. She had plans to start an art consultancy, matching Delhi's rich with works that would earn them the greatest cachet at the lowest cost. Appeals poured in from charities, requesting her to help raise funds—and from time to time she would feel that she really ought to do what she could. She wondered about moving abroad, perhaps to a Mediterranean island, where she pictured a new and simple life: a large white sun hat, late-night dips in coves, harvesting her own clams. Nothing ever came to fruition. Now in her mid-fifties, the dreams of a new life had waned completely and any new endeavors were modest and infrequent.

One year she had decided to learn Persian and engaged the services of an Iranian tutor. This seemed as though it would be the most successful of her ventures until the young man began to unburden himself to her as they sipped mint tea on her balcony.

His family had fled Iran immediately after the revolution and, having been cheated out of their Paris apartment by a business partner, were forced to seek refuge in India. It was only the beginning of a chain of indignities. He would speak yearningly of the turtle doves that had flitted around the walnut trees in the garden of their Tehran mansion. There had been two servants whose sole duty was to look after the chandeliers. Would it surprise her, he wanted to know, to discover that he went to school in a Daimler?

"And now look," he said, gesturing at the gulmohar-lined Khurana drive. "I have to come here on a secondhand scooter I bought from a butcher."

Renu tried to be sympathetic, but her interest in Persian sprang from a desire to read enchanting verses steeped in romance. She had not really reckoned with the despair of an embittered émigré.

"They used to bow before us and lie on the ground. And then they chased us out like stinking rats," he told her.

Renu couldn't help but feel that this would have sounded a little more palatable in Persian.

WHILE ANIA LOVED her bua's presence in the house, finding in her someone even more indulgent than her father, she was stricken by what she saw as the tragedy of Renu's life. A firm believer in the elemental nature of soul mates, Ania felt that it was never too late.

"I've set up a discreet profile for you online, and I'll monitor the responses," she had told her recently. "Don't worry, I haven't used your real name. And there's no photo. I'm just looking at what's out there. You don't have to do a thing until I put together a short list. You have no idea, bua, but there are tons of creeps out there. Even in your age bracket."

Renu didn't take Ania at all seriously and supposed she would tire of this new pastime as soon as something more diverting came along. In any case, Renu had assumed a long while ago that she would remain single for the rest of her life. She allowed herself no measure of hope: it was too wounding.

While Ania trawled dating websites, squealing or groaning at the expectations of solvent men in their fifties, Renu continued to leaf through wine auction catalogs, even though Dileep allowed her no part in the acquisitions for their cellars.

While Ania's websites yielded nothing, events soon proceeded in an unexpected manner in that most unlikely of locales: the waiting rooms of the city's leading oncologist. Delhi's smart set would not let anyone other than Dr. Bhatia anywhere near their tumors, and the parking area of his specialty hospital was choked with Bentleys and Jaguars. Ania was an occasional visitor too. She considered public service commitments important to her personal growth and would drop in at Dr. Bhatia's hospital whenever she had a commitment-free weekday that took her in that direction. He was, after all, her father's close friend and had assured her that his patients were among the most desolate and blighted creatures in the National Capital Region. It seemed natural that Ania should visit and spread a little cheer in the wards and waiting areas, distributing handmade get-well-soon cards to bewildered patients and chatting with distraught relatives. No one who favored their privacy was likely to object when they discovered that she was Dileep Khurana's daughter.

On one of her missions, Ania was delighted to meet a trim

man with a face like a genial frog, who managed a buoyant air in those most funereal surroundings. Colonel Suraj Singh Rathore, formerly of the Garhwal Rifles, had an aunt who was grimly hanging on to what was left of her life in a south-facing room on the top floor.

"It must be *so* terrible for you, all this waiting," Ania said as a waiter brought their coffees in the hospital canteen.

"Yes, it's about time. Sad to say, but the poor lady should just go. It's much worse for her children, of course."

"Naturally, naturally."

"Just thinking of the fights they'll have over their inheritance is causing them all to break out in hives."

Ania discovered over the next hour in the canteen that he was widowed, with no children, and owned a few bungalows scattered around the Kullu and Kangra Valleys of Himachal Pradesh. He had also been shot in the knee during routine training.

"In India, dear girl," he said with a loud chuckle, "the enemy is very much closer than you suppose."

Ever since Ania could remember, she had played a game with female friends, cousins, anyone of her age who might be around, called "that's your husband." Their gazes would alight on the most uncouth boy, the vilest man, the male most likely to bring forth a great snort of laughter, a shriek equal parts delight and disgust. Leering men with sweat patches under their arms, pimply louts, smelly layabouts with bad teeth: the grosser, the better.

"That's *so* your husband."

But occasionally the game would be flipped, and one of the girls would gesture to a shining specimen and say with a sigh, "You know what, he really *is* my husband."

In spite of the colonel's looks, Ania was bewitched by him and felt that he really *was* a husband, specifically, one who would be ideal for her bua. On her way home, as the driver sped down the expressway, a plan began to fall into place. There would be no problem inviting the colonel to her home—she had already discovered at least half a dozen mutual family friends. The difficulty would be her dear, wretched bua, who seemed determined to spend her days like some sort of long-suffering abbess, albeit one with a colorist trained by David Mallett in Paris.

A drinks evening was arranged, followed swiftly by a dinner, but matters were not progressing to Ania's satisfaction. The colonel and Renu would need a little push.

Ania discussed the problem with her new friend, Dimple, as they returned from their obstacle course training one weekend.

"Arre, it's simple, why don't they go for a picnic in Lodi Gardens?" suggested Dimple.

"Are you crazy? A picnic in a public place?" asked Ania. "But I like the idea of al fresco. Maybe we could have a little quiet something in the gazebo here, or I could get them to open up the private garden at the Tapi museum. Maybe Jérôme will be able to cater. Not a bad thought, Dee."

Dimple almost glowed with pleasure. She had met Ania only a few months earlier at a PR event and was still unaccustomed to the idea that she could be privy to plans involving the Khurana family. She could remember discovering the existence of Ania Khurana on a gossip website a few years earlier in the gloom of her tiny bedroom in her hilltop hometown. To think that they were now friends still seemed an occurrence of great wonder.

In due course, a little table was set up under the jacaranda tree behind the Tapi museum, and lanterns were hung in its branches. Renu barely touched her salmon, and at the moment when the colonel's knee grazed hers, the little garden seemed to turn vast and soundless. She didn't think he looked like a frog at all. A few teas and one lunch later, the colonel proposed.

Dileep was astonished by this turn of events. Years ago he had suffered bouts of minor irritation at the thought that Renu would be a permanent fixture in the house. But he had learned to appreciate how she always deferred to him, and eventually it became impossible to imagine her living anywhere else. He came to view Renu like the rosewood furniture that he had inherited from his grandmother: handsome pieces with sturdy legs that represented a precious link to the past.

And now Renu was leaving to become the wife of a well-liked and charming ex-army officer, a new status that seemed to delight her. The other day he had actually heard her humming. He couldn't help but feel a little overlooked, although he tried hard not to show it. Renu's departure was just another manifestation of the monstrous tick of time.

They all had their reasons to desire a small wedding: the colonel because he hated any kind of fuss, Renu because she thought drawing attention to herself in this way at her age would be unseemly, Dileep because he was not sure how he felt about these developments, and Ania because enormous Indian weddings were gross.

But a small wedding would have been impossible in Delhi— news would get out, and in no time there would be widespread agitation for the right to participate in a Khurana wedding, no matter how antiquated the bride. So they decided to have a quick ceremony in that most unfashionable of foreign locations: London. Everyone knew that the Russians had ruined the place; it was unlikely that it would be overrun by friends and relatives.

The colonel's visa was fast-tracked after a call to a contact at the British High Commission, and they gave the Kensington and Chelsea Register Office notice of their intention to marry. Dileep and Ania would fly in for the ceremony but had been careful to impress upon the new couple that they would be leaving the day after. There would be calla lilies, there would be tears, but Ania was determined that there would also be a grant of privacy and discretion.

Renu and the colonel stayed at the Khuranas' company flat on a little lane off Fulham Road, opposite a shop that sold fountain pens. On their second afternoon they unlocked the gate to the residents' garden in the square but were dismayed to see a sign that said that dogs were prohibited. There seemed little point in being in a park with no dogs, so they took a quick, sullen tour of the paths and left, wet leaves sticking to their boots.

The idea of having any kind of itinerary quickly lost its appeal, and the discussions about museums and matinees petered out. They also soon discovered that a large number of their acquaintances were still unaware of London's outmoded status and, as usual, had come to vacation on Bond Street. Instead of ducking into shops to avoid the Mehras and the Chhabras, Renu and the colonel spent their days mostly in the warmth of the upper deck seats of various buses, gazing out at the quiet streets of Pimlico, making out the Royal Courts of Justice through the drizzle, watching people struggle with their umbrellas on a blustery

King's Road. In the window of Peter Jones, there was a wedding dress that looked as though it was made of cobwebs. The colonel gave Renu's hand a little squeeze. This anonymity felt like a freedom that would not be available to them again. So they kept changing buses and returning to the upper deck to look at London in the rain.

CHAPTER THREE

In Delhi, the winter smog had descended—though in restaurants and clubs there persisted the delusional insistence that it was only fog. People continued to sit on patios and lawns, their eyes stinging and temples throbbing.

In Mehar Chand Market, along one ledge of a café's terrace, giant chrysanthemums and dahlias, planted in ceramic urns in different shades of blue, jostled for attention.

At a large table, a business meeting was in progress:

"We are looking for a range that will have a sophisticated, corporate vibe. But it will be worn by people who aren't very sophisticated, so you have to bear that in mind."

"I'm thinking a palette of grays with a pop of magenta and maybe yellow."

"Done."

Ania sat down at the next table, having set aside most of the morning for some work on her novel. Her main character was a less beautiful and more philosophical version of herself. She nursed a dark secret, as did most of the other characters. These were all to be eventually revealed in the book-lined office of a psychiatrist, the novel's narrator. Before long Ania was deep in contemplation, weighing up the benefits of different venues for her book launch.

Her tisane arrived in an impractical pot with a choice of tiny cups to match the drinker's mood. Ania picked "playful."

Just as she returned to the mysteries to be revealed, she spotted a man in a navy jacket fiddling with the clasp on his case. She recognized that same jacket, worn day after day; the satchel with a broken zipper; the fraying above the shirt pocket: she was convinced it was all an affectation, a way of indicating to the world that their owner concerned himself only with matters of sublime worth and not mere flummeries. Ania and Dev had practically grown up in each other's houses. The two families had spent innumerable childhood holidays together, Dev exhorting his brothers and Ania to look at the scenery while they all ignored him and squabbled over a video game. She now felt that she could almost predict his every gesture. She snapped her notebook shut and called him over.

He approached her table and gave her a stiff peck on both cheeks.

"You," he said.

"You could at least pretend to be pleased to see me."

"You know that it's always a delight."

He turned her cup slightly.

" 'Playful.' I see," he said.

She brushed his hand away.

"Could we please not have some kind of commentary on my character," she said. "We all know how astute and clever you are."

"Don't worry, I wouldn't dare attempt anything so complex," he said.

He turned the cup back to its original position. She noticed the down on his wrist and the network of veins on his forehand. His nails looked as though he still bit them.

"Where have you been hiding? I haven't seen you for ages," he said.

"We're all exhausted and lying low."

"And how is married life treating Renu? I heard the wedding went well."

"Oh, it was a *beautifully* intimate ceremony and she's *gorgeously* happy. It's the most gratifying thing to see."

"You must miss her though."

"Yes, but I'm not even sure I fully believe she's gone. Just this morning I was on my way to her room to ask her something. Then I remembered. But I still call her all the time."

"Is that wise? Shouldn't you be giving the newlyweds a little space?"

"Please. Poor bua would be completely lost without me. I mean, how do you think this marriage even happened?"

"Well, she met colonel sahib, and I suppose one thing led to another. I'm not sure how you're responsible for the whole thing."

"Without me, they wouldn't have met. Actually."

"You can't say that for certain."

"Of course I can. Bua hadn't left the house in about a hundred years. I was the one who introduced and encouraged them and organized all those teas and pushed her and comforted her and told her it would all be wonderful. If it wasn't for me, the poor thing would still be up there watching *MasterChef.*"

"So would you say you were an agent of destiny?"

"You know your sarcasm does nothing for me. I'm not sure why you can't just admit that they came together because of my efforts and be happy for them."

She took a delicate sip of her tea and added, "But I'm sure you have your reasons."

"I am happy for them. But even happier for you. Congratulations," he said. "I'm sure there is a place assured for you in the glorious hereafter. Now, I'd better head back to work."

"Have fun."

"That seems most unlikely. Another afternoon of banging my head against university bureaucracy."

"But don't they just do whatever you say? You being one of their brightest stars, I mean."

"Very amusing. You've never tried to get funding for a lecture series from an academic institution, have you?"

"It's on my bucket list."

Dev smiled and shook his head. Ania caught the resignation in the gesture.

"Wait, tell me, what lecture series?" she said.

"I've been planning a series of lectures on important archeological discoveries that we've made recently. If we don't make an effort to drum up public interest and pride in this kind of work, we'll lose the battle against institutional apathy. All those venal assholes in charge."

"I've never heard you say 'asshole' before."

"You should come to work with me one day."

"So about these archeological discoveries, how are you going to get people interested?"

"I'm going to talk to them."

Dev's voice was louder now. He had straightened up, and he seemed more alert than she'd ever seen him. It reminded her of the times when Sigmund spotted a squirrel in the garden.

Ania wasn't the only person who was taking a keen interest in Dev's alertness. An attractive woman at the next table was eyeing him with an indulgent smile on her face but looked away when Ania glanced at her.

She supposed women did often find an allure in Dev's brand of shambolic intensity. He was tall and occupied space rather imposingly when he was in full flow. His gray-flecked tangle of hair softened his face; there was a light in his eyes that seemed to come from deep within.

"Did I tell you about the find in Maharashtra?" he asked.

"Yes, of course," said Ania, not remembering.

"Didn't you think it was exciting?"

"Oh, completely."

"That's the kind of buzz I'm talking about. If people knew, they'd be so eager to help us. Just think about it: if our preliminary conclusions are correct, we have found the remains of an ancient Buddhist monastery that no one knew about. It could tell us all sorts of things about the spread of Buddhism, trade routes, the tail end of the Gupta dynasty."

He was leaning forward, shoulders tensed, as though surrounded by the ghosts of the Gupta emperors. She felt an immediate ripple of sympathy: partly a desire to help him with a project that he considered vital but also compassion for the fact that these were the matters that governed his inner life.

"Look, I'll call some people. Let's see if we can find some private sponsors for your lecture thing," she said.

"Who will you call?"

"Does it matter? You wouldn't know them even if I told you. You don't know anyone. At every party you stand in a corner, being sarcastic, talking to the same four people. Even your sarcasm is too subtle for Delhi."

"Kamya said the same thing."

"Kamya?"

"Kamya Singh-Kaul."

"You know her?"

"Yes, she's back in town for a bit and happened to witness my terrible attempts at small talk. Maybe I should ask her to help. She seems to know everyone too."

Ania looked for signs of mischief in his face, any hints of a deliberate reference to the frustratingly ubiquitous Kamya Singh-Kaul. But she saw only a clear-eyed earnestness.

"You can ask her if you want to, but there's truly no need," she said.

"You really think you can find some sponsors?"

"Of course I can. Before you know it, the whole country will be stampeding to find out about your monasteries."

"Thank you. I mean that. You're really very lovely when you put your mind to it."

He gave her an awkward kiss on the cheek and walked away, raising his hand high above his head to say goodbye. It did not occur to Ania that the funds for Dev's project could come from her family or indeed his own; their charity extended only to long-standing, prestigious causes. More minor ameliorations to society would have to be accomplished on someone else's dime.

She poured herself a little more tea. The day was getting warmer. She slipped off her jacket and closed her eyes, turning her face up toward the hazy winter sun. The woman at the next table continued to watch her.

CHAPTER FOUR

THINGS SHIMMERED. OR they glittered. Or they gleamed.

Dimple understood that there were fine gradations in the luster of objects, that some kinds of dazzle were far more acceptable than others. But she worried that these nuances would always escape her. In the Khuranas' drawing room, there were silver photo frames and lamps; on an occasional table lay an antique brass candle snuffer. She presumed that these all gleamed in a legitimate manner. But in some Khan Market shop windows there were those resplendent dinner sets at which Ania and her friends would roll their eyes: the wrong kind of radiance.

This business of rightful shine seemed to extend to almost all areas of life. There were saris and belt buckles and curtains and cell phone cases and pen tops and earrings and table legs, all of whose sheen had to acquit itself in an appropriate manner. Dimple looked around the room once more. She supposed she would learn.

Heels sounded on the parquet, and Dimple stood up.

"Hello," she said to the tall woman in the doorway, who was holding a bunch of long-stemmed hydrangeas.

"Do you know if anyone is here?" the woman asked.

"I think Ania is coming down now."

"Oh, well, I'll just carry on."

Dimple had run into Marina before. The woman came to the Khuranas' twice a week with an assistant to see to the flowers in the house. She could probably have dispatched the assistant to replace the arrangements, but if someone had free run of the Khurana house twice a week, why wouldn't they take advantage of it?

Dimple wondered whether it was appropriate at this stage in their friendship for her to make her own way up to Ania's bedroom. They had spent hours there in the past months, but she had always been led there. It was difficult to know what to do.

She could hear the clack of claws on the stairs as poor, ancient Sigmund made steady upward progress. There was a low growl and a snuffle. The clacking stopped. Sigmund had reached the first floor.

Dimple walked to the entrance hall and admired Marina's handiwork on the center table. Through an open door came a faint, comforting waft of furniture polish. Soon she returned to the French doors and, using her phone, took a picture of herself with her back to the garden. Sitting on a bench on the patio, she cropped and sharpened the image, applying various filters. And then she deleted it.

One evening as a guest of the Khuranas at the Delhi Gymkhana, Dimple had overheard the infamous socialite Nina Varkey describing a village in Austria: "It's pleasant, there is a lovely view of the lake, a clock tower, and those charming wooden houses. A picturesque village, but I would say there is absolutely no need to stop there—it's a place to pass through on one's way somewhere else."

Dimple pictured the village as Nina's words ran through her head. They were oddly familiar words. They seemed to her a perfect articulation of how these people viewed her. She had made herself picturesque over the past couple of years, slimmed down to achieve the correct angles, learned to appreciate the value of a great blow-dry. But still the gaze was always fleeting, the interest already on its way elsewhere. Even Dev, the most attentive of Ania's friends, had a dutiful set to his face when he spoke to her, as though he were listening to a hospital patient narrate her symptoms.

These people. She couldn't believe she was in their midst. These people who seemed to have been created to sell newspapers. At best, they allowed themselves to be glimpsed getting into a sleek car or being ushered through a faraway door. But she had got much closer.

Led by Ania, Dimple had seen so many sights for the first time, her face remaining impassive only with great effort. Elderly women, wild with drink, being led down the stairs by a waiter, their diamonds catching the light; duffel bags full of cash heaved onto a table after a game of rummy; girls in high heels asleep in men's laps; a woman made up for a photo shoot breast-feeding her five-year-old son.

She thought of her mother, rail thin, clinging to a personal brand of austerity that even their poorer relatives could not understand. A plea for an ice cream on a hot day was to be refused not because of the expense but because acquiescence was the thin end of the wedge. Her mother was nobody's fool. If there were treats to be had, she would decide when to buy them. When Dimple was ten, she had once stolen loose change from her mother's purse, bought and eaten three bars of chocolate, one after the other, and then vomited them all up in terrified heaves in a gutter outside the coaching center.

She heard her mother's voice again, pitched soft and low, so that the students on her verandah would be forced to concentrate to catch every word. The young men with bobbing Adam's apples and downy mustaches, heads bowed over their texts, creatures of such habit and discipline: early-morning prayers and patriotic songs, the raising of the saffron flag, an allegiance to all that was pure and righteous. Her mother reveled in their shared beliefs, that India was an exclusively Hindu country and should return to its former Hindu glories. And in the room on the other side of the open window, Dimple would also be listening to her mother while using a razor blade to sharpen her pencils, each shaving cascading into one flawless curl.

"I THINK I'M going to try a shorter style for the summer," said Ania.

Dimple immediately stopped her exasperated account of a colleague's idiosyncrasies. She had noticed that Ania, like many in her circle of friends, would change the subject with a startling abruptness whenever it suited her.

"Even the thought of another Delhi summer is making my neck itch," said Ania.

"The summer here makes me long for home. There's nothing like the cool breeze that comes off the lake first thing in the morning."

Dimple hardly ever referred to her hometown but felt comfortable enough doing so with Ania, who had displayed a genuine curiosity about her life rather than a sneering disdain. It was true that Dimple had been surprised at the extent of Ania's ignorance. But she also felt energized at the unusual prospect of being the person who could finally impart some useful knowledge.

"Actually I was in the hills this last weekend," said Dimple.

"Where?"

"Simla."

"Ugh. Why?"

"Ankit and his sisters asked me to go along with them, and I thought, haan, why not?"

"What the hell is wrong with you? You went to Simla with *them*?"

"They're the first people I met when I moved to Delhi, and they've all been really sweet to me. You know, they're not stupid or anything. You can have really interesting conversations with Ankit. And we all went to a fun fair. It was really good fun."

"I can't believe what I'm hearing. Seriously? A fun fair, for God's sake?"

Dimple put her hands in her lap and widened her eyes in apology.

"I'm sorry, but I didn't think there was anything wrong with that," she said.

"My God, if there's anything you've learned from me, surely it's the meaning of irony and context. I mean, we've all done completely ridiculous things but always *knowing* that they are ridiculous and awful. But to actually do them thinking they're normal and acceptable . . . What were you thinking?"

"It was just a bit of fun."

"You're insane. Anyone could have been photographing you. Imagine turning up on someone's Instagram looking like you're having the time of your life at a fun fair in Simla."

"People take pictures of you, not me. Anyway, I was happy to be there."

"Life isn't always about fun, Dee. We have responsibilities. To ourselves."

At the Khurana home, Dimple had seen a small Chola bronze of a reclining Parvati that cost more than the entire apartment building where she lived. Ania owned a sapphire ring that had once belonged to a famous German aristocrat. Dimple's interest and anxiety were not motivated by envy but by a vast greed for knowledge. Who made these things? When? At whose request? Who sold them? And how did they end up in a mansion on Prithviraj Road?

The move to Delhi had been difficult and daunting. When Dimple had first arrived four years ago, there had been everyday arguments in the dirty flat she'd inhabited with five others; a long commute often sharing a single metro seat with two other women; the knowledge that she was being cheated on every transaction by brokers, agents, and middlemen; but now, at last, there was a measure of contentment. She felt that these days she laughed more and worried less, although sometimes when she was with Ania and her friends she had begun to worry more again. At least she no longer fretted constantly about jobs in other industries that paid more and offered increased job security. Her own job was fine, and she found it interesting, mostly, and it had given her the opportunity to meet people who would never have crossed her path before. Her greatest stroke of luck was meeting Ania at the launch party of a restaurant she was promoting at the time. Knowing her tastes now, it was astonishing that Ania had even made an appearance.

"I think a short style for the summer would be perfect," said Dimple.

ALONG WITH HER acts of mercy at Dr. Bhatia's hospital, Ania also paid occasional visits to a shelter for stray cats and dogs in East of Kailash. She never seemed to have enough time to contribute to the paperwork or to help with the cleaning or feeding, so she pitched in by taking selfies with the most photogenic inmates, which were admired by her many thousands of followers on social media. The shelter was grateful for her efforts, as each post inevitably led to substantial publicity and at least a couple of animals finding caring homes.

In some ways, Ania's initial interest in Dimple's affairs could be placed on the same spectrum of charitable instincts as the one that led her to the animal shelter. When Dimple stared in confusion, widening her large brown eyes, Ania's heart gave a little flip. But over time she had become genuinely fond of Dimple and didn't see why the girl shouldn't reap the rewards of a superlative Delhi social life just because of her unfortunate beginnings. These handicaps could be overcome, provided one had an excellent instructor. Ania would be able to impart the gloss that Dimple required, acquaint her with the necessary culture, mention her to the people who mattered. Her experience with dear Renu had taught her that people were often unaware that they required assistance; when they found themselves the subject of a kind intervention, they were usually overcome with gratitude.

In the study fireplace, there was a flare and crackle as the last smoldering log settled. The empty glasses smelled of scotch, and a cold draft pressed its way around the closed door. As she called for one of the maids to turn off all the lamps and prepared to go upstairs, Ania wondered what she could do about the Ankit situation.

She wondered if she was being harsh but knew that she was acting in Dimple's best interests. It would be altogether too depressing to see her end up with someone like Ankit, after all her progress. Dimple would defend him, it was in her nature: he had a lovely face, but more than that, he was respectful and honest; she owed his family many kindnesses. Besides, their business was doing so well; in fact, they were opening a second branch of Tip-Top Fashions soon. But poor Dimple, it would all be such a terrible waste.

Ania saw the cheap cardigans and gaudy shawls in the shop, the nasty sequins strewn on an ill-fitting pair of jeans; she could picture, unwillingly, the apartment upstairs with extra chairs and gas cylinders crammed onto the balcony; the cycle rickshaws outside the shop, their drivers throwing their bidis into the churned-up mud; the sapling outside the door almost dead in its pot.

It was up to her to make Dimple see all this too: that life with Ankit would soon thrum with disappointment, and, even worse, contempt. Ania's Delhi was unforgiving. If it saw a scar or a wart, it turned away for good.

She knew that she had to be realistic. There were men in her circle who would try to unbutton Dimple's blouse in the back seat of a car but would be horrified at the suggestion that they might date her. Dimple had to be protected from those beasts. What was required was a good-looking and charismatic man whose family was not too overbearing, someone who would appreciate Dimple's qualities: her curiosity, her loyalty, her good sense.

She had to arrange matters to Dimple's best advantage. She would make the people she knew accept Dimple in the way she herself did.

Now, who?

Bunty was still unattached. He was sweet and very attentive in bed, apparently, but there was that reptile of a mother to contend with.

She hadn't seen Sohail for a year or two: could he have left Delhi? He was presentable and well-mannered but had an inept air about him. Maybe it was the way his eyes bulged slightly, but he had the look of a man who had never made a woman orgasm.

Satpal was nice enough and from a reasonably cultivated family who wouldn't consider themselves too grand for a girl like Dimple. But God, that earnestness and all those bloody Rumi quotes.

Savio was lovely but too sarcastic to be straight.

Shantanu was probably one of the most handsome men she had ever seen, but, of course, he was all too aware of that. Plus, it was embarrassing to go out with him, he was so weird about tipping.

Fahim.

Ania had known Fahim for two or three years now, perhaps longer; it was so hard to tell. As a journalist, there was a time when no one knew who he was and then, all of a sudden, everyone knew him. He was seen at rooftop parties in Jor Bagh; he would wave from across the room at receptions in foreign embassies; some haughty dame at the next table was always pressing him to have the steamed ginger pudding at the India International Centre. Of course, it was around the time one of his big stories broke, and people did want to know about how he managed to go undercover and whether he was shot at and that sort of thing. But then people lost interest quite soon; and in spite of that, Fahim was still seen everywhere that one went. Perhaps he was still doing stories on unspeakable things. Ania felt terrible that she didn't know and resolved to take a greater interest in his life.

She began to prepare for bed, pinning her hair back, making sure the air purifier had been turned on.

Since her triumph with the colonel and Renu, she was more convinced than ever that providence left little clues for mortals to find, encounters and opportunities that would glow at the right moment in a world humming with hazard. There was, after all, a reason she had recently run into Fahim at an art fair. Someone a few years younger might be preferable, but he was a fine choice.

The hot-water bottle had been filled for her and tucked under her quilt. She put it in her lap as she dabbed some serum under her eyes. The warmth flooded over her lap and rose up into her chest, a little like the warmth she felt when she knew she had been intuitive enough, humane enough, to transform someone's life.

Across the room her phone beeped.

She picked it up, read Dimple's message a few times, and walked slowly back to the bed. Ania forgot that she hadn't yet applied night cream on her neck or her arms and got under the covers, her hands pressing down on the roiling heat of the hot-water bottle. In the dark she listened for another message, but none came after the one she had already read.

"Oh my God, Ankit is here, look don't worry, everything's fine. But I think we're just about to do it. See you tomorrow!!"

CHAPTER FIVE

IT HAD BEEN another bad night for Fahim. The first shades of light were leaking into the room through a gap in the curtains. He dared not look at the time again. His insomnia was always worse when he slept in a strange bed. His eyes throbbed, and he was conscious of the heavy thud of his heart. He swung his legs to the ground and walked to the door. The corridor was silent, the stairs in complete darkness. There were probably still a couple of hours left before morning definitively arrived. It seemed wrong, indecent, to be awake.

The interview with Altaf Masood was a coup not because he was a newly elected MP but because he was an ex-cricketer, a superstar whose number 9 jersey could still be seen on train platforms and street corners all over the country, a name breathed with awe in all the cricket-playing nations. This would be a special profile, filmed in the garden of Altafbhai's constituency home, a relaxed and engaging portrait of the man who promised in his speeches to bring to the legislature the focus and energy he had once brought to the crease.

For months Fahim had persevered, drawing on all his charm and determination to set up the interview. He had met Altafbhai a number of times over the years and had even joined him as part of a raucous drinking group one humid night in Mumbai. On occasion he had told people that they were related in order to get closer. He had courted Altafbhai's managers and publicists, and had asked a mutual friend to introduce him to Altafbhai's wife.

And now there he was in Altafbhai's huge house, in the dusty plains of Uttar Pradesh, so far from Delhi, welcomed like a guest, waiting for someone to bring him a cup of tea. His crew would arrive later that day and begin their checks. Altafbhai had agreed to a quick breakfast to go over the format of the interview. Fahim walked to the window and soon saw the first signs of activity. A man was raking leaves on the front lawn; a wheelbarrow full of firewood had appeared on one of the paths. The curls of mist began to disperse as a hint of gold tinged the clouds.

Some distance away from the main house was a guesthouse, converted into a sort of reception center for supplicants and sycophants. Fahim had spent a couple of hours there as soon as he had arrived, asking those waiting a few discreet questions. They squatted on the verandah floor, they stood around in groups on the hard-packed earth outside, a few stood waiting outside the main gates. From time to time a select number were allowed into the outer room and permitted to perch on the cane chairs. Women were ushered into the stifling air of another anteroom, where the fan refused to budge from the lowest speed.

Sometimes tea was served, sometimes it was not. One lucky visitor might be plied with four cups while the others had to look on. Since these dispensations were an indication of probable success in Altafbhai's office, the scrutiny was relentless. Everyone knew that a grain wholesaler from Kairana was given two Nice Time biscuits on every visit.

This domain was presided over by Altafbhai's assistant, a man whose face bulged in rather odd places, like an angry cauliflower, his countenance matching his bellicose nature. He sat at a desk in the inner room, grunting into one of his numerous phones, glowering at his minions when they knocked on the door and then opened it to peek inside. By some mysterious internal process revealed to no one, he decided who would be granted passage to the main house to lay a request before Altafbhai. Seemingly undeserving petitioners were marched to the house within minutes; others were cast out of the gates for relatively minor infractions, pacing up and down or laughing too loudly.

They came with genuine grievances or solely to spend a moment with the great batsman. Others knew of his personal generosity and arrived with plans for personal development, empowerment, betterment. Altafbhai was renowned for drawing out wads of cash from his pocket on a busy street and handing out money to anyone with a sorrowful tale. His party colleagues were appalled. Patronage and largesse were essential tools in politics, but they could not simply be squandered on the poor.

Fahim was also in search of patronage, and this weekend it looked as though his industry in cultivating Altafbhai would finally achieve some success. But he had not realized that there were others even more eager to show him their generosity.

Ania had called Fahim earlier in the week.

"You need to come over this weekend. It's really important."

"I can't. I'm going to be in Saharanpur."

"Why, for God's sake?"

"I'm interviewing Altaf Masood for a TV special."

"But why can't you interview him in Delhi? And why the whole weekend?"

"He's an MP now. We're doing it in his constituency. It was his idea, actually. It's an in-depth kind of thing. We'll chat in his home environment, where he's comfortable. I'll get to see the kind of work he does there. He's a hospitable guy."

"This is really inconvenient, and I'm sure it's on purpose. Okay, let me know as soon as you get back."

Half an hour later she had called again.

"Fahim, listen, I'm a huge Altaf fan. Can I come to your interview thing? I really want to meet him."

"Since when?"

"Since, like, the first time he batted, okay?"

"Right."

"Fahim, I'm serious. I want to come and hang out with you guys. I think he's amazing. Please, you can swing this."

"I'm *working*, not hanging out. You can't just show up. There are protocols and security arrangements. He's not just some dude."

"Look, tell him about me; he must know Papa. He's not going to say no, and it'll be so much fun. Please, just ask him and see what he says."

"Ania, no."

"You know I'm just going to harass you until you do it. So, speak to him and call me this afternoon?"

Fahim had seen it many times, this appetite for entertainment among her set. It emerged as a hot flare, an acute and insistent demand. And if it wasn't immediately satisfied, it dissipated just as quickly and then rose elsewhere. They were young, rich, groomed, and bored. Their gazes alighted on anything that promised a little diversion, but the moment there was a dip in their enjoyment, their absorption vanished. They often did not mean to give offense; having so many admirers and devotees, they simply did not consider it a possibility. On they went, with their careless endearments and excited intrusions. But as much as he was flattered by Ania's attention, this interview was too important. He would not do anything that might displease Altafbhai and ruin his plans.

Ania had called again late that night.

"Well, you're completely useless. So I've arranged it myself."

"What?"

"Altaf is expecting us on Saturday afternoon, so we'll see you then."

" 'We'?"

"Yes, me and my friend Dee. Dimple? You remember her. We're so excited!"

"But what the actual fuck; you're really just turning up there?"

"Please don't swear. It shows a real lack of vocabulary. And no, we're not just turning up. Altaf has invited us, and it's going to be amazing, so relax. I'll text you later."

He had felt a surge of anger. It had taken him months of positioning and planning to gain this special access; he had barely slept in weeks. Even now he carried with him the feverish prospect that the interview would be called off. And a girl like Ania had been able to inveigle her way into Altafbhai's home with one phone call. It would have been simple, a question only of identifying the most advantageous conduit, and Altaf would hardly refuse the chance to offer his hospitality to a Khurana. A flimsy yarn would have been spun: Ania's interest in television production, her newfound enthusiasm for cricket or politics.

Anything could have happened. Altafbhai could have postponed or even canceled the interview, saying it was no longer convenient. Dileep Khurana's daughter was coming over to play. In that moment, Fahim hated her, hated them all.

But over the past few days his rage had abated. Nothing adverse had happened. The interview schedule remained unchanged. And it seemed as though there was a curious providence at work. He hadn't believed for a moment that Ania cared about meeting cricketers. It had seemed as though this was a sudden amusement, a jolly trip into the provincial hinterlands. But there was something more. He thought of the dark gloss of her hair and her fragile-looking limbs. There could be a real opportunity to become much closer. She had been so much more attentive of late; she had begun to act as if he was a real friend rather than one of the cast of extras in her life. A chink had opened up.

"All you need to do is work hard, put your heart in it, and anything is possible," Fahim's mother would always say, her head bent over a customer's embroidery.

It was not true. Or only partially true.

Fahim had learned that diligence had to be applied not necessarily to a person's work but to the people who enabled that work: the authorities and benefactors, the sovereigns and their gatekeepers. The first step was that most precious of grants: an introduction. Then followed a careful ballet, the choreography of further encounters, managed with constant vigilance and forethought.

The technique could be learned by anyone with a bit of

intelligence and a huge appetite for success, even by a boy who had grown up in the shadows of a tire factory in Meerut. Some judicious flattery, hints of familiarity with their world while taking care not to be caught out in a lie, no sense of challenge, an impression of loyalty, a willingness to acquiesce, a ready laugh. Good looks helped as long as they were the kind that might be glimpsed on an office staircase or in a supermarket queue, not the kind that dazzled on a billboard.

When Fahim first started as a journalist a decade earlier, he had been avid and enthusiastic. He had been punctilious about counting the number of bullet holes in the wall of a military outpost in a remote Kashmir village. A police lathi had left welts on his legs as he had entered the fray at a demonstration in Manesar. He had received death threats for refusing to reveal a source. He had still been in thrall to his mother's advice then, and he did everything with a sense of great responsibility. He felt that he was in touch with a certain kind of honor. As soon as he'd left college, he developed a lightly sarcastic tone that did little to disguise his anger at being the token Muslim, a boutonniere pinned to a lapel to set its wearer off to best advantage.

And then it had slowly crept up on him, the eradication of purpose. The exhaustion had begun to take over, limb by limb. He discovered that his mother had been wrong. He saw capable and industrious colleagues lose their homes and wreck their marriages, and he also noticed the untalented networkers who suddenly began to achieve every kind of success.

Over time, he taught himself their ways. He talked about garden parties and private members' clubs he hadn't been to. It was simple these days: everywhere was photographed and reviewed, some Instagrammer was bound to have violated the sanctity of every secret domain. He learned the easy manner of the young men he sought out, the sudden bright guffaw, the devotion to their immaculate side partings, the cuffs allowing only a glimpse of a superior silver watch. He found the fraud came to him all too freely.

He googled assiduously and scrutinized connections on social media. He studied photos with care: jungle spas in Vietnam; a music festival in Spain; yacht decks in Sardinia, the water almost painfully blue. There were pictures of table centerpieces in Aspen—it was preposterous that someone would find the time and opportunity and inclination to take this photo, but they had. And at such a moment, his eyes would feel like cinders, as if at the end of some long, sleepless night.

Now, he spilled out opinion pieces and had his nose powdered under studio lights. It wasn't so bad being the Muslim of choice, the liberals' darling. But it was not enough; it was never enough. He was still exhausted, sleep still eluded him. His greatest fear was that his background and ruses would be discovered, that mediocrity had a smell that would break through. He had taken credit for the work of others and cast false aspersions on colleagues and rivals as his career had progressed. These had been dispensations he granted himself to balance out the handicaps in his life. There had been no school tie, no foreign degree, no early introduction over a whiskey at the club.

He had made the decision to work only for personal reward— the promotions and esteem that were due to him—rather than any nobler cause. He continued to pursue powerful people, even though the reasons for his attempts were sometimes foggy and inchoate. Having lost sight of what they would do for him, the pursuit had become an end in itself. But he wasn't sure how long he could keep going. A tendon would snap, a capillary would burst: he was sure of it. Even a man with his patience and perseverance could stay wise for only so long. In a short while, during the course of some interminable party, he would hurl a glass across a crowded room.

CHAPTER SIX

DIMPLE LIT HER cigarette as they waited for the driver to return, enjoying the scandal she felt she was creating in the small town where they had stopped. Schoolgirls with ribbons looped around their braids stared at the film star smoke she blew into the air. She and Ania leaned against the back of the SUV, both dressed as though they were going on safari, all taupe and khaki with a hint of animal print. Across the road, a man adjusted the crotch of his trousers.

"Please don't tell me you made a sex tape," said Ania.

"Of course not!"

"Let's see, you used protection, there's no documentary evidence, it's only his word against yours. Not great, but at least I can work with this."

"Poor Ankit, I really don't know what you have against him."

"And how was it?"

"It was strange. I mean, it was fun and all that. But also comforting, as if we had done it before even though we hadn't."

"In other words, boring. What did I tell you?"

"It wasn't boring."

"Yes, well, it doesn't matter what it was. We just have to make sure that he doesn't get the wrong idea about you and become a total stalker."

Market traders had begun to set up stalls behind them, emptying out sacks of cauliflowers and potatoes onto their patches. They indulged in a good-humored joshing and occasionally threw glances at the two women standing by the side of the road in their sunglasses. There was a fat sizzle and the smell of garlic hitting hot oil.

The man across the road was joined by a friend, and they both continued to stare.

"Let's get back in the car," said Ania.

Dimple took a long, final drag and stubbed out her cigarette, her theatricality unabated.

"I still can't believe we're going to Altaf Masood's house," she said, gathering up the magazines that were strewn all over the back seat as she climbed in.

"Okay, listen, I told Fahim I was a huge fan, so if he asks you, just say we're both crazy about him."

"But I actually *am* crazy about him. My God, you remember when he scored that double century against Sri Lanka at Headingley? I didn't breathe for a week."

"You're such a loser. But actually it totally worked that you started hyperventilating as soon as I mentioned Fahim's interview with Altaf. I just knew that I had to call him back. All your cricket knowledge is perfect for what we need. It'll make you shine in front of Altaf and, more important, Fahim. I have such a good feeling about this."

Dimple looked as though she was about to say something.

"What?" asked Ania, her tone sharper than she had intended.

"Nothing," said Dimple.

The driver appeared with bottles of cold water, and in a minute the SUV sped off, showering pebbles and gravel onto the verge. One of the schoolgirls stepped away from her companions and continued to stare until the car disappeared from sight.

ANIA AND DIMPLE arrived just as the crew was wrapping up for the day. Altaf had disappeared a couple of hours ago, and there was a strangely festive atmosphere. Ania took in the house's enormous façade, stippled with columns, porticoes, and balconies, all insisting on their artistry. An underling was dispatched to turn on the fountain as they approached the front entrance, but the water supply had unfortunately run out.

There were innumerable introductions, refreshments were offered, their bags were taken to their rooms. Fahim was at his most charming, and Ania knew she had made the right decision. She thanked him for all the trouble he had taken, urged Dimple to tell him all about the fistfight they had seen en route, and assessed the pair with a practiced eye. As they sipped their drinks, the late-afternoon sun freckled the verandah floor. Squirrels darted across the lawn. Overhead they could hear a tiny rustling in the trees.

A short while later, Altaf walked into the room and everyone stood up. He was more handsome than he appeared in the advertisements for the dozens of products he had once endorsed. It was true that the physique of a sportsman in his prime had made way for a different kind of build: there was a thickening around the waist, a softening around the belly. But if he represented any kind of decline, it was a magnificent one, a replacing of one kind of allure with something gentler, more accessible.

"New friends," he said, smiling at the group. "This month has really been the month to make new friends."

Fahim made the introductions as though this gathering had been a long cherished ambition.

"I'm so pleased to meet you finally," said Ania. "You know, I've watched all your matches."

"Welcome," said Altaf, turning to smile first at Ania and then at Dimple. "No, no, it is my pleasure, thank *you* for coming. You have made me very happy."

Dimple let out a soft, low sound like a wounded animal.

"Come, let us sit and talk. But not here. Out on the other side, near the rock garden. It is beautiful at this time. Unfortunately my family is away on holiday in California. They would have loved to meet you too. I have just come back from there, in fact. My wife only likes these places where no one plays cricket as it means I am left in peace."

The group trailed after Altaf through the public parts of the house as he pointed out improvements he had made or mentioned his plans for his constituency. He carried a sense of spectacle around with him from room to room. His strides were long. He looked as if he might execute an elegant swing with an imaginary bat at any moment. On the verandah Dimple continued to be mesmerized, wiping her clammy palms against her seat, nodding at anything that was said. Ania too felt herself swept along by his charisma. He had a deep chuckle that delighted her. He used it often and indiscriminately, seeming, more than anything, to be laughing at his own good fortune, at all this abundance that he now wished to share.

"You are a writer?" he asked Ania.

"Yes, I'm working on my novel, but who knows," she said with a modest shrug.

"I am sure it will be wonderful. I will read it. I will ask all my party workers to read it."

"Oh, thank you so much, you're too kind."

Altaf turned to Dimple. "Fahim said you are a member of Miss Ania's staff?"

"No, I am not her staff," she said, casting a nervous look at Ania.

"Not at all," said Ania. "Dee is a very dear friend. Did you really say that, Fahim? There must have been some misunderstanding."

"Oh, yes," said Altaf. "These misunderstandings are very common, especially in Western UP. So, Miss Dimple, you're also a writer?"

"No, no, I don't write anything. I mean, some things obviously, but not like her. I work in PR. Publicity for start-ups."

"Excellent. I am very much in favor of start-ups. This is how our country will come forward, through the vision of our young people who are all so brilliant. I will take you to the engineering colleges of this area. You will see what brilliance we have here."

"Yes," said Dimple, the word catching in her throat.

Altaf's phone rang, and he excused himself with a delightful bow. They all watched him leave, vaguely aware that this was how infatuations began. But they also knew that Altaf was a man accustomed to infatuation and that he would treat theirs with kindness and understanding until it retreated and settled into mere adoration. Ania never voted, but here, finally, was a politician who could win a tick in the box from her.

THERE WAS STILL quite a bit of filming to get through the following day. The crew had been put up in one of the outbuildings, and Fahim spent the morning there, preparing for the shoot. Ania's time was taken up with a lengthy search for her tofu extract face-cleansing capsules, which had slid to the bottom of one of the two large cases she had brought on the weekend trip. She had also carried a vintage hat box, thinking that it would contribute to a charming picture if paparazzi photographed her anywhere en route. The hat usually housed in the box was unsuitable for the trip, so the box was empty.

"What's in the round box?" Dimple had asked as they set off.

"Nothing, it's empty," Ania had said without further elucidation.

For Dimple, it was another mystifying aspect of Ania's life, a practice to try to decode later, during a break in her office work.

Ania and Dimple had buttery parathas for breakfast, hoodies thrown over their pajamas. Then they walked to the guesthouse, amazed at the number of petitioners there, the queue that stretched toward the front gate and did not seem to move.

"It reminds me of Shivratri in Nainital, all the people waiting to enter the Mukteshwar temple," said Dimple.

Ania looked on in generalized sympathy. It reminded her of nothing. She had not stood in line for anything since boarding school in England.

Later they lazed about on the verandah, chatting and checking their phones. Ania mentioned Fahim from time to time, nimble little references to the awards he had won and the friends they had in common.

"So what do you think of him?" she asked finally.

"He seems so great, such a professional at all this."

"You know that's not what I mean."

Dimple knew that Ania's actions were often influenced by a range of motives, all benign but involving a complex network of social obligations and strictures. At first, on their way to Saharanpur, she had not even bothered to try to puzzle any of them out. The imminence of the encounter with Altaf Masood had been too overwhelming. But now Ania's intent had become clearer to her, and she found herself swept along with the general euphoria.

She said, "No, what I meant is Fahim is really great. Funny, handsome, great."

Ania looked satisfied and swung her legs off the sofa.

This was no longer the real world. She was on an adventure and felt able to suspend all normal rules. The house had a touch of theme park for her—it was a place where she could sit and shriek in a giant teacup or eat sweets until it was time to go to bed with a stomachache.

"Let's have a look upstairs," she said to Dimple.

"I don't think we can just wander around his house."

"Why not? He's a public servant, and we are taxpayers. We have a duty to see what he's up to. Come on."

The first-floor corridor was lined with large framed photos of Altaf, in cricket whites, in the national team colors, at the wheel of a sports car, a formal portrait with his wife and children.

"She's pretty," said Dimple.

"Fabulous eyelash game," said Ania.

They caught a glimpse of what looked like the master bedroom: a bedspread of pink silk, a white dressing table, touches of gold. It was difficult to imagine Altaf in that boudoir, his large male presence among those frills and tassels—he was a man who looked like he would happily bed down in a barn.

At the end of the corridor a servant asked them if they were lost.

"No, not all," said Ania. "Altafbhai has sent us. You carry on."

Dimple was aghast at the liberties they were taking but managed to find it within herself to follow Ania through the house, her gait determinedly casual.

They walked through a family room, leatherette sofas mushrooming from every wall, a games console in front of a giant screen. Up a short flight of stairs, they could see another corridor, curtains drawn over its windows. This part of the house looked largely unused. A musty sourness seeped from the ceiling.

They walked on, peering into rooms. In one they saw a roll of bedding and a plastic clothes horse, in another a mass of bathroom fittings—taps, rails, brackets—all scattered across the floor. A room at the end of the passage contained a life-size bronze statue with angel wings, its head crowned with a lampshade.

They walked into the room for a closer look.

"Do you think she turns on?" asked Dimple.

"I can't see a switch," said Ania.

"Her ass is even bigger than mine," said Dimple, giving the statue's bottom a sharp slap.

The bulb under the lampshade sparked alight, and both women screamed.

"Oh, do it again. No, let me," said Ania.

They took turns at turning the lamp on and off, rapping the bronze buttocks with their knuckles, choked with laughter. A maid heard them and hurried into the room, panic written all over her face.

"Is something wrong?" she asked. "Shall I fetch sahib?"

"No," said Ania, composing herself, "we just came into the wrong room. Is there a way out at the bottom of that staircase?"

They left the house, still snorting and setting each other off, their faces freshly beautiful with their abandon. Again they were asked if they were lost or whether they needed anything. They passed through the vegetable garden and spotted a door set in a high wall. It was unlocked and led to steps bordered with potted palms and tubs of marigolds. Here the grounds felt cut off and private.

They walked around a hedge and saw the swimming pool, an egg-shaped affair, its green water a little murky. A head crowned with a great rosette of hair was making its way up to the far end.

"Wonder who that is," said Dimple.

The head turned around and began its return journey.

"That pool looks like it hasn't been cleaned for a hundred years. She'll probably be dead by the time she finishes her next lap," said Ania with a shudder.

They both squinted as the head approached the near end, its neck still firmly erect, chin raised high. The breaststroke was stiff and tentative, the kicks feeble, as if the swimmer was as disgusted by the water as the spectators.

"That can't be his wife. Didn't he say she was away?" said Ania.

"Do you think it's his *mistress*?" asked Dimple.

"I don't think she would be allowed to swim up and down in front of everyone like this. I mean, there are party workers and constituents and, for God's sake, a TV crew."

The head reached the pool ladder, and two slim arms emerged from the water to adjust the rosette. The resettling complete, the head turned around and set off again.

"She's too old to be his daughter," said Ania.

"Sister?"

"Does he have one? No idea. Let me google," said Ania, reaching inside her handbag.

The sun dipped behind a cloud, turning the water a cloudy gray. The frail kicks continued.

"Two brothers, no sister," said Ania.

"Maybe she came with the house," said Dimple.

They walked back to the house, arms linked, looking forward to lunch.

FAHIM HAD FINISHED filming for the day and was on the front lawn telling Dimple about his preferred techniques to draw information from an interviewee. Ania joined them where they stood under a giant neem tree; matters seemed to be progressing well, but she had to guard against any complacency. According to Fahim, it had been a great day; and when the interview aired, they were really going to break the mold. Audiences were accustomed to seeing politicians thundering at them from a podium or looking stiff and surly in a studio. Earlier that day, they had filmed Altaf rustling up some eggs in the kitchen to make him seem even more accessible and unassuming—though the cook had been on hand to help, as Altaf had never handled an egg in his life.

Dimple appeared to be listening to Fahim as though he might ask her to repeat it all verbatim. Ania took the opportunity to leave the room and slip upstairs.

Everything in their guest room was oversize: the twin beds with the massive headboards, the reams of heavy curtains, the fruit basket covered in printed cellophane. The spikes of the enormous pineapple had easily broken through. Ania sat on the edge of a bed to perform her facial yoga and then allowed herself to lie back.

She called Renu to give her an update.

"I'm supposed to be going on a short trip tomorrow at sunrise with Fahim and Dimple. There's some sort of fort here that everyone keeps insisting that we see; poor things, it's their one tourist attraction. So I'm going to pretend I'm ill and drop out. I'm sure that if they're left alone for a couple of hours, something will definitely happen."

"Still matchmaking? I'm the auntie, remember, not you."

"Oh, but, bua, if I didn't bother, where would you and the colonel sahib be?"

"Yes, of course, you hardly need to remind me. Without you, my dear colonel would never have come into my life. Although, I should probably tell you that it all happened a lot sooner than you think."

"What do you mean?"

"Well, very soon after that first meeting, we both knew. And at our age it's really not advisable to dillydally. So we were meeting each other at various times and places right from the start. Mostly at my friend Mona's home."

"But, bua, how terrible of you. How could you not tell me?"

"You're not really surprised. You had an inkling, didn't you?"

"I promise you, I didn't."

"I'm sorry, you seemed to be having so much fun arranging all those teas and whatnot. Neither of us had the heart to spoil your fun, and we were, of course, so grateful to you."

"Well."

"You're the sweetest thing. Now, I think you should go ahead and see the fort tomorrow. You've gone all that way, after all. It would be such a shame to miss it. If Fahim and Dimple are interested in each other, things will proceed naturally once you all get back to Delhi. Now, call me again whenever you can, darling. Lots of love."

Ania couldn't help feeling a tiny bit annoyed with her bua and the colonel for their chicanery. There really was no need to creep about behind her back. It seemed a little unappreciative after all the trouble she had taken.

On a whim, she called Dev. It was a habit that annoyed him, since he preferred only to text, but she felt cajoling him into conversations would make him less socially awkward, another helpful endeavor she had embarked upon.

"Are you busy? You sound distracted," she said.

"I was just getting ready to go out."

"Where to?"

"On a date, if you must know."

"How *thrilling*. Anyone I know?"

"No."

"Don't be ridiculous. I know everyone. So who is she?"

"I'm not telling you. By tomorrow morning it'll be all over Delhi."

"Wow, this secretiveness must mean that she's a major embarrassment. But I really won't judge you. Is it a proper date or are you just hanging out?"

"Is there a point to this call?"

"You're always saying how I never travel within India and I'm so out of touch. So I wanted to tell you that I'm in Saharanpur and it's pretty amazing."

"What are you doing there?"

"Social work."

"You?"

"Really, I am. Putting all my efforts into a great cause. But coming back to your date, could I ask, what are you going to wear?"

"A kimono."

"Oh, shut up."

"When have you known me to wear anything other than what I always wear?"

"So, who is it? Is it that psycho you were dating a while ago? The one who bit you?"

"No."

"Is it Mimi Faujdar?"

"Definitely not."

"Oh my God, could it possibly be Ariana?"

"What is wrong with you?"

"I can do this all night."

"I can't. Good night. I hope the good people of Saharanpur realize how fortunate they are to have you in their midst."

THE WEEKEND HAD gone from being a theme park visit to a camping holiday. Dinner was set up in a clearing in the mango orchard, lights glimmering in the trees, a bonfire casting a fierce glow. One of the television crew members got out his guitar. Ania did her best to secure a quiet spot for Dimple and Fahim, but the evening was far too loose and chaotic. Altaf drifted around, chuckling into his phone, and Fahim would appear at her shoulder, urging her to have another drink and then disappear, just as she managed to get tipsy Dimple to one of the outdoor sofas, arranged there for the evening.

As a server brought her another drink, she saw Altaf emerge through the trees. She followed him, emboldened by the weekend's enjoyment.

"I'd like to thank you again for all your hospitality," she said.

"Please don't mention it. My pleasure."

"It's been so lovely. We spent some time by the pool this afternoon. There was another lady there too."

It was as though a veil came down over Altaf's bonhomie. He stayed silent.

"We didn't get a chance to speak. Is she a relative?" she asked.

After a pause, he said, "She is a friend who is having a difficult time."

He gave her an almost imperceptible nod and slowly turned away.

Even his reproach had been perfectly executed. Ania felt diminished all of a sudden, aware that her sense of abandon had led her into a mortifying lapse of decorum. When she looked toward the bonfire, Altaf was nowhere in sight. In spite of the people walking past and the loud talk and the clatter at the buffet, she had the unwelcome sensation of being all alone. She walked around the clearing and finally spotted Dimple on a sofa, her head lolling about.

As soon as they got to their room in the main house, Dimple fell asleep facedown on the bed, one shoe still on her foot. Ania slipped it off and covered her with a blanket. She began her nightly cleansing and moisturizing rituals, a routine that had only been interrupted once, during her bout of appendicitis. Many of the older women she knew flew to Innsbruck for periodic rejuvenating blood transfusions, apparently the only foolproof skincare regime. But Ania had opted instead to supplement her tofu extract face-cleansing capsules with seaweed skin patches and an oxygenated mist in a sheathed canister couriered to her from a hilltop in New Zealand.

She slid open the balcony door and stepped outside. The temperature had dropped fast, and she wrapped a shawl around her, covering her head and ears. She scanned the grounds and could see groups of men huddled around braziers, dogs rooting under the trees. A quarter moon hung weakly in the distance. What she felt at this moment in her life was a deep sense of satisfaction. Its warmth came to her from many directions, and she was enjoying it too much to look closely for its precise source.

All her plans were progressing in the right direction; it was only a question of patience. There was a sense of everything being on hold till the next day, insects *click*ing and *whirr*ing to mark the time until the petitioners and the officials would return to the waiting room and the sweet tea would begin to flow again.

CHAPTER SEVEN

DIMPLE WOKE THE next morning to loud moans from Ania, followed by an earnest explanation that she was suffering the worst cramps of her life. There were anxious offers from Dimple to cancel the trip, each of which was met with a stoic and determined refusal. This was probably the only chance Dimple would have to see the surrounding countryside; it could not be foregone.

Dimple did not dress for a date, but she took far greater care than a morning visit to a fort merited. It was too early for makeup, but she gave her eyelashes a lick of mascara; there was a quick spritz of the more expensive perfume; her top was simple, white, suggestive of advertisements for healthy juice drinks. Ania approved because she thought it would be what Fahim would appreciate. Ordinarily, her rule was to dress for one's shape and personality, never for boys; but once in a while a girl could toss a boy a bone.

Dimple followed Ania's advice with care, but she was equally cautious about appearing to imitate her or wanting to *be* her. In any case, it would be a futile exercise. Ania was a good few inches taller, her features so much more delicate and precise, and her hair was a tumble of rich and complex browns, as though it was always catching the sunlight, so unlike Dimple's own weekday ponytail, jet-black and severe. And Ania carried herself like a dancer, even when she was barely moving, even if her hands were simply gesturing to emphasize another one of her confident assertions. It was all so far removed from Dimple's own stiffness, never knowing what was required, a handshake or a hug, one breezy kiss or two, or simply a respectful nod of the head from a safe distance.

Naturally, Dimple had been convinced that many of Ania's secrets would be uncovered in her bathroom. But when Dimple finally saw it, she was only further confounded. Half a dozen steps descended to the contoured tub. On the other side of the bathroom, complex sets of nozzles and faucets gleamed behind an enormous glass wall. For some reason a divan lay under the window, in the shadow of clusters of white roses. Dimple's disloyal prying had made her heart thud as she opened the cabinets to examine the great assemblage of bottles, tubes, and sprays. The most surprising fact of all was that Ania did not shut the door when she disappeared to use the bathroom. As Dimple sat in the bedroom, Ania's conversation would continue, a gentle tinkle hitting the porcelain, followed by the sound of the flush. Dimple would have assumed that this kind of exhibitionism was a sign of complete vulgarity, but it showed how wrong she was in so many areas of life. She tried it in her own home when her roommate was out. She settled down with the bathroom door wide open, trying to relax, her gaze fixed on the wall's peeling plaster. And then moments later she heard her roommate's key in the front door. She scrambled and stumbled to slam the bathroom door, her underwear still around her shins, almost breaking her nose in the process.

As Dimple waited for Fahim, she doubted Ania's wisdom for the first time. There was no convincing reason why Fahim would be attracted to a woman like her, obviously provincial, still at times cloddish, when he had the pick of those sophisticated gazelles at media parties. Ania had kept insisting she could see the signs, but Dimple was worried about the dangers of being wrong. It had taken her months of discipline and training to calm the anxieties that assailed her—worries about her position as some kind of interloper—and now her equilibrium was again wrecked. Ania was too fearless and her friendship too effortless, spilling from her without consequence, leaving a trail of easy generosity and advice. For Dimple that same friendship offered elation and play but also apprehension and uncertainty, a fear that it would all collapse and crumble to dust. She felt a brush against her shoulder.

"Sorry, I'm a bit late," said Fahim.

Dimple explained that Ania was unwell, and he showed the greatest sympathy.

"I think we should cancel," he said. "It doesn't seem right, merrily sightseeing like this when she is so ill."

"She's not exactly ill but, yes, I think you're right."

Behind them, a throat was cleared. In spite of their protestations, a guide had been foisted on them, and he was not going to be done out of this opportunity.

"What do we do? He came ages ago. Maybe we should just go. Ania really won't mind," said Dimple.

Fahim looked at the guide, who maintained his steady gaze.

The guide and Dimple headed off in the direction of the car. Fahim followed.

He seemed to sleep most of the way in the car, although the dimness made it difficult to tell. As soon as they arrived at the road approaching the fort, the guide began his recitation of its history, heedless of his audience's attention. On Fahim's side, the car door slammed.

They walked up the narrow path, Fahim shining a flashlight and turning to make sure Dimple did not need his help as she followed. Behind them, the guide continued to name dates of key battles and conquests. The first wash of light seeped over the battlements. Birdsong filled the air, dense layers of animated conversation; but as Dimple looked around, from the lush foliage of the neem trees, across the craggy outer wall of the fort to the scrub beyond, there wasn't a bird to be seen. They stopped for a few moments to watch the light strengthen with a kind of guile, the sky taking on a little more pink, fine tints of ochre appearing across the towers.

The guide's tale had moved on by a couple of centuries. They followed him through a narrow gateway and past an empty water tank. He scrambled up a little path toward the gaping arches of a row of caves.

"There is an underground spring that flows above these caves. It was first discovered some three hundred years ago," he said.

He beckoned them over to the farthest cleft in the rocks.

"No matter what the season, the water flows right overhead and into a sacred pool in the cave. Of course, during the monsoons, the water pours down, but even in the driest summer, there is always a trickle. During our worst drought, the water never stopped. Truly, a miracle. You can go inside and see," he said.

Dimple looked at Fahim and asked, "Do you want to?"

"You must," said the guide, "never again will you get such an opportunity."

Dimple took off her shoes at the narrow entrance and stepped into the cave. It was like slipping into a dark lake, the chill washing over her. The splash of the water echoed around the small space, making it difficult to know where it flowed, through some distant fissure deep in the cave or down the walls around her. She ran her hand across the cave wall, smooth and damp, broken by sudden knots and ridges.

As Fahim stepped in behind her, she discovered that he was close enough to smell. She caught a hint of citrus cologne and something else, a smell she imagined to be his warm skin, the night's sleep not yet scrubbed off him. She turned, her shoulder grazing his arm. In the curve of light stolen from the day outside, she could see the paleness of his shirt, the way it creased over his chest.

"I think we have to crouch down and go farther if we want to see the water," she said, her voice rushing at her ears.

He did not respond. They remained immobile, listening to the whoosh and gurgle. In that moment, all her doubts vanished. She knew that if she lifted her head up and closed her eyes, he would take her face in his hands.

Echoes sounded in the dark space: the burbling of the water, her own short breaths. The chill now rose up through her, beginning at her feet, a combination of desire and caution.

"I think we should leave," he said.

He turned and ducked, making his way out of the cave.

She stayed for a moment longer and then followed him, certain that the long pause in the darkness, the silent contemplation, meant that he had felt it too.

ANIA TRIED TO catch up with her social media but gave up, realizing how ridiculous it was to dart from the balcony to the bedroom window and then out again to the staircase and then to the front lawn, all in an attempt to get a proper signal. She took her magazines with her to the verandah and flicked inattentively through them, her eyes drawn to the activity on the grounds. Already small groups were forming for little conferences under trees and outside the guesthouse. Several members of staff asked her whether she required anything, and even after she had smiled them on their way, she knew that they were keeping a watch on her, as though she was an unpredictable, skittish creature who could take a sudden turn.

Fahim and Dimple were still not back from the fort, which could only be read as a good sign. Ania wondered whether women often found flimsy pretexts to arrange appointments with the handsome journalist, made errors and forgot vital details as they lingered in his presence, addled with desire. He certainly aroused no such feelings in her: there was an odd gnawing presence about him that made him seem ill at ease, unable to tell when a conversation had ended or to register anything said in irony.

She had also noticed that he would proffer names—politicians, broadcasters, actors—as though he were testing people's reflexes. He seemed to think that he was doing it with a winning breeziness, but it was all a bit pointless and hardly to be encouraged in the long term. She would have to think of a subtle way of bringing it up at some point. But for now, she thought it was oddly endearing. All this bluster, whether true or not, was obviously for Dimple's benefit. He was confident that he could grandstand his way to her heart. Men were such unevolved creatures, and it was a matter of serendipity that women were often won over by their bungling guile. Certainly, Fahim was lucky that Dimple was impressed by famed personages, or at least had the good grace to pretend. Ania stretched her legs out in a patch of sunlight. Every time she thought about Dimple and Fahim, she felt a warm rush of gratification.

And in addition, Dimple excelled at something men prized in women: the ability to listen. She leaned forward and drank it all in, her eyes limpid, with barely a blink. She made her speaker feel extraordinary, essential. She was also surprisingly adept at plainspoken one-liners. Ania knew that Dimple did not even intend to be witty, but her lack of pretension often cut through the imperious bombast that surrounded them. The reason Ania had remembered her from their first meeting and decided to invite her to a brunch was because of her deadly but inadvertent diminution of the corporate blowhards who were running the event.

The birdsong that surrounded her, the rhythmic sound of a hammer wielded nearby, the rustle of the magazine pages as they fluttered under the ceiling fan, the occasional tinkle of wind chimes: it all gave a slowness to the day, lengthening the hours, keeping anything unexpected at bay. Ania was confident of success. She could already imagine the interest rising in Fahim, turning to love, the great churn of it all when they returned to Delhi. And when they mentioned it to her, Ania knew it would be proper to give them a modest shrug and deny that she had played much of a part.

CHAPTER EIGHT

DILEEP HAD THOUGHT the feelings would settle in a few days or even weeks, but he continued to be troubled by a vague malaise. He was happy for Renu—she had found a remarkable match in the colonel, an affable man who seemed to be able to get on with everyone. Did he miss her? He could not really say. But her departure had brought about a definite shift, a crumbling.

He was reluctant to speak to Ania about his feelings. She would feel sorry for him, chastise him for being silly enough to feel alone, and smother him with a sincere but distracted love. It would be humiliating to be pitied by his daughter.

He went up to Renu's old wing and for some reason knocked on what used to be her door. He opened it and looked at the drawn curtains and the dustsheets on the headboard. Her books were still there, but the photographs had gone. He closed the door and went back down to the kitchen. The pantry spotlight splashed the tiles with a tinge of blue—it looked as though the room were slowly drifting underwater. He ate everything he could find: he cut himself wedges of Parmesan, emptied packets of cashew nuts into his palm, chewed on cookie after cookie, standing at the window. Later that night, he was in so much discomfort that he had to lie on the floor in the study, waiting for the stomach cramps to subside.

In the morning he weighed himself and spent forty minutes longer in the gym. And then he did what came most naturally during times of crisis. He called Nina Varkey.

DILEEP AND NINA had slept together on four occasions. The first time was on his eighteenth birthday; the second time was the following morning. Nina had claimed that they were both part of his birthday present but in reality she was taking revenge on a boyfriend whom she felt was treating her shabbily. Many years later they had tumbled into bed in a Los Angeles hotel after finding themselves on the same flight. And, finally, a few weeks after his wife's death, Dileep had found himself at Nina's door late at night, begging to be let in. She had taken off her rings and allowed him to lie on top of her, sobbing into her neck, his head hot and heavy. It had rained softly all night, the wind whimpering at the windows.

Nina woke up on most days expecting bad news. It took her hours to get out of bed, and it was only the thought of her lineage that managed to hold her up, like a corset. A catalog of careless investments and endless litigation meant that most of the family money was long gone. Her two divorces had left her with the small apartment in Vasant Vihar and an indifferent income, in addition to a few heirlooms and half a dozen Wikipedia entries. She often pursed her lips before spitting out the words "these days." It was a trenchant expression of everything that had gone so horribly wrong in her world.

"Oh, these days," she said, "the only way you can tell the difference between loud women in the cafés and their maids is by the quality of the diamonds in their ears."

At the age of nineteen she had insisted on being allowed to spend a year in Paris. That summer she had been coming down some stairs near the Place de l'Opéra and was almost at street level when she had stopped to adjust the strap of her sandal. She had looked up in the instant that a photographer from *Life* magazine took a picture of her from across the street, a loose strand of hair over her eyes, her irritation with the strap giving her face a perplexed look. In the years since, she had given countless interviews about the photograph, changing the circumstances of the day as the whim took her. She had been a model in Paris; she had been a student of architecture; she had lived there for years; the photographer had been a friend; she had never set eyes on him before; she was adjusting her sandal; she was picking up a purse; she was nineteen, seventeen, sixteen.

"Is it true that you had many letters asking if you were Italian?"

"Yes, I answered them all explaining that some of us Indians are stunning too."

As expected, she had matured into a formidable beauty with an elegant neck, unblemished skin, and the mouth of a vamp. Her first newspaper column was called "Dirty Laundry," and she dictated it to a woman called Rose, who would come to her house every Tuesday afternoon. A prominent gossip column was an effortless hobby that she could use to torment her enemies. Rose would go on to become the editor of one of India's first luxury goods magazines around the time that Nina's first divorce was being finalized. A few months later Nina remarried, changing her surname and the name of her column. It became "Nina Varkey's Grapevine."

"OF COURSE IT'S an adjustment for you, but you really must try to pull yourself together."

It was as close to a comforting cluck as Nina would ever be able to provide. She glanced at the clock and lit another cigarette.

"No one, absolutely no one, was as surprised as me. I mean, Renu of all people. I know she's your sister, darling, but those hideous kurtas and that hair. She's a terribly sweet thing, but who wants sweet these days, if they ever did. Luckily she found the one man in the world who apparently does. Anyway, good for them, and it could have been someone so much worse."

"He's a very fine man, Nina, I have no complaints with that at all. It just feels like everything changes so suddenly and so quickly. Before we know it Ania will be leaving too."

"I should jolly well think so. I hope you're not going to try and turn her into a Renu replacement and feed her all your awful butter chicken and strand her on the top floor."

"We don't serve butter chicken at our house."

Nina began to do neck exercises, still smoking, barely listening to Dileep. He stayed on the phone for a little longer and said he wanted to drop by later. She said she had plans but she would call him.

She picked up the ashtray and took it back to bed.

It was extraordinary how a little thing like marriage had made

Renu appear interesting to the whole world. She could certainly vouch for the fact that Renu had never been interesting. Clever, placid Renu, who had never even accidentally provided an amusing anecdote in her life. She had a vague memory of seducing one of Renu's boyfriends many years ago, but perhaps it had been someone else. Now Renu had found herself a colonel. It would be so easy to sweep into her home and enchant her new husband. An elegant blouse and a dash of flattery was all it would take. But what would be the point? They were not twenty-one any longer.

And now she would no doubt have to suffer the visits of poor, idiotic Dileep and pretend to tend to his wounds. She wondered whether she should marry him—it would certainly ease her way in life. He had never asked her, but she knew that the proposition was there, had been there for many years, furled tight, ready to spring open at one touch. It was tempting: there was so much ground she could reclaim as his wife, so many scores she could settle. And of course, the security of all that money. But he would need so much attention and counsel, such constant reassurance, that even the thought of it brought on a huge wave of fatigue. She stubbed out her cigarette, picked up another one, and then paused, distracted, pressing its tip against the cushion of her finger.

DIMPLE'S OFFICE WAS on the second floor of a royal pink block in Shahpur Jat. It was difficult to know if the choice of color had been an adherence to some family tradition by its former occupants or whether it was a splash of deliberate kitsch. On the ground floor, a minimalist cupcake bakery was flanked by a dress-material store and a little grocery, sacks of black gram and red chilies propping open its ancient wooden door.

Across the narrow lane, Ania waited for Dimple in a new café, vintage birdcages dangling down from its beams, hand-dyed mosquito nets strung up against the walls. She had spent the past couple of weeks trying to persuade Dimple to take the initiative. But Dimple had said that she wasn't the gritty kind of girl who invited men out for a drink: she would have no idea how to begin. Even more maddening than her obstinacy was Fahim's diffidence. She had heard, mainly from him, she now recalled, that he had skirted around land mines and narrowly missed being killed by a sniper. Yet it appeared that the intrepid reporter's greatest fear was the prospect of rejection by a potential date.

And so they had all been to a Chinese restaurant in Defence Colony, steam rising above the hot pot, as they reminisced over their sublime weekend with Altaf Masood. Both of their accounts of the trip to the fort had been infuriatingly bland. Fahim had come over for Saturday afternoon beers, but neither he nor Dimple had got tipsy and disappeared to dangle their legs in the pool. There had been group messages and funny videos and long trains of banter. Ania felt like a researcher at a captive-breeding facility trying to cajole a couple of pandas toward a secluded spot under the bamboo. In spite of their mild deception, the colonel and Renu had acquitted themselves with so much more panache.

Dimple came through the door and rushed to give Ania a hug.

"Do I look terrible? I've had four hours of sleep," she said.

She explained she was exhausted by the demands of one of her new start-up clients, even though she truly believed in their unique product, a newly designed fabric with cutting-edge anti-stain technology.

"So it's a bib," said Ania.

"It's not a bib," said Dimple. "It's a personal stain guard. It's especially useful for Indian food, which is full of turmeric and chili powder and other especially staining ingredients."

"It's a bib."

"It's *not* a bib. This is a sophisticated product for adults. It is what is known as utilitarian chic. I'll get you a sample so you can see. I promise, you'll start wearing it at once. Please don't tell me you don't spill dal or coffee or wine sometimes. And actually, what's that on your scarf now?"

"That's not dal. It's a fleur-de-lis motif."

"The point is that this is a very common problem in India, and our client is providing a low-cost, environmentally friendly solution."

Ania lowered her head and bit her lip.

"Oh God, why the hell has she turned up here?" said Ania.

"Who?"

"Don't turn around."

"But who?"

"Act casual, smile."

"But who?"

"I said, *don't* turn around."

Ania stirred the dregs of her coffee and then examined the light trace of froth on her spoon.

At the same moment a tall woman, her hair in a long, tight braid, her outfit a collection of beautifully mismatched prints, left the café, walking past them on the other side of the glass. Ania waited a couple of seconds and then turned to watch her cross the road. The braid swung with every step.

"Who was that?" asked Dimple.

"You don't know her. Kamya Singh-Kaul."

"But why are you avoiding her?"

"It's sort of hard to explain."

Ania turned again to have another look at Kamya, but she was out of sight. Crossing the road toward them, however, was another unwelcome sight.

"Isn't that Ankit?" she asked.

"Oh, yes, it is."

"Why is the whole world in this bloody café today? Wait, did you tell him we would be here?"

"I didn't invite him. I just mentioned that I was meeting you here after work."

"But why are you even in touch?"

There was no time for a response as Ankit had come in and, not knowing what else to do, shook hands with Dimple and then Ania.

"What's up, dudes?" he asked.

The greeting sounded forced and exaggeratedly jovial. Ania almost winced.

He seemed so pleased to see Dimple that he gave her a sideways hug as she beamed at him. Ania almost winced again.

His hair rose with a bouffant zeal that was not unfamiliar among the young men of North Delhi—but the deep furrows beneath his eyes made him look older. His nails were bitten right down. He ordered a Coke and finished it in three or four great gulps as he leaped from topic to topic like a lemur. Almost every other sentence was a non sequitur. It was exhausting. But she also had to admit he had a guileless charm, which was disarming. She glanced at Dimple, who seemed to have forgotten about her poor night of sleep and was squirming in her seat with delight.

Ania looked across the street again, in case Kamya was still loitering in the area. The early-evening bustle had closed in on her, and all Ania could see was the crush of traffic broken up by throngs of pedestrians weaving in and out of the chaos. Headlights glared, neon pulsed above shop signs. The *shang-a-lang-langs* of a doo-wop track had started up in the café. Ankit was still talking, apparently all too aware of his intoxicating effect on Dimple.

Ania could see that matters were spinning out of control and that it was time to take charge again. Another scheme clicked into action.

"I'm really sorry, but I'm going to ask for the bill. I have to be somewhere," said Ania.

Dimple gave her a little shrug, pasting onto her face an apology about Ankit's sudden appearance, which Ania knew was completely insincere.

"I'm having a small party at our farmhouse on Saturday. Just a very casual thing; a friend of mine is visiting from Lisbon and he's going to DJ. Dimple's coming; you should too. If you're free," said Ania to Ankit as she stood up.

Dimple stared at Ania, as Ankit looked stunned and then delighted.

"I'll text you guys all the details," said Ania.

She turned to wave to them from the street and saw that their heads were bowed toward each other. It would take a little more effort, but she was confident that Dimple would see sense. It was Ania's job to point out that ambitious girls did not fall in love with garment shop owners from Lajpat Nagar. When Dimple came to the farmhouse with Ankit, she would discover that this was Delhi's most undeniable truth.

CHAPTER NINE

IT TOOK WELL over two hours to reach the Khurana farmhouse from Dimple's home. Ankit and Dimple had been forced to negotiate a broken-down gas truck, a series of dug-up roads, and a demonstration demanding a resolution to the city's power crisis. As they finally arrived at the approach road to the farmhouse, they could see a few photographers leaning against their motorbikes, ever alert to events there. Flashes blazed as they waited to go through the gates and give their names to the security team. Dimple sucked her cheeks in a little and looked pensively at the dashboard.

Once they were on the other side of the vast perimeter walls, the neem-lined road seemed endless. Feathery lights wound around the tree trunks and twinkled from the hedges on either side. The headlights raked over forks in the road leading to separate annexes and outbuildings. They dipped down a slope, and as they climbed again, they could hear the pounding of the music under the stars.

The house emerged into view on the crest of the hill, its immense boxlike symmetry startling in that remote landscape. Lights shone behind a precise geometry of glass panes, punctuated by timber and granite, the roof sweeping across the whole structure in an elegant, shimmering curve. Ankit brought the car to a crawl.

"Yaar, no way," he said.

"Come on, it'll be fine," said Dimple with a reassurance she did not feel.

From the parking area, they climbed the steps to the house, anxiously seeking Ania. Along the paths, staff in golf carts delivered ice and cocktails to the various groups gathered in gazebos around the property. A man waded through a pond looking for something as a woman shrieked with laughter at its edge.

"I thought it was you," said Ania, coming up behind them. "Welcome. Someone has to get you some drinks ASAP. Let's go around the other way; these useless acrobats were such a mistake."

When a visiting nouveau cirque troupe from Vietnam became available at short notice, Ania thought booking them would be an interesting way to jolly up proceedings. But as they flipped and flew and hurled their wooden props across the main lawns, they were mainly ignored by the guests. Ania nudged a waiter toward Ankit. Then she took Dimple by the hand and led her to the other side of the lawn, where people sprawled on divans under grapevine chandeliers.

"You have to meet some of my Bombay friends who are here," she said. "I've mentioned them to you loads of times. There's Kamaira and Mridul, who are both jewelry designers, and Alleenna, who thinks she's an influencer—poor thing, literally no one cares what she does, but when you get to know her, she's really very sweet and warm."

"Let's go back for Ankit, he was here just now," said Dimple.

"He'll find us when he wants, I'm sure."

"But he doesn't know anyone here."

"That's why I invited him. So he can make new friends. Will you relax? I'll go and find him in a second."

They passed young men in shirts damp with sweat, a woman who was already holding her gold high heels in her hand. The music was louder here, and the lights strobed across the garden, turning petals silver, hurling pink flares across the ferns and vines.

Ania deposited Dimple among a group of aspiring documentary makers and then headed back to the house. On her way, she found Ankit and introduced him to a bunch of hard drinkers, overgrown schoolboys whom she invited to parties because occasionally her female friends liked to have sex with one of them. As she approached, she could see that they had all had plenty to drink already, whooping and egging on one another.

She spotted Dev moments later and linked arms with him. It was something she did to put him at ease, but she was never sure if it had the desired effect.

"So you've deigned to leave the city and come out to the sticks. Thrilling, really," said Ania, leading him away from the thundering music.

"I like to see how the other half live," he said, his voice wry.

"Do you know people? Would you like me to take you around and introduce you?"

"I have a drink; I'll be fine. And this is wonderful. I'm treating it as a bit of an anthropological study. But I probably won't stay long. Flying out to a conference tomorrow."

"Which reminds me, your lecture series thing is coming along very well. I have a great feeling about the Mehras stumping up all the cash."

"Really?"

"Yes, I mean, I had to change the gist of the project because all that stuff you sent me was useless. No one would have gone for it."

"What do you mean, 'change the gist'?"

"I'm really sorry, Dev, but these people aren't like you and me. They are just not going to get super-excited about a lost monastery in God-knows-where. So I googled some archeological whatnot and sent them a different pitch."

"Pitch? What kind of pitch?"

"So, please don't overreact, try to stay calm, but you know, all those seals and symbols that have not been deciphered from Harappa and Mohenjo Daro? Well, all that stuff is *fascinating*. And I thought it would be a great angle, so I told the Mehras that you've almost cracked the code and are on the cusp of translating the Indus valley script."

"You did *what*?"

He suddenly stopped walking and looked at her in utter bafflement.

"I'm sorry but would you please be reasonable? I'm trying to help you. Look, you know all about archeology, but I know about Delhi society, and what excites them most is anything that says first-time-in-India. The moment I told them that no one had deciphered the inscriptions before, and you've now managed the first truly significant deciphering, they were hooked. Now they're desperate to be associated with the world-famous decipherer and sponsor the talks across the country. Trust me, the Mehras won't care what you actually say at the lectures, they'll just want their name all over the invitations," she said.

Dev was about to ask her if they could discuss the matter in the house when they were interrupted.

"Oh my God, you totally look like someone I know," a girl in a spangly headband said to Dev.

Dev's look of confusion persisted.

"Keep walking, Scheherazade," said her male companion.

"I have no idea who she is, but she was totally hitting on you. We'll talk about all this later," said Ania, heading off toward the bar.

"I don't think she was," said Dev softly, even though he knew Ania was already out of earshot.

She headed to the bar area, where Ankit stood alone, one hand gripping the back of a barstool. She took his arm and led him to one side.

"A double scotch," she said to the bartender.

Ankit's gait already had a little wobble; his eyes narrowed as he tried to focus on what Ania was saying to him. The price tag of his new trousers still hung off one of its belt loops.

"Look, this party's really flagging. There's just no atmosphere. You'll have to help me get things going again," she said.

He looked at her uncomprehendingly.

"Dimple's told me you're an amazing dancer. Could you, you know, raise the temperature, give us a little show?"

"Me?"

"Oh, come on, it's just for a bunch of friends. And don't pretend to be shy or anything. I already know you too well for that."

She gave him a nudge.

"Just tell me what you want the DJ to play, and I'll sort it out."

"I'm not a good dancer. I don't know why she told you that."

"Will you stop with all this modesty? Look, it'll impress the hell out of her. Just go out there and do your thing."

She slid his glass toward him and clinked her own against it.

"Come on, if you won't do it for me, do it for her. Drink up and let's go."

He downed his drink and widened his eyes. He had never looked more eager to please. They approached the large terrace, the speakers booming into the night. In front of them were long limbs and dark heads and beautiful faces, all caught in a net of light.

Ania led him through the crowd, smiling at friends as she passed them.

"Stay here, have fun," she said in the middle of the floor. "I'll be right back."

She said to someone who offered her a sip of his drink, "That guy, you've got to make sure he shows you his moves."

Turning around to take a last look at Ankit, she disappeared through the mass of bodies.

He stood still. The heat closed in around him, and he wiped his forehead with his arm. A man backed into him and gave an apologetic kind of shrug. Ankit began to wave his arms in time to the beat and took a few steps. The floor was sticky with residue.

"Hey," said a voice next to him.

He rolled his shoulders and staggered to one side. A woman moved away from him. He tried to say something to her but then stopped mid-sentence. People in the distance had their arms in the air. He swung his arms too.

A small space was beginning to form around him.

"Sexy," shouted a male voice near the wall. "Take your shirt off."

A few women near him collapsed into giggles. The cry was taken up around the terrace with enthusiasm.

"Take. Your. Shirt. Off."

Ankit looked confused at first; and then, hesitant. He staggered once again and continued to swing his arms, now more energetically, in response to the crowd's chant.

"Shirt. Off. Shirt. Off."

Comprehension flashed over his face, and he began to respond to the crowd, pointing at them and pointing at himself. He had pleased them in some way. They wanted more.

"Off. Off. Off."

He pulled the tails of his shirt free of his trousers and a roar swept around the terrace. The bass thudded. He began to undo the shirt buttons, staggering again as he tried to keep his feet moving. More people had gathered on the terrace. A champagne cork sailed over the timber railings and landed on the grass.

Dimple walked up the pathway, its pebbles glowing silver in the moonlight. The house was lit up, like a ship sweeping through the night. The shouts of the crowd became more distinct as she climbed the stairs to the terrace. A couple stumbled on the top step and shook with laughter. Behind her, twists of light hung down from the trees.

She stood at the edge of the group on the terrace and looked over their shoulders at the spectacle in their midst. When the bare-chested figure spun around, she felt a horrible lurching, as though she had been swung too high and had lost her grip. Ankit was staggering over the flagstones, trying to undo his belt, a smile struggling to stay on his face. He veered to the left, finally managed to pull his belt off, and then stared at it in surprise. The group roared. He flung the belt over the terrace wall and began to cheer too, delighted at their reaction.

Ania came up to Dimple.

"Here you are," she said.

"Oh my God, what's he doing?" asked Dimple.

"Is that Ankit?"

"Yes, but what's he doing?"

"I have no idea," said Ania. "Is this some sort of party trick of his?"

"Of course not. I'm really sorry; I'm so embarrassed."

"It's not *your* fault."

"Let me go and pull him to one side."

Ania stopped her.

"No, don't. He might resist, and it'll cause a scene. And it will all be horrible, in front of everyone."

"Someone's got to stop him. Look at him."

"He'll just get tired. Look, people are getting bored and turning away already."

"Oh God, he's so drunk. I've never seen him like this. I'm really very sorry, Ania. I don't know what to say."

"It's fine, really. Maybe he gets like this all the time. How would you even know? You haven't been with him that long. Just forget about it."

"Off, off, off," yelled the crowd.

Ankit began to fumble with the fly and button on his trousers. He lifted his head, as though he needed assistance. The look was on his face again, the eagerness to please, and then a gratitude that he had been welcomed and favored and applauded and accepted. He began to wriggle out of his trousers, struggling to push them down past his thighs. His white boxer shorts gleamed in the flashing lights.

Dimple turned away.

"I've got to stop him," she said, her voice wavering.

In that moment, there was a loud groan of disappointment from the crowd. Dimple turned to see Dev with his arm around Ankit's shoulders, leading him away from the music, toward the stone bench at the edge of the terrace. She moved through the crowd and stood in silence as Dev helped Ankit settle on the bench.

"You just need to get him home," said Dev.

"He drove us here in his car," said Dimple.

"Are you ready to leave? My driver's here. We can drop you off, and he can see about his car tomorrow," said Dev.

She nodded. "I'll get his shirt," she said.

"Come on, you can walk," said Dev to Ankit, helping him up.

Dimple followed them as they labored down the steps and along the pathway. She reached for Ankit once or twice, as though she felt able to help, and then fell back again. Their steps crunched over the pebbles, the sound echoing as they moved toward the parking area, farther away from the music. Ania came rushing down the steps a few minutes later, holding her empty glass.

Dev and the driver helped Ankit into the backseat of the car, pushing his legs clear of the door. Dimple climbed in next to him, without a word.

"If you think he's going to be sick or anything just say, and we'll stop," said Dev.

He straightened up and turned to look at Ania. He said nothing for a few moments and then climbed into the front seat.

She put her glass down on the hood of a car. No one said anything to her. The two front doors slammed, and the car pulled away. She watched its taillights disappear around the bend in the road. Laughter and a thumping bass continued to fill the night air behind her. In a couple of hours the music would stop, and the silence would lie close for a while, upon the chrysanthemum buds in the flower beds, spreading over the terraces and gardens, settling above the crests and slopes of the grounds. It would be broken soon after dawn by the rustle of hares in the undergrowth and the long wails of peacocks. But for now the noise thundered as Ania remained standing alone in the driveway, still staring into the darkness.

CHAPTER TEN

THE GAHLOTS' FOUR-STORY house, with its great stone façade, had a number of entrances and staircases—and visitors were normally escorted to the correct room by a uniformed member of staff. Ania, of course, knew exactly where she was going. The top floor had been converted into an apartment for Dev, the rest of the family feeling that he should be free to populate it with journals and fellow academics without any embarrassment.

She stood in the doorway, her arms folded. It was a mission of repentance, and so she had dressed entirely in black, from her crepe wrap dress to the leather cuff around her wrist. As she looked into the room, she thought grimly that if she had been able to procure a hat with a long veil, she would probably have worn that too.

"I came to say I'm sorry about last night. Thank you, it was really good of you to take them home," she said.

"You can come in, you know," said Dev.

"I mean, it wasn't that bad, what happened. Some people just can't handle their drink," she said, taking a few steps into the room.

She watched him as he picked up the newspapers strewn across the sofa and looked for somewhere to put them. He walked to the bookcase and then the dining table and finally dumped them on the credenza.

"Next time, we'll need to make sure he sticks to fruit juice," she said.

"There's going to be a next time?"

"I don't know."

"Please stop, Ania. I saw you plying him with booze. I think we both know what you were trying to do."

"What was I trying to do?"

Dev did not reply. The *whir* of a lawn mower drifted through the open windows, rising and falling as it moved up and down the garden. The clock in the hallway began to strike. They stood across from each other until the twelfth chime sounded. And then Ania sat down on the sofa.

"If you're not careful you're going to turn into one of those vicious old bags who sit in people's drawing rooms with their dark glasses on, taking note of every bit of gossip. Maybe you need a new interest in life," he said.

The lawn mower fell silent. Prickles surged across her skin.

The look on Dev's face was unfamiliar, almost hostile. A mist seemed to pass before her eyes, and she scrambled to regain the thread of their conversation.

"I get that you're almost a decade older than me, but do you have to patronize me as if you're the village elder?"

"What's patronizing about telling you that you've got everything going for you but you're still wasting your time on all this socialite nonsense? May I ask what happened to the book you're working on?"

Ania stood up.

"I came here to say I was sorry, not to be subjected to a personal *attack*."

"Will you calm down? I'm just asking about your book, because if you're serious about writing it, shouldn't you be, well, writing it?"

"If you must know, I've got a place at a writing residency in Italy. An extremely well-regarded one. They've seen samples of my work."

She preferred to leave out the influence of Clarence Lam's effusive letter.

"That's great to hear, congratulations," he said.

He moved as though intending to give her a hug, but it turned into a few enthusiastic pats on her back.

"That's all I had to say. I'm leaving now," she said.

"I'm sorry, I didn't mean to be harsh and I didn't mean to lecture you. Please, let me take you out to lunch to make it up to you. I just need to send an e-mail and then we can go."

"If you insist."

"I do."

He looked down at her wrist.

"Your thingie is loose. It might fall off."

He took her hand and, for someone who paid such little attention to his own grooming, reknotted the cuff's ties with great care.

"That's better now," he said.

She looked at her wrist. It almost brought a lump to her throat.

"I'll be back in a minute," he said.

Ania walked around the room, adjusting a hydrangea that threatened to tumble out of its vase, folding the jumble of newspapers. Unwanted items from the rest of the house were often sent up to Dev's floor, as it was assumed that he would not care or perhaps even notice: a coffee table fashioned from an old cartwheel, a bust of some morose ancestor, and in the corner, a battered upright piano. Books and journals were piled on most of the surfaces, including the floor. But the walls were bare: no shelves and no paintings. Dev seemed to live a life in opposition to everyone else.

She felt a sense of unease, as though there was some vital task she had forgotten. Her mind was foggy, her dignity injured by her own actions of the previous night. She needed, more than anything, to rake over the conversation she had just had with Dev.

A breeze brought with it the smell of freshly cut grass. There was a time, she suddenly remembered, years ago, when she had lain in the long grass and listened to Dev's voice, unable to make out all the words but content to stare at the passing clouds as he spoke. He had been reading out loud; she was sure it had been something funny, maybe comic dialogue from a book or jokes from a magazine. A tennis match had been in progress somewhere behind her, and she could hear the *pock, pock* of the rackets against the ball, cries of "out" and "your serve," the occasional cheer, but mainly Dev's low voice wrapping itself around the knoll on which she lay.

It was the same summer that she had asked Dev whether he remembered anything about her mother. The scandalous

circumstances of her death meant that Ania received only nervous
and evasive replies on the occasions when she brought up the matter. She had wondered whether Dev would be any different.

A graveness had pooled in his eyes.

He had said, "I remember her laughing and always smelling of
the same perfume. It was so subtle but distinct. There was a time
when I got into a fight at school and somehow ended up at your
place. She took me upstairs and told me about all the fights she
had got into at school. I didn't believe her, but I remember standing with her at the bedroom window, both of us laughing at the
wild stories she told me."

He had said no more. And neither of them had spoken of her
mother again.

She put the folded newspapers on the coffee table and began to
look through the other bits of debris: vinyl records, pages torn
from note pads, fliers for university events. Also lying there, in
plain sight, was a copy of Kamya Singh-Kaul's book. It winked in
its glossy jacket, a row of silver skyscrapers catching the light. He
seemed to have given it a degree of prominence—it was not
shoved into the recess of some obscure bookcase, the natural
home for copies of unappealing books pressed into one's hands by
acquaintances. Ania's own novel, which she had introduced into
conversations with such confidence a few months ago, now felt
like a burden that oozed reproach, a secret failure accompanied by
a rush of anxiety and hopelessness every time she thought about
it. Dev's questions had reminded her that she often felt a deeper
apprehension that she had left unexplored.

She picked up Kamya's book and felt an unpleasant contrac-
tion in her chest as she read the cavalcade of breathless quotes

from distinguished authors. Her author photograph—dark lips, cheekbones, all with the glaze of a museum piece—was exactly what Ania would have expected. She turned to the back of the book, looking for the acknowledgments page, eager to see exactly what combination of nepotism, flattery, and abuse of position had resulted in the book's outstanding success. His name leaped out at her as though it had been scrawled with a marker pen.

"To my dearest Dev Gahlot, for all the love and inspiration across four continents."

There were probably dozens of Dev Gahlots who could have drifted into Kamya's life to provide inspiration and love. Ania flipped to the front pages and found the signature: "To Dev, thank you for the big ears and the little ones. With love, forever, KSK." Horrified at what she might find, Ania turned the pages looking for the dedication.

"For GN," it read.

While it was a relief that Dev's name was absent, Ania wondered whether the initials could refer to some revolting little nickname for him. She returned the book to its place and walked to the other side of the room, as though moving away from its toxicity.

She was astonished that Dev had chosen to form some sort of close bond with Kamya. They shared private jokes about ears. They had pursued each other across four continents. She had never credited him with much intuition, but she was surprised by the extent of his misjudgment.

Ania believed herself to be an impartial and dispassionate judge of character, certainly fairer than the majority of people in her set. She had befriended all kinds of people and felt she had displayed a distinctly generous spirit. But Kamya had always defeated her. She presented a glassy indifference to anything Ania had to offer, whether an invitation to dinner or an acidic retort. She volunteered nothing, disclosed nothing. Attempts to draw her out or share a confidence were futile. People were "sweet" or "nice," places were "great," and a few times she had used the word "simpatico." Her gaze was cool and hard. As others spoke, her eyes would dart from the keepsakes on the mantelpiece to the fringe of a Persian rug to the prints on the wall, as though she were a bailiff compiling an inventory.

She also had an infuriating habit of stating the obvious. Ania was at a loss to understand how a person who apparently wrote the most incandescent prose and displayed searing insights into the human condition could catalog the most banal observations in that low monotone. The state of the traffic, the time of day, the end of the rain, previously noted and then dismissed by everyone else, were all pronounced upon with new authority.

And to add to all these considerations, there was Kamya's unbearably tiresome long braid, which emerged from her crown like a glossy declaration that its owner was straining to return to her roots and attain the purity and authenticity of a simpler time. It swayed and swung, or lay glossily over her shoulder, or was on occasion coiled on her head like some sort of primitive coronet. Sometimes Ania felt that it was the braid, more than anything, that she detested.

And now Ania was faced with the discovery that her old friend was perhaps in love with this creature. Poor, sweet Dev. Even if any of this was true, she felt sure that he had been manipulated and misled. She pictured his puzzled face, the lines on his forehead creased into an innocent appeal. A few years ago they had danced at a wedding, and he had moved as though he was trying to shake a randy dog off his leg. She had tried to help him, taking his hand, trying to get him to match the rhythm of her arms and hips. He had looked at her in utter helplessness.

She supposed she could simply ask him; she had never hesitated before. But how was she to phrase such a question? Do you like her, Dev? Are you into her, Dev? Is there something going on between you, Dev? What's the matter, Dev? Are you just sleeping with her, Dev? Ania felt an odd physical reaction, a snag, a sharp jerk somewhere within.

She was quiet during the drive to the restaurant and continued to be subdued as she slid into an ivory-colored banquette and opened the menu, barely registering its contents. Dev sat opposite her, enthusiastically reading out the names of the dishes he fancied—"duck with, what's this, caramelized apple ravioli, well, it's always hard to resist a duck"—and listened to a waiter announce the specials with great attention. A pianist played lunchtime jazz standards, his foot a little overenthusiastic with the pedals. A vertical garden rose up the wall opposite them, starbursts of silvery alyssum splashing through the ferns and trailing moss.

The restaurant manager hurried over to greet them and to ensure that the table was to their satisfaction. Complimentary tastings were sent over, frothy concoctions in little glasses or agglomerations perched on porcelain spoons, all of which Dev consumed unthinkingly.

When her salad arrived, Ania slid the endive around her plate.

"So have you read Kamya's book?" she asked.

"Yes, it's wonderful. What did you think?"

"Oh, I haven't read it."

"I should lend it to you. In fact, it was right there, on my coffee table."

"Oh, what a shame, I never saw it."

"It's set in Manhattan over the course of twenty-four hours. I think you'd like it. She has a strikingly detached tone when she writes about exile and the despair of belonging everywhere and yet nowhere. It takes the sentimentality out of it and turns it into something very nuanced and polished. Crystalline. That's a good word for her work. Crystalline."

Ania scrutinized Dev as he spoke about Kamya. His eyes were bright; his hand gestures animated. He even forgot to ask for more bread. She felt thoroughly deflated.

"Do you think she actually wrote the book herself?" she asked.

"Stop being so absurd. We're hardly talking about a bit of maths homework that she could have copied from a friend. You're being catty now."

"Honestly, I'm not. I just find it surprising that she's able to absorb and convey these insights so well. I've always found her uncommunicative and wholly absent. There's a real emotional disconnection, do you know what I mean?"

"Well, she's certainly reserved and private. And never talks about her work in public. Maybe that gives the impression of disconnect. But she's incredibly astute and sensitive and so wonderfully precise with her language."

The intensity of Ania's envy was new, blinding, hateful. She had never envied anyone before; there had been little reason. This new resentment was especially dismaying since it concerned an accomplishment that Ania was slowly beginning to suspect might always evade her. But her thoughts instantly turned to the possibility that it might not, and the antagonism blazed anew.

She was relieved that Dev seemed oblivious to her feelings.

A woman in a brocade sari waved at Ania from the doorway and blew her a kiss. Ania nodded at her with the briefest of smiles before looking away. The woman continued to stare in their direction but eventually trudged behind the restaurant hostess toward her own table.

"Thank God, I thought she would come over. You can never go anywhere in this stupid town without seeing some moron you want to avoid. And who dresses like that for lunch? Anyway, what were we talking about? Oh yes, I had no idea you know Kamya so well," she said.

"Not really surprising, is it? We've always moved around with the same people. In Delhi. And New York. And then she was in London at the same time as me. I'd say she's a fairly close friend. She can be brilliantly wry when you get behind the reserve. I remember when we found ourselves at the same hotel in Rio a few years ago. She had come with a boyfriend, but then they split up right there, on the way to Ipanema Beach, the day they arrived. He took a flight back home, and she decided to stay on. She was very funny about the whole thing," he said.

"You've known her on virtually every continent. Dev, do you think this might be some sort of disguised walnut? I can't bear them," she said, holding up her fork.

"I'd swear on my life that it's a walnut."

"Anyway."

"Anyway. You should read Kamya's book."

"After everything you've said, I'm so looking forward to it."

"Are you being catty again?"

"Here, have my walnut."

CHAPTER ELEVEN

SOME OF THE talk was exaggerated, but the exact truth was known in many parts of Lutyens' Delhi, the few square miles of broad avenues, pristine gardens, and forbidding gates where so much of the country's power was concentrated. Properties purchased by the dozen; astonishing transfers made to offshore accounts; cash metamorphosing into bullion and then back into cash; vast portfolios of bonds, equities, options, and futures. In this charmed world, the Khuranas knew that an invitation was equally valuable currency.

Planning a party was a delicate operation. Dileep, ordinarily so preoccupied with his private obsessions, brought his full attention to the matter at hand, his assessments quick and sharp. Renu was often ignored on important matters; but here, with her fine memory and intimate knowledge of Delhi family trees, she came into her own. Even Ania, in spite of her youth, was considered essential to the process. Fine politicking, it was assumed, ran in the blood.

There were questions of future utility to be balanced with the danger of current solecism. Favors sometimes had to be returned, but in the correct measure and on the appropriate occasion. Acts of censure were necessary and inevitable. The creation of a guest list was not dissimilar to the use of valves and gauges to control the addition of a precious liquid into an experiment of great complexity. A crucial equilibrium had to be maintained at all times.

And when rising Slovenian opera star Agata Župan agreed to give a private performance at a residence in New Delhi, the stakes were even higher. Dileep had met Agata at a party at his town house in New York—she was his chiropractor's date—and had been impressed by her quiet modesty and sublime cheekbones. She had just won a major international award, had signed a contract with the Lyric Opera of Chicago, and was being persuaded by her agent to write a memoir with plenty of photos. Agata told Dileep that she had always been fascinated by India. While she was, of course, delighted that the Iron Curtain no longer existed, she could not help but feel that the West was a corrupting influence. True happiness lay in the sanctity and temperance of the East.

Dileep agreed, and his kind invitation was accepted almost immediately. The more prosaic details involving her fee and travel arrangements would be dealt with by others; what really mattered was that they felt sure their encounter on that crisp spring evening would be the beginning of a dear friendship.

The dates for Agata's trip were finally confirmed, and she wrote to say that she was now a vegan. Dileep, Renu, and Ania sat at their dining room table with their diaries, phones, and tablets. Strewn around them were Post-it notes and sugar-free bonbon wrappers. Dileep's hair stood up in an uncharacteristic tuft as he absently ran his hand through it. Renu had refused the fennel tea and started on the red wine. Ania chewed the end of a hair-grip. Every so often, Sigmund dragged his aged body to each of them, and they gave him a distracted stroke or two. It was, in essence, a wartime cabinet meeting.

So far, Serena Bakshi, the head of marketing for a major French fashion house, was in.

Restaurateur couple Krish and Candy Mehra, having decided not to fund Dev's lecture series, were out.

The colonel's expedited visa was still fresh in everyone's minds and, as a result, the British high commissioner and his wife were in.

Historian Mingel Andrade had not been forgiven for an injudicious tweet and was out.

There were renewed rumors that famed architect Flavia da Costa had received a fabulous commission to build a new presidential palace in Kazakhstan. She also happened to hail from one of Goa's most prominent land-owning families. Naturally, she was in.

One question mark was the big builder from Noida.

"We have to invite him," said Dileep. "He seems to be buying up entire sectors. And I've heard he's going to be funding quite a bit of you-know-who's election campaign."

The builder from Noida was in.

"What are these names?" asked Dileep, adjusting the size of the font on his tablet, too vain to use reading glasses. "Fahim? *Dimple?* Ania, I'm not bringing Agata all the way over here so you can have a party for your random friends. We have very limited places."

"Oh, Papa, please. They're such close friends, and they'll never get a chance like this again. They'll be so thrilled," said Ania.

"Oh, let them come, what difference will two seats make," said

Renu. "I need one place for the colonel's nephew, Nikhil. But it's a bit of a question mark. We're not sure when exactly his sabbatical starts and when he'll get to India."

"Is he hot?" asked Ania.

"I haven't met him yet, but I have been led to believe that he is indeed hot," said Renu.

"Well then, he can come. Now, who else?"

"What about Kamya Singh-Kaul? I hear she's back in town."

"Over my dead body."

"But why, darling? She seems lovely, and her father is now something even bigger at the UN. And she's a writer, like you."

"Look, no way. Let's just drop it. What about the Kannaujia crowd?"

"Here, take my list," said Dileep. "Why don't you two just cross out the whole damn thing and invite whoever you like—your butcher, baker, candlestick maker."

Renu took a long look at the list.

"You've got both Silky Chhabra and Anita Malwani on here. One of them will have to go or there will be blood on the floor."

It was commonly known that Silky Chhabra had warned Anita Malwani against arranging a home birth for her first grandchild. The whole process, she had announced, was uncivilized, dangerous, and disgusting. Anita had ignored the advice, and her daughter had gone on to give birth to healthy twins in the upstairs reception room of their Malcha Marg home. Silky had never forgiven her for this affront and had spread it about that the twins were a little simple. Anita had retaliated by posting unflattering pictures of Silky on Facebook, taken in her home during happier times.

"I don't know," said Dileep with a heavy sigh. "Of the two, Silky's probably nastier. You better cancel Anita then."

Renu gave it a moment's consideration and thought it would be more entertaining to have them both there after all.

THEY EYED EACH other: Dimple and the cardboard cutout. The figure's eyes carried a joyful gleam that had stopped Dimple on her way into the shopping center. She ran her eyes over the flight attendant's uniform—the tight red skirt, the natty scarf, the pillbox hat—and tried to imagine herself in it. Years ago at school she had been convinced that she would never get the marks required for a good university and that her only option to make an independent life for herself would be to take to the skies. The language in the recruitment advertisements mimicked the trajectory of the flights and spoke only of soaring dreams and looking up to the heavens and the sky being the limit. She had been on a flight only once at that stage and had spent the entire time scrutinizing the serene faces of the women as they handed out drinks and checked on passengers' seat belts.

A strong wind shook the cutout, and the woman nodded at Dimple. She took one last look at the woman who seemed to be so vehemently happy with her life as a flight attendant, her hand grasping her waist with such confidence. Dimple was aware of what she had escaped, and felt that she had escaped it by the narrowest of margins. She had heard about the long hours, the aggressive male passengers, the late payments of salaries, the summary sackings, the MP who had beaten a member of the cabin crew with a shoe for not allowing him to sit in an empty business class seat. The girls were coming in from even smaller towns, their accents and deportment requiring so much more work, their perspectives far more naïve than hers had ever been. It wouldn't have been an escape route but rather a trap.

Dimple walked into the pharmacy in the shopping center. Standing a few feet away was none other than Nina Varkey. Nina put her reading glasses on and began to look closely at the tube she was holding. Even when reading a label, she looked magnificent and imperial, in a gray dress that wound about her body and pearls at her ears. Dimple had first met her in the foyer of Ania's house, and they had run into her again at the club. Dimple had, of course, read and enjoyed many of Nina's old columns, and Ania had later rattled off some of the scandals in which Nina was said to have been the prime offender. When they met, Dimple had almost curtsied.

Nina put the tube back on the shelf and looked up. Dimple's instinct was to duck down and appear to be in search of an item on the floor or perhaps even dash out of the shop. But this was not how polished persons conducted themselves. It was entirely possible that Nina would say a few kind words to her, make a polite inquiry, maybe say that she would like to meet her properly someday with her good friend Ania. After all, when they had been introduced, she was sure that Nina had given her an appraising but approving look, a sign of having passed muster.

Nina turned to speak to the man behind the counter while Dimple loitered by the dental care products, following her progress. It was Dimple's turn to pick up tubes and look at the small print.

"Exceptional relief for symptoms of lichen planus."

She had thought that lichen grew only on trees and walls, but here was evidence that it could sprout on bodies too. Unless this had nothing to do with the other kind of lichen. She replaced the tube hurriedly and walked toward the door.

Nina picked up her packet and put her sunglasses back on. Dimple stood a few feet in front of the door, at first gazing into the distance in a casual manner and then deciding to look at Nina and give her a broad smile.

Nina settled her handbag on her shoulder. She walked out of the door as though the only thing around her was the chill air of the shop, with its vaguely floral odor.

"SHALL WE STRETCH our legs a little? I love it when the weather is just about to change," said Dev.

Dileep was a little taken aback that he should suggest walking anywhere in Delhi, but since they were by Lodi Gardens he supposed it would be all right. He was often surprised by Dev's proclivities and never sure whether they were just an attempt to garner attention. Perhaps it was only natural for him to make a virtue of his peculiarity.

The Khuranas had known the Gahlots for three generations, ever since a senior Khurana had managed to obtain an insurance premium at a favorable rate from a senior Gahlot. Both families' business interests had prospered in tandem since those early days, and their lives had become entwined socially and professionally. Precious contacts had been shared, favors exchanged, and bad news obligingly suppressed.

Dev had three older brothers, all of whom had gone on to

distinguish themselves in business and industry. Their endeavors were presented as exemplary case studies at management schools, and their square jaws and rimless glasses often adorned the covers of business magazines. Dev was the only one who had banished himself to academia, imparting and adding to a body of knowledge that appeared to be of value only to those who published books in the field, books bought exclusively by Dev and his colleagues. Dileep had never understood the attraction of this circularity. It seemed a dismal way to proceed through life.

Nonetheless, Dileep enjoyed being with Dev. He could let down his guard a little and not feel he was in competition for anything. Dileep's fetishes sent him hurtling toward youth, and Dev's disposition made him seem like a visitor from an older era. It was a curious fit. They played tennis, and Dileep always won. They would have dinner occasionally, one anxious about the fat content, the other happy as long as the food was plentiful and didn't take too long to arrive. They could indulge in easy silences over a drink, breaking them only to remind themselves of a much-repeated joke, the punch line familiar and snug. There was no secret that had not been shared between the members of their families, no celebration unattended, no crisis where they had not all come together.

They set off through the park, away from the rush hour commotion on Max Mueller Marg, a thin moon nestled above the tree line. The evening cold had descended, the change from the mellow warmth of the day always as sudden as a dousing. They saw the bobbing of a flashlight through the tracery of hedges and shrubs. A spaniel came rooting around their feet, exploring Dileep's loafers with great interest. They both squatted to make a fuss over their new friend, tickling him under his ears and chin.

"Swarovski," called his owner.

"Swarovski?" said Dev.

Dileep chuckled.

"Here, Swarovski, now. We're going home," came the frosty reply.

They continued up the path, past the rose garden, through small copses where mynas and weaverbirds were returning to their nests. Glittering in the gravel a few feet ahead were a handful of beads; a necklace had snapped earlier in the evening as its owner hurried home, perhaps later fretting at the bad omen.

"How's work?" asked Dileep.

"Can't complain," said Dev. "And you?"

"Me too. Same as usual."

The steady crunch of gravel receded on an adjacent path, and somewhere behind a ruined wall a woman stifled a laugh. Shadows lay along their path: the dark spike of a palm, the thin lines of palings. As they crossed the bridge, the pond caught a splash of moonlight, and there was a flash of white feathers in the reeds.

"Where are you off to after this?" asked Dev.

"I thought I'd drop by Nina's," said Dileep.

"How is she?"

"Good. You know Nina."

"Things any better with the son?"

"No, he still won't talk to her. They haven't spoken for over ten years. But she e-mails him once a week. Every single week."

"And he never responds?"

"Never."

The darkness was now complete. It felt as though the ice cream sellers had gone home to be replaced by ghosts that had trailed through this city for thousands of years. The two men wandered off the path and toward the yellow haze that surrounded the tombs. Beams of light flooded through the arches. The scars on a turret looked as though they were stained with purple; near their feet a cracked tile glimmered blue.

"How are plans going for the party?" asked Dev. "Ania has been calling to give me updates, but I don't always understand them."

Dileep smiled.

"I've never met two people as different as you. What exactly do you talk about when she calls you?" he said.

"I must confess, it's mainly her doing the talking."

"Don't say another word against my darling girl. The consequences will be extreme."

"The consequences are already extreme. I have to come to another one of your parties."

Dileep chuckled again.

The starless sky had turned a deep indigo, and rows of lampposts poured their sulfurous light onto the benches, the flower beds, the pathways. At the top of a craggy set of steps they could see two pairs of legs stretched out and almost entwined. They exchanged a glance, smiled, and turned to leave the park.

"Ah, the folly of youth. But the mad desire to be that foolish again . . . ," said Dileep. He thought he had displayed a particular courage to joke about it in this way. And while he expected a reassuring response from Dev—"but you seem younger than most men I know"—none came.

THE ARRANGEMENTS FOR Agata and her accompanist were complete. A request had to be lodged at the highest level of the

Central Board of Indirect Taxes and Customs to ensure that the accompanist's harp would reach the Khurana home without delay. If all went well, their contact knew he would find himself the recipient of a bounteous Diwali hamper later in the year.

The save-the-date card went out eight weeks in advance, providing hardly any information but accompanied by a box that contained a tiny pair of opera glasses. A low thrumming turned into a surge across the social circuitry of South Delhi. People who had not been in touch with the Khuranas for months made a sudden reappearance. Dileep was questioned at various holes around the golf course and, in one instance, followed into his chiropractor's clinic. Renu enjoyed herself by telling a couple of close friends about their visitor's international acclaim and then switching her phone off for the rest of the day.

There was a daily enumeration of invitations already received and those that might simply have been delayed. Rumors spread. Dileep Khurana was finally remarrying—and he had picked a European *singer*. The Khuranas were flying a few of their close friends to Vienna. Ania was involved in a new business, and it had something to do with the opera. An exact picture of the guest list eventually emerged, and Agata Župan was discussed over lunches and dinners as though she had been a South Delhi fixture for years.

A few days later on the far western side of the city, past the cranes that thrust up at the grubby sky, beyond rutted lanes choked with garbage, on the other side of an illegal settlement, a bridge collapsed into a heap of rubble. But on Prithviraj Road no one really noticed.

CHAPTER TWELVE

WITHIN AN HOUR of the first guests arriving, a few reputations had been destroyed and the prospect raised of a marriage bringing together two revered families in the petrochemical industries. The caterer had flown in from Rome with his team the previous day and was overseeing rows of marinated quails in the kitchen. Across the lawn, groups began to form, their composition influenced by the prevailing currents of business rivalry, sexual entanglements, and the poaching of domestic staff. Some of the men had worn burgundy or navy velvet jackets instead of tuxedos, unaware that Dileep would be certain to take a dim view. The women trailed their deconstructed saris or previously unworn couture through the rooms. Marina had managed to source parfum de Provence white roses and orchids whose large petals blushed a ballet slipper pink in the foyer and reception rooms. She had hiked up the total cost as much as she dared. In her invoice, she added a "special dispensation fee."

Nina Varkey was one of the last to arrive, even later than Silky Chhabra. Nina and Silky had served on some of the same boards and committees and had enjoyed sparring over the years. They were well-matched: Nina had the pedigree, but Silky's husband had earned an extraordinary fortune through improperly obtained mining concessions. Silky had come of age in an era when international flights were still unusual and glamorous, a time when wealthy businessmen routinely married air hostesses. She had met Raj Chhabra as she served him coffee high above the Arabian Sea, and as a consequence, Nina rarely passed up the opportunity to make a joke about in-flight security procedures in her presence. But today, she was not in the mood.

"Good evening," said Nina to Silky, before moving on. That would be all that Silky would get.

Serena Bakshi made her way toward Renu and Ania. She was known for her unerring taste, and since her compliments were rare it was presumed that they were sincere.

"You look stunning," she said to Renu, who beamed and gave Ania's arm a squeeze.

"Do you see Dileep anywhere? I have something important to discuss with him," said Serena.

It was clear to Renu and Ania that she would reveal nothing more.

"He's probably in the house," said Ania, "come with me."

Dileep had excused himself and gone upstairs to get one of the servants to see to his jacket sleeves with a clothes brush. As he left his room to return downstairs, he saw a shadow pass across the landing.

"There you are," said Serena, "hope you don't mind me coming upstairs."

"Well, look, quickly, come in here."

He led her into one of the bedrooms and shut the door.

"The house is full of people! You know what they're like; if they see you heading toward my room . . ."

"God, why would you care? I'm sorry but I just can't stand all that."

"I really need to explain?"

"I thought . . . never mind. But I wanted you to know that I've heard back from him. He's agreed to see you."

"I'm sorry, after all you've done to help me, but I just have to be a bit careful. We'll find a time to talk, I promise, just not tonight."

He left the room and went downstairs as Serena waited a few moments, pacing, halting, never letting her gaze leave her reflection in the mirror. She was not a flirter. She had always found it difficult to maintain the correct balance of effervescence and intent and, in any case, had married early and believed that she would no longer need to trouble herself over other men. But as her marriage had begun to fail, she had turned her attention to Dileep Khurana. Like so many other women, she had seen a strong measure of safety in his impeccable manners and unimpeachable status. She had finally decided to try to flirt. But her approaches had elicited no reaction, and she had wondered whether he was gay. There had been no known dalliances with other women, no girlfriends or mistresses. But there had never been any rumors about other men either. Over the last decade, she had accepted that Dileep was simply uninterested in romance and would remain only a friend; even that was much more than most people could claim. But now they had discovered something to bring them much closer. The temptation to achieve a greater intimacy with

Dileep had far outweighed any reservations she had about revealing the source of her great inner calm.

A GROUP OF six were seated on the terrace that overlooked the back lawns, Dev and Flavia among them. They had known each other for years, Flavia having restored Dev's family's holiday home in Goa before buying the plot next door to build her own internationally renowned tree house.

"Why am I even here? I know they like to keep the numbers low for this kind of event—they should have invited someone who appreciates the music. I have no ear for this sort of thing," said Dev.

"Nonsense," said Flavia, "just close your eyes. How can it not move something in your soul?"

She stood up and shimmied, passing her hands over her hips and then running them over her close-cropped hair.

Dev looked unmoved. Everyone was accustomed to Flavia's bouts of exhibitionism.

"Honestly, I feel nothing but mild irritation. And boredom. Suddenly the seat seems hard or someone's face looks really comical or I just want to have a loud coughing fit. And it's not just this opera stuff, it's all music. Jazz just sounds like furniture being moved around, Hindustani like cats being tortured, and please, let's not even start on Carnatic."

"Stop trying to be controversial," said Flavia, sitting down again.

"I really mean it. I don't like music, but I'm not allowed to say it. You all jump down my throat as though I plan to drown a sack of puppies. Music annoys me. I *like* silence. And yet I'm forced to come to these events. There's so much noise in this country, wherever one goes. What's wrong with a bit of silence?"

No one could think of a fitting response, and they all drifted off the terrace and descended into the garden, leaving Dev dandling a tumbler of whiskey at his knee, relieved. A man in a handlebar mustache clapped him on the shoulder, mistaking him for someone else. When he realized, his apology was spiked with annoyance, as if he had been hoodwinked. Waiters appeared bearing platters of delicate offerings that looked like they had been magicked out of a fairy story. Dev helped himself unthinkingly.

The colonel came up to him and shook his hand.

"So?" he said.

"So," said Dev.

They stood and gazed at the lather of guests on the patio, the flash of white collars, the gleam of pearls, until Renu approached and grabbed the colonel's arm.

"Darling, you can speak to Dev anytime. Come with me," said Renu.

Renu was not blind to the sudden rise in her stock as a married woman and was keen to show off the colonel to as many people as she could. She led him onto the lawn, nodding at friends in a manner that was, for the first time in her life, almost queenly.

When Dev had finished his drink, he went upstairs. He had always had free run of the Khurana house, and as a child it had on occasion been a refuge from his rambunctious older brothers. He remembered the sweltering summer that the gazebo had gone up, days of hammering and clanking, white dust that flew onto the terrace in hot gusts. And then one afternoon work had suddenly stopped and the builders were sent home. An alien still-ness had invaded the house. He'd wandered through the rooms and spotted Dileep in the study, drawing the curtains against the glare. When he turned around it was clear that he was weeping. Dev had backed away and then leaped down the stairs. It was the first time that he had seen an adult cry, a terrible vision. Later that afternoon on the way home in the car, Dev's mother told him that Mrs. Khurana had died in the hospital from her injuries.

The study door on the upper floor was open, and Dev walked in. A table lamp threw a cone of light over Sigmund, asleep on the rug, his jowls in a miserable droop. Dev wondered what he had done with his glass; he was on his third whiskey, maybe fourth, and he was warm, fuddled, and content. He walked toward the Goya etching that had always fascinated him. Two muscular fig-ures in a grapple, fingers pressing into an abundance of flesh, ten-dons strained with supreme effort. They were confined in that small square space, the awkwardness of their stance almost too much to bear. As a child Dev had imagined that they would crash out of the frame and brawl their way through the house. They would continue their macabre dance down the street, past horri-fied watchmen and drivers, whirling madly under the golden rain trees, the whole avenue a blur of high walls, wrought iron curli-cues, and brass nameplates. And here, after all these years, the two figures had still not escaped the frame.

"You're always skulking around miles from the action," said Ania from the doorway.

Dev turned around. "Oh, hello. I came up to look at the Goya. I've missed it. What are you doing up here?"

She joined him in front of the etching.

"Our dear minister of land reform has asked to lie down for a few minutes. Apparently he shouldn't have been drinking with his antidepressants."

"Is anyone here not on antidepressants?"

"I'm not."

"Yes, I would imagine that your natural jauntiness wards off all dark thoughts."

"Funnily enough, I only have dark thoughts when I'm in your presence."

He pretended to cuff her on the shoulder, but it was a mistimed and awkward gesture.

"You're looking pretty amazing. What are all these silver bits? They look like the things you tie curtains back with," he said.

"It's a fringed dress. You're supposed to gasp at the way it catches the light."

She twirled.

"Gasping as we speak," he said.

"Thank you. You'd better come down. Agata's about to start."

He watched her go downstairs, deliberate in her heels, one hand pulling up her hem by a couple of inches. He continued to linger on the landing for a few minutes. On one side the sweep of the banister ended in a beautifully burnished volute; through the open door to his left he could see the corner of a gilt frame and a pile of books on a faded ottoman. He leaned over the balustrade. Murmurs floated up the staircase, a loud titter. A woman with an elegant topknot began to climb the stairs, a silver handbag dangling from her wrist; a few steps later she changed her mind and went back down. Staff in white jackets carried fresh glasses across the foyer.

He turned to give Sigmund a last look and then closed the study door. His glass was on a table by the stairs. He picked it up and went downstairs in search of a waiter.

THE CHANDELIERS IN the house's largest reception room were reflected in the arched windows, and the air was thick with the fragrance of Marina's white roses. At the back of the room stood the walnut Steinway, barely used in the ten years since Ania failed her grade 5 piano exams. The guests were seated on rows of chairs upholstered in bronze velvet, clutching the program notes, which had been bound with a black silk ribbon. Agata walked in, her face calm and expressionless, a black lace dress hanging off her body almost as it had trailed off its hanger. She was followed by the doleful-looking harpist, whose harp had successfully made it through Indian customs.

After the initial applause died down, there was a long pause before Agata began. A few heads turned; there was a hint of alarm, and in one or two cases, a hastening toward schadenfreude. But then Agata lifted her chin and sang the first lines of an aria from *Rodelinda*. In that instant, the light around her seemed to splinter. Her neck was bare but a thin silver bracelet glinted at her wrist. The harpist's fingers moved with a barely perceptible precision, as though making music from the air.

Every seat was taken but a frigidity filled the room, a chill occasioned by an absence of interest. There existed an unspoken acknowledgment that the important proceedings were the ones that preceded and followed the performance, in the foyer, on the lawn, at the table. Oblivious, Agata sang on. Her body was still, stiff even, but her face blazed with expression—coquetry and joy and regret—all directed at an imaginary person stationed at the back of the room.

Ania had seated herself where she could keep an eye on Fahim and Dimple. She thought she saw Fahim stifling a few yawns, but Dimple was completely focused on the performance, leaning forward, for once not self-consciously fiddling with her hair. Instead of taking in the music, Ania observed the other guests and their reactions, part of a careful assessment of their suitability for further invitations. It was an appraisal that came as naturally to her as it had always done to Dileep.

In the second row, Renu's eyes were almost closed. The world had become a gauzy film, shot through with spots of light, Agata's stately form in the center. Her voice rippled and then flinched and then soared. Renu, unlike so many of the others, was listening. She recognized the strange helplessness in Agata's voice as a great sadness. How had someone as young as Agata captured a feeling that Renu felt was reserved for the old or the dying?

Renu was overcome by an awareness of her exceptional good fortune, and she felt her heart clench. She had enjoyed so many towering advantages, and she had taken them all for granted. And now, late in life, she had stumbled upon a profound love that she had assumed she would never know. Her shoulders began to shake. She squeezed her eyes shut, but this forced the tears down her cheeks. She took a deep breath, trying to stave off sobs.

The colonel's hand was in her lap, holding out a handkerchief. The pale blue square was perfectly ironed, and a darker blue stripe ran around its edge. It seemed to represent the colonel perfectly.

She buried her face in its vague smell of lavender.

The first part of Agata's performance came to an end, and she lowered her head. The applause drowned out the last of Renu's sniffles.

"Oh God, I'm sorry, I'm such a mess," she said, dabbing at her eyes.

"No need to apologize at all," said the colonel. "At least your snuffling sounds might have stopped some people from texting."

Renu returned the handkerchief, and for a couple of seconds put her head on the colonel's shoulder, the wool scratchy against her ear.

In the last row one other person had been transfixed by the performance. For the first time in Dev's life, music had collapsed the space and sights around him. Perhaps he had really listened for the first time. What he found astonishing was that the final silence could hold within it even more significance than the music it followed. He kept his eyes closed until the sound in his head died away. When he opened them, they locked with Ania's. She stood up and looked as though she was about to approach him. Embarrassed, he looked away.

GREAT CARE HAD been taken with the name cards placed on the fifteen tables, but the builder from Noida found himself next to Agata for a moment as they looked for their places.

"Welcome to India. I hope you have been enjoying yourself here," he said.

"It is a beautiful country," said Agata, lowering her head, the same gesture that had marked the end of her performance. "Such dignity, so many truths."

"Yes. My cousin is a producer in Bollywood," he said. "He hires many Slovakian dancers for his films. Indian men go crazy for Slovakian women."

"I'm Slovenian," she said.

"Oh yes, from there too. They are also highly appreciated."

Waiters began to serve the main course. Anita Malwani had been seated next to the colonel and at a considerate distance from Silky Chhabra. The colonel was a stolid chewer. He had experienced long periods stationed in the mountains with little comfort—and would never forget. He was greatly appreciative of the benediction of good food and liked to eat without distraction. Anita Malwani, however, had come to the party to chat.

"What a shame it is that you two didn't meet years ago. What wonderful children you would have had," she said, taking advantage of Renu's brief absence from the table.

"We've both been perfectly happy without children," said the colonel. "In all honesty, I find them quite boring. All those dull games and the repetition. I much prefer them when they are adults."

"Nonsense. Renu would have loved children. Look at the way she dotes on Ania."

"Well, I also have a nephew whom I am terribly fond of. But I can assure you I have not been pining for any of my own."

"It's different for women. Nature has created an urge within us," she said, pointing to her breasts with her fork. "There is no use fighting it."

She looked at him for a response and then made an attempt to drive the point home by indicating her cleavage again, the repository of her maternal urges. The colonel returned to his lamb. A few tables away, Silky was being commended for having had the same husband for more than thirty years.

"All these years and nothing has changed in the bedroom department. We still rock," said Silky.

The British high commissioner's wife gave her a weak smile and reached for her glass of Chablis.

On the next table, Renu watched Nina holding court. Even at this age, she was magnificent, her face sculptural, the cheeks softly hollow, eyes still glimmering with possibility, a beautiful shadow at the base of her thin neck. She whispered theatrically and then let out a thin, cruel laugh. The man next to her stared down at his hands.

Renu knew Nina would not have missed her emotional scene. She was far too worldly to mention it now, but it would have been cataloged for future use. Nina's neighbor was looking up at her in some sort of wordless appeal; she was ignoring him, intent on a conversation on her other side, hand toying with the stem of her glass. She could be so much kinder, thought Renu. It was all such a waste, such a terrible waste. And in the next moment it occurred to her that people must think the very same of her own life too.

ANIA HAD BEEN warned not to Instagram the event—Dileep liked to maintain what he saw as a kind of Khurana mystique— but her fingers lingered over her phone. She looked up as she saw Silky Chhabra waving to her.

She called out, "Ania, I've been meaning to speak to you properly all night. I have the most wonderful idea for your novel."

"How clever of you. Later, maybe," said Ania.

Silky had a son who was so uncouth and dissolute that even Delhi's most ardent gold diggers steered clear. This was in spite of the fact that the family was rumored to own, among other business interests, almost half the gas stations in Punjab. For the last year, she had been on a mission to try to burnish his reputation in Ania's presence, explaining that he was callow and misunderstood, requiring nothing more than the love of an intelligent woman to bring out his finer qualities. Silky patted the empty seat next to her and beckoned to Ania, who blew her a kiss and turned to look at her phone.

Ania was delighted with the progress in her plans. She had caught Dimple watching Fahim as they came down the stairs: a look of complete absorption and something else, a sort of resolve. And she had never seen Fahim be so charming, feigning interest in the most tedious conversations around them, teasing old dowagers with some beautifully timed banter, flattering Dileep's tiresome golfing friends.

After dessert there were two empty places at Ania's table, the wineglasses drained, a napkin dropped on the parquet. She smiled to herself and pushed her chair back. She hadn't seen Fahim and Dimple leave the table, but she could see that now would be the perfect time. There would be easy chatter and the warmth from the wine, a stroll to the quiet spot on the steps that led to the pool, above their heads the Moroccan lamps swaying slightly. She slipped off the strap of her sandal and rubbed her heel.

On the other side of the house, in a downstairs cloakroom, the harpist wept, counting the days before he would be on his way home.

CHAPTER THIRTEEN

IN ONE SENSE, Ania's trip to Italy was poorly timed. She would be away from Delhi for four weeks. It felt like a dereliction of duty at a crucial point, when Fahim and Dimple would welcome her oversight and encouragement. On the other hand, perhaps what they needed was time on their own, unfettered by other distractions. It seemed a bit of a gamble, but perhaps her absence would allow a natural momentum to build.

In any case, the time away was non-negotiable. A disquiet about her manner of living had been taking hold of her over the past few weeks. The feeling was unwelcome, but there was little she could do to dispel it. She could see a future where she did nothing, achieved nothing, had only the vaguest recollection of all the promises that she had made to herself. She thought about turning thirty in a few years. There might be nothing left of her ambitions, perhaps only something tepid and watery, melted ice at the bottom of a cocktail glass. She often started awake in the middle of the night. More years would pass and she would be the next matron in the room on the top floor.

She was also determined to prove her serious intent to Dev. While she certainly did not need his approval, she often thought about his reprimand. She had tried to couch it in other terms, but that was indeed what it had been.

An Italian literature foundation funded residencies for international writers with an impressive publishing record; others could pay their way, as long as they could provide a weighty letter of recommendation and a huge, nonrefundable fee. The writers would travel to the restorative environs of Lake Garda and spend four weeks closeted in the rooms of a fifteenth-century villa. They could sit by the promenade in the nearby village or walk in the villa's terraced gardens, camellias and rhododendrons tumbling all the way down to the winding road. There was to be a rich exchange: ideas, opinions, interpretations.

"More realistically, dark looks," Dev had added.

Ania arrived at the villa on a gusty evening in early spring, the wind flattening her yellow floral dress against her as she got out of the taxi. When the porter opened the door to Ania's room, she could see traces of frescoes in the lamplight, a jeweled scepter in an alcove by the window, on the opposite wall the outstretched arms of an angel. Her welcome letter was printed on stiff cream paper, its envelope sealed with the foundation's crest. The sheets on the four-poster bed were taut and crisp. On the terrace she caught the scent of lemon flowers and, after a few seconds, rosemary. Everything was just as she had imagined it would be.

"We have already received a package for you," said the porter.

She ripped open the envelope to find a calf-leather notebook from Dev. He had scribbled a note on a postcard, but the words were bland and brief: they could have been addressed to anyone.

In her disappointment, she almost forgot to turn the card over. But when she saw the image, she read everything that he had failed to say. It was Vermeer's *The Lacemaker*, a woman with her head bowed over her work, in complete absorption, bringing all her attention to the intricacy of her task. Ania could see that the immersion was a reward in itself. The woman had dropped out of time in the intense beauty of the moment. She realized that his conversation with her in Delhi had not been a reprimand. It had been an expression of faith.

The villa was run by an English editor and his Italian wife, both of whom brought up Nobel laureate Clarence Lam's letter in almost every conversation they had with her. They divided their labors according to their dispositions: he had the unctuous patience required to deal with artistic temperaments, and she had the iron hand needed to terrify the staff. Ania found their first encounter distracting; there was about the man a suspicion of body odor. Ania hated to make such a damning judgment without being certain. As he chronicled the history of the villa, she waited to be accosted again by that ripe smell. It took a quiet patience. But when the whiff arrived, there could be no doubt. His quarters, she soon discovered, were not on her floor.

Lodged in the neighboring room was a short story writer from Brooklyn who often spoke fondly of his time working in lumber mills in the Appalachian Mountains. He called her "Anna." Across the corridor was Nemesia, a Chilean poet, who took all her meals in her room by special request. It was three days before Ania met her, having heard allusions to her bizarre working practices: an espresso machine installed in her room; midnight runs through the olive groves; a cell phone, possibly not her own, that she had thrown into the pond. They met on the stone stairway late one night, and Nemesia grabbed her by both arms. She seemed thrilled to see her.

"What is going on?" she asked.

Ania had no idea what to say, so she smiled and shrugged. Nemesia smiled back and rolled her a cigarette with special cinnamon-scented paper.

It took Ania a couple more encounters to establish that no response was expected to Nemesia's question. This was merely her customary greeting. Every day Ania spent half an hour studying the few poems by Nemesia that she could find in translation online. The next time her arms were gripped and she was asked what was going on, she wanted to tell Nemesia, out of some sense of solidarity, out of a respect for her manic diligence, that she had understood and loved her poems, and that *that* was what was going on.

ALSO IN RESIDENCE was Adrian Thurley. Ania was astonished to find herself writing on the same floor as one of her favorite authors. She was lucky enough to be seated opposite him at dinner on her first evening. Even in the soft candlelight, his skin was chalky, his eyelashes pale. The skin on his nose was peeling. He looked as though he was weathering in a noble sort of way, taking it on the chin.

She watched him over the next couple of days, as he had lunch on the terrace and, later, in conversation over cocktails. Two deep furrows would often appear across his brow along with a tightness around his jaw, as though he was struggling with a hangover, which he often was. He seemed to have a signature gesture: a compact shrug and a shake of his head, often when his work was mentioned, as though the prospect of considering it was unbearable, as though he wished to throw off his fame and reputation, perhaps even his whole identity. She googled him to discover that he was only forty-eight, about ten years younger than she had thought.

Facing the picture window in her room, she tried to write, forcing fragments on to the screen, her page littered with sentences and parts of sentences but no coherent paragraph. The following day she would salvage what she could and then begin the attempt all over again. She wrote pithy impressions of her day in her new notebook. She made elaborate chapter plans and then scrapped them. She considered beginning a fresh novel. She could not bear the weight of her hair on her neck, so she piled it on her head in a tight knot. An hour later she took the pins out and let it tumble down again.

After a few days she received a message from Dimple, a short line hoping that she was well and feeling productive. Ania had barely given Dimple and Fahim a thought; life in Delhi seemed so far away. She felt a singe of guilt and replied instantly, saying that she wanted to hear about all developments the instant that she returned.

One breakfast she discovered that Adrian had left her a few doodles on her napkin, caricatures of three of the more annoying residents. She secreted it into her journal, flushed with delight. He lent her his copy of *The Book of Disquiet* and, a few days later, *The History Man*. After a day's work, they began to go for walks on the lake promenade, past the ice cream–colored façades and the fruit market. He read her lines from a Sylvia Plath short story after dinner, his voice rich and low. Lights winked at them across the dark hillsides. When the writer from Brooklyn joined them uninvited, she felt a jab of annoyance. Her finite time with Adrian was being encumbered. She was sure that Adrian felt it too.

That same evening he offered to have a look at her work. She thanked him but knew she would always be too terrified to show him a word.

Late that night she wrote an e-mail to Dev, a galloping stream of words, ostensibly to let him know that she was enjoying her stay, but in reality to tell him that one of the world's most gifted writers had shown interest in her work, listened to her ideas as though she could in some sense be considered an equal, and avoided the company of established authors to discuss books with her. She fell asleep before she could send it.

One day, Ania and Adrian played hooky and ordered champagne hours before lunch. After their second bottle, they staggered into the village and had lunch in the piazza, Ania reveling in the writer's outrageous literary gossip. As the sun began to dip, they lost their way in the cobbled alleys and then stumbled back into the piazza. Everything seemed funny: the marble pout of a saint, the ridiculously long inscription on a building, the way they felt they had to stifle their laughter in the sudden hush of a colonnade.

She tried on hats in an old-fashioned milliner's shop as he egged her on. When they emerged, she was wearing her purchase: a white straw hat with a navy ribbon that trailed off the wide brim. When he put his arm around her shoulders, she noticed its surprising heat and heft. The gesture felt kindly and genial. Great barriers had come down, and she now had a new, immensely accomplished friend. He patted her arm and guided her across the road with his hand resting on her lower back. She herself had on many occasions been accused of being too tactile, grabbing the arm or wrist of some delighted male in her eagerness to drive home a point. At the rickety stairs that led down to the ancient castle wall, she let him take her hand.

THAT NIGHT THERE was veal at dinner and too much wine. She wasn't much of a drinker, and the excess of the last few days was taking its toll. She said good night to Adrian and the others and took the back portico to the stairs. A few moments later he called out to her, and she waited for him to catch up. Flames flickered in their lanterns. At the end of the passage an arch framed an orange tree in an urn.

"You left this," he said, holding out her room key.

As she reached for it, he closed his hand over hers.

There was a slick of sweat in the dip above his upper lip. His eyelashes looked white. When he came closer, his breath was thick with whiskey fumes. He put his arms around her and whispered into her ear: "Principessina."

She held her arms stiffly against him and turned away from his breath.

He moved closer and nuzzled against her neck. She felt his hands glide from her waist, downward, to form a grip.

"Please," she said.

She pushed him away, her breath coming fast in fear and disgust, and walked down the passage that now seemed endless, her footsteps sharp, their echoes thrown up to the vaulted ceiling.

ANIA DID NOT see Adrian the next day. It was a day filled with uneasiness and frustration. She left the room briefly for a swim, but when the water closed over her head, she felt a sense of panic. The smell of the chlorine gave her a headache, and the water made a horrible sound as it slapped against the side of the pool. She felt as though she had lost something precious and did not understand how a friendship could flourish and then sour so quickly. It was, of course, his fault, but she was sure that in some irrefutable way it was hers too.

She knew that men were elementally predatory. It had been a fact that she had absorbed from a young age, expressed to her in both categorical and more subtle ways by Renu, her friends, her teachers, almost all the women she had known. There had been a few men in her life who had been pushy and sexually demanding, but she had always felt in control, forewarned, and able to repel them instantly. She had believed that there was a protection that emanated from her status, as though a special symbol existed next to her name. But at the villa, the bulwark had crumbled. And at the same time, she had been blinded by Adrian's renown and apparent solicitude.

She found the e-mail that she had written to Dev and winced at her smug, crowing tone. At first, she felt relief that she had not sent the e-mail and that Dev would never come to know of her foolishness. Later, she was filled with shame that she had written it at all.

Toward evening her appetite returned, but all she really wanted was sashimi. She managed to locate a restaurant nearly forty miles away that was prepared to send her a delivery. When it arrived there was a tear in the plastic container, and the fish was a lurid pink and smelled foul.

Two more days passed. She changed the times she went down for her meals or had them in her room. Once in a while, she wondered if she was being exceptionally stupid. She caught a glimpse of Adrian from her window, walking along one of the tree-lined paths. The writing had come to a standstill. She lay on her bed staring at the faded blues and reds of the frescoes. She caught up with her e-mails.

Late one night, Adrian finally knocked on her door. She was preparing to go to bed, already in her pajamas, and was reluctant to let him in, especially when she saw he had a glass in his hand. He insisted, saying that he had something important to say.

She gestured at the chair and took the sofa opposite.

They sat in silence. She was desperate for him to leave and at last looked him in the eye. The skin on his nose was still peeling.

"Look, you're the most beautiful thing here," he said, pulling his chair nearer.

He touched her face, his thumb lingering against her cheek. His hand brushed against her neck and came to rest just below her collarbone.

She froze.

His hand felt cold and scaly. He looked like a different man, a pleading selfishness narrowing his eyes. When his irises focused on her face, they glittered.

Just as he leaned in toward her, she sprang up off the sofa. The fear and disgust crashed through again, but this time there was a cold fury that he had persisted, that he had felt entitled to do so with someone like her.

He was thrown off guard, lost his balance, and crashed to the ground. The chair screeched against the stone floor. His glass reeled across the room before coming to a gently rocking halt by the baseboard.

As a pass, it was grotesque. As an act of will, it was inept. Spots of whiskey stained the rug in a wide arc. He lay on the floor, looking at her like an injured animal, limbs strained, frozen in an effort to redeem himself, but the exertion proved too much. His body seemed to cave in, and his head hit the floor with a sad *crack*. He blinked rapidly: it looked as though he expected some ministration, some sympathy. Ania left the room and walked into the corridor. Anyone walking past would see his corduroy legs through the open doorway, his feet in the scuffed shoes. But there was no one about. She pulled a coat over her pajamas and ran down the corridor. After she had knocked on Nemesia's door, they hurried together to find a security guard.

MORNING EVENTUALLY CAME. She was still shaken and in the grip of that same cold rage. During the long sleepless night Ania was sickened to realize that even in this temple of art and culture, where she had secured her entry using all her advantages, she could not make herself safe. In the morning, she asked to meet the center administrator in order to make a complaint. She made sure she was calm and clear-eyed as she described Adrian's conduct in bald terms. He nodded at her every word and pushed a box of tissues a couple inches closer to her, tissues she did not need.

"I am truly sorry that this unfortunate incident occurred here, and I can fully understand your concerns. But I think we all have the same objective, do we not? We all want an amicable resolution," he said.

"I don't want an amicable anything," said Ania. "Either he goes or I do."

"Miss Khurana, everyone here is an artist, part of a threatened breed, doing our best to confront the challenges of a world that is, at best, indifferent, at worst, hostile. We are all on the same side, and it is essential that we remain so."

Ania remained silent.

"It's also worth pointing out that Mr. Thurley is a huge figure in the literary establishment. I need hardly tell you about the prizes he has won, the regard in which he is held all over the world. If any public unpleasantness results from whatever has transpired between you, it will certainly be troubling for him. But for a young, talented writer like you, just about to launch herself into this world, it could be a complete disaster."

He pulled at each of his cuffs.

"I will speak to Mr. Thurley," he said, lowering his voice. "I will make him understand that nothing of this sort must be repeated while he is here."

As he continued to provide assurances, Ania left the room.

That afternoon she walked to the village to clear her head, her eyes still prickling. She held the two books Adrian had lent her. From an outside table at a café on the promenade, she gazed across the lake. It all seemed ruined. An oppressive humidity had descended; the shops in the village now looked crammed with vulgar souvenirs and an enormous tour bus blocked the road leading up the hill. The lake waters were choppy and gray. Somewhere, bottles smashed. She was going to throw the books into a trash bin, but she found that she did not have the heart. In the end, she left them facedown on a wall above the jetty.

She had shown a flash, a mere flash, of resistance but did not have the stomach for any more. She felt betrayed, winded. She wanted to leave at once. As she packed, she saw that she had a message from Dev. She would not read it until much later; there was no telling what effect it could have on her at the moment. Early the next morning, having changed her flight to New York, she was in a taxi on her way to Verona. Deep in her suitcase, secure in a cylinder of tissue and sticky tape, was the cigarette that Nemesia had rolled for her on the sunniest day at the villa.

CHAPTER FOURTEEN

DIMPLE KNEW THAT Ania had strong opinions on food but was unlikely to have ever prepared anything that required more than the addition of a dressing. And she knew that food was cooked in the Khuranas' house, vast quantities of it, but not even a whiff reached the parts where the family spent their time. It seemed remarkable. She mustered up the courage to have a quiet word with the Khuranas' housekeeper, Dina. She wanted to cook a meal that was not too difficult but stylish, a couple of courses with class. Dina had overseen enough dinners; Dina would know.

Her office was a windowless room off the kitchen, from where she administered the Khurana household. Her sagging appearance belied her energy and efficiency. The bags under her eyes were pronounced and capacious. Her neck rested in folds. Her clothes sagged too; baggy trousers and a series of smocks with large pockets that hung loose. And her words sagged as they fell in a despondent trickle from her lips, which also tended to droop.

Dina, unsurprisingly, had a keen sense of social distinction and was able to rank individuals by the pitch and tone of Dileep's voice when he mentioned them. She settled her own behavior accordingly. She spoke to Dimple as she sorted out the week's receipts into neat piles; there was no need to get up.

"Who is the guest? Is it a man?" asked Dina.

Dimple mumbled that it was a man but not that kind of man. Dina looked at her over her reading glasses and turned back to her receipts.

Her instructions were sound and delivered like proverbs.

"Don't make something for the first time. You'll definitely get it wrong.

"Give him something filling and make sure it's hot.

"And make sure there's plenty of it.

"And there should be bread on the table. Men love bread."

THE TIME HAD come for Dimple to show herself that she was modern. It was interesting, that word. At home it had been used with derision to describe any woman who wore lipstick in the daytime or had an acknowledged boyfriend. But she had also heard it used by young men to refer to their hopes for IT careers in large cities, and by family members to describe relatives who had moved abroad and now owned two fancy cars. In her case she decided that it meant a certain kind of courage, to be able to ask a man home to dinner, to buy and cook the food, to encourage him to make his feelings known. Her heart thudded at the prospect. When Ania spoke to her about Fahim, she was easily convinced of their mutual attraction. But during her absence, apprehensions returned. Now Dimple was going to be modern. With her roommate away for a while, she would have the apartment to herself. It was the right time to approach Fahim.

He accepted her invitation immediately and sounded thrilled to be asked. Dimple felt a twinge of guilt for having doubted Ania. She decided on chicken cacciatore with rice. She had not cooked it before, but she was confident about her abilities in the kitchen. It sounded hearty but sophisticated: she said it under her breath a few times in her cubicle at work. "Cacciatore" meant "hunter" in Italian, according to one of the recipes. It seemed like the kind of food that would appeal to a man, along with the two loaves of bread she intended to buy. Dina's advice was to be at least partially heeded.

Dimple went shopping for the ingredients at Khan Market. The capers came in a jar with a little booklet tied to its rim, the balsamic vinegar had a castle stamped on the top of its cork. She looked at the labels with care. Didn't *all* salt come from the sea? Wasn't that why Gandhi had to march all the way to the seashore at Dandi?

She took the day off work: this day had to be kept separate from other days; it could not be corrupted by her normal routine. But then she was at a loss. The shopping was already done; the cooking didn't have to be started till the early evening. She unfurled her yoga mat on the mosaic floor and then simply sat on it. The room was filled with an unfamiliar mid-morning light; on the mat lay a square of sunshine, patterned with the swirls of the grillwork. In a few minutes she had rolled onto her side and fallen asleep, her snores barely audible.

She opened her eyes to the yellow stains on the ceiling, the result of the vapors and sighs of dozens of previous tenants. For a few seconds she had no idea where she was—then she sprang up in horror, certain that she must have slept through the day. She grabbed her phone to see that she had been dozing for only a few minutes.

He could want to have sex. The thought struck her like a blow. She had been so preoccupied with the apartment and the food that she had not given it any thought. She was practical: there was a packet of condoms at the back of her underwear drawer. But she did not even know how he really felt about her, so wasn't it presumptuous to assume anything along these lines? On the other hand, she had been led to believe that men always wanted sex. Would she have sex with him even if it became clear that he was just looking for a fling? The last time had been with Ankit, and there had been no tortuous rumination. They had drunk too much Old Monk and maniacally shed their clothes on her bedroom floor. Her mood dampened as she thought of Ankit, and she sprang up to busy herself in the kitchen.

She browned the chicken, enjoying the sizzle in the pan, still trying to force Ankit from her mind. Then a wave of anxiety washed over her again. Fahim was a television personality, someone who would be recognized by half the city. It felt as though his world had flipped itself inside out and somehow come to include her. These sorts of thrills occurred in the lives of wide-eyed girls in soaps *on* television. She wondered if her landlord would spot Fahim on his way in. He was the kind of man who would barrel upstairs a few minutes later, full of a stammering admiration, panting for a selfie with the celebrity. And then the next day he would try to grill her about the nature of their relationship, warning her about these TV types and Fahim, a Muslim.

She returned to her bedroom to have another look at the dress she had picked. The problem was what to do about her feet. She couldn't open the door barefoot: it seemed too casual and might suggest that she was expecting nudity in due course. But it would be unseemly to shuffle around in front of him in her house flipflops. High heels would make it look like she was trying too hard—and she might slip and drop a bottle. Should she pad around in socks?

She returned to the kitchen to make the sauce, growing more confident as it began to smell right. Her mother was an indifferent cook: nearly everything she made tasted of some watery vegetable and an excess of garlic. Her primary concern was with wastage. Nubs and chunks from the back of the fridge were grated and chopped, jars were swirled with water and then scraped dry. Dimple had once borrowed a rolling pin for a game and lost it. Her mother had made her roll out chapatis with a Thums Up bottle for days afterward.

She opened the windows to air the room. In the street below, one of her neighbors rushed out holding a pressure cooker, plonking it down on the repairman's cart, and announcing that it still would not whistle, she was tired of waiting by it like a fool. Dimple decided it was time to shower. She wished that there were other friends who could send her a few spirited messages, Ania being out of bounds for the time being. But none of her other friends knew about Fahim, and their minds would simply boggle at the thought of her dating someone like him. As she lathered her hair, she remembered the coffee and almost cried out with annoyance. She had forgotten to buy a cafetière and now Fahim would have to do without. She finished up as quickly as she could and ran downstairs to the kirana store, her hair still wet, damp patches on the old kurta she had thrown on. She bought a small jar each of Bru and Nescafé. If she used half a spoon of each, it might not be so bad.

HE WAS TWELVE minutes late so far, which was nothing. She had spent the last hour or so wishing it was all over, whatever that meant. But now her heart was palpitating again. She checked all his social media to see if there were any clues as to his whereabouts, but he had posted nothing for a day. She tried to think about it like a crisis at work, contemplating the worst that could happen, and then making reassuring contingency plans. They would have little to say to each other, and he would look bored and distracted. He would wolf down the chicken and leave early. Or he would hate it and push it around on his plate, eating all the bread. She would laughingly ask if he wanted to order a takeaway instead and try to alight on some new and interesting topic of conversation. He would never call again. But then she remembered the moment in the cave, the certainty she had felt as the sound of the water echoed around them.

When the knock on the door came, she almost froze.

It sounded again, cross and insistent.

She leaped up, gave her palms a quick wipe against the skirt of her dress, and opened the door.

It was her landlord.

He said that he was going to be out of town for a couple of weeks but not to worry, his brother and sister-in-law would be staying to keep an eye on everything, presumably meaning her. The rent would be due while he was away, but she was under no circumstances authorized to hand the cash over to either of them, and, for obvious reasons, there was no question of a check. He would come and see her as soon as he returned to take the cash. Dimple nodded as he spoke, beginning to inch the door forward as much as she dared. He continued to talk, bringing up the boy who cleaned the common parts and the person he suspected of always leaving the front grille unlocked and the fate of her broken-down air-conditioning unit, which he could not afford to have repaired at the moment. She was assaulted by a surge of rage so violent and unexpected that she had to grip the door and stare at the floor to steady herself.

When she finally closed the door, she was exhausted. She headed toward the bedroom to take yet another look at her face and then felt she couldn't go through with it. She went to gaze at the chicken instead, which appeared remarkably like the photo in the recipe, although its casserole looked far more eye-catching than her battered steel pan. She moved back to the divan, but she would have to plump up the cushions again so sat instead on one of the hard dining chairs.

She stared at her phone screen and in that moment, as though by an act of her will, it lit up. She read Fahim's message, saying that he would not be able to make it—a major breaking story, really sorry, these things happen—as though she had been expecting it all along. He said nothing about trying to reschedule. She told herself that in a way it was a great relief: at least she wasn't still waiting, checking her breath, looking to see whether the ice had firmed up in the trays.

Dimple took off her dress and hung it up in the wardrobe. It would still smell of her perfume the next time she wore it. She returned the wine to the kitchen cupboard and filled a few plastic containers with the food, wiping the rims. There was still a little chicken left over, too little to bother to refrigerate. She spooned it onto a plate that was not much bigger than a saucer and took it to the divan by the open window.

There was due to be a wedding in the house opposite, and strings of yellow lights cascaded down from their balcony. A cycle rickshaw came to a halt, bringing the old couple to the building across the road. They returned at the same time every evening in the same rickshaw. It took time, the man carefully stepping to the ground and then turning to help his wife down. They checked all their belongings and then looked back into the rickshaw to be sure. When they had made their way to the door, the rickshaw driver tinkled his bell twice as a way of saying goodbye. She listened for it. He did it every time.

CHAPTER FIFTEEN

ALMOST A COUPLE of months had passed since Fahim had heard from Ania. His last message had gone unanswered, but he was not worried. He knew that she had been abroad, tending to one or other of her indulgences. She would be in touch soon.

It was one of those metallic Delhi days when the light seemed to have no source, just a mineral haze through which millions of people found their way home. On the street corner, there was a whirl of yellow and pink as a sudden breeze sent a hawker's pinwheels into a spin. Fumes rose; men jostled. Every edge of the pavement was trampled on.

At the edge of the flurry, Fahim was deep in thought. He had always known how to make himself useful. He was able to change a tire in under ten minutes; he could affect a sympathetic ear; he was familiar with obscure corners of the city and could provide information in no time; he would give his arm to someone's grandmother for a whole evening, aware of who would be remarking on his attentiveness. Now, he felt he was on the way to making himself indispensable.

Ania's pursuit had been relentless. When he thought about the public praise, the constant communication, and the welcome into her home, it seemed almost starry-eyed. He was surprised by the awkward use of Dimple as some sort of fig leaf. He had never imagined that a girl like Ania would need the presence of an inconsequential friend to maintain a sense of propriety. But he had humored them. He knew that every incident was pored over and that men were judged by how they treated a woman's close friends. There had to be warmth and interest but no sexual curiosity. So he had directed his charm at Dimple too, in spite of her earnestness and insignificance. In a moment of weakness a few weeks ago, he had even accepted an invitation to dinner from her—but later come to his senses and canceled. Delhi was full of these girls: lost, eager to please, pointless.

He and Ania had danced around each other enough; it was time to be frank. With her by his side, he would finally be secure. Would it make him happy? It was so easy to let himself believe that love was imminent. For the first time in years he thought about what it meant to be loved, to have an unqualified attachment to a woman, to be assured of true affection, to be free of anxiety and alienation. It seemed an extraordinary and stupefying prospect.

He had to stop walking as he was assailed by a feeling that was physical, a tremble in his joints, a burst of vertigo. He held on to a lamppost while he waited for normal sensation to return to his body. Commuters hurried toward rickshaws in the rush; a woman pulling a suitcase tutted that he was in her way. Young men, touting for fares, hung out of bus doorways and yelled their destinations. He felt worn out and stupid, continuing to lean against the lamppost, still waiting for some kind of relief.

DIMPLE SAT AT her desk, unable to concentrate. She had spent much of the morning thinking of the grand hotel in her hometown. As a child she had been inside the hotel only once, the spring she had snuck in to try to catch a glimpse of an actress. It had tormented her, the fact that a film crew was at the hotel and that for hours every day the actress would be visible, sitting on a bench in the garden or perhaps walking along one of the shaded paths, a lackey holding an umbrella over her head—and in a few days she would vanish like a popped bubble. There was no point in even trying, her friends had told her. Security guards swarmed around the hotel, angry blasts sounding from their whistles whenever they saw stragglers trying to approach the film crew. Even those hardy souls who had camped out by the gates only glimpsed the darkened windows of her car as she swept in and out.

At the age of twelve, for the first time in her life, Dimple had schemed. She was convinced that the actress's arrival was fated and somehow yoked to her eventual ability to escape the town. She had heard that they were filming in the hotel ballroom at all hours. Her mother stayed up late reading and marking papers, and so the best time to slip out of the house would be in the early hours. It was certain to be Dimple's only chance.

She left the house before dawn, wheeling her bicycle beyond the light cast by the streetlight. It had seemed wise to wear her blue velveteen dress in case the actress invited her to her room, but now, as she pedaled up the hill, she knew it would be tragically creased. She left the bicycle at the bottom of a slope behind the hotel. Everyone in school knew about the breach in the bamboo fence through which waiters smuggled girls into their rooms. She made her way up through the pines and deodars, twigs cracking under her feet, the faint warble of thrushes already audible above her head.

It was easier than Dimple could have ever imagined. Even as her heart hammered, she skipped up the front steps, buoyed by the recollection that she was in her blue velveteen dress, and said confidently to the guard on duty, "My mother is waiting for me."

He smiled and nodded, perhaps accustomed to the strange habits of the rich on holiday, whether late-night frolics or early-morning rambles.

There was no one at reception, and she hurried across the parquet and stopped near the foot of the stairs. She had to make her mind up in the next few seconds. She decided to go down the dimmer of the three corridors. Halfway down she paused and then slipped under the cordon, from which hung a sign that read "No Entry."

At the end of the passage, crates and boxes were stacked next to a pair of double doors. She tried the handle, and the door remained shut. She tried again, pushing against it with her shoulder, and it swung open. The room seemed to extend into a distant darkness. Light was beginning to seep around the edges of the heavy curtains, and she could make out the shape of a grand piano in one corner. There were rugs in different shades of maroon and an ornate sofa against the wall. To her, everything looked opulent and irreplaceable.

On a table in the middle of the room, a pale plastic sheet shrouded a dark object. She skirted around the room, past lighting equipment, taking careful, tiny steps over the cables. On the other side of the table, the plastic covering gaped, and as she approached, she could see what it was meant to hide—a cake, a three-tiered chocolate cake, with delicate swirls of pink and silver icing. Dimple stopped. She knew just how it would taste, the way each bite would disintegrate to fill every crevice in her mouth. She wanted to sink her arms into the cake elbow-deep, the blue velveteen dress now forgotten. The temptation was too great. Even if she were to jeopardize her future, it was a risk worth taking. She stretched out her arm and swept the side of the cake with her finger. It was cold and hard. The cake was carved out of wood.

Disappointment flooded through her. At least there was no one there to witness her humiliation. She left the room, closing the door behind her, and walked back down the dim corridor. Opposite the stairs a door leading to a verandah was now open, kept ajar by a cleaning trolley. Dimple crept out and climbed over the railing, jumping into a flower bed. She tried to regain her bearings.

And then the miracle happened. On the third floor, opposite where she stood, the actress emerged on a balcony. Dimple crouched down. The actress had her hands on the balustrade as she watched the sun creeping over the distant hills. She looked as though she was still dressed from the night before: her long silk dress fell like water, a horseshoe sparkled at her throat. Dimple stared at the actress, incapable of standing or waving or calling out, her shoes sinking into the soil. The sun continued to rise, shafts of light lancing through the trees on the hillside, their reflections aflame in the glass balcony doors. The actress turned her head toward the room as though someone had called her name, and her expression cracked into one of revulsion. In the next moment, she coaxed a smile back on to her face and disappeared through the doors.

At school later that day, Dimple's story was heard with disbelief, suspicion, and, eventually, a grudging acceptance. She had never been one of those girls who spun tales to draw attention to themselves, and the ardor with which she described the actress could not be faked. As unlikely as it seemed, of all the girls at school, Dimple was the one who had gotten closest. Once this had been established, there was a quiet acknowledgment of her success in the classroom, a concession that was ominous from the start.

The next day there was a new development. A few girls in Dimple's class said that the film crew had passed a request on to the school: they were looking for children to be extras in a scene to be filmed on the bandstand and would pick up volunteers outside the school gates the following Sunday. Hasty plans were made around the playground to gather at the appointed hour, and girls who in the past had barely looked at Dimple asked her anxiously if she was going. It was extraordinary how one little triumph had transformed her fortunes.

She decided not to risk asking her mother for permission and simply left a note wedged under a pickle jar on the table. On Sunday morning she wore the lucky blue velveteen dress again and was outside the school gates by six o'clock. She was the first to arrive. She walked up and down the road for a little while, not wanting to sit on the stone benches, in case they left streaks on her dress.

A cart carrying potted plants trundled past, followed by a rickshaw. Rolls of brightly colored blankets went past on another.

The silence returned until a man sped down the hill on a motor-bike. Dimple perched on the edge of a stone bench and then stood up again, craning her neck to see the back of her skirt. Another rickshaw rolled by.

She ran through the range of complicated reasons why the film crew bus could be late. Several times she walked to the end of the road and back. She had no watch and could only tell that she had probably been waiting for hours when her stomach began to rumble. Crows began to caw above her head, and she felt a quiver run down her spine. She wondered whether she was being watched, but there was no one in sight. She looked again at the line of the school wall, the pink rhododendrons that swept down the hill, the stone bridge above the culvert, the bend in the road. The tug of suspicion grew stronger and turned into a near cer-tainty. There was no bus; there never had been a bus. She had been punished for her ascendancy. Eyes had gathered in nooks all around her to observe her disgrace, hidden behind trees, perhaps in a parked car or peering from the other side of the high wall.

When she returned home, the note was still under the pickle jar. Her mother must have rushed out to one of her meetings without even seeing it. Dimple screwed it up and crammed it into her pocket.

She had been punished then and, as she deleted Fahim's num-ber from her phone, she realized she had been punished now.

HIGH ABOVE MEHRAULI, there was a pause in the conversation. A remote, clamorous reality unfolded in the narrow lanes below. Deities were lifted onto a bier, and the procession threaded its way through the throngs. Flower sellers bellowed. At the sweet stall, a ladle sank slowly into a giant pot of ghee.

At the rooftop club, a sense of seclusion drifted around like a haze. Ania had keyed in her password and been escorted to the top floor by a man with a walkie-talkie.

"Is that real? What's it actually for?" she asked.

He looked injured.

"Important staff communications, ma'am. For your safety and security," he said.

Fahim was waiting for her at one of the tables under the vine-covered pergola. She stepped around the dark waters of the rooftop pond, grasses quavering at its edge in the evening breeze. It wasn't much of a breeze. The weather had begun to turn warm and muggy. It had been only a few months since she had embarked upon her project to bring Fahim and Dimple together, but it seemed like so much longer.

From the villa at Lake Garda, she had gone to New York, hoping to be revitalized. But she had stayed only a couple of days: their town house was too quiet, the streets too busy, her friends too annoying. She had returned to Delhi a fortnight ago determined to think no more about Adrian Thurley. The rage had abated. But there was a deflation, a lethargy that she had not been able to shake off. She had found it difficult to plunge back into her social life and had spent much of her time in her room with Sigmund, whose rheumy eyes seemed to share her melancholy. She had dropped by Dev's home and discovered that he was away at a conference. Eventually she met Dimple, who tried to be breezily evasive but in the end gave a full account of those dire hours waiting for Fahim.

Ania was furious. She felt personally snubbed but was even more enraged that Fahim had manipulated Dimple and treated her with such disregard. She ignored his calls and messages at first; her anger turned into a chilly contempt. Of course, stories did break and journalists did have to cancel plans at short notice. But her recent introspection had made her sense that there was some greater ruse at work here.

As Fahim's appeals continued, however, she began to wonder whether she should agree to see him. She had been fond of him, she reminded herself. And perhaps he was sincere in his desire to give her an explanation. Whatever happened, it would put an end to the ridiculous, uncertain choreography of the last few months.

Fahim stood up as soon as he spotted her approach the table.

He seemed anxious. He had twisted the napkin into a coil, and it had dropped onto the floor. She read that to be a good sign: he would be contrite and responsive.

"Is this table okay? Is it too hot for you here? Shall we go inside?" he asked.

"I'm fine here."

From their table, Delhi was a maze of treetops and sandstone, arches glimpsed through foliage, balconies nestled high up against weathered façades, dark thickets of acacias. A pair of boys, still in their school uniform, emerged on a pitted wall, their arms outstretched as they took careful steps over the clefts and niches. They leaped off the end of the wall, raced up a half-ruined staircase, and crawled into a tunnel. Minutes later they reappeared on a neighboring rooftop, giddy and triumphant.

As Ania watched them, she could feel Fahim's eyes on her.

It was still early, and only one of the other tables was occupied. A waiter polished glasses, his back turned.

Fahim continued to be uncomfortable. He gabbled about some inconsequential election, changed his drink order, undid and retied his shoelaces, went off to wash his hands. When he returned, he gestured to the other side of the terrace.

"Come and have a look at the sky; it's amazing."

She picked up her handbag and followed him.

The sun was a pale disk at the center of a grand purple billow. There was a great rustle and heave, an endless thrash as a tide of pigeons rose into the air. The light changed again. A mauve tinge seeped over the cracked white domes of an abandoned mosque.

"Listen," said Fahim.

She turned, and his face was far too close. And then she felt the rough scrape of his skin against her lips and then the warmth of his mouth, a wetness.

"What are you *doing*?"

She pushed him away with all her force.

His face crumpled, overwhelmed by hurt. And then it reconstituted itself, shock and anger etched into his features.

An image of Adrian Thurley flashed through her mind—the chalky skin, the pale eyelashes, the whiskey breath, and the hoarse whisper of "Principessina." With all her force she swung her handbag, hitting Fahim in the chest.

"What the fuck is your problem?" he shouted.

The other couple turned around, a waiter stopped in the middle of the terrace.

Ania hurried past the tables, through the door, and into the waiting elevator. A sharp pain ran through her finger as she jabbed at the button. The doors closed. She was beginning to sweat, a cough making her chest hurt. At the exit she walked past the desk and then had to return. She mumbled the car's license plate number to the valet and mauled the inside of her bag, looking for a tissue as the elevator made its way up again. An arrow flared in the dim light as the lift began to come back down. She was still coughing, still sweating. She spotted the car nosing its way up the lane and rushed out to meet it. A motorbike swerved to avoid her. She stepped in a pothole, and the water seeped into her shoe. Reaching the car, she yanked at the door handle, her cough now hurting her chest. The cold blast of its interior made her feel feverish. It was the same fear and disgust that she had felt in Lake Garda. But this time, thoughts of Dimple also crowded into her mind.

She managed to let the words out: "Thanks. Let's go home."

She laid her head back and looked at the row of tiny perforations that ran the length of the headliner fabric. The car went past the dark doors of the club but she did not turn to look. They reached the main road and waited for a gap in the traffic. She had stopped sweating. But the cough remained trapped in her gullet.

PART

TWO

CHAPTER SIXTEEN

IN ANOTHER FEW weeks, summer arrived with all its ferocity. From the pool there came sounds of a ferocious splashing and a wail cut short. Ania rushed across the lawn, through the horseshoe arch in the wall, and down the steps, wondering whether Sigmund had been nosing around its edge and tumbled in.

As she approached, she saw that the splashing form was Renu, her limbs crashing through the water as though she were powering a turbine. Her head swung from side to side with an uncharacteristic violence. The colonel stood by the side of the pool in shorts and a Hawaiian shirt, making encouraging noises. Ania had never seen his pale, thin legs before. She tried not to look and instead stepped nearer to the edge of the pool. Its ultramarine tiles were made more vivid by the white tadelakt-plaster walls that surrounded the pool area. Jasmine cascaded over the roof of the pool house, built in the style of a Moroccan riad, hand-carved wooden doors at its entrance and lanterns from Fez hanging in its many niches and alcoves.

Ania settled on one of the vintage daybeds in front of the pool house.

"Oh, it's you in the pool," she said to Renu. "I thought Siggy was drowning."

The colonel gave her a wave, and Renu stopped mid-hurtle, rising to stand in the shallow end.

"It's my new life, a sort of baptism," she said, her chest heaving.

"All right then, time for a break," said the colonel.

Renu waded to the steps and climbed up them on her hands and knees. The flouncy little skirt of her floral one-piece was now plastered around her hips.

"I'm exhausted. And starving. I never knew swimming brought on such an appetite."

"Bua dearest, that was hardly a swim."

Renu giggled.

"That's a huge improvement, you should have seen me yesterday."

"Where did you get that swimsuit?"

"Isn't it just adorable? I've missed it. I haven't worn it since the days when that horribly rude woman would come home to wax me."

"So what's with the swimming, all of a sudden?"

"I've finally decided to learn. Well, it all began because I wanted to restart my Persian classes and the colonel said that he would like to come too. But sadly my tutor, you remember him, the young man who went to school in a Daimler, he said that he doesn't have time at the moment because he's writing his memoir. So instead, I started teaching the colonel a bit of French. And it's been so much fun. Although the poor darling's pronunciation is atrocious."

Ania tried to ignore the swell of annoyance she was beginning to experience. Even though she was responsible for Renu's marital euphoria, she was not in the mood to witness it. Her efforts to bring Fahim and Dimple together having gone so horribly wrong, she felt she deserved some time to wallow.

"Well, you better be careful the colonel doesn't get too fluent in French. Lots of women find it a real turn-on, you know. He might end up running off with someone else," said Ania.

Renu's confidence had soared to such an extent that she found the prospect hilarious.

"Oh, they'd just send him back after they'd seen what an utter grump he is first thing in the morning." She giggled.

"In return for the French classes," she continued, "he's teaching me how to swim. He was appalled when he found out that I couldn't. He demanded to know what on earth I used our pool for. I told him that on occasion I used the water to wet a tissue when I needed to clean my glasses."

"Aren't you supposed to be off to Australia soon?"

"We've postponed the trip. Nikhil has finally confirmed that he's coming for a few weeks. And you know, he's really like a son to my dear colonel. I'm just praying that everything goes well."

"But why wouldn't it?"

"I'm terribly apprehensive. They have a very special relationship, and what if Nikhil finds that he doesn't get on with me or thinks that his uncle made a wrong choice or something like that."

"Bua, stop being so absurd. Even if you don't get on, it hardly matters. How often do they even see each other?"

"That's not the point. These are deep bonds, and it's important that we all come together as a family. You know, it's really quite nerve-racking. I'm not sure what I have to do to appeal to a young man."

"Oh my God, would you listen to yourself. So what do we know about him? Give me the essentials."

"Well, he's lived in America all of his life, and he's very close to the colonel because he has a difficult relationship with his own father. He's smart, handsome—although I don't know, he looks handsome in photographs, I should say. I learned a lesson or two when they were trying to get me married years ago and kept sending me all those boys' pictures. And then finally I'd meet them in the flesh. Uff."

"What does he do?"

"Something to do with financial responsibility. Is that what they call it, or is it corporate responsibility? You know, these large companies, they make them spend some of their money on forests and malaria and zoos."

"And I remember you saying he's very attractive?"

"Shall I turn matchmaker for you this time?"

"I'm sorry, darling, but you'd be completely terrible at it. Let's see what he's like when he turns up. I still can't see how his approval matters so much when you're already married, and he doesn't even live here."

"I suppose you're right. But still."

"Listen, bua, I need to ask you about a hypothetical situation. Strictly hypothetical."

"Go on."

"Have you ever tried to improve someone's life, you know, out of sheer kindness, lift them up, but then realized that the way you went about it was all wrong, but because of other people's awfulness and not because of anything that *you* did?"

"Have you been interfering with Dileep's wardrobe again? I'm telling you, he's so stubborn, just let him wear those suits with the funny checked trousers. He'll tire of them in another week."

"Enough chitchat," called the colonel from the far end of the pool, "time to get back in."

He took off his shirt, folded it as though he might have to return it to a shop, and laid it on a lounger. In a flash he turned around, dived off the edge, and sliced into the water with perfect grace. A few seconds later his gray head emerged in the middle of the pool, a quiet pride washing over his face.

"Oh my," said Renu, "how wonderful, did you see that? Well, I had better carry on with my lesson. Darling, come round to dinner at ours. If I spend any more time here, Dileep will think I never left."

She stepped into the shallow end and waded through the water, her arms aloft, as though she were delivering some precious cargo.

NINA REACHED FOR a pair of scissors and cut the invitation into little strips. She swept these off her desk straight into the wastepaper basket. So much was trickling out of her hands, but she could still safeguard and ration her most valuable possession, her presence. She lit a cigarette with a great sense of satisfaction that she knew would dissipate in a few moments.

The apartment owners' association had finally settled on a figure for the refurbishment of the building façade and common parts. She had no idea how she would pay it. An oleaginous letter from her bank had not been able to disguise its malevolent intent. As a result of her recent defaults, her loans were being recalibrated to assist her in abiding by their terms. The mechanisms of this conversion were set out in opaque terminology, but it was clear that the outcome would be stricter vigilance and higher interest payments.

And now Silky Chhabra was throwing a wedding anniversary party in St. Petersburg. She could imagine the jollity, the fountains and marble floors, the stony looks on the bodyguards' faces. A hundred people were being flown to Russia to witness her tawdry tsarina dazzle. But Nina would not be in attendance.

Year after year, Nina had watched Silky inhabit her role as Mrs. Chhabra, settling into its splendid nooks as though she had been born to it. She had traded in her social insecurities for a jangly new personality, in whose service bad manners masqueraded as benevolent plain-speaking. She made her female staff dress like French maids. She renamed all the Chhabra houses, and now one of them was called "Rhapsody."

Once a year Silky gave a lunch for her lesser relatives and friends, usually in the third week of June, when many in her close circle had not yet returned from their summer holidays. After dessert, but before the coffee was served, she would clap her hands, and they would all troop into one of the spare bedrooms. Hanging on a couple of rails would be a selection of Silky's clothes from the previous year: a sari that had been widely admired at a party and therefore could not be worn again, a pair of slacks that had proved to be a little baggy at the hips, a skirt whose bold print in the clear light of day had proved to be a misjudgment.

"Help yourselves," she would announce with another dainty clap.

Silky was at least a couple sizes smaller than the most petite of her guests, but no one dared point this out. The group would sullenly pick out items that they could at least try to resell. Silky would make enthusiastic suggestions, pressing a lace blouse into a pair of resistant hands or tying a foulard around someone's neck, the knot a little too tight. The guests would thank her for her generosity, and Silky would say that it was the least she could do, which, in fact, was true. They would have coffee and then leave with their new acquisitions, some of them swearing to themselves that they would not return the next year. Invariably, they did.

Nina reached for the invitation envelope and scribbled a few calculations on its flap. She drew a line across the final figures, the nib ripping through the paper. It was clear that her situation was impossible. The cigarette's long finger of ash crumbled over the onyx edge of the ashtray. She began an e-mail to her ex-husband, describing her financial predicament in vivid and not altogether truthful terms. It was a note that, on the whole, was conciliatory, although she left in a couple of subdued accusations. She decided she would send it the next day, after reading it one more time, even though it hardly warranted such careful attention. He would read it in a few seconds and make up his mind instantly, his face hardening. His voice rang in her ear, the one he used to cut people down to size. Even after all these years, it was as though he was in the room with her.

She began another e-mail, addressed to her son's doctor at a treatment facility in Utah, even though she knew that her entreaties would be rebuffed. Her ex-husband, as the named guardian and the person who paid the bills, would have left strict instructions. But trying to renew contact with her son had become as much a part of her routine as the tortuous enumeration of the people who had wronged her. It had been years since she had heard his voice.

When he had been born, she could scarcely believe that he was hers, that pink, wrinkled creature with the skin flaking off his tiny fists. All his life, she had continued to search but she had found nothing of her in him. Perhaps a few antibodies coursed around his blood, that was all, the result of those horrific few weeks of breastfeeding, her eyes screwed tighter with each agonizing suck. There had been moments when she recognized some trait—a stubborn refusal to be embarrassed, a distaste for public displays of affection—but in the end they turned out to be something completely different. It had always been disorienting: feeling such anguished, helpless love for a creature that could just as well have hatched in a pit or grown from larvae.

Nina shivered; she was always cold these days. She checked to make sure that the maid had not turned on the air-conditioning and pulled on a pair of thick socks. If she had a little bit more work done to the apartment—a new bathroom, an overhaul of the ancient wiring—surely it would be worth far more. The last valuation had been a few years ago and all anyone talked about was Delhi's galloping real estate prices. She might even be able to borrow some more.

For the time being, however, she needed a rapid fix. She would have to go to lunch with Dileep and employ her breeziest manner to allude to her financial difficulties. He would, of course, come to her assistance with the delicacy and discretion that she had come to expect. But she did not imagine that it could continue forever.

ANIA ARRIVED AT the restaurant early, still mulling over her phone call with Dimple. She had apologized once again for the fact that Fahim had turned out to be so disgraceful, but had kept the incident at the Mehrauli club to herself. There had been a strange pause over the phone, and a conversation that was meant to reassure them both had been taut and unsettling. Even the sight of the restaurant's famous flummery pudding on the menu failed to lift her mood.

Once a year Ania had lunch with CS Dayal, one of Dileep's numerous legal advisers but also the trustee of a primary family trust of which Ania was the sole beneficiary. They met at a restaurant of excellent vintage on the outer circle of Connaught Place, apparently once graced by Lady Willingdon, in one of her many mauve dresses. They were led to the same table each time, the leaded window behind it still unwashed; he always ordered the pork cutlet, followed by a double portion of trifle.

Ania was never sure of the purpose of this annual meeting. It took place in public so no trust affairs could freely be discussed; and besides, Mr. Dayal was not a voluble man. He would ask her how various members of the family were keeping and then fall silent. After these preliminaries, Ania was left to take charge. She felt, during that gloomy hour, that she had to account for her life in some way. So she told CS Dayal about her work at Dr. Bhatia's oncology department and at the animal shelter. She mentioned any travel plans and skirted round one or two of the better-formed ideas she had for a novel. CS Dayal would nod and try to dislodge a shred of food stuck in his lower right molar.

She persisted with the meetings because they gave her a sense of stability and significance. She had first experienced a far cruder version of this sensation as a child, accompanying her father to a bank in Zurich. They had walked into an enormous room with mottled marble floors and tiers of foliage cascading down around them. At the far end of the room sat a severe-looking woman at a desk, the authority who would decide on admittance farther into the building. Even at that age Ania knew what confidence and courage it would take to cross the vast distance toward the woman, exposed and conspicuous, the sound of footsteps echoing through the cold air. But her father held her hand and approached the woman with an easy stride. They had a right to be there. And today she took strength from that same awareness.

Far away from the inconsistencies and eccentricities of her family, there lay in place binding arrangements to secure her future. Trust deeds in impregnable language were locked in a vault. And once a year, CS Dayal, a man with complete knowledge of their terms, came to meet her for lunch.

"Did you just ask me something? I'm so sorry, I've been a little preoccupied," she said.

CS Dayal shook his head.

She took a sip of water and continued.

"Mr. Dayal, if you don't mind, could I ask you something? You may think it's a little strange. But has there ever been a time when you let a friend down? I mean, a time when you were genuinely convinced that you were acting in their best interests but in fact made a total mistake."

CS Dayal stared at her. His gray mustache was always a little unkempt, making him look like a melancholy seal.

She sighed.

"I'm not expressing myself very well. What I mean to say is, have you had a situation where other people behaved terribly, and so out of no fault of your own, or maybe just a small fault, but really, an unforeseeable situation, you have ended up hurting a dear friend? That sort of mistake."

CS Dayal licked the mustard sauce off his fork, examined it to make sure there was none left, and then laid it down.

"I would say, with friends, once or twice," he said. "Professionally, never."

CHAPTER SEVENTEEN

THE OLDER RICH had ways of perturbing the newer rich. A direct snub would be too foolhardy, given the unpredictable places where political influence now arose. So they shut them out with ambiguity, glances shot across the table, a stifled smile, all the signs of a beautifully preserved way of life. It was true that this way of life had been handed down in part by the English upper classes: a tenacious respect for hunting-and-shooting rituals, moth-eaten bits of taxidermy, a boarding school brutality, a fitful promiscuity that pledged, and often failed, to be discreet. But there were other more ancient codes that were wholly their own, alive as far back as anyone could remember, which raised their self-belief to near divinity.

There was an artistry in disconcerting the newly rich and immense satisfaction in its correct execution. Invitations would be accepted but apologies would be sent at the last minute due to unavoidable circumstances; or events would be attended for a mere fifteen minutes; or a proxy from the extended family would be dispatched, a lisping second cousin. One dowager from Civil Lines would come to dinner but not eat, asking in the most charming way if her food could be sent over later: her doctor had told her not to consume anything after six in the evening and so she would have it for lunch the next day.

Perturbing the newly rich also involved praise—lavish praise. Everything was lauded. A lazy, practiced rapture flowed over all their choices. But the compliments were so profuse and inflated that they were bound to raise doubt, which was, in any case, the intention. Later, after the last guest had left, there would be a reckoning, an anxious attempt to separate the sincere tributes from the insincere, identify the failings and the missteps, correct them for next time.

Dileep was no exception, but he was more cautious than many in his set. He was all too aware that power reared up in unlikely places, and he made a point of weighing up his actions carefully. But Dileep would also admit, only to himself, that there were other reasons for him to show himself. He loved making an entrance. He looked forward to the way people would jump up from their seats when they spotted him; to the fact that married women gave him compliments about his clothes when the trill in their tone made it obvious that they were referring to what lay under them; to the glances from young people to whom ordinarily a man his age would be invisible.

At the wedding of a billionaire meat exporter, Dileep turned up exactly two hours late. He congratulated the bride and groom, he posed for photographs, he told his host that the mock Times Square was the most beautiful wedding venue he had ever seen.

He accepted and held a drink, which he deposited on a passing tray five minutes later.

On his way out, he pulled out his phone and walked quickly, not making eye contact with anyone. No more could be asked of him.

Serena Bakshi answered after one ring.

"Are you on your way? One thing about him is that he detests people being late," she said.

"I know, I'm sorry, yes, I'm on my way. But I won't pick you up. Can you meet me there?" he said.

"Why?" she asked.

"We've been seen together. God knows how. People are starting to talk," he said.

"Who?"

"I'll tell you when I see you."

"Shall we go at separate times?" she asked.

"No, just separate cars. I feel much more comfortable if we're there together. If you don't mind."

"Of course I don't mind. You're probably the only person I trust in this nightmare city."

"You park in their building and message me when you're there. I'll get dropped off there and ask the driver to park somewhere else," Dileep said.

"Done."

UNTIL RENU WAS married, she had never spent the night in an apartment. Sleepovers with school mates had unfolded in mansions of varying sizes, and holidays were spent in hotel suites or friends' villas. She'd moved into the colonel's apartment as soon as they returned from their honeymoon, conscious that it was a place where he had lived for more than twenty years; whatever she felt about its interiors, it was not for her to breeze in and transform it. The color scheme ranged from tan to rust, and in the hallway there was a ghastly brass plaque depicting some gruesome battle. His mother's many watercolors hung in almost all the rooms, the usual dragonflies and riverbanks, and in one surprising instance, what looked like a nude couple playing badminton. She was relieved that the master bedroom contained little apart from the bed, whose mattress provided excellent lumbar support.

Renu discovered that the most extraordinary feature of living in an apartment was the close manifestation of other people's lives. When sounds drifted in through her windows in the Khurana mansion, they tended to be only the wet hiss of the sprinklers or the steady crunch of the security guards walking down the gravel paths. The colonel's building, however, rattled and hummed all day long. There were titters in the foyer, squabbling in the corridor. The doorman made calls all day to someone called Dolly, which were hurriedly interrupted when he heard the elevator doors open. At around four in the afternoon several times a week, the young girl in 2B went off in a red BMW with a much older man. The occupant of 1A seemed glum and secretive, barely acknowledging her in front of the mailboxes. He always wore a black fedora and muddy boots. Occasionally, on an active day when Renu took the stairs, she lingered for a few seconds as she passed his door, listening out for the strange thumps that she sometimes heard. Bodies, perhaps.

She took her tea out onto the balcony at the same time as the two aged sisters in the apartment downstairs. Their rasping voices carried, and she felt a delicious thrill at being their unseen guest.

"They are very strict on airlines these days, no cutlery allowed in your bag, no knives, nothing."

"I wonder how Pankaj Uncle manages now. You remember how particular he was about having fresh food. He always used to travel with a servant on international flights. The servant would sit in economy and cut up all the fruit for his salad and then take it up to him in first class."

"I don't think they allow you to carry fruit anymore either. It's all so sad, the way the world has become."

"How are your knees today?"

"Better. Yours?"

"Not very good."

Some afternoons she would open a bottle of merlot to share with Clara Ruiz Salinas, the eighty-year-old occupant of 3B. With each glass Clara's memories of her time as a Communist activist in her native Mexico became ever more wistful. As the evening smog closed in and the light dimmed in the apartment, she swallowed various pills and capsules, throwing her head back in a determined way with each swallow. All of this mixing of drugs and alcohol worried Renu, but she felt that it was hardly her place to point out these dangers to a woman who claimed she had spent her youth shooting at fascists. The colonel took a dim view of revolutionary activity, and so these tête-à-têtes were conducted while he was away at the tennis club.

"My nephew will be here in a couple of weeks. It'll be lovely to have a young person around again," said Renu.

"I don't understand the young anymore," said Clara. "They seem so docile and colorless. At their age, we were planning the liberation of the country, singing and dancing and making love under the stars at El Pedregal."

"I think they are still doing some of that. Many of them take sex videos and put them on the Internet."

Clara patted her on the hand and said, "It's not really the same thing."

Now that Nikhil's visit was imminent, Renu felt emboldened to make a few changes in the guise of readying themselves for their first guest. She had the interior of the apartment repainted in alabaster and duck-egg blue, ordered new curtains, and asked Dina to send over the chaise longue from her old bedroom. The brass plaque was stowed in a cupboard in the utility room.

Then, on the afternoon of Nikhil's arrival, she had a hefty drink, mostly gin, hardly any tonic, while she waited for the doorbell to ring. The colonel had never told her that he regarded Nikhil as a son, but she had read his strength of feeling. She had never yearned for children; after a point, she had not expected to have them and had dwelled on the matter no further. She had stepped in, with great joy, as a parental figure whenever Dileep had deemed it necessary, always aware that father and daughter took primacy in the Khurana house.

The question she had asked herself most often was how much Ania knew of the circumstances of her mother's death. She had never dared discuss it even with Dileep, and it would have been unthinkable to broach the matter with Ania without his permission. Ania's quests for perfection had always worried Renu. The thought came to her in disquieting flashes that she would have been a much better friend to Ania if she had been honest and allowed her to see how much rot always lay under the surface.

ANIA HAD PREPARED herself for the worst. There was every possibility that Nikhil would be a cocky, high-achieving East Coast nuisance, determined to disapprove of darling Renu just because she had the temerity to marry his uncle late in life. He would try to condescend at any opportunity and be an expert on everything. He would probably chew gum. By the time Ania arrived at Renu's flat, she had almost convinced herself that she had already met and detested Nikhil. Her body was stiff with disapproval; she had worn her hair up; she was dressed for a fight.

But she had been disarmed in every way. It helped that he looked so unthreatening—he was handsome, of course, but in a quiet and almost apologetic way. He blushed readily and covered his mouth with his palm as he listened. There was a puppy-like effort to lay things at people's feet: compliments, inquiries, the occasional terrible pun. And what recommended him most of all was that he seemed to have developed a deep affection for Renu in no time.

When Ania first saw them, they were doubled up in laughter listening to something on his phone, sharing a pair of earphones. And for a moment she felt that it might be Renu who needed a quiet word. There was no real pressing need to leap into *this* kind of conviviality.

"So I hear you're writing a novel," he asked in a low voice, sitting next to her at the table for lunch.

"Sort of," she said.

"I won't ask," he said. "I'm sure it's really annoying for you."

She smiled and said nothing more.

She agreed to meet him for coffee the next day, after her game of tennis. As he walked into the clubhouse, he saw a board that listed strict rules on apparel, cell phone use, and the conduct of maids or nannies accompanying patrons.

Ania waved to him as he approached.

"Can you believe that shit?" he said, giving her a warm hug. "Did you see all those rules?"

"Some of them are a bit over the top. But you do need rules in a chaotic world. Otherwise, the center cannot hold. Things fall apart," she said, shrugging.

"Wow. So you have a lot of rules of your own?" he asked.

"Obviously. Loads. Let me see. Never go through life without a dog. Never go to sleep without taking your makeup off, even if you can barely stand. Never let a man see you cry, that gives him all the power. Never trust someone who is rude to drivers or photographers," she said.

She emphasized each rule with a tap on the table, inches away from his hand.

"It's okay to toss a boring book after the first fifty pages. What else? Never drink alcohol on long flights. Never, I mean *never*, date a man with long nails. Never tell anything private to your Delhi hairdresser, the whole town will soon know."

He held up his hands.

"See? Neatly trimmed nails," he said.

"Good for you, although I really don't see the relevance," she said, trying to keep the smile off her face.

"You will," he said.

The following day Dileep took them all out to lunch at a

restaurant famed for its signature egg dish, poached at sixty-three degrees and bathed in heart-of-palm foam. Ania continued her vigilance, but there were no chinks in Nikhil's charm, no shift from his voluptuous civility. It would all have been too much, too schooled and apt, were it not for the gaffes. The gaffes were superb. At a dinner party he told a wonderful story about Kitty Malhotra's honeymoon in Fiji, unaware that her aunt was on his other side. He repeatedly mistook the elder Mr. Bandopadhyay for the younger Mr. Bandopadhyay, a galling act as they had not been on speaking terms for more than a decade. Ania remained enormously amused and hoped that his knowledge of Delhi society never improved.

He spoke often of personal growth and emotional intelligence and living absolutely in the moment. It was a vernacular of self-help that normally made Ania and Dev howl with derision—but Nikhil made it seem acceptable, appealing even, in its naïve but noble intentions. He referred often to family, not just in the sense of kinship; but in its broadest possible sense, as some kind of comity of nations. It sometimes showed even in his physicality, in the way he used his hands, as though he were urging people to come together and listen a little more, in the way he shifted in his seat and gave people his full attention, his lips pursed in concentration.

His most appealing quality was that she could sense no hidden motives behind his warmth. At no point did she feel that he was befriending her to be able to position himself closer to Dileep, to bask in her presence on social media, or to ask for the use of the Khurana beach house in Mauritius. Ania shuddered at the vulgarity of people who bragged about their money or celebrity—but the fact remained that she was wealthy and well-known. Many of her boyfriends and flings had ultimately wanted her to erase herself in some way. She had found herself making excuses for her connections and supporting those boyfriends unquestioningly in all kinds of idiotic endeavors—at least, until she had tired of them. She had been required to present a certain dullness to set off their weak shine. But Nikhil did not need any coddling or validation. He appeared to be delighted with her true self. It seemed little short of miraculous.

Ania recognized the weight of her interest in him when she found herself squirreling away funny incidents and anecdotes to tell him. She did not pause to think about what he was doing away from home for so long and the nature of his sabbatical. It seemed perfectly natural to her that a young man would be at leisure trying to wring every ounce of beauty and pleasure from the world. When the colonel questioned Nikhil on their morning walks, the response that came back was that he was exploring opportunities. This seemed like a sensible thing to be doing, so no one felt the need to say anything more about it.

He joined Ania and a group of her friends on safari in Madhya Pradesh. During the day they swam in waterfalls and watched sloth bears rubbing themselves up against tree trunks; at night they drank martinis outside their tented suites and tried drunkenly to identify constellations. When he roused himself one night to stagger back to his tent from hers, she almost pulled him close and asked him not to go. But her courage failed her.

A couple of weeks later Ania and Nikhil flew to Hong Kong to go to a masquerade ball, her bespoke Medusa costume having been couriered ahead. When she walked into the hotel ballroom, his hand on her back, she had felt a sudden warmth flow from the roots of her hair to her bare shoulders. The three nights in Hong

Kong were spent in a whirl. He had wanted to change hotels on a whim, had taken her to an illegal underground casino, had a couple of grams of coke delivered to him in a cigar lounge.

Even though she had booked separate hotel rooms, Ania had convinced herself that she would sleep with him there. But somehow it had not happened. She had been drunk and exhausted in the early hours after the party, the next night the moment had seemed wrong, and on the final night he simply disappeared for hours. She wondered whether he was punishing her for something or simply trying to be elusive. When he eventually called her, she had been too proud to ask him where he had been.

On their way back, they barely spoke in the car. But in the airport lounge, his good humor returned. He began to clown about in a gentle way as they raked over the events of the weekend.

"Did you notice something about the hotel?" he asked.

"What?" she said.

"The elevator music."

"I don't remember. What about it?"

"It was really scary. Like the music from *Jaws*."

"Why would they use scary shark music there?"

"I don't know, maybe it hadn't been serviced for a while."

Hours later, on the flight, when she lifted her window shade, the darkness was strangely comforting: they were cocooned in velvety shades of black. When she stood up she could see over the partition that he was wholly absorbed in a syrupy family drama. When at last he saw her shadow fall across the screen, he lifted his head, smiled without any embarrassment, and touched her arm. She slipped her hand under the sleeve of his sweater and felt the warmth of his forearm. She felt that she had reclaimed him.

CHAPTER EIGHTEEN

THE FAMILY TROOPED into the Khurana dining room but had to pause to adjust to the dim light after the glare outside. The room's décor was inspired by a Hammershøi that hung in their Manhattan town house, the painting divided by thin streams of light, shadows in pewter and slate and oyster. A woman in a black dress was seated at a table; the door behind her was ajar; the floor shone. This room had the same sense of space and texture. Its brightest point was the pale yellow ceramic bowl on the ebony dresser.

"Can't we eat on the patio or in the kitchen? Sitting around this table is like being at a board meeting," said Ania.

"It's much cooler here," said Renu, "and it's all been laid. Plus Dev has just dropped in so I asked him to stay for lunch. It'll be easier to add a place there next to the colonel."

"Interesting how you always drop in around meal times," Ania said to Dev as he walked into the room.

"Ania, don't say such things, he might think you're serious," said Renu.

"Not to worry, Renu, this is how we always talk to each other," said Dev, "although I'm always defeated by Ania's rapier wit."

"Now we're just waiting for Nikhil," said Renu.

The grays of the room seemed to affect the family's behavior whenever they took their meals there. Conversation was muted. Heavy foliage blocked much of the light from the windows, and the room had a somber and stately aspect. A clock ticked, cutlery clinked. The door to the kitchen would open and close as a servant passed through. Every so often water would glug into a glass.

Nikhil's entrance meant today would be different. He bounded in, went around the table greeting everyone, and then rushed out again to get something from the car. When he returned, he sat down with a great deal of bluster, commenting on the food and the delicious coolness of the room and offering a protracted explanation for his slight delay. Then he addressed a remark or two to each person, as though he were hosting a conference. All the while, Dev barely looked at him.

Dileep's special meal was being served in small china bowls next to his plate: chunks of tuna in a seaweed marinade, dehydrated broccoli, a baobab fruit salad. His attitude to his food was unpredictable. He would either spend an hour evangelizing about his latest superfood discovery or sink into a cold sulk if he read any interest in his current diet as an attempt to mock him. The others had learned to maintain a cordial silence with only the occasional peek at his plate.

The rest of the family were being treated to a special Kashmiri lunch, Dina having managed to engage a cook originally from Sonamarg for the day. The lunch would allow the Khuranas to feel that they were doing their bit for national unity, given the conflict in the troubled state. And it would also ensure that they sampled the sought-after cook's offerings before their neighbors, the Mehras, who were known to be dreadfully competitive in culinary matters.

Renu introduced the dishes as though she had cooked them herself: a delicious yakhni made of tender lamb and flavored with cardamom and mawal flowers; a pulao studded with dried fruit and almonds; a bowl of goshtaba, rich mutton meatballs fragrant with ghee. Dileep could not help feeling that she was being inappropriately proprietary, given that she no longer lived in the house.

"Nikhil, you must try the guchhi, wonderful and rare Kashmiri morels, completely delicious," said Renu.

"Yes, Nikhil, you really *must*," said Ania.

Renu threw her an injured look.

"Hey, guys," said Nikhil, "here's something I wanted to ask you."

They all turned to look at him, apart from Dev, who hardly raised his head from his soup.

"I want to know from each of you: what's your earliest memory?"

"Why?" asked Dileep.

"No reason, just a fun thing to do."

Dev broke his roll in two, buttered one half lavishly, and popped it into his mouth.

"All right, mine is from when I was about four, I think," said Renu. "I was wearing these patent leather shoes, bright red and gorgeous, but they were too tight. And I was scared that if I told my mother how tight they were, she would give them away. So I kept them on, even though I was in so much pain. I remember trying to loosen the buckle for ages and then trying to slide my finger into the side of the shoe. Uff, it was agony. In fact, even the thought of it, I'm sorry, I'm going to have to slip my sandals off for a minute."

Dileep speared a piece of baobab.

"We got them in that adorable shop that we used to go to on Kensington Church Street; do you remember, Dileep? What was it called? Something to do with transportation . . . Tiny Trucks?"

"What about you, uncle?" asked Nikhil.

"Someone had died. I remember standing there looking at all the people dressed in white at the funeral. Lots of wailing," said the colonel.

"Darling, what a dreadful first memory to have. Couldn't you come up with something a bit more peppy?" said Renu.

The colonel shrugged.

"Ania?" asked Nikhil.

Ania had often imagined her mother at thirty, the age at which she had given birth, the age at which she had died. She had convinced herself that this ought to be her first memory. She pictured a woman who was beautiful in the way of a woman on-screen, a perfect play of light and shadow, the camera panning away from her face to her silhouette as she walked into the distance. It was a perception of shape and motion that could not be openly discussed and certainly not a vision to be aired in this company over lunch.

She conjured up a different memory.

"Painting. My hands were covered with paint, and I was

making palm prints on a blank sheet of paper. I can remember the smell and seeing my own tracks appear slowly over the page, like a little animal's," she said.

"Wagon Wheels!" said Renu. "It was called Wagon Wheels."

"What's yours, Dev?" asked Nikhil.

"I don't have one. And yours are all inaccurate too. Psychologists have done lots of work on these mental functions. What we claim to be an early memory is usually a fiction."

"All righty, I guess that's that then," said Nikhil.

"Oh, Dev," said Renu.

She sounded genuinely hurt and disappointed.

"It's true," he said. "These sorts of autobiographical memories are fraudulent by their very nature. We don't just reach for a snapshot from a filing cabinet in our brains. We cobble together mental reconstructions using different sources, images we might have seen or stories we might have heard much later. We readjust them for trauma, for convenience. We superimpose emotions and senses. The whole process is notoriously unreliable."

He spoke with a forceful clarity that made Ania look at him longer than she had intended. His words made perfect sense to her. She had not articulated it to herself in these terms before, but he had expressed precisely the way in which she thought about her mother. She could not possibly have a memory of her, so she had layered other people's recollections, family anecdotes, the swish of her old saris, the heft of her jewelry, the scenes in photo albums, to create a film of impressions.

Dev's mouth was stern; the lines on his brow deep. He looked as though he were trying to find his way out of a predicament.

She also had the impression that he was deliberately avoiding her gaze. She wanted to agree with him, but he was all too willing to take an intractable position to spoil Nikhil's harmless line of questioning. His mulishness could sometimes be infuriating, and she didn't want to let him know he was right about yet another thing.

"Well, you can't dismiss everyone's memories just like that. Some people may in fact remember things accurately," she said.

"I'm pretty sure mine is a hundred percent correct," said Nikhil. "I have the clearest memory of being high up somewhere and seeing dozens of boats in a marina. We might have been in the Caribbean, I'm not sure, but I can really see the sunlight on the water and all those white boats."

"That's lovely, the way you put it. I can just picture them," said Renu.

Ania rolled her eyes, but Renu pretended not to see.

Dina appeared through the kitchen door.

"Dina, we are all discussing our earliest memories," said Ania. "You have to tell us yours."

"No, no, ma'am," said Dina, "I really can't remember."

"I don't believe that at all. You've never forgotten a thing in your life."

"No, ma'am. I'm sorry, I can't tell you. It's not suitable."

"We've all shared ours. Please, Dina. Come on, stop being so mysterious, you've got to tell us now."

"No, ma'am, please, I have work to do."

"You are absolutely not allowed to leave this room until you have told us," said Ania, reaching for Dina's hand.

Dina eased her fingers away and sighed. She put her hands

into the deep pockets of her smock. Her gaze seemed to travel around the room and finally settled on a carafe on the table.

"I can't remember how old I was, but I was still in a cot. The kind that have metal bars. I was standing, and I remember holding the bars, trying to push my face through the gap. My parents were on the bed just a few feet away. They were under a sheet with big pink flowers, and they were having relations."

The colonel put down his fork.

Dina's expression was trancelike. Once she had started to tell the story, it looked as though she was powerless not to finish it.

"Of course, I didn't know what was happening. I must have thought they were having some kind of fight—it looked like they were trying to kill each other. I was trying to reach them through the bars. I was shaking the bars, putting my arms through them. Those pink flowers kept jumping up and down. I was so frightened. It was horrible."

She took her hands out of her pockets and inspected what looked like a scratch on the dresser then reached for the empty wine bottle.

"Another bottle, ma'am?" she asked Renu.

Renu glanced at the colonel and shook her head.

Dina left the room, closing the door behind her with a quiet *click*.

There was a brief silence.

When Dev spoke, his tone was sharp. "Ania, did you have to insist in that way? She clearly didn't want to say. And now we know why."

"Well, I didn't know it was going to be *that*. Anyway, it was all Nikhil's idea. He got us on to the subject."

"But how was I supposed to know about the jumping pink flowers?" asked Nikhil, raising his hands in protest.

He smiled and then began to giggle, clapping his hand over his mouth.

"Oh stop," said Ania.

The next instant, she was in fits too.

"Stop it, you two," said Renu. "Poor thing, she might come back any moment."

"I'm sorry, but tell *him*!" said Ania, her voice still choked. "Oh God, why did she have to mention the pink flowers?"

" 'It looked like they were trying to kill each other,' " said Nikhil.

He and Ania exploded into fresh sputters.

"Thank you for lunch," said Dev, standing up. "I must make a move."

"Dev, so lovely to see you," said Renu. "I'll call you soon."

"Goodbye, all," said Dev, nodding at Dileep and raising his hand at no one in particular. He left the room through the other door, and they could hear him stride through the hall. A few seconds later, the front door slammed.

Renu pushed her chair from the table and signaled to the colonel. Dileep stood up too and went into the hall.

The sun had moved to this side of the house, and a few flecks of light trembled on the dark wood of the table.

"That went well," said Ania when they had all left. "Any other sparkling topics of conversation you have up your sleeve?"

Nikhil leaned forward and said, "Let's do something really *bad* this afternoon. Something bad and *expensive*."

"You are such a terrible influence," she said. "Come on."

She smiled and stood up. Dev's irritating, old-fashioned ways made her want to provoke him with some imprudently silly behavior. He ruined everything by pointing out the harm in what everyone knew were harmless follies. She fussed with her hair as she left the room, her thoughts drifting back to the slam of the front door.

CHAPTER NINETEEN

THE LINE OF vehicles looked endless, hot metal and dusty windows in every direction. There was a great burst of revving and hooting; they all moved a few inches and then halted again. Ania regretted having offered Renu and Anita Malwani a lift to the Imperial on her way to the vet's. They were all crammed into the car, Renu in the passenger seat googling the causes of gum disease in dogs, Ania in the backseat, sandwiched between a glum Sigmund and a sleeping Anita. Her head was thrown back, her lower jaw had fallen open, affording a clear view of her darkly pitted molars.

"Can't we have a blast of the AC for just a few seconds?" asked Renu.

"No, Siggy goes crazy if his window is up," said Ania.

"All right then. I must say, it never fails to surprise me how amazing Google is. No matter what you are looking for. It's quite frightening, actually."

"Have you ever googled yourself?"

"Oh, no, I wouldn't dare; but I caught the colonel doing it the other day. He was horribly embarrassed."

Ania shot Anita a dark look as she began to snore. Her thighs seemed to spread on the seat, the dark silk of her skirt straining across them. On Ania's other side, Sigmund shifted heavily.

"Will you sit still, Sigmund; stop all this bloody wriggling," she said.

"How terrible. It looks like gum disease in dogs may be a precursor to heart trouble or other organ damage," said Renu.

"There's no point in you trying to diagnose him online. We are literally on our way to the vet."

"Also, a sign of diabetes. Oh dear. You know there is so much diabetes in the family. I wonder if dogs in South Asia are as high risk as the humans."

"Can we please stop discussing this?"

"You're in a funny mood. I'm just trying to help poor Siggy."

They had hardly moved at all. Fumes from a bus drifted in through the open window on Sigmund's side. Anita and Sigmund both let out a wheeze within seconds of each other. Ania could feel the tickle of sweat trickling down her back.

"Bua, do you remember Fahim? He was here that night when Agata sang. God, inviting him was such a mistake," said Ania.

"Yes, I think I do."

"It really doesn't matter if you don't. Anyway, I've just heard that he's got married."

"Oh how wonderful; what happy news."

"It's not happy news at all. It's quite irritating news."

"Why? Did you have a thing for him?"

"Ugh, no. It's too complicated to explain. But I just don't understand how a guy can be single one day and then suddenly married in no time to somebody that no one has ever heard of. Men really are so disgusting."

"I'm a feminist, but I really don't think it's fair to go around saying things like that. I know plenty of very nice men. This friend of yours, is he the one who was on TV? The journalist?"

"Yes."

"Maybe there's something about the wedding online. Let me google it."

"Do you really have nothing better to do? How are the French classes going?"

A commotion of hooting started up again, and the driver craned his neck to get a better look. It felt as though there was a steady tick underneath it all, the approach of a furious confrontation. All around them the air seemed to shimmer.

"This is just unbearable," said Ania.

"Oh, look, it's on some funny gossip website. They got married in England, it says here. In a castle. His wife is English. Did you know that? It appears that she's very well known in Jaipur. She's writing an intimate memoir of one of the royals somewhere in Rajasthan," said Renu.

Ania reached for Sigmund and tickled him under the chin.

"You're not very well known in Jaipur, are you, my darling little wretch."

Sigmund turned to face her and drooled.

"Oh God, your breath," said Ania.

He barked, and Anita woke up with a start.

"We haven't moved at all," she said.

"Nothing more about her," said Renu. "Just that she's from England, has been living in India for a while, and has a keen interest in our royal families."

"Everyone's a royal today, my dear. As long as you can point out a turret or two on your house and find a ragged photo of a turbaned ancestor on a horse, or better still, an elephant. Much more distinguished these days to say you hail from a line of butlers," said Anita.

She leaned her head against the window and within seconds was snoring again.

"Now I do remember this Fahim chap," said Renu. "But wasn't he the one who was after your friend Dimple?"

"Well, apparently not, as we can see."

"Shame, what a sweet girl she is. How is she, anyway?"

"I haven't really seen much of her recently. We've both been busy."

Ania turned to face the road, trying not to touch Anita Malwani's warm flank. Not a leaf stirred; there were no pedestrians on the verge; in the far lane a truck had been abandoned. Drivers had turned engines off and one or two were standing in the middle of the traffic.

She had let it drift for long enough. There had been a series of lackluster messages, vague promises to meet. For weeks, Ania had repeatedly nursed and then suppressed the fear that Dimple would find out about her last encounter with Fahim. She was not to blame; most of the time, Ania was certain that she had done nothing to lead him on. But a doubt would crash through, and she would become convinced that Dimple would accuse her of being a treacherous friend, greedy for all the attention. The thought filled her with a combination of defiance and shame.

And now she had made it worse by avoiding Dimple, one more failing to add to the awful chain of events. She got out her phone and made a list of things she could take Dimple soon—peace offerings, but nothing excessive that would look like an admission of culpability.

DIMPLE BIT HARD on her lower lip as she attempted to stifle her giggles. She and Ania were in their bikinis, lying facedown on adjacent massage beds in the pool house. A curl of incense unfurled around their heads as the Khuranas' regular masseur, Anasuyaben, performed her preliminary rituals. She muttered an incantation, shook a bamboo rattle, and then ran around the massage beds clockwise. Dimple buried her face into the firm surface of the bed.

Anasuyaben was a tiny woman with a tight gray bun whose anklets jingled as she moved. Her unique massage technique— she sometimes stood on their backs and barked—had at first been looked upon with some suspicion by the Khuranas. But the effects had proved to be so potent and enriching that she now visited twice a week. On this occasion, since Dimple would also be present, Anasuyaben was accompanied by her sister-in-law, a woman twice the size of Anasuyaben and apparently equally skilled. She had looked at the house and the pool with disapproval but had saved her most vinegary expression for Dimple.

Dimple was unaccustomed to strangers being paid to pummel her body. She was squeamish about being touched in at least half a dozen places. She managed to counter her natural inhibitions during sexual encounters with the assistance of alcohol and a fervent application of her will. Ankit was the only man who had made her feel like an equal participant.

She had only agreed to the massage session because Ania had been so insistent and sincere in her wish to make amends.

"But Fahim probably does this to lots of girls. Or maybe it was just me he didn't like. It's a hundred percent not your fault," Dimple had said to Ania.

"Why the hell shouldn't he like you? You're the one who's far too good for him. Ugh, hateful creep. Anyway, you have to experience the magic of Anasuyaben. It'll make you feel so much better. She reorders the inner cosmic force of our beings, you know."

Anasuyaben's sister-in-law continued to look at Dimple as though she was an urchin who had shinned up the drainpipe to gain entry into the house. It was as though she had known in an instant that Dimple had no business lying around the Khurana pool in a bikini and intended to punish her for it. While she hadn't stood on Dimple's back, her technique seemed harsh and condemning, like the pecks of an angry bird. At one point Dimple was convinced she had felt a hard pinch. And now the woman had begun to press into the lower half of Dimple's bottom. It was a tender spot that threatened to release all her suppressed laughter.

She concentrated hard on dark, frightening thoughts: the possibility of losing her job, the death of her mother, someone breaking her newly acquired ceramic dinner set. But the laughter kept welling up. The woman now seemed to be shaking the bamboo rattle over her head. It was a vision that sent another giggle hurtling into her chest.

"Isn't this amazing? She learned it all in some obscure village in the Kutch desert," said Ania, turning to her.

Dimple cackled but tried to make it sound as though it was a groan of pleasure.

"I knew you'd love it. If you want, I can arrange for the lady who's doing you to come to your place every week."

"No, no, that's too much; you've already done more than enough."

"It's nothing. I just wanted to get your mind off you-know-what. And please let's agree that we are never going to mention his name again. Anyway, I have another surprise for you. Your mind is going to be blown. Are you ready? I've arranged with an amazing artist to do your portrait. Sunflower Parathasarathy? Have you heard of him? Very cool, very up and coming."

Dimple stayed silent for a few moments before saying, "Wow, thanks. Sunflower. Is that a boy or a girl?"

"Boy. His real name is Parashuram, but you can see that he needed something with impact. Fabulous artist. He's doing this as a special favor. He'll make you look amazing."

"So, portrait, like a painting, in a frame?"

"What else would it be in? A bucket?"

"No, I mean, that's really sweet of you but it's just too much, too grand for me."

"Oh please, you hardly move without taking a selfie. This is just a step up. I'm doing it for you."

"It's really, really sweet but I can't. I have nowhere to hang it anyway. My landlord still hasn't fixed the leak in the hall and the bedroom walls are so thin. If I tried to hammer a nail there, the painting would end up in Bubbly Auntie's kitchen."

"My God, Dee. This is a chance at making history. He'll be

huge one day, and you'll have a portrait of yourself *by him*. All you have to do is arrange with his assistant about going to his studio. You might have to sit over seven or eight days."

"Eight *days*? How can I do that? I have a job, in case you've forgotten."

There was a moment when something seemed to swell in the air around them. Dimple felt heat creeping up her neck. She had been too blunt.

Ania let out a long sigh.

"You're right. It's the sitting time, isn't it? I hadn't really thought of that. Although you're lucky. At least you only have one job. I feel like I'm being pulled in a hundred different directions, all the things people want me to do for them. It's true, you know. If anyone asked me to sit for a portrait, I really wouldn't have a clue when I'd do it."

Anasuyaben let out a whoop.

The bamboo rattle was hurled into a corner of the room.

"Look, I'll just arrange it with Sunflower, and if you do have some time, get in touch with him. Otherwise, I'll ask him to give you something else he's done. Apparently, he's great at flora and fauna too. He's famous for his frogs, I think."

IT HAD ALL begun in Serena Bakshi's sensational Maharani Bagh apartment. Dileep could not have thought of a more unlikely place for his discovery. Serena displayed, in every way, a tyrannical focus on aesthetics. She worked for a major French fashion house, but her obsession with what she considered essential to the eye went far beyond devotion to her work. Acquaintances found it difficult to relax in her presence, even though she was far too well mannered to criticize. They became conscious of the creases in their skirts, the ugly contents of their handbags. Serena's dedication naturally extended to every square inch of her home: the wrought iron balusters cast a sublime shadow on the checkerboard floor, her Edward Weston photographs were all perfect whorls and sinews, the white curtains came from Milan.

One evening as Serena took a call in another room, Dileep had begun to toy with the boxes on an occasional table, delicate rosewood caddies whose lids had to be twisted and pried open. In one of the boxes he found some fingernail clippings; in another, some coins, a snip of hair, and a shriveled red chili; in a third box, a mound of ash-like powder. A revolting odor wafted from this substance, and he recoiled, dropping the box on the floor.

Serena rushed back into the room and stared at the streaks of gray on her white rug.

"Oh my God, what have you done?" she said, her voice almost a whisper.

"I'm so sorry. How clumsy of me. Don't worry, we'll get it cleaned up, I promise. But what is all this stuff? It smells disgusting. Have you become a witch doctor in your spare time?"

Serena was silent for a moment. And then she let out a terrible sob and sank into a chair. She buried her face in her hands and her shoulders shook. Dileep's instinct was to turn and flee. He knew he had committed an appalling blunder but was at a complete loss.

He only knew Serena as a woman of inscrutable composure, guarded and driven. She was a wonder, a miracle worker, a woman who had managed to persuade the iron-fisted old families of Delhi to accept the Bakshis back into their fold after years of disgrace; a disgrace that was so much graver than embezzlement or graft, since it involved a woman descending into the most sordid of worlds.

"That Nirmala Bakshi."

Every so often in a Delhi drawing room an aged matriarch who survived mainly on the nourishment provided by old scandals would mumble the name of Serena's grandmother. The Bakshis were known to have a preponderance of daughters, most of them doe-eyed nymphs who would go on to make advantageous marriages. Nirmala, however, had been struck with asthma and buckteeth and was considered of little consequence by the rest of the extended family. Bright and capable, she was an English literature gold medalist and was offered a lectureship at one of the city's prestigious arts colleges for women. It was 1962, and even in conservative Delhi, the world seemed full of possibilities for an ambitious young academic. One evening, at a reception hosted by the college to celebrate the strengthening of ties among the countries of the Non-Aligned Movement, a South American diplomat put his hand on her knee.

"There is to be friendship between our countries, yes?" he asked.

"No," said Nirmala, standing up swiftly.

But Nirmala was not, in fact, feeling that unfriendly: an idea had begun to form. The college was full of quick-witted, liberated girls who were long on ambition but short of cash. They wanted to travel, accumulate a nest egg; the more daring ones even wished to move away from home. Nirmala was confident that some of these girls would have no objection to a quick fumble between lectures or after classes. New five-star hotels were sprouting up near the college, full of itinerant politicians, diplomats, and bureaucrats from around the globe. Nirmala had the organizational skills to bring the girls and the men together for a small commission.

Over the next year her scheme was such a success that she rented a small office and went part-time at the college: she still needed an excuse to be on the premises, even though the salary barely paid for the imported gifts she gave her more popular girls. She married a meek man who would do as he was told, and gave birth to Serena's mother soon after. In a few years she had become Delhi's most influential madam, making contacts at the highest level, party to the most unorthodox predilections of senior statesmen.

Inevitably, as her wealth and power grew, so did her own hubris and the envy of others. Her eventual arrest made headlines around the world, but she parlayed a guarantee of absolute secrecy for a conditional discharge. Nirmala disappeared to set up an ashram for widows in Rishikesh, leaving her daughter with one of her sisters. While her considerable assets in Delhi remained safe, the rest of the Bakshi family were cast into the wilderness.

The Bakshis had been ignored for a generation, but Serena's international success had allowed them a revival. The mistakes of the past were laid to rest. It helped that Serena was single-minded, secretive, charming. She dressed always in black, allowing only a flash of pink lining or the hard green of a gem on her finger. Even with the greatest application, it was hard to see how she could have been kept out of the fold.

And now trembling before Dileep was the woman who had made the Bakshis acceptable again.

He let her cry, looking down at the mess on the rug, not daring to ask her why she was so upset.

"I'm sorry," he said eventually, "would you like me to leave?"

She waved her arm at him, and he had no idea what she meant. She stood up and stumbled into the next room. He picked up the caddie, screwed its lid back on, and wondered if he should call for one of the servants.

Serena emerged from the room, calm, pale, her eyes still puffy.

"Wait, Dileep, I may as well talk to you," she said.

"I'm really sorry; I had no business touching these boxes."

"You think I'm crazy, don't you?"

"No, of course not. But I really don't understand what just happened."

"I'll get someone to clean that up, but I can't bear to be in the same room. Come with me."

He followed her down the stairs into the formal sitting room. It felt absurd, as though he had committed a gross infraction and was being asked into a grand chamber to receive his censure.

She asked him to sit but remained standing.

"About a couple of years ago, everything started going wrong. I thought I was going to lose my job, my friends, my sanity, everything. I was on antidepressants, seeing one of the best shrinks in New York every week on Skype, nothing seemed to help. And I knew Amar was cheating; I had no idea with whom, but I just knew. And then he said he wanted a divorce, and I really thought that was the end."

"I'm sorry; I had no idea."

"That was the whole point, making sure no one had any idea. I thought about it all the time, you know, how I would do it.

Maybe buy a hundred sleeping tablets online or just drive my car at top speed into a building."

"Serena, this is awful."

"But then someone told me about Mr. Nayak. I was completely skeptical, but I was so desperate that I went to see him."

She paused.

"I haven't told anyone this. All of you will think I'm crazy. I don't even know how to describe him. He's not one of these typical godmen or astrologers. There are no saffron robes or mantras. All I can say is that it's all so professional. It's like a real service."

"But what does he do?"

She sat down to face him.

"I'm so glad to be able to talk about this now. It's a little like I felt when I first met Mr. Nayak. He just knew about my problems and didn't make me feel like a crazy person. He was so reassuring about everything. And he knew things about my life that no one could possibly have known. You're already looking at me like I'm insane, but he just has this sense. And after that, things began to change. Of course, it seems weird, all this superstition, these odd rituals. But I promise you, they work."

"He makes you keep those things in the boxes?"

"Not just that. I have to keep an old broom under my bed, and he's blessed an amulet that I now wear all the time around my upper arm. I see him regularly, and every time there's something different. It really is so hard to explain. Sometimes when I speak to him, in that moment I doubt whether he can ever help me. But later when I'm on my own and I've had a chance to think about what he said, look at it from different angles and apply it to my life, I realize that he's given me the greatest thing anyone could give me: hope. Amar and I decided to try harder; work has never been better. All I can say is that Mr. Nayak has transformed my life."

Dileep turned to look away.

"Do you think I'm crazy?" she asked.

His throat was dry, and he asked her if he could have some water. Serena rang the kitchen and then looked at him, her eyes still pinched, her mouth anxious.

"No, I don't think you're crazy," he said. "I get it. More than you think I do."

"Thank you," she said. "I really mean it."

The water arrived, and they sipped it in silence.

"Would you mind if I met him too?" asked Dileep.

DIMPLE LOITERED IN the gloomy corridor, unsure whether she should go into the room. Others had no such compunction. They came in pairs or in little groups, the men in their navy jackets, smelling faintly of mothballs, the women fiddling with their chunky silver jewelry made by tribes in remote hills. They peered down the passage in both directions and then strode into the hall. They walked with the confidence of people whose ancestors had roads named after them or whose likenesses were captured in busts in parks around the city. The roads might have since been renamed, the busts might have been bespattered by crows and defaced with graffiti, but their gait remained unchanged.

"Have you seen my daughter?" asked Silky Chhabra, swamped by her silk patchwork coat.

"I'm sorry, who is your daughter?" asked Dimple.

"Oh, never mind," she said and disappeared into the hall.

The famed Belgian art collector Herman Van den Broeck, now a cherished member of the Delhi art scene, had enlisted Ania's help to secure a respectable audience for his talk. Always eager to help him, she had rung a few of her friends to remind them that if they did not show Mr. Van den Broeck some appreciation, it was possible that he would return to Antwerp for good. As it happened, the audience was greater than was usually expected at these events: the subject of Mr. Van den Broeck's talk was the appreciation of the nude in classical Greek sculpture.

"I can see that Ania strong-armed you into coming too."

Dimple spun round to see Dev smiling at her.

"Hello," she said, greatly relieved to see a friendly face. "I thought it sounded interesting. I've not seen that many nude sculptures."

"Haven't you?"

"I have so many events to go to after I leave work."

"Well, I'm sure Herman will make you feel that you've seen enough for a lifetime. Shall we go in?"

"Sure. I just got a message from Ania saying she's going to be late."

"I got one too. Something about logistical problems. Whatever they might be."

Dimple giggled. "It's actually a wardrobe issue."

"Really?"

"She was about to leave but her cape got caught in the car door and ripped."

"Her *cape*?"

"You wouldn't know. It's a fashion thing. And then she got

changed, but Sigmund jumped on her with his muddy paws. So she had to go and change again. And now she's caught in traffic."

They sat down in the last row, behind a man wearing an ushanka to brave the fierce air-conditioning, the fur flaps hanging down like a spaniel's ears. Dimple and Dev had seen each other only once, briefly, since the night of Ankit's drunken display at Ania's party.

"You know, I wanted to thank you properly for being so nice that night after Ania's party. I really appreciated it. It was all so embarrassing," she told him.

"Not at all, please don't mention it," he said. "How is Ankit?"

"I think he's okay. I've not seen him much."

They watched a few more people arrive and take their seats.

"It really wasn't a big deal, what happened. Everyone's had too much to drink at times and got a bit silly," he said.

"It was more than that. It was just terrible." She paused and then lowered her voice. "I felt so humiliated."

"Look, I don't know what Ania has said to you about it, but trust me, she doesn't hold anything against Ankit, nor should anyone else. She thinks the world of you. I know that. And she really wouldn't want you to be upset over something so slight."

Dimple twisted the straps of her purse in her hand and nodded.

Herman Van den Broeck made an appearance at the front of the room, refusing to acknowledge anyone in the audience. It was an essential part of a performer's mystique that the public be recognized only when the show had truly begun.

"I'm starving," said Dev.

"Me too. Work was so busy, I've had no lunch," she said.

"Nothing at all?" he asked.

"Half an apple," she said.

"I've had lunch, and I'm still starving."

"On my way here I passed this little kebab place that I know. I nearly fainted, the smell was so good."

"What kind of kebabs?"

"Dora kebabs. They are incredibly awesome."

"Tell me about them."

"What?"

"The kebabs. What do they taste like?"

"Uff, so tender, and that delicious smoky smell just as you pull the string off."

"Are they spicy?"

"Just right. So fragrant."

"Oh God," he said, louder than he had intended. Dev put his head in his hands. And then he stood up. "Come on."

"What?" she said.

"We're going," he said.

"Where?"

"To your kebab place."

"*Now?*"

"Now. We're both starving. Come on, before Ania gets here."

"But she'll be so mad." Dimple hesitated.

"We'll get her some too."

"I don't know if it's your kind of place. It's tiny. And not somewhere Ania would go."

"It sounds exactly like my kind of place. Hurry, or we won't be able to escape. I'll send her a message. She'll understand. That smoky flavor, I can smell it."

Dimple continued to hesitate. She did not want to offend

Ania, their friendship only recently having regained its former equilibrium.

"I really don't think we should," she said.

"You're actually prepared to see me starve to death in front of your eyes? I'm telling you, she probably won't even notice. Let's go," he said.

Dimple stood up and followed him into the passage, hurrying to keep up with him as he made for the elevators.

A few minutes later Kamya Singh-Kaul emerged from the staircase and made her way into A17. She scanned the room before sitting down in the same row that Dimple and Dev had vacated.

Finally, the chair of the arts society ascended the dais and breathed into the mic. After a lengthy elucidation of Herman Van den Broeck's many achievements, he was invited to begin his talk. An image of a nude Zeus hurling a thunderbolt flashed up on the screen as Mr. Van den Broeck's staccato introductory remarks filled the room.

"Nudity. Lust. Titillation. *Engorgement.*"

Ania walked into the room, hot and harried by the misfortunes that had delayed her. She had been further annoyed by Dev's message telling her that he and Dimple had already left. And she was embarrassed to see that Herman had already begun his talk.

It was only when she had sat down that she spotted her neighbor adjusting her long glossy braid. Kamya was gazing straight ahead, and it was impossible to tell whether she had noticed Ania's arrival. Ania's temples were beginning to throb. She looked straight ahead too, failing to register any of Mr. Van den Broeck's marvelous examples of Greek musculature. The rest of the audience was rapt.

She glanced at Kamya, who turned to look at her.

"Kamya, *hi*," said Ania, "I didn't *realize* it was you."

"Yes, me neither."

"How are you?"

"Good."

"Great."

"Are you here on your own, Ania?"

"Yes, I was supposed to meet Dev here. But the idiot's gone off somewhere."

"I know. He was the one who asked me to come. And now he's not here and not answering his phone. Do you know where he's gone?"

An expression of annoyance colored Kamya's face, usually so cold and unflinching. Ania felt that the evening was finally looking up.

"No idea. How terrible of him. He must have completely forgotten about you," she said.

Mr. Van den Broeck raised a finger in the air, and they all raised their eyes to gaze at it.

"You will note the obscuring, I could almost say, the *erasure* of the male genitalia, in this period of sculpture. Why?" he demanded.

A woman in the front row gave a terrified shrug.

"I will tell you why. It was to deny them their potency, since these appendages had the power to distract from artistry, from beauty, from what was, after all, a tribute to *God*."

The woman on Kamya's other side leaned toward her.

"Excuse me, dear, if I'm not mistaken, are you Kamya Singh-Kaul? The author?"

Kamya turned to her and nodded, her features having returned to their stony normalcy.

The woman grabbed her hand and continued to whisper: "I simply can't believe my luck. I knew it. I was telling my husband, Jolly—this is Jolly—it had to be you. It's just unbelievable to see you in the flesh."

Once again, Kamya nodded.

"Your book has changed my life. I feel like you somehow climbed inside my head and articulated the world for me. Ask Jolly, he was there when I was reading it."

Ania shot a look at the others seated around them. It was an outrageous breach of courtesy, and she hoped that someone would furiously shush the woman.

"How do you do it? How *do* you do it?"

Kamya shrugged and mumbled something into the woman's ear.

"No, it was perfect. The intricate facets of the human condition captured in that beautiful way. You have written a perfect book."

Ania glanced at the aisle. Even her admiration for Mr. Van den Broeck could not persuade her to tolerate any more. She shifted in her seat and gave him a last guilty look.

He pointed at the image of a bronze sculpture, a doleful youth reclining against a rock.

"There is, of course, a crucial difference between nudity and nakedness. If I were to strip in front of you, stand on this stage without a stitch on, I would be merely naked and not nude."

From somewhere in one of the middle rows, there came a hiccup.

"The next slide will show us why."

He frowned as the next slide failed to show. Waving an arm, he summoned an assistant who began to fiddle with the laptop on the desk.

Ania used the break to slip toward the back of the room.

The assistant muttered an apology and hunched farther over the laptop. Another woman left the lecture. Herman had taken careful note of every departure. It proved, if nothing else, that the barbarians really were at the gates.

CHAPTER TWENTY

"So who else lives with you there in Delhi?"

It was the kind of question that Dimple would not have found objectionable when she was younger: she would even have expected it to be asked. But now she found herself bristling. A couple months had passed since the debacle with Fahim, and she had felt ready to make the periodic visit to her mother. It had been a mistake to take a shared taxi from the station to the small hill town. There were a good forty minutes to go along the narrow road that clung to the slopes, still a smoky blue at this early hour. She closed her eyes and leaned her head against the car window, hoping the stranger would think she had fallen asleep.

"No close family in that kind of city? How can that be safe?" he asked.

She faked a gentle snore. Ordinarily, she tried to slip back into old ways when she came home, knowing that people would be on the lookout for newly acquired airs, affectations, extravagances. Her mother would, of course, be the most vigilant. It was always best to trudge slowly up the last hundred yards toward their house, her case rattling over the ruts in the road, the signs of a long journey apparent on her face.

Dimple let herself in, and she could hear that her mother was up: the sound of water drummed into a bucket in the bathroom, and the radio was playing its early-morning devotional songs. Boxes from the printing press sat on the dining table and on each of the chairs. Dimple's mother was not a history scholar, but she wrote and distributed history pamphlets that she said were far more legitimate than those that relied merely on historical evidence. What was evidence? Anyone could dig up a worthless nugget, misinterpret a dusty manuscript, quote pointless statistics. Her words were emotionally authentic. They contained a greater truth since they outlined the damage to the psyche of the nation, battered by wave after wave of invaders, humiliated and enslaved. And her version of history encapsulated the future too: it showed how the route to self-sustaining glory was to repel the invaders, reclaim the purity of a Hindu nation, and erase that shameful past.

Her mother emerged from the bathroom, drying her thin hair.

"You gave me a shock," she said. "I've got so used to being here on my own."

They stepped toward each other and executed an indecisive hug.

"You've lost more weight," her mother said.

Dimple took a box off one of the chairs and sat down.

"Good journey? You'd better rest for a couple of hours. And then what are your plans? A few children have volunteered to distribute my pamphlets, but it's the first time for a couple of them. I think I'll go with them part of the way. You should come too; it's your first day back; it will give us a chance to spend some time together."

"I'm really tired," said Dimple. "And I'm getting a headache. I don't think I'll be able to walk around for that long."

Her mother nodded, her mouth crimped with disappointment. "Have some rest then. We'll speak later."

She picked up a box of the pamphlets and went into her bedroom.

A few years earlier Dimple would pretend to take an interest in her mother's politics, but her move away from home had given her the confidence to bat away all overtures. Dimple's mother regarded the English-speaking snobs who had run India for so many decades with a violent contempt. She could barely control her voice as she spoke of them, their staggering arrogance, their vanity and greed. They were traitors whose supremacy had been ruinous, and even though she was only a teacher in a small hill town, she intended to fix them. And for that she would use their own glittering weapon: English.

She impressed upon her students the importance of their own culture and traditions. But she also made it clear that to unseat the hateful patricians they would have to be able to expose and disgrace them in the language that had allowed them to reign. As she made each point, she enclosed her fist with her palm, her eyes bright, the strands of her thin hair plastered to her temples.

She raced through Shakespeare and Wordsworth, she skimmed over Dickens, but where she exacted a punishing concentration was in her grammar and oral classes. Her declaration echoed in the little schoolroom with its view of tin rooftops jumbled on the slopes: the most powerful ammunition in the world was correct communication. They had all heard the English of complacency; now she was tuning it for action.

Dimple had never intended to unseat any patricians. Her greatest desire for most of her life had been to escape that brittle voice with its terse injunctions. But she was profoundly grateful to her mother for her insistence on the importance of English. Her proficiency had helped her steal into a distant world and had offered her a choice of new identities.

Even while still at school, Dimple had tried out different manners of speech, sometimes unconsciously, absorbing syntax and vocabulary from American sitcoms, online makeup tutorials, travel blogs, advertising copy on fliers, romance novels. It was only after her move to Delhi that she realized the value of her advantage, as she watched people her age sputter and pause, return to Hindi, drum up some more courage, recall another nimble English phrase, hear it emerge from their lips, the words hesitant and mangled, and eventually clam up in public. She came to regard the English language as her savior and, whether she liked it or not, her mother was the prophet who had led her there.

She had not eaten for hours, and before that she had only crunched on a couple of mints. She walked into the dark kitchen. Its one small window looked out on to whatever was hanging on the clothesline, a dimness made up of the faint flowers on a sheet or the threadbare check of a towel. She opened one of the cupboards and saw packages of biscuits stacked high. She suspected that her mother rarely cooked now; she had always hated the waste of time that it entailed. Bodies needed fuel, and she now probably received most of hers from the biscuits that she bolted down only when a dizzy spell reminded her that she hadn't eaten. They were the cheapest kind, full of sugar and artificial flavorings, packed in thin shiny paper. Dimple closed the cupboard door; she had not realized that it was possible to feel so alienated by a packet of biscuits.

But her mother had obviously made an effort today. A ball of dough had been left on a tray to breathe, covered with a clear plastic bowl. Boiled cauliflower cooled in a pan on the gas ring. She could almost taste it from where she stood; cooked to a mush, it would slither down her throat.

She left the kitchen; the smell of the cauliflower was making her stomach turn. From her bedroom window she could see straight into the verandah of the house next door, wedged a little way down the same hill. A pregnant woman paced its length, caressing her belly, crooning to her unborn child. She had been in the year below Dimple at school, a skinny little thing with oily plaits, chapatis smeared with pineapple jam in her lunchbox on most days. Reaching the end of the verandah, she turned and stood still, fingers spread wide across her bulge, eyes closed as she sang. It was her third pregnancy or possibly the fourth. Her husband was a jawan in the army, and every time he came home on leave he seemed to impregnate her. She looked joyful and healthy, her hair long and thick, still oily. She opened her eyes and looked startled to see Dimple standing at the window. She raised her head. Dimple ducked down and crouched on the bed.

She had no idea why she should behave like this, like a sneak, a spy, her heart racing.

Pots of marigolds lined the steps from their front door to the road. Dimple made her way up the hill, her gaze sweeping from shop fronts to windowsills to open doorways, looking at the changes but also keenly aware that she was being noticed too. The Good Luck Beauty Parlor had now become a unisex establishment and plastered to the window were photographs of men running their fingers through their glossy locks. A few steps farther up, the clock repair shop was selling cell phone accessories. The sign advertising "Kailash Wonder Balm" still swung over the pharmacy, even though no one in the town had ever been able to find it and avail themselves of its extraordinary properties.

Away from the smog-shrouded lights of Delhi, she could see it all so much more clearly. She had never known or desired Fahim— he had always been a mirage; how strange it now seemed that he had managed to singe his way through her thoughts for so long. Perhaps he had behaved badly, extending her only a deft insincerity, but she had seized on him for her own ends too. The idea of a boyfriend of consequence had seemed so enticing, someone to moor her to that shifting world, a man by her side as she walked into clubs and restaurants in her new clothes with the slits and the silk straps. And she was finally able to admit to herself that she had been thrilled at the idea of breaking the news to her mother: a Muslim boyfriend. Even now, her face grew warm, her cheeks felt an exquisite tingle.

Night after night, her mother would laboriously scroll through the long messages she received on her phone and then deliver a précis.

"By 2050 the Muslim population of India will have overtaken the Hindus.

"There is a hit list of Hindu temples in the state. They plan to damage idols and desecrate the temples, one by one, in a systematic way.

"Good-looking Muslim boys are sent out by mullahs to snare decent Hindu girls, to dishonor them and then make them convert to Islam."

And Dimple pictured herself interrupting her mother with a nonchalance that could never come to pass, saying that she ought not to say such things anymore, now that her daughter's boyfriend—potentially a son-in-law—was Muslim. And, in fact, it was her daughter who had seduced the good-looking Muslim boy, entertained him, captivated him, and, she might as well be frank, had her way with him.

It was difficult to predict what the exact reaction would be. Dimple pictured long minutes of disbelieving silence, a choking, spluttering rage, hands trembling as they looked for a hard edge to grip, a chair being knocked over in fury. Her mother had given her the occasional smack on the leg or a rap on her palms with a ruler, but could she turn decidedly violent? Was she capable of lunging in fury, grabbing Dimple by the hair, and dragging her into the street, closing her hands around a human throat?

She was so caught up in the fantasy that she had to remind herself that there was no Muslim boyfriend, no horrifying transgression that she could lay at her mother's feet. The worst Dimple had done was to stretch out the period since her last visit to eighteen months and call her mother with decreasing regularity.

She arrived at the lakeshore where the vendors were setting up their stalls, laying out socks and scarves in jewel colors, now that the weather was turning. A man was fussing with his easel, the lake a churn of blue flecks on his canvas. Behind her there was a series of pops as children took their turns at the balloon shooting range.

She knew that she had let Ania down. All the time wasted, the energy expended, the long nights of advice. Perhaps it was true that a real friendship with someone like Ania was impossible. Dimple would always fall short, no matter how much she learned. She would put the stress on the wrong syllable, buy an offensive dress, admire a terrible painting, reveal a crude fact about her upbringing, be tasteless, improper, or coarse in a hundred different ways. It was a question of information, and people like her would never have enough: a crucial nugget would always be withheld.

Or perhaps Ania was the one at fault. Dimple had never forgotten the Sunday when she had waited outside the gates for the film crew in her best dress, believing what the girls at school had told her. Were all her friendships doomed to end in some kind of deception? Had Ania decided to pursue an interesting experiment knowing all along that Fahim had no interest in her? Her scalp prickled.

She dismissed the thought as nasty and uncharitable, and as a form of penance, sent Ania a series of messages, which said nothing at all. When she looked up from her phone, the man had finished stippling the blues on his canvas and was dabbing little spots of orange to make a boat. Behind her, a balloon popped.

A group of schoolgirls walked by in their uniforms, a jumble of whispers and laughs and linked arms. She remembered sitting by the lake many years ago, hearing the conversation of a few older girls drift down to her from where they stood.

"As dry as month-old mutton bones."

"Like a coconut husk, and the same color too."

"And smelly, like rotting fruit."

It was a few minutes before she realized that the girls had been discussing her mother's vagina.

She felt a stab of guilt when she remembered that she had been far more upset with her mother than with the girls. She had felt that her mother deserved the opprobrium for her failure to be more conventional, more feminine. She remained obsessed with her political projects and continued to wear the same old snuff-colored saris, allowed her greasy hair to stay stuck to her scalp, ignored the dark down on her sallow cheeks. If she had not been her mother, if the girls had ever allowed Dimple into their huddle, she would probably have nodded in agreement too.

A woman had sat down on the bench next to Dimple. With a toothpick she was picking out pieces of fruit from a plastic bag and chewing them with great satisfaction. She found a new toothpick and offered a slice of apple to Dimple, who smiled and shook her head.

Dimple stood up, and the lake looked exactly the same as it always had: the same curls of smoke drifting over the shore, the same ring of dark hills, the same silvery light. She was caught by surprise because all day she had been so focused on noticing the changes. But it remained the place where at anytime there might be a jovial slap on the back, a greeting shouted from across the lane, an inquisitive face at the window. When she was younger Dimple would often hire a boat and pedal it to the middle of the lake, as far as possible from the day-trippers and honeymooners. The boat was in the shape of a swan, painted white. And they would drift in the blue, the girl and the swan, looking out at the crests of the surrounding hills.

CHAPTER TWENTY-ONE

THE WEDDING RECEPTION had been held in a castle near Salisbury, complete with flaming torches and a horse-drawn carriage. At first, Fahim's heart had thrilled at the extravagance. He'd felt that it was a vindication of his headlong dash into marriage with Mussoorie and a mark of her family's acceptance, since they were paying the bill. But it had turned out to be an odd affair. The venue was too large for the number of guests, and they huddled at the foot of a large staircase, looking up at the vaulted ceiling. Sudden drafts gusted through the reception room. The air smelled of mildew.

At dinner the conversation had depressed him, as it settled on a series of inconsequential niceties. He had come to England to get to know her family, but it appeared that they barely knew one another. There were polite inquiries about jobs and vacations. Waitresses brought salmon smothered in sauce. Wineglass stems were fingered, phones checked. Within days of the reception Fahim was having to fight off the realization that he had made an appalling mistake. His insomnia had returned, and he used it as an excuse to explain the sudden interruption to his and Mussoorie's sex life. The truth was that he had lost all desire for his new wife. He could barely admit to himself that she had deceived him. His own meticulous duplicity made it even harder to stomach.

THEY HAD FIRST met at a senior bureaucrat's garden party in Delhi, a gray afternoon, overcast but warm, standing around wondering when the speeches would end. Fahim had once been told that people at these parties were never asked what they did since everyone either already knew or simply assumed that it would be significant. Nevertheless, he asked her what she did.

Looking him straight in the eye, she said: "Whatever I'm asked."

She had made numerous trips to India, but this was her most involved visit: she was writing an intimate history of the Maharajahs of Somwari and, apart from her forays to Delhi, was spending much of her time in residence at their palace, interviewing the family and exploring their personal archives. The Somwari clan were politically active and owned vast tracts of land—and as a result, often failed to recall that they could not act like they were in charge of a sovereign principality.

"I know they have a bit of a reputation," she said, "but they do an awful lot of good work. It's been terrific getting to see this other side to them."

At first he wrote her off as another white girl who had arrived in India with memsahib fantasies, eyes ablaze at the thought of palanquins and peacock feathers. But she seemed to have more substance than that. Her knowledge of Indian history was impressive, and she appeared to have traveled widely in remote districts of Rajasthan and Gujarat. And most impressive of all, she had gained access to places that it would normally take years to infiltrate. Part of this was obviously the result of fawning half-wits desperate for attention from an attractive Englishwoman. But Fahim was beginning to be convinced that there was far more to Mussoorie Hughes.

One evening she invited him as her date to a party at the mansion of a retired brigadier. She seemed completely in her element, gently flirting with the septuagenarian army crowd, beating an almost ceremonial retreat when their wives interceded. There was no clue that she was visiting the country to research her book—she acted as though she had grown up in the care of this company.

At one point, she walked past him on the verandah and whispered into his ear, "Come with me."

He followed her through the foyer and up the stairs, into a room with a heavy wooden door.

"I just needed a break," she said, reaching for her cigarettes. "They're sweet but it can all get a bit much."

She led him into a dimly lit study, made even gloomier by the greenish tinge of its cabinets' glass panes. Someone had been applying a muscle relaxant—the tube was still on the sofa—and the room reeked of synthetic camphor.

"Christ, got to let some air in. There's a lovely balcony where no one will disturb us," she said.

"You seem to know your way around here very well," he said.

"Oh, I'm always in and out of this house. Adorable of them, they've sort of adopted me."

They squeezed onto the tiny balcony and balanced their drinks on the rail. It would take only one expansive gesture to send them crashing to the ground below, possibly finishing off some frail field marshal. Fahim watched her blow smoke into the air, her eyes not leaving his face.

"So, Mussoorie?"

"It's the first thing anyone asks me here. I was wondering what took you so long."

"You're named after the place?"

"It was my parents' favorite hill station. They've always loved everything about India, but Mussoorie was always the most special."

She leaned forward and kissed him. She tasted of tobacco, vodka, ice—and a delicious licentiousness that he had not encountered before. He slipped his hand under her blouse, she leaned back, her arm knocked against the rail. The two glasses shook but did not fall.

He learned that two of her ex-boyfriends had been at Sandhurst, and she gave the impression of having been a regular at military balls. It was a natural assumption that her background had the upper-class solidity of the high-ranking officers that she had known. One uncle had been an Olympic skier, another had been caught doing something unsavory in Kenya. From the books he had read, it all seemed typical of a certain kind of Briton who gravitated toward the former colonies.

He studied pictures of her on society websites, clutching a champagne glass with a few other apple-cheeked blondes in satin dresses. In one "Around Town" column, she was described as "the India-born writer and beauty, who was the toast of the party for being able to read palms and give frighteningly accurate insights."

He saw Mussoorie whenever possible, encouraging her to

spend more time in Delhi. After the debacle with Ania, he felt that there was a great urgency to this new alliance, a perfect opportunity to propel himself forward. Fahim's insomnia was worse than ever. He would sit up at night, carrying his humiliation in his stomach like an ulcer.

"Never hold a grudge," his mother would warn him, "it will kill you first."

He was making every attempt; he knew she was right. And in any case, what would a grudge held against Ania Khurana achieve? She would spring up every few days in the papers, on social media, and, if he was lucky enough to be invited, at some cocktail party, where he would watch her refuse canapés while she pretended not to have seen him. He was convinced that he was now the butt of jokes shrieked across the Khurana pool on those lazy Saturday afternoons.

"Would it be completely mad for us to get married?"

It was Mussoorie's idea.

They gave the court notice of their intention to marry, neither one quite sure if it would really come to pass. But it did. On the appointed day, they waited for hours on a wooden bench outside a grimy office before they could get the marriage registered. The additional district magistrate had been called away to cut the ribbon at the opening of a new classroom at the local school. Their witnesses—Fahim's old newsroom colleague and a taxi driver—signed the papers in advance and left. They drank cup after cup of sweet tea, possessed by a mild hysteria as they gazed at the dusty files and the trunks full of old election papers. It was their wedding day.

As if to restore some sense of balance, the honeymoon was at a magical hotel on the edge of the Rajasthani desert. A former palace owned by one of Mussoorie's friends, its rooms were filled with a golden light. Even the slightest breeze sent the sheer curtains into a billow; and beyond them, through the latticed doors, the pool gleamed an outlandish blue. The evening sky was the same lilac as the fragments of quartz they found in the sand.

Her brassiness was wonderfully at odds with the prissy coquetry of the women he knew, who would gaze up at him through their lashes and then act wounded if he tried to touch them. He thought her strong-willed charm might rub off on him. It was just the boost he needed: the attention lavished by a well-connected woman who would introduce him to a new world. Perhaps she would even prove to be the gateway to a new country, where he would be ready for new professional conquests.

BUT HE WAS flooded with disappointment when their cab pulled up outside her parents' home. She had often referred to the place as their "manor," and it was only now that he realized that she might have been being playful—or duplicitous.

The manor turned out to be on a drab crescent in a Basingstoke suburb. The front garden was almost entirely paved over—a sole cypress tree stood to one side of the detached house. The door-knocker was in the shape of a smiling Buddha, and there were more Buddhas sitting inside the bay window. Mussoorie's parents had never had anything to do with the armed forces. Former hippies, they had settled into unspectacular respectability by way of a successful key-cutting and shoe repair business. Simon shook Fahim's hand and pulled him into a hug as Ann stood behind them, patting her husband on the back, as though impatient for her turn.

The warmth of their welcome made him feel even more wretched. Conversation was like sitting through a slide show of holiday snaps as Simon and Ann recalled their time in Goa and Rishikesh.

"It must all have changed so much," they said every so often.

"Yes," he said.

They seemed impressed by his broadcasting career, which Mussoorie seemed to have embellished.

"It's an honor to have an Indian celebrity as part of the family," said Ann. "Now what can we get you to drink? There's everything: wine, beer, gin, scotch."

Then her face creased with embarrassment, and her hand flew to her mouth.

"I'm so sorry," she said. "How insensitive of me. You're Muslim."

"Mum, he drinks like a fish," said Mussoorie.

"Oh what a relief," said Ann, her face righting itself. "Red wine all right then?"

There hung a large portrait of Mussoorie on the landing, her hair tumbling in pre-Raphaelite curls, an orchid nudging her shoulder. She had the largest bedroom in the house. From the window he could see the roof of the house next door, a wide overhang that held an assortment of balls and cuddly toys flung out of an upstairs window. The slightest movement made her brass bedstead shudder. He opened the cupboards to find a tangle of tights, sweaters, and balled-up tops. She laughingly explained what they were: the purchases that were lapses of judgment, the clothes that she hoped she would fit into again, those she had forgotten she owned.

"I've told Mum not to worry, I'll make some space tonight," she said, kissing him on the side of his head.

When she had gone downstairs, he lay on the bed, his shoes still on. He had to concede that it was a fitting turn of events. While Mussoorie had wheeled in place glittering façades to impress him, he had also created a few illusions of his own. He had fabricated a kinship to the Nawabs of Baoni, discovering that they were not the subjects of much researchable material. He described occasional visits to their palace before a fire destroyed it. She had been charmed when he described the Baoni coat of arms, on which the escutcheon was supported by two otters, the kind of detail that he knew would delight her. She reveled in the paraphernalia of Indian royalty like a puppy in a puddle.

There were other lies about his life: major news stories he had broken, his friends in the media, his plans for the future. He was an only child with no surviving parents: it was easy to inspire a sense of sympathy for someone who was unmoored by family. And there would never be any relatives who would come forward to lay bare his claims.

"You're not going to have a nap now, are you?" Mussoorie shouted from the bottom of the stairs.

He sat up. The bedstead let out a long creak. Slowly he lay down again.

THERE WAS LITTLE sign of Mussoorie's glittering London social life. The pictures in the society pages were not borne out, and quite a few of the evenings were spent in the local pub. Mussoorie was a different woman in Basingstoke, much more subdued, perhaps now chastened by the reality of having led him on. He felt a lull the first time they walked into the pub, a strange suspension as his presence was absorbed. And then the music and the clatter and the chat all sped up again.

The regulars were friendly enough, but it was an arrested sociability, so different from the voluble enthusiasm of Mussoorie's parents. The staff displayed a hard professionalism, and he wondered how long it would take to secure the cheeky amiability they showed the other drinkers. Perhaps he would never be allowed to experience it. That was the enigma of being an outsider: the reasons for exclusion were rarely made clear.

Some of Mussoorie's friends complimented him more than once on his fine English. On other occasions they would treat him with an exaggerated camaraderie designed to reassure him that, while many would readily believe he was a terrorist sympathizer, *they* were not among that number and were eager to be absolved and, in some sense, applauded.

Every other evening a couple called John and Susan would pop in for a drink, looking almost embarrassed to find Fahim still in the house. John never met his gaze, rarely started a conversation, and when he did, spoke mainly of his suspicions of mismanagement at the golf club. Susan told Fahim that he reminded her of Omar Sharif, her mother's favorite actor. She took to calling him Omar.

During these visits, his sense of having been entrapped was so acute that he would excuse himself and slip into the bathroom. The frosted window had a little vent with a nylon cord to slide it open. Every time he pulled, it made a smart *click*. The sage green guest soaps by the wash basin were for show; family members were supposed to use the liquid soap that was in the cabinet. There was a framed sketch of a giraffe on the wall, made by Mussoorie when she was six. When he returned to the sitting room, they all turned to face him with broad smiles. He could not bear the thought of settling down again, being sucked into the large sofa cushions, so he stood in front of the French doors for a few moments, as though admiring the sad, sparse garden. There was a hot tub on the deck. He imagined them all sitting in it.

CHAPTER TWENTY-TWO

THERE WAS NO adornment in the Khurana office boardrooms and banqueting halls, no artwork on the walls or specially commissioned sculptures, no tributes in bronze or glass to the traditional values of the company. There had been a deliberate attempt at emptiness and sterility, as though in reaction to the excesses that the company otherwise encouraged. In one of the meeting rooms, sunlight streamed through the skylights onto the large white table. The men seated around it all stared at the video screen on the wall waiting for their interlocutors in Guangzhou to resolve their technical hitch. No one looked at their phone in meetings unless absolutely urgent: another Khurana decree.

Dileep glanced around and closed his eyes. In meetings he often gave the impression that he was preoccupied with his own thoughts, gaze fixed on some distant point. But then he would seize on some feeble or imprecise formulation and interrupt without any hesitation. He paid professionals handsomely to order the company's affairs, and he was always vigilant about the value he received. He had a nose for accounts and an interest in technology.

His legal training meant that he was practiced in the pliability of language, the fragile surface through which a loophole could be gently bored. But that day, as they all focused on the blank screen, the minutes dragging, he began to feel the soft swell of an incipient panic.

He left the room, saying that they could finish without him. He needed some sense of motion and vitality. He took the stairs to his office, leaping up them two at a time, and keyed in the code for his private bathroom. The lights, sleek and yellow, sparked to life. He pulled the magnifying mirror toward him and examined the skin on his face. Two hairs were longer than the rest of his short stubble, and they showed brilliantly white against his skin. He reached for some tweezers and pulled them out, enjoying the twinge. He looked at his chin in profile, searching for but not finding any bagginess. He lowered his head by a couple of inches to make sure.

He had taken risks and either grown or transformed the businesses: the mills had been replaced by pharmaceutical companies, the trade magazines were now globally integrated financial risk management service providers. As a single parent, he had raised a beautiful, accomplished daughter. He had provided a home for his sister and was convinced that he had saved her from some kind of deathly insanity. For the most part, he had lived his life in the way that the dead men of his family had lived theirs, or perhaps would have wished to live theirs, or perhaps would have wished him to live. These questions of legacy were complicated. But now every day he faced a seeping dread that there was nothing more to do. Incomplete, irrelevant, he would slip into an early death.

He had wasted no time in getting Mr. Nayak's number from Serena and arranging to see him.

Dileep's interests did not extend to conventionally religious matters. Given Serena's endorsements, he merely craved a glimpse into this mysterious world, since it seemed to be available. His upbringing had not been religious. His father had been an atheist who would attend religious ceremonies when expedient to do so. And his mother's connection with God involved a series of lies, exaggerations, and threats, which made it no different to her relationship with her husband. She did the puja every morning while her sari blouse was being freshly ironed. Dressed in one of her magnificent silk saris, spilling out of her demi-cup bra, she stood at the top-floor shrine, tinkling a little silver bell at any point that she felt required particular emphasis. When she had finished, a tremulous waiting hand would hold out the ironed blouse on a hanger, and she always associated its warmth with the Almighty's munificence.

During Dileep's first visit to Mr. Nayak's office, the small degree of skepticism had soon dissipated. Serena introduced them and gave Dileep a little reassuring pat on his arm. Mr. Nayak smiled. There was none of the garish and obvious paraphernalia of the shady godman. He wore a well-pressed white shirt and gray trousers, a slim gold pen tucked into his breast pocket. His secretary was in a navy skirt, white blouse, and thick glasses. They could have been middle-ranking employees of an insurance company. It was clairvoyance, but its appeal was that it looked managerial. Mr. Nayak's business card offered an emergency out-of-hours number. Appointments were promptly confirmed by text message.

"I am a professional, Mr. Khurana. I do not want any kind of misunderstandings between us, isn't it? From the very beginning, I will confirm to you what exactly I cannot do. I am not able to predict the future and tell you whether you will get some contract or when your daughter will get married or when party X or party Y will become deceased. That is clear, isn't it?" said Mr. Nayak.

"Yes," said Dileep, his voice low.

"I am in the business of people's energies, the forces that they emit, positive or negative, both for the alive and the deceased. And I will help you reconnect with those energies and improve your relationships with those people. You are a busy man, there are countless demands, many people depend on you. Correct, isn't it?"

"That's correct."

"I may provide you with a remedy—some powder, some vegetable matter—or I might ask you to use some substance or article to assist me. Please don't misunderstand this as some kind of black magic or witchcraft."

"No."

"I think you have understood me. Symbols are very powerful instruments in dealing with energies. What I will give you are representations of this power. Temporarily containing these energies. I am being clear, isn't it?"

"Yes."

"I can already see that you have some unfinished business with a deceased person. There is a serious matter that has not been resolved for many years. She is waiting. And I will help you."

Dileep stayed silent, stunned with this divination.

It was clear to him that Mr. Nayak had quickly become aware of the torment he suffered. Dileep still thought of his dead wife every day. He had never discussed grief or mourning with anyone but had heard others speak of their struggles. They seemed to agree that the irritating memories faded: the tiny nuisances that would rankle for days, the tiresome habits that inevitably led to a confrontation. This had been his experience too. He had made a conscious effort to cultivate only the recollections that would act as a sudden sunburst on a grim day. It was difficult, but year after year he had managed to avoid dwelling on the fact that she had died only as a result of her own treachery.

Mr. Nayak patted him on the shoulder as he showed him out, a hopeful, professional gesture.

"I will help you, Mr. Khurana, I will help you."

NINA HAD BEEN asked to attend a friend's perfume launch party, an invite that held little allure but no clear escape, which was how she found herself in a hotel lobby with distinct and inimical constituencies. Near the fountain there stood a group of tall women in short skirts who, to all appearances, inhabited the hinterlands of prostitution. A group of Korean tourists waited their turn at the front desk, quietly seething about something. Couples from the Middle East occupied the sofas by the windows, the women in burkas, the men dressed like jocks on spring break in floral board shorts and slogan T-shirts, earphones trailing out of their back pockets.

At the concierge Nina asked the way to the Ruby Room. As she turned, she spotted Renu, walking through the sliding doors. Her instinct was to spin back around and head toward the shopping arcade, linger among the gaudy, overpriced scarves and trinkets until she could safely emerge again. But Renu caught sight of her and began to approach, her arm linked with that of a handsome young man.

But there was a difference. Renu was strutting. Or at least,

Nina could see an approximation of a strut. Renu's hair was shorter, her chest was puffed out with pride, a hen in charge of a splendid egg. She was marching the poor man along as though he would try to make a break for it at any moment. Poor, plodding Renu had finally been blessed with everything she had ever desired, and it was almost too painful to witness.

"How lovely, Nina, I didn't expect to see you here," said Renu.

"I could say the same," said Nina, offering her cheek.

"This is Nikhil," said Renu.

Nina looked blank.

"The colonel's nephew."

"So you're the famous nephew," she said. "We waited and waited but you never came. It was all getting terribly biblical. And now you've arrived. I was wondering when Renu would let the rest of us have a little look."

"Like a new toy?" he asked.

"I wouldn't be quite that optimistic."

He grinned, and she could see his body relax into the fun that she would provide. He had his head slightly cocked; he took his hand out of his pocket and let it fall by his side. It wouldn't be long before Renu's dullness would become unbearable.

"So how has Renu been entertaining you?" asked Nina. "Bridge parties?"

"Nina! I've never played bridge in my life," said Renu.

"Oh, she's been wonderful, allowing me to tag along, introducing me to all kinds of people," said Nikhil.

Renu gave him a sweet little pinch.

"How marvelous," said Nina.

There was something in his manner that reminded her of the

young men who would wait to give her a ride home from college—
clear-eyed chaps who tried to pass off their nervousness as a kind
of friendly impatience. She could see that he was trying to settle
into his manliness: there was no telling what it would turn into
after a few years.

He had the kind of American accent that she associated with
preppy students at good universities, the rounded enunciation of
earnest debaters. Renu was looking at him with fond pride, nodding in agreement, her arm almost twitching to be in his again.

Nina thought briefly of her own son. A huge crack of thunder
had woken her up before dawn. She had lain in bed, feeling anxious and dislocated—the water drumming against the walls and
roof, the wind rattling the balcony doors—wondering if he would
ever speak to her again. This is what it would be like in a few
years, she thought: too tired or ill to get out of bed, making sense
of the world through its sounds; a woman lying in a mausoleum,
listening out for leaves being raked across the paths.

It had been raining in Utah too; she had checked. On the
website of his addiction treatment facility she had found the daily
patient schedule, photographs of the staff, and information on
pro-recovery diets. Her son had always been a fussy eater; for a
couple of years he had lived on ham and raisins. And then his eating habits had crossed into squalid chaos, like all his behavior. She
would find him late at night, standing at the fridge, eating out of
serving bowls with filthy hands. He had picked at a scab and bled
all over the pale roses on the silk that covered her wing chair.
There had been broken syringes, a stench of day-old vomit, the
certain knowledge that he had scrabbled around on the urine-
spattered floor of a public toilet looking for a pill. She had at least

been spared the indignity of having her house burgled by her son, not an uncommon occurrence in their set, she had later come to discover. Although, what difference would it have made? He had shown some restraint but nonetheless there was precious little left in her life that was worth plundering.

A loud laugh sliced through the air. They turned to see a young woman on her phone. Her handbag was the size of a duffel bag, and the neck of her dress scooped low. As she spoke she faced one way and then turned around and then shifted back, as though ensuring that she could be appreciated from every angle. A diamond pendant dived into her deep cleavage. Nina and Renu looked at it at the same time and then caught each other's eye. A momentary warm current passed between them but it was nothing more than that. The woman laughed again, louder this time. Nina looked away.

"Lovely to meet you. Here, take my card," said Nina.

She patted Nikhil on the arm, offered Renu her cheek again, and walked out through the sliding doors. As she waited for her car, she felt unusually self-conscious. She had not given anyone her card for a long time. One of the phone numbers it listed had been disconnected, and she hadn't checked the e-mail address for months.

Two days later, he called her.

"You really must be at a loose end," she said. "I can't think what you want with me."

"I enjoyed meeting you; I think it would be wonderful to have lunch."

"Presumably everyone else is busy today."

"I'll let you in on a secret. I've canceled everyone else today."

"You're not pretending to flirt with me," she said, intending it to sound like a command.

He laughed.

But she knew not to trust a young man's laugh.

They agreed to meet for lunch—and it was a surprise to Nina that neither of them canceled.

The restaurant was almost empty, and she felt a prickle of disappointment. It would be rather fun if a concerned well-wisher reported their lunch date to Renu. It was so tempting, so easy, to lure someone away from her, even, if ultimately, so dull and unrewarding.

She watched Nikhil speak, feeling she could stay silent for the rest of the afternoon and he would not even notice. He had not needed much of a prompt to begin talking about his childhood in New Hampshire. It began early with boys, the belief that their speech had an intrinsic weight and exigency. She knew that it had begun early with her own son although it had taken her a long time to realize it. They were more or less the same age. She thought of a phrase that her son had often used and was on the point of mentioning it when she felt her heartbeat speed up, a sharp warning. It would be better not to mention her son.

"Northern Spy. Early Joe. Wolf River. Maiden's Blush," said Nikhil.

"I'm sorry?"

"The names of the apples. They used to fascinate me. We would drive past the orchards and end up in a village that was having a fall festival. A white church in the distance, pumpkins piled high, horses and carts for show. A whole bunch of stuff. And tables lined with boxes of apples, with their names on signs."

"Wolf River is an apple?"

"Makes the best pie."

"Dear God, it's like having lunch with some American salesman from the 1950s."

He laughed and tried to top up her glass of wine. She shook her head.

"Well, I'm kind of like a bad salesman. I try to make people buy or do things that really aren't good for them."

He crinkled his eyes and took a large sip of wine.

The waiter brushed the crumbs off the table with a smart, circular motion, making a soft *whoosh*ing sound. After he had retreated, it felt as though the entire room had fallen away and they were seated in a wide open space with only the pristine tablecloth between them.

Before Nina could reflect on the question, she had already asked it: "I'm going to Kolkata for the opening of a photography exhibition. Why don't you come too?"

He considered her offer, eyes lowered.

The room seemed to return. She caught it through the tail of her eye. The kitchen door swung shut; a shaft of sunlight hit a row of copper pans. A few feet away a businessman rose and did up the top button of his suit jacket. Somewhere behind her, there was a clatter of ice cubes into a sink.

"You know what," Nikhil said. "I think I will."

CHAPTER TWENTY-THREE

IT WAS ONE of those changeable Paris days when a gauzy shower spattered the newspapers left on café tables, even as the sun continued to shine. Umbrellas in pastel shades were raised and lowered and raised again. One of the fashion label's publicists led the way through the crowd at the Jardin des Tuileries, and Ania followed close behind, eyes downcast, occasionally glancing at items in the splashy parade for the photographers: a brocade coat, a pair of gold boots, some inflatable trousers.

As she approached the VIP entrance, a fashion blogger stopped her to ask a few questions.

"Do you think the rise of populism in countries around the world will have an impact on forthcoming collections?"

"I think fashion works very much as a reaction against the mainstream, so I believe designers will respond creatively and instinctively, finding new ways to make alternate conceptions come through."

"Thank you. Is there anything that has really grabbed your attention this season?"

"I loved the asymmetrical beaded headdresses at Balenciaga."

"Thank you. Do you think we will be seeing some affordable versions of them soon?"

"No."

"Thank you."

They showed their passes, and Ania was escorted to her seat, a glitchy bass pounding from the speakers, the black walls and floor shimmering with a blaze from the overhead lights. The chair was tiny and uncomfortable, even by Parisian standards.

Ania should have been looking out for friends and casting her usual discreet glance at the celebrities in the front row across from her—but she was preoccupied, raising her hand to her mouth several times to chew on the side of a fingernail before remembering that she was being filmed. The day before her departure she had seen a message flash up on Dev's phone. The phone was locked, but she had managed to read the first sentence of the message from Kamya before the screen went dark. Dev was nowhere in sight, and her urge had been uncontrollable. She pressed the home button, the message illuminated again, and she took a photo of it with her phone. She still felt small and grubby.

"Darling! We're having dinner tonight. Pick me up? Got something for you. Kiss-kiss."

The message had repulsed her, and she had been unable to dismiss it. She had looked at it several times on the flight, trying to decipher its codes. Dev had already told her that they were only friends—across four continents, if one were to be precise—and she had never known him to lie. There was no reason why they should not be having dinner together. But the message was steeped in a cunning ambiguity, as though it was, in fact, a trap.

"Darling!"

It was an odd choice of word for someone as chilly and unde-
monstrative as Kamya. The exclamation mark was even odder, an
attempt perhaps to convince the recipient of the sender's warmth
and vivacity. It looked as though heavy equipment had been used
to move it into place.

"We're having dinner tonight."

It was virtually a command. Ania bristled.

"Pick me up?"

Kamya had departed from her usual glacial imperiousness to a
disgusting coyness. In the spaces between the words, Ania could
almost see the flutter of eyelashes. It was an unmistakable act
of manipulation. Kamya had a driver. Why did Dev have to pick
her up?

"Got something for you."

This did not even bear thinking about.

"Kiss-kiss."

In a curious way, this was the most redemptive part of the
message, since no woman in possession of all her faculties would
ever say this to a potential lover. Why was there a hyphen? It almost seemed ironic. It was Ania's best hope.

There were forces at play here that made her deeply uncomfortable. She had always been uneasy with Dev's girlfriends, even
after she had taken great care to ensure that her assessments were
fair and objective. When she looked back at her own relationship
history, she could recognize the small mistakes she had made, the
impulses she could have curbed. But overall, there had been suf-
ficient distinction; no one had been mortifying or disgraceful.
Dev's exes were a different matter.

There had been the social climber with the nasal whine who taught at the London School of Economics. She was a historian, working on a book that applied Gandhian principles to the new world order. She often spoke about "post-capitalist social ecology" and "anarcho-pacifism" but would have clawed out the Mahatma's eyes to get an invitation to a Khurana cocktail party. After they had split up, Ania had been brazen enough to ask Dev what he had seen in her.

"Intellectual rigor," he had said.

"Oh, please."

"It's what I always look for."

A look had passed between them, filled with a kind of mischief, which suggested that they were talking about something else entirely, and she had not known what to say.

His next girlfriend had been jealous and possessive, an absurd creature who sulked for days if he appeared to enjoy a conversation with another woman. On the occasions they had all met, she had been stiff and uncommunicative, relaxing only when Dev's remarks were directed *at* her but were also *about* her. Dev had later told Ania that she had once bitten him in the bath—not a lighthearted nip, but an unprovoked gnawing that had required antiseptic—so one wondered what other terrible details he had kept to himself.

After that he had been engaged to a beautiful psychiatrist who lived in her parents' mansion in Defence Colony. She dressed in mannish shirts and waistcoats and had a permanently distracted air, as though her patients' voices were running through her head at all times. Ania was disgusted to see that she stubbed her cigarettes out on dinner plates. She had never seen Dev as unhappy as he seemed to be in the months after the engagement. He worked all hours and never wanted to leave the safety of his university. He slumped silently on sofas, had dark circles under his eyes, and, worst of all, listened to everything Ania said with a terrible earnestness. She had never discovered what transpired between Dev and the psychiatrist during that year, but the engagement was called off a few days before Christmas and his spirit had returned by the new year.

Ania could now see that all these women had mistaken his kindness for pliability, his patience for unworldliness. It was clear that they had seen him as an old, gentle soul at their service. They had no appreciation for the happiness he gained from his esoteric enthusiasms, nor did they see that a bit of gentle joshing could turn him into a boy again. They had never walked up a mountain trail with him, inserting inappropriate lyrics into Beatles songs; they had never been to see a hilariously bad off-Broadway play with him; they had never watched him try to roll out pastry. And now Kamya's unpleasant proximity meant that Ania would have to renew her vigilance and protect Dev from the negative repercussions of his own fine nature.

She thought of the journal he had sent her in Italy. For a moment, it seemed like the only sign of his existence. She had written in it for the first few days and then abandoned it. That guilt-ridden fact seemed like a dark premonition, and she resolved to return to it as soon as possible.

"Excusez-moi," said a voice ravaged by cigarettes.

Ania was brought back to the room and to the reedlike woman who was making her way past. The show was now over an hour late. She glanced at her neighbors on either side, but there was no sign of a shared frustration with the moment. On the other side of the catwalk, all along the front row, she witnessed the same bored, courtly rigidity. The celebrities sat there like figures in a play, legs crossed at similarly elegant angles, fanning themselves with their programs, silent and pale like porcelain.

The venerable buyer on Ania's left finally let out a weary sigh.

Ania broke her own rule and ventured a whisper. "Do you know what's going on?"

"It's the muse," said the buyer, one eyebrow shooting up. "She's been delayed at customs, and the show can't begin without her."

"Wonder what she was trying to bring in."

"Oh, her mother's ashes, apparently. I've just had a couple of messages. Her mother died recently and loved the Paris shows, so she wanted her ashes to be present here to appease her soul. Something like that. Can you imagine? The urn gets a front-row seat."

The eyebrow shot up again.

"She's still at the airport?"

"She must be on her way here now. But it looks like the customs people didn't make it easy. The French find this kind of American sentimentality horribly vulgar."

"But how long will we wait?"

"As long as it takes, my dear. The bloody woman won an Oscar last year."

THE DESK WAS a mess: a ball of tissue smudged with lipstick, a medley of postcards, a ring dropped into a pen stand for safekeeping, a saucer with a faint edge of gilt. On the other side of the room Sigmund was licking a butter dish as though he were trying to bring it to life. Ania had no idea how he had got hold of it but decided that it was easier to let him continue. Her bedroom door was shut and would remain so for the rest of the afternoon.

The day after she returned from Paris, Dileep had said something about bullet-proofing the doors to the house.

"Aren't you getting a bit carried away?" Ania asked.

"You have no idea what this country is turning into."

"We live ten minutes away from the prime minister's residence. It's not the Wild West."

Nonetheless a van full of security specialists had arrived at the house, and Dina was guiding them through the rooms. Strange men kept appearing on the landing or in the doorway, asking if there was a balcony at the end of the corridor or if there was a false ceiling in the study. For hours they had been reinstalling alarms and testing cameras.

Ania had begun to notice odd strains of behavior from Dileep: a heightened sense of paranoia and periods of unexpected indecisiveness. She had spent much of her adult life reassuring him about his insecurities—his looks and pastimes—but there was an unfamiliar element to his current disquiet. In the past there had been occasional difficult episodes involving his businesses, but he had never seemed overly troubled. She wondered whether there were serious money problems that he was keeping from her; she wondered for a mad instant whether they could lose everything. It seemed too absurd a prospect to contemplate: like a shoddy dream sequence in a B-movie. Perhaps it was only a prolonged adjustment to the absence of Renu; he missed her much more than he would admit.

Ania shut her bedroom door on the security experts. She and Dimple would emerge only when it was all over.

"What was that Japanese candy in the kitchen called again?" asked Dimple, flopping down on the bed.

"Amezaiku."

"I couldn't believe how beautiful and delicate they were. Like real works of art."

"It was fabulous to see. Can't believe how quickly he worked, all those translucent horses. And he must have been jet-lagged, because he only flew in this morning."

"I thought he was quite hot."

"The chef?"

"Yes. There's something about chefs, na? I don't know why. Is it because of their hands, all that kneading?"

"Do you think so? I don't know. As long as they don't smell of their food."

"But who is all the candy for?"

"Part of the dessert buffet. For a supremely dull dinner tonight, some American think-tank people. I don't need to have anything to do with them, thank God, so I'm going to be at Dev's, making him watch *The Umbrellas of Cherbourg* with me."

"Have you stopped seeing Nikhil?"

"I wasn't *seeing* him. But I have no idea what we're doing. We had such a fabulous time when we went away. And there's definitely something there, I know it. I really felt that after we got back, it would all happen, but I've only seen him a couple of times since then. Maybe he got busy; I've been busy too. All we seem to do is like each other's posts and send flirty messages all the time."

Ania neglected to mention that she had been scrutinizing his social media interactions with other women too, trying to judge his intent.

"But you like him?"

"Of course I like him. But he does these strange disappearing acts."

After a pause, she said, "He's the only guy I've met in a long time where I don't keep thinking, is he okay, have I said too much, should I reign myself in some more?"

"But is there something going *on*?"

"There's not enough going on, and I'll have to do something about that. If I don't make things happen, nothing ever gets done."

It seemed like an opportune moment.

"So have you met anyone, Dee? Any guy on the scene?"

"No one."

"Really? No one at all?"

There was no response from Dimple. She was lying on her back, looking at the ceiling, her eyes half closed. There was a tiny droplet glistening in the corner of her eye. It happened to Ania too—her eyes watered for no apparent reason. But she couldn't be sure; perhaps Dimple was still upset about the men in her life, about Fahim. Ania had held herself out as a smart, knowledgeable friend who knew what was best for Dimple. She still felt an ache to somehow be proved right.

"You heard about Fahim?" asked Ania.

"What about him?" said Dimple, turning toward her.

"Getting married."

"I saw something on Facebook."

"What an asshole."

"It's a free world. Let him get married to whomever he wants."

"Yes, but to pretend that he's into someone and then suddenly, ten minutes later, he's married to somebody else. Honestly, no one has heard of this woman, and none of us can even imagine where he picked her up. I mean, how could we have known that he'd turn out to be such a creep."

"You know what, we really don't need to discuss it. Not because I'm all upset. I realized that I probably didn't even like him that much. I just thought I did. Does that make sense?"

"Of course it does. But it doesn't change the fact that he's an asshole. I'll keep my eyes open. There's got to be someone else."

Ania thought it best to change the subject.

"How was your trip? Did you manage not to kill your mother?"

"Uff. I left early. Made up an excuse about being back at work. It was like being trapped in childhood again."

"I can totally see that."

"She was just so difficult, as usual. Pushing her crazy politics down my throat, disapproving of everything I do, but not openly. I couldn't stand it. And now I feel guilty for leaving early."

"I'm dying for a cigarette. I'm allowing myself one a week. I'll just have one quickly on the balcony. Stay here if you want, it's baking outside."

She slid open the French doors and perched on a rattan chaise longue, slipping into a practiced performance, leaning back as she exhaled and stretching her long legs out, even though her only audience was Dimple.

"We should do something next week."

Dimple nodded and sat up. Among the debris on the desk, she spotted a framed photograph of Ania's parents that she hadn't noticed before. Dileep did not look greatly different; today there was more of a tightness around his features and his hair was trimmed short, having lost what he had probably once considered a charming rakishness. Ania's mother was everything Dimple had imagined: hair swept back, a shock of red lipstick, the long strand of pearls. The lights were blurred in the background, and they were both dressed for a party. There was a stiff formality to his gaze as she leaned in to him, one hand curled awkwardly against his chest.

Ania came back into the room and closed the French doors.

"You really look so much like her," said Dimple. "You didn't know her at all?"

"No, I was just a few weeks old when she died."

"How did she die?"

At last, she felt able to ask the question.

Ania returned to her spot on the bed.

"I'm sorry, that sounded so nosy," said Dimple.

"It's okay. You can ask. It was a car crash. For years I didn't understand what she was doing in a car on her own, late at night, on a lonely road near Manesar. And so soon after I was born."

Ania lay back and looked at the ceiling as she spoke.

"But she wasn't on her own. She had gone for a drive with her lover, and that's when it happened, a head-on collision. He was dead on the spot, and she died a few days later in the hospital."

"Oh my God."

Ania nodded.

"Your dad knew about this?" asked Dimple.

"I don't know. He obviously found out when the accident happened. But maybe he knew all along."

"You've never talked about it with him?"

"Of course not."

"Then how did you find out?"

"Nina told me. Nina Varkey, she's a friend of my father's. A poisonous bitch of the first order, but she has her uses. I'm sure she couldn't wait to tell me."

Ania rolled over onto her front.

"Her lover. He told her he was an artist, a painter, and a sculptor, the kind of thing she would have lapped up. But he was nothing of the sort. He would take her to a friend's studio and pass off all the work there as his own. She paid him crazy money for the pieces because she was so in love with him. And that's all he was, a con man. She threw it all away for that. Everything, including her own life."

"My God, this is so sad."

The song playing on the laptop faded into nothing, and a deep quiet settled over the room, broken only by Sigmund's gentle snores. The lilies on the desk were drooping, a dusting of pollen on the pile of books next to the vase. Dimple let her head fall back on a cushion. Ania's arm dangled off the bed, and her finger strayed up and down a groove on the parquet.

"She tried to abort me. They had ended their affair, and she decided that she would try to rebuild her marriage by getting pregnant. And then a couple of months later, he reappeared and they started up again. He was furious about the pregnancy. He punished her for it. He would make her pose for hours but never draw anything. She would be on the floor, naked, on all fours, like a dog, waiting for him to tell her she could get up. And worse things, such degrading things."

Dimple laid her hand on Ania's arm.

"Really, it's fine, darling," said Ania. "I've known all this for a long time. I got the whole story from Nina. My mother confided in her."

"I wonder if your dad knows that you know."

"How would we ever talk about these things? And how could he think I wouldn't find out one day? Nothing ever stays a secret in Delhi."

They lay on the bed, listening to Sigmund's snores, the steady rhythm of that deep rumble, a remarkably human sound. Dimple thought it would be wrong to look at the photo again after all she had heard, as though she were trying to satisfy an insensitive curiosity, but she could not stop herself. The way Ania's mother leaned in to her husband looked even more mannered, a prominent vein traveling all the way up her neck. She looked straight at the camera. Her eyes were huge and blank.

FAHIM AND MUSSOORIE were back in Delhi. There had been a whirl of dinners, with friends demanding a proper wedding in India, a party at the very least: they would not be cheated out of their chance to celebrate their union. Mussoorie had regained her sangfroid almost as soon as they returned to India. She teased, she charmed. Her laughter rang out in rooms already filled with music and chatter.

"Well, we have to decide what sort of event we want: a low-key celebration with friends or more of a showcase," she said, working at her laptop in the sitting room of Fahim's apartment.

"A showcase for what?" asked Fahim.

"For us."

She decided that the latter, in spite of the expense, would reap greater dividends and began to put together a list of people who ought to attend. He looked over her shoulder, scanning the document.

"It'll be pretty embarrassing if half these people decline or just don't show up," he said.

"I don't see why you have to be so negative. The trick with these sorts of things is you've got to make people desperate to come. Get the right sort of people talking. You need to build it all up. You need buzz."

He knew that he had to get back to work. There were urgent stories he ought to pursue. A fifteen-year-old boy's skullcap had been ripped off his head moments before he was stabbed to death on a train. Claiming to have discovered a cow's carcass, a mob dragged a dairy owner from his home and set it ablaze. Two young men were found swinging from trees.

But he was flooded with despondency and trepidation, struck by an acute paralysis. It had been so long since he had nosed around in the field, he worried he would ruin what was left of his reputation, cutting corners, failing to notice clues that would be obvious to any good reporter. Years earlier, he had heard that another journalist planned to head out to Gujarat early the following morning to cover the discovery of an enormous stash of arms at a private warehouse. Fahim had managed to get the last seat on the last flight that night and then traveled by taxi, potato truck, and a hired moped to arrive at the village on the edge of the Thar Desert by daybreak. The scoop was his.

It seemed like someone else's life. Even the memory was elusive.

A few days ago he had been offered the opportunity to host a show called *Indian First*, in which Muslims would be invited to declare their love for and allegiance to the country. The aim was to show them in their home environments performing patriotic tasks—cheering on sports teams, petting cows—which would lead to a greater sense of national unity.

"I've decided about the show," he said.

Mussoorie looked up from her laptop.

"I'm not doing it," he said.

"Why not? Darling, it's exposure, isn't it? And we do need the money. Come on, they're desperate for you. It really doesn't matter whether it's for your talent or because they're so relieved you're not some bearded Saudi-supporting lunatic. You just have to make the most of it," said Mussoorie.

"That's offensive," he said.

"Oh please, you said to me yourself that you'd got lucky, getting gigs playing the acceptable Muslim. How is this any different?"

He stalked out of the room, nearly losing his footing. He bristled at his own words being used against him, words uttered in moments of self-doubt, not intended to erase the years of genuine dedication and accomplishment that he had once brought to his profession, and certainly not offered to her with any kind of license to comment on his aptitude or merit. She had no understanding of how difficult it had been to get this far.

He walked into the bedroom and looked at the tea tray on the floor, the curtains still drawn, the unmade bed. His libido had not returned. Mussoorie would lay her arm over his or nuzzle against his shoulder, and when he did not respond, curl herself into his body. There was no point in pretending to be asleep; she knew that it was improbable. She tried more subtle approaches: tracing light circles on his palm with her little finger, pressing gently against him with her hip. He feigned headaches and stomach upsets, but minor infirmities could grant only a certain degree of abstention. Always present were the accusatory memories of their rampant premarital sex life, the sidling of a hand in the back seat of a car, the frenetic thrusting in a spa's shower room.

Eventually he had to confront the stark fact that he no longer desired her. He initiated the conversation, and he could tell that she was grateful; he admitted that it was a physiological affliction, probably caused by stress, and assured her that she was in no way to blame; he agreed to go and see a doctor. It bought him some time. That night, for the first time in weeks, he slept straight through for five hours.

One night he had a clear vision of her future infidelity, as though it were being projected on the bare wall in front of him. There would be ostensible research trips and meetings with important contacts, probably in other cities: a couple days spent in a hotel where the blinds would silently close at the touch of a button. Mussoorie would always be one to explore all options. They were so similar in that respect. He was surprised to discover that he felt no anger or jealousy. He felt a sort of relief. It would make time for him to think. And perhaps it would even benefit him in some way. Mussoorie would pick her lovers with care. She was in her own way generous and pragmatic. Her ambition and industry would carry them both.

He picked up the tea tray and returned to the sitting room.

"I think it's going to be cooler today," he said.

"Yes, not so sticky."

He sipped the last of his cold tea. Trivial conversation seemed to be the best way to keep from unkindness.

CHAPTER TWENTY-FOUR

ANKIT TOOK DIMPLE's hand and led her off the pavement, glancing at the upper floors of the buildings.

"Take care, okay? These bastard children are throwing water balloons," he said.

Spotting a couple of shadowy figures crouching behind some plastic sheeting, he yelled: "I'm warning you, I'll break your legs if you try anything."

He kept his gaze directed upward. Perched on a ladder was a young man tinkering with a jumble of electricity cables. His elbows jutted out at awkward angles, and for a moment it seemed he might topple off and come crashing to the ground. Ankit and Dimple stopped just as a starburst of gold and blue flashes sparked out of the tangled wires.

"This street is full of barbarians," he said. "But at least they're barbarians I know. They're easy to fix."

He gave her a playful nudge.

It had been a morning of errands. Dimple had sat in the passenger seat fiddling with the radio as Ankit had sped recklessly across overpasses, wheeling in and out of snarls of traffic, swerving into empty side roads. He would park in front of a staircase or in the middle of an auto stand and then dash out to pay a supplier or pick up a package.

"I'll be back in two seconds. If anyone starts shouting, just look helpless, okay?" he said, leaning in through the window to plant a kiss anywhere on her face.

Dimple had found a station with a sensational playlist, and together they had belted out the numbers, a theatrical extravaganza in Ankit's battered van, attracting amused looks from hawkers and traffic police. She knew she could hold a tune, but Ankit's voice was exceptional, inhabiting a saucy falsetto for a whole verse and then in the next breath plunging into a disconsolate baritone.

For weeks after his night of shame at the farmhouse, he had tried to apologize to her in person. Eventually, the messages stopped coming. She had realized over time that what she nursed was not the memory of her humiliation but her disappointment that he had resigned himself to her absence. The time had come for her to be modern again. She bought a bottle of Old Monk and went to his shop one evening at closing time. He saw her just as he was pulling down the shutters. They had ducked under the half-closed shutter into the shop and sat on the counter, drinking out of plastic cups in the pale gleam from the streetlight.

Ankit continued to hum as they walked up the stairs to his family's flat. At each landing they caught a glimpse of the old man on a balcony across the street, wrapped up in a shawl and wooly hat in his rocking chair, even on a warm autumn day. Ankit had told Dimple that his mother and sisters would be away at a wedding, but when he opened the door, music blared out of the back room and the whole flat smelled sharply floral and metallic: hair spray, deodorant, and nail polish.

"They must still be getting ready," he said.

The door to the back room swung open, and his mothers and sisters emerged in a haze of silk, gold, and lipstick.

His mother stopped when she saw Dimple.

"Oy, one of you turn that music off," she shouted.

The bass stopped thumping and silence flowed into the room.

Dimple stepped forward and gave them each a hug, an awkward negotiation of shoulders, elbows, and handbags. It had been months since she had come to the house, and it was clear that they had settled upon some sort of wary explanation for her absence.

"Aren't you going to be late?" asked Ankit.

"Oho, since when have you cared so much about people being on time?" asked his elder sister.

"Eesh, Ma, did you pour the whole bottle of perfume over yourself? That's not going to help you find a husband," said the younger sister.

"You shut your mouth," said her mother, reaching out but failing to give her a cheerful smack.

There was a shuffle around the room as Ankit cleared newspapers off the sofa, his mother looked for her keys, and the sisters took turns in front of the long mirror in the hallway. Dimple stayed standing. She could tell that they were treating her like a suspicious package; even if the contents were not liable to explode or burn, they would at the very least produce a nasty shock.

"Stupid, look what you've done," shrieked the younger sister.

She held up a gold tassel that had come off her pallu.

"I knew you were stepping on it."

"You did that. I didn't even come near you."

"Stop it, you two, you're making us late," said his mother.

"But, look."

The tassel was waved in her face.

"Here, give it to me. This will take one minute," said Ankit.

He rummaged in a drawer and pulled out a needle and a couple spools of thread.

"This one," he said, settling on the lighter gold.

In one deft movement he had threaded the needle.

"Don't move," he said, reaching for his sister's pallu.

They watched as he reattached the tassel, his hand sailing through the air in quick, exaggerated motions, as though conscious of its audience.

"There," he said, bending to snip the thread with his teeth. "Now stop screaming and go."

"Oh thank you, bhaiyya," she said, spinning 'round to give him a hug.

"Beta, sorry we have to leave you, but come again soon, okay? Don't leave it so late next time," said his mother, putting one hand on Dimple's shoulder.

They trooped down the stairs without a backward glance.

"I thought they'd never go," said Ankit, closing the door. "Why are you still standing?"

Dimple picked up the needle and spool of thread and put them back in the open drawer.

"Lajpat Nagar aunties are the scariest customers in the world. If you're selling them clothes, you learn how to fix zips, buttons, and hems in under thirty seconds flat," he said.

He climbed up on the sofa.

"Sorry, always so dark in here," he said tugging at the curtains, even though it was clear that they had been pulled back as far as they would go. He switched on the overhead light and then blinked.

"Is it too bright?" he asked.

Before she could say anything, he had switched it off again.

"We could go and sit in the back room, but I think it's a real mess. They've been getting ready in there. Blouses and petticoats everywhere. Sorry."

Dimple felt a terrible wrench. A great sense of tenderness welled up in her. She followed him into the back room as he picked up clothes and tried to bring some order. She wished more than anything to protect him from the cruelty of the world that she knew, the meanness and the spite.

PART

THREE

CHAPTER TWENTY-FIVE

THREE MINUTES INTO her morning meditation routine, Ania had a profound sense that her attention was required elsewhere. Her wrists itched, and a tingle made its way down her leg. She reached for her phone and saw that she was right. Leaping up from the floor, she scrolled through the dozens of messages she had already received from friends eager to be the first to alert her to alluring calamities.

The news had broken a couple hours earlier on social media, just as the morning rush was heaviest in South Delhi. Ania turned on the television in case there was anything on some of the trashier news channels. She could see that reporters and photographers had thronged into the small lane where Kamya lived, just a few yards away from the embassy of Luxembourg. Security guards blew their whistles, passersby swelled the crowd. There were a series of altercations involving traffic police, a dog walker who tried to control his agitated bullmastiffs, and a woman who emerged on her balcony with rollers in her hair.

The wife of a prominent film director had taken her grievances to social media that morning, accusing acclaimed young novelist Kamya Singh-Kaul of trying to wreck her marriage. A tide of posts had warned Singh-Kaul of dire consequences if she continued her sordid affair with the director. She was accused of stalking him, being a depraved she-devil, tormenting the couple with her obsessive behavior. The language and punctuation of the tweets and posts became increasingly bizarre as the hours went past. And then, there was a sudden halt of all activity on the wife's social media accounts.

The reporters checked their phones every few seconds and then squinted up at the upper floors. The front windows of Kamya's apartment merely reflected the glare of the afternoon sun. No one from the family came or went through the gates. The maids were nowhere to be found, the watchman was surly and uncooperative. Inquiries revealed that the two cars were still in the basement parking lot. It looked as though it would be a long wait.

Ania sat down again in the posture she used for meditation. But this time she faced the television, phone in hand, her face a beatific vision that no mindfulness had ever produced.

NINA HAD DECIDED that she needed to secure her future and there was no point in wasting any more time. She had heard the rumors about Dileep's affair with Serena Bakshi from several sources, and the whole thing seemed absurd enough to be true. Marriage to Dileep was now Nina's only realistic option, even if it meant that she would have to be more discreet about other aspects of her life.

She had just returned from Kolkata, where she and Nikhil had woven their way around the photography exhibition, not speaking, barely noticing the images or the people around them. As the rain had begun to fall in the cobbled courtyard of the gallery, he had led her into a dark passage, his arm around her waist. Water drummed down as they kissed. But the boy would not solve her problems. Now that she was back in Delhi, she knew she had to act before Dileep embroiled himself any further with Serena.

Nina arrived to see him on one of the few golden autumn days before Delhi's smoggy winter set in. Her sunglasses gave the garden a warm lilac glow, making everything seem even more benign. Even Dileep gave the impression of being handsome and charming rather than a vain, anxious fool. Nina had had a full night's sleep, and she knew she looked better than she had in months. Her mouth was gentle and full; her hair shone. She stretched and let the cream linen of her dress grow taut over her breasts. The leaves in the hanging baskets appeared to be made of soft velvet and the long flowers drooped, as though in longing.

"And how's your son? Still in New York?" asked Dileep.

She nodded.

He lowered his voice. "Are things any better?"

"I'd rather not discuss it, if you don't mind." Then she added, "Which, of course, you'll take to mean that no, things are not better."

"I shouldn't have pried. I'm very sorry," he said.

"No, you're not," she said.

Parakeets wheeled around the garden, landing on the branches of the gulmohar trees. Their trills turned into a questioning sort of cluck. Gardeners were watering the borders, and she thought she could hear the earth crumble and crack as the moisture soaked through. Vines on the trellis cast a lace of shadows across Nina's face.

"Do you ever think about old age? You know, dribbling soup, waiting for someone to come by with the meds, not knowing whether it's day or night," she said.

"I'm surprised to hear you mention it."

"I try not to boast about it, but I am, in fact, a few years older than you."

"No one would ever know that."

"Thank you. You're always right on cue."

"Of course I think about old age. To be honest, it seems to be all I think about."

"Is that why you're thinking of getting married again? You need a glamorous little nursemaid?"

"What?"

"Serena Bakshi?"

"Oh for God's sake, not you too. I don't know who comes up with this nonsense."

"It's not true? Just a fling then?"

"Not even a fling. Nothing."

Dileep shook his head in exasperation and drained his glass. The wedge of lime in his drink looked violently green.

"Fabulous. That leaves the way clear for me then," Nina said, taking off her sunglasses so he could see her eyes.

"What? Us? You and me?"

Dileep laughed. He brought his hand to his face and covered his eyes. His perfect teeth gleamed, and he showed a little bit of gum. His shoulders shook. It was a belly laugh: lavish and de-meaning.

He looked at her as the amusement faded.

"You weren't serious, were you? For a second there, you looked as though you might be serious."

"Of course I wasn't serious. How ridiculous do you really think I am?"

"I know, I'm sorry."

And then she laughed too, knowing in that moment she hated Dileep more than anyone she had ever known.

THE RESIDENTS OF homes across South Delhi had been follow-ing the story unfolding on social media with great delight. Ania had missed her barre workout class and instead was hunched over her phone, still in her pajamas, having ice cream for breakfast. It felt like a holiday.

When the doorbell rang, she flew down the stairs, powered by sugar and adrenaline.

It was Dev, and she could not have been more pleased.

"Isn't it just too awful? Poor Kamya. How is she coping?" she asked, dragging him into the study. "And why aren't you taking my calls?"

"Yes, it's pretty awful. I thought I'd just come round instead."

"I'm so glad you did. How is she? The media has gone com-pletely berserk. Will you have some breakfast? Ice cream?"

Dev looked with confusion at the carton that she held out.

"I've just eaten. Any coffee?"

"Of course there's coffee; I'll ring for some. Anything you want, just say."

"Look, Ania, I've been speaking to Kamya, and she is really terrified."

"Oh, I can imagine."

"She's not a celebrity, she's never had to cope with anything like this before."

"So dreadful."

"Now, I need your help but you have to promise me, you aren't going to tell anyone. Absolutely no one."

"Of course not."

"I'm serious, she's in hiding and this can't get out."

"I completely understand."

"The press will lose interest in a few days and move on to something else. She's gone to our house in Goa until all this blows over."

"Has she now? That's a bit odd. Why didn't she just go back to New York? I mean, no one over there would care about her affair with some Bollywood zero. Or even know who she is."

"Are you serious? People from here have already sent reporters to her Manhattan apartment and to speak to her neighbors there. Anyway, she says she can't face the thought of a long-haul flight. Even the thought nearly brings on a panic attack."

"Well, if she won't fly, how did she get to Goa then? Roller skates?"

"Try to be a little sympathetic. Do you have any idea what's it like to be hounded by every media channel in the country?"

"Of course I do. I'm papped almost every day, in case you didn't know. This morning there are nearly a hundred comments on Undercover Coutourista about a belt I wore yesterday. A belt, Dev."

"I'm worried about her. All this media harassment, you have no idea what it's like until you see it up close."

"Sleeping with married men though? Well, I suppose a famed writer like her has to get her ideas somewhere."

Dev's tone was sharp. "A bit sanctimonious, don't you think? Anyway, it isn't true. She's told me that they were just friends and that the wife has got it all wrong. Apparently she's quite unstable."

"That's what the cheating husband and the floozie always say about the poor wife."

"She's not a floozie."

"No, I suppose she's not."

Ania wished she hadn't already smoked her weekly cigarette. This would have been a good time to light up, busy herself with finding an ashtray, contemplate the smoke rising into the air.

"She's all alone there, although Flavia's next door and she'll help her with anything she needs. And there's the caretaker. I told her I'd fly down in a couple of days, but I can't now till the weekend."

Ania reached for Sigmund and tickled his jowls.

"Could you go?" Dev asked.

"Go where?"

"Go and keep Kamya company until I get there. Please? She probably shouldn't be alone right now."

"My God, Dev, doesn't she have any friends?"

"I've told her not to tell anyone she's there. That's the whole point. You never know who can be trusted at times like this. People will do anything for a bit of cash or publicity."

"But would she even want me there? Have you asked her?"

"I will. I'm sure it'll be fine. You'll calm her down, I know you will. I'll tell her. And anyway, I'll be there as soon as I can get away on Friday."

A strip of stubble on Dev's chin was now gray. She wondered how she had not registered this before—he was hardly the most punctilious man in matters of grooming. His fingernails looked gnawed and raggedy, as usual. There was a bit of fluff clinging to his collar.

"I don't know," said Ania. "Speak to her, and if you both still want me to go, I will."

"Thank you," he said, clasping her hand.

"Uff," she said, giving his hand a squeeze.

CHAPTER TWENTY-SIX

THE TAXI SPED down the road that led away from the coast into the quiet interior of Goa, far from the tourists that thronged the flea markets, the Jet Skis that bobbed on the waves, the newly-weds posing for photographs by a picturesquely rustic boat. The local news rumbled softly from the car radio, the driver letting out an occasional exasperated sigh at each instance of municipal mismanagement.

Just as they came around the bend toward the village, the sun slipped from behind a cloud. It was as though one of the elegant watercolors sold in the souvenir shops had come to life. The palm trees leaned at a gentle angle and the white roofs of the churches formed a perfect slant against the sky. They went past the Sunshine Bakery, the Natraj General Store, and the rose-pink school building, from which a woman emerged, shaking a bell in her hand.

Ania felt a surge of excitement, which had been building ever since she had boarded her flight about three hours ago. It was, she told herself, simply the thought of getting away from the smog of

Delhi, the pleasures of a few days in a Goan village. It had little to do with the anticipation of witnessing Kamya's confined state and the opportunity to show her a splendid generosity of spirit, however undeserved. Ania's light-headedness was undeniable: if there had been a banister nearby, she would have slid down it.

"Anna-Maria."

Ania turned to see where the cry had come from. Two men on a motorbike cruised by, slowing as they peered into front gardens, and then turned into the dirt road that led to the old step well.

The man riding pillion cupped his hands around his mouth again and shouted again: "Anna-Maria."

A boy wheeled past on his bicycle, pointing to a ramshackle building in the distance.

"Have you tried the field behind Oswald's place? She goes there sometimes," he said.

"What's happened?" Ania asked the driver. "Is someone missing?"

"Yes, every few weeks this happens. She's getting very old now. She disappears, and the whole village spends the day looking for her. Last time we found her asleep by the reservoir. Any closer, and she would have fallen in," he said.

"Anna-Maria," he added, "Mrs. Elsie Machado's dog."

"Oh, the poor thing."

"Yes. If Mrs. Elsie Machado herself was missing, I can tell you no one would care."

He laughed so violently that the seat shook, his head lolled about, and his hand pressed hard against the horn, outraging a stately woman who was crossing the road.

They arrived at the two-hundred-year-old villa, its lime plaster walls the color of buttercups, broad white pillars framing the verandah that ran across the front of the house. Ania wished the driver all the best in the hunt for Anna-Maria and walked up the path from the small wrought iron gate. Bees circled the oleanders in the front garden, a magpie swooped down onto the ancient sundial. She stood on the verandah for a minute, wondering what she would say to Kamya. This would be the first time they had been in the same room without a noisy gathering present. The late-afternoon light was glinting off the mother-of-pearl windows, and there was a waft of incense from inside the house. She ran the back of her hand along the azulejo tiles to feel their perennial coolness. The caretaker burst through the door with apologies; he had only just seen the taxi disappear down the road. He took her bag, and she followed him into the hallway.

Nothing in the house had changed since her last visit almost a year earlier: the palms swayed in the inner courtyard, the red floors threw off their familiar sheen, a cat was asleep on the swing on the verandah. Through one of the open bedroom doors, she caught a glimpse of the corner of a four-poster bed, azaleas in a brass pot, a swell of muslin in the breeze. The kitchen was silent, fresh figs in a bowl, a few empty bottles by the door. Through the open windows, she caught the smell of woodsmoke.

Ania had expected Kamya to be cloistered in her room, dark circles under her eyes, face wan. Perhaps the braid would have come loose. But Ania found her lying on a chaise longue near the pool in a typical bikini—bold zigzag print, beads—skin fresh, with her usual apathetic expression, her enormous headphones giving her the look of a regal insect, a queen waiting for the workers to arrive.

Kamya shaded her eyes from the sun and looked in Ania's

direction. She stayed like that longer than was strictly necessary and then swung her legs off the chaise longue. She reached for a bottle of water and took a long sip. Then she walked toward her.

There was about her physical presence, Ania had to admit, a distinction. She carried herself as though awestruck men had painted portraits of her, softening her strong features out of love, and submitted them nervously for her approval. Framed in dull gold, a woman with stern eyes and a long neck, expecting some entertainment.

"Hey, Dev mentioned you'd be coming," said Kamya.

"Hey."

There was no kiss or hug. The business of greeting was dispensed with after a mutual cocking of heads. Kamya tossed her headphones onto a garden chair and adjusted the waistband of her bikini bottoms. Her breasts were small but perfectly in proportion; her stomach was as flat as a tile. Ania wondered whether she would dislike her less if she were squat and flabby; she thought, on balance, not.

"Listen, I'm sorry about what's happened. It sounds like it's been awful. Hope you're okay," said Ania.

She shrugged. "It's all copy."

"But still, I suppose there are worse places to be in hiding."

"There's cold stuff in the fridge, the booze is over there in the bar, and if you want anything stronger, I guess Flavia can hook you up," she said.

With great difficulty Ania managed to restrain herself from saying that she knew about the booze since she was often the one who put it there, that she had been a beloved guest at the house for well over a decade, and, in fact, hardly a guest, as she had her *own* set of keys.

"If you need anything else, just shout. There's a couple of people around."

Kamya went into the house, stepping lightly over the hot flagstones.

The gifted author did not seem at all troubled by recent events. She certainly did not seem to need or even desire company; no kind soul was required to rail on her behalf at the cruelties of a celebrity-driven media industrial complex or reintroduce her to the small joys of life. As usual, Dev had completely misread the situation. Ania began to berate herself for making the trip and then remembered that, in spite of his ineptitude, she was doing it to make Dev happy. The thought of her loyal sacrifice gave her a sudden warm charge.

And there would be the opportunity to see them together and discover what cryptic messages Kamya and Dev liked to exchange, the kind of friendship that could blossom over four continents. She felt a tiny pang of loss. He would be in Goa the next day, and then she would leave. She thought of his eyes, bright with amusement, his gentle ribbing. Then it occurred to her that she had never seen him tease Kamya on the few occasions she had observed them together. It was Ania who was always teased. That was something.

She settled into one of the planter's chairs on the verandah and sent Dev a message saying that Kamya seemed to be fine. She had a full view of the most famous house on the road, the tree house built by Flavia da Costa, which still attracted the curious and obsessed from all over the world. The house was all elevation and retreat, a human shelter that had opted for a different realm. It looked as though the beams and struts and panes of glass had insinuated themselves into the tree cover, achieving a natural state in spite of the construction's hard angles and clear surfaces. Ania had been inside the house a few times, and it had been like stepping into a transparent nest, suspended in the crook of a branch.

Over a decade ago it became known that Flavia had won an important commission from Kazakhstan, leading to much speculation on whether it was a museum, a concert hall, or a vast new presidential palace to break up the terrifying emptiness of the steppes. No substantive progress appeared to have ever been made, but rumors about the project would surface from time to time, particularly when a group of Kazakh men began visiting the village once a year. Their shiny black cars would pass slowly through the narrow lanes and deposit the men outside Flavia's house, dressed in what looked like their holiday outfits: pale slacks, bright floral shirts and moccasins, and chunky gold bracelets.

"It's like an oligarchs' tea party," Dev always said.

But the grand Kazakh edifice remained unconstructed, and Flavia continued to come and go from the village, her talents apparently untapped.

She was in residence now and appeared at the edge of the verandah in ragged trousers and a sun hat that had lost all shape.

"Everything all right here? Just checking in."

Ania leaped up, thrilled at the sight of someone who could provide relief from the strained atmosphere in Dev's house.

"Let me get you a drink," she said.

"No, darling, I'm busy in the garden," said Flavia, waving a pair of pruning shears. "My boys are all useless. I just popped in to make sure you weren't burning the house down."

She turned to leave. And then turned back.

"But if you girls fancy a bit of an adventure later tonight, let me know. I'm going on a secret mission. Wear old clothes and comfy shoes," she said.

She waved again and disappeared down the steps.

Ania's mood lifted. If she was to be denied the sight of Kamya in torment, she would happily settle for some late-night entertainment in the wilds of Goa.

ANIA HAD MADE sure that she was on time so that she would be able to sit up front and not be relegated to the backseat like a child. Kamya had finally emerged, wearing enormous dark glasses and sneakers emblazoned with gold medallions. Flavia had given her a look of dismay.

"You better take those glasses off, darling, we will be back before the sun comes up," she said.

"Are you sure you want to come?" asked Ania. "It could be quite a late night. And you might need your rest, you know, after everything."

"I'm fine," said Kamya. "I'm curious. I'm a storyteller."

It was well after midnight when they set off in Flavia's tiny hatchback.

"I have to give you a bit of background or else you will think I'm crazy. There is an old lady called Mrs. Cardoso, Evelyn Cardoso, who lives on the other side of the village. She has not been feeling very well these days—back problems, arthritis—so she is mainly confined to her bed. Her children are abroad, and it's getting difficult for her to manage her house and garden. There was a vacant plot next to her place for many years, but now some people have built holiday homes there—three ugly houses crammed next to each other. Delhi people," she said, looking pointedly at Ania.

"Oh dear," she said.

"Yes, but that is not the problem. In Goa, we are used to outsiders with no taste moving in." She shifted gears noisily. "The problem in this case is that they know Evelyn Cardoso is not well, and they are dumping all their garbage into her garden. I went to see it yesterday. Mountains of it, poured into the corner of her garden as if it is a dumping ground. The arrogance, the inhumanity."

"That's absolutely terrible; can't Mrs. Cardoso complain to someone? The police?" asked Ania.

"The police do nothing, the panchayat does nothing; they have either taken money or they are too lazy to bother anyway. No, this is a case for citizen action. And that is why we are going on a secret mission. It will be great fun, I can assure you."

" 'Fun' probably isn't the word, but let's see what happens," said Kamya.

They parked some distance away and slipped into Mrs. Cardoso's garden through the side gate. Flavia turned on her flashlight.

"Careful, now. There are roots and twigs all over the place. If either of you fall and break your neck, I'm leaving you here."

They made their way over piles of dried leaves, clumps of weeds, and sudden tussocks, the pale rings of light trembling over the ground and tree trunks. The cicadas were loud and active; above their heads, there came a low hoot. At the bottom of the garden, Flavia stopped.

"Look," she said, the beam from the flashlight flailing wildly over a great sea of trash: bottles, cardboard, blocks of polystyrene, a great slope of plastic bags.

"Disgusting. See, they throw everything over the wall because they know she is too sick to do anything about it. Bastards. From Delhi."

"Yes, you did say. Such terrible people," said Ania, who considered herself a native of Prithviraj Road rather than Delhi.

"Careful here," said Flavia.

She slipped through a narrow gap between the wall and a thorny hedge. They followed her, staying close to the wall, before crossing the lawn to the back porches of the houses. Flavia took the rucksack off her back and reached inside. With great care, she pulled out a large bag of eggs.

"I know some poor servant will be made to clear it up. But these fuckers don't listen to reason, and we need to send a sign. This will be their warning," said Flavia in a low voice.

"Isn't it a bit of a shame to waste all these eggs?" asked Kamya.

Flavia and Ania ignored her. Having seen her let a bottle of champagne topple on the lawn earlier in the evening, a third of it soaking into the grass, they were unconvinced by this sudden display of thrift.

The first egg hit the French doors with a satisfying crack, the mess taking its time to slither down to the ground. They listened for a moment to see if the security guard had heard anything. Flavia picked up another egg and tossed it up toward the top half of the windows.

"Better to have even coverage," she said.

Ania picked up an egg and aimed for a spot a couple feet away from the last splatter. She watched it sail through the air and smash against the glass. It was lunatic, unseemly, and delicious. She felt as though a riotous laugh was stuck somewhere in her chest and would come gurgling up at any moment. She picked up another egg. She was contributing to the administration of local justice, a redressal of a fundamental imbalance.

"Look at these monstrous houses," said Flavia. "No embellishment is too much, no adornment is left out. Money, only money, nothing else."

The splatter of her egg was especially violent.

The flashlight shone on Kamya's gold medallions. Ania turned to see that she looked bored and disappointed, obviously having expected a more eventful, or perhaps less parochial, adventure.

"What happens if the police show up?" Kamya asked. "I can't get involved in anything like that right now."

Flavia giggled. "Police awake at night."

Ania decided to emit a supportive giggle too.

They heard a noise, and Flavia turned off the flashlight. The owl hooted again. But no one came striding around the corner.

"I know that watchman. He'll sleep through a storm," said Flavia. "Now, let's give the upper walls a nice coating. Get some eggs onto the balconies. They'll have a lovely smell and beautiful clouds of flies when they arrive tomorrow."

Kamya finally picked up an egg and let it drop to the ground. That was the end of her participation. She lit a cigarette and watched the operation proceed, her features settled into renewed tedium, flicking the ash into the wind.

When every egg had found its way to a target, they crept out the way they had come, Ania wiping her fingers on leaves that they passed.

"Come in and have a drink to celebrate a successful mission," said Ania to Flavia at the villa, worrying that she would leave immediately.

Handblown glass pendants swung lightly in the breeze over the stone decking by the pool, their dim light lapping at the foliage and purple-tinged rocks. The cream parasols had been secured for the night.

Bottles were opened under the stars; ice emptied into a bucket.

"Vigilantism is, of course, dangerous, and every vigilante will swear that the righteousness of his convictions justifies the aberrant behavior," said Flavia, putting her arms behind her head, settling in to her lounger.

"But there are some situations where we must recognize the absolute repulsiveness of certain behaviors; we must concede that we are not dealing with civilized people. And, you know, there are people who question my right to voice these opinions in the village. Because I am internationally celebrated and spend so much time abroad, they challenge me on my local credentials, try to make me out to be an unwanted interloper."

Flavia reached out and took a long sip from Kamya's glass.

"But I waste no time in telling them that my mother was born in this village, my grandfather was born here, there are six generations of my family that have known this area. Even when the Portuguese were ruling, ours was one of the few families they respected and came to for advice. My ancestors have founded villages here in Goa; they have built temples, churches, schools, libraries. And I have built *that*."

She waved at the dark contours of her house in the trees.

"I have every right."

She made a fresh round of drinks and gave Ania a little stroke under her chin.

"I want to tell you a few things about my life," she said.

Kamya pulled her glass nearer, laid back on the lounger, and closed her eyes.

Ania, now brimming with affection for Flavia, felt a sense of outrage against this rudeness.

"So, Kamya, did you get any stories out of this? You know, as a storyteller?" she asked, forcing her to open her eyes again.

"No, what I write about is dislocation and liminality," said Kamya, and closed her eyes again.

The cat appeared at the edge of the patio, green eyes gleaming, disconcerted by this unexpected nocturnal activity. When Ania called to her, she raced into the garden, a white streak in the night. Flavia continued with her anecdotes, her voice measured and soothing, like the sound of water swirling over pebbles. Before long, she had poured herself another drink.

At daybreak when the house staff emerged from their quarters, they spotted the three women still by the pool, each asleep on a lounger, as if they had been taking in the rays from the moon.

CHAPTER TWENTY-SEVEN

ANIA WATCHED AS Kamya lay in the sun, warming her cold blood, occasionally unhooding one eye and then letting it close again. The surface of the pool winked and sparkled. Ania had agonized over her choice of poolside reading matter, aware that it would be scrutinized and judged. But in the end all she had read were updates on her phone, her eyes flitting to Kamya's supine form, the braid trailing over a rattan stool. She turned away from her and looked for the latest news on the scandal. The director's wife's account looked as if it had been suspended, and his spokesperson had insisted that it was a clear case of malicious hacking. But the speculation continued. Kamya and the director were said to be at a secret location engaging in crisis talks. Memes and jokes were flooding the Internet. The wife's former psychotherapist issued a damning statement, sparking a nationwide debate on patient confidentiality.

Ania glanced again at Kamya and thought that perhaps she was more disturbed than she looked, her coldness nothing more than unfortunate habit. She suggested lunch at a nearby restaurant, a shabby, family-run place, famous for its crab. Kamya agreed. They walked the short distance in silence. Ania asked her for a cigarette. It was her fourth that day. It seemed the only way to cope.

By the time they arrived at the restaurant, the brief goodwill that she had felt earlier had dissipated. Once again she saw Kamya as a performer in a pantomime, a ham playing the difficult, inaccessible artist. A caricaturist would show her eyes creased into little lines of dissatisfaction, her nose in the air.

They ordered and then waited, as the paper lanterns above their heads swung in the breeze.

"So you do know this director? It's not like they completely made the story up?" asked Ania.

"I know him. We've had a couple of meetings. He was interested in adapting a short story I wrote. And, of course, after the novel's success, he wanted to talk about that. But I've no idea where that crazy woman got the idea that we were sleeping together."

"You know how it is, you get seen together in public a few times and then that's it."

"I went to his office both times. We talked over green tea. Only about the book."

Ania looked across at the open countryside, a canal and a footbridge, paddy fields in the distance with cows grazing at their edges. She did not intend to give Kamya the satisfaction of asking about her book. Infuriatingly, however, Kamya showed no interest in talking about her work either. It was as though she had decided that it was hardly worth the effort, secure in the knowledge that there were many others in her circle, far more accomplished and discerning, with whom those conversations would unfold. Ania felt a misery she had never felt before.

She glanced up to see that she and Kamya were reflected in a mirror that hung on the opposite wall. Kamya looked serene as she stared at the fields, toying with the straw in her glass; she looked almost happy. The surprising thing was that it was Ania who looked troubled in the mirror—a little pinched and diminished.

BACK AT THE HOUSE, Ania paced from the patio to the cool hush of the bamboos at the bottom of the garden and back to the front of the house, where the sun beat down on the white walls and the bougainvillea. It would still be a few hours before Dev arrived, and Flavia rarely surfaced before the late afternoon. This intimacy, which she had stupidly inflicted on herself, was suffocating. She had seen a long black hair in the sink and stubs of candles in their holders on the side of the bath. In the sitting room Kamya had lain with her feet, toenails painted lime green, resting on a table where family photographs were arranged, an irritating and disrespectful act. The cloying smell of her deodorant lingered in the passage outside her room.

When Ania went back inside, Kamya was nowhere to be seen, her bedroom door open, the pool deserted, the verandah restored to order by the cleaner. Ania felt relaxed enough to take a long nap in the hammock, drifting off as she watched the dappled green of the trees overhead, occasionally imagining that she heard a male voice murmuring nearby. When she woke and went to the kitchen for a glass of water, it looked as if Kamya was still away. She wondered whether she had packed her bags and disappeared. Perhaps her distaste for Ania's presence had been even worse than anything Ania had felt.

"Have you seen Kamya, the other guest?" she asked one of the gardeners tending to the flower beds.

"Yes, I saw her about half an hour ago," he said, "as I was riding past the cemetery. She was outside on the road, talking to a man."

"A man? What kind of man?"

"A man. A normal kind of man."

"What did he look like?"

"I can't say. I saw him from the back for a second."

"Could it have been Dev?"

"Maybe. Has sir returned?"

"*I* don't know. That's why I'm asking."

"I don't know either."

He returned to the oleanders with a sad shrug.

Kamya did not know anyone in the village and had certainly not been wandering through its lanes making new friends. A flirtation with a local lothario seemed most unlikely. Ania wondered whether Dev had arrived early and some sort of preliminary meeting had been planned. She grabbed a sun hat and then wheeled one of the house bicycles through the gates.

She rode through the village, left the bike leaning against a tree, and walked through the cemetery. It was empty. Wilted marigolds lay near some of the graves; an ancient hearse stood under a portico, its iron wheels stippled with rust. There was no sign of Kamya, no indication that any secret rendezvous had taken place. She looked at some of the names on the tombstones: Eleutheiro Saldanha, Teodoline da Gama, Petornila Lobo. This was not a place that seemed to have any connection with the present.

She walked toward the church, its white façade shimmering in the heat. It had been a mistake to venture out at this time. The expanse of red earth in front of the church was baked hard; there wasn't a sliver of shade. Her sundress clung to her thighs. Two dogs lay, as though in complete surrender to the heat, not caring if they were charred into brittle remains.

In a corner, the statue of Saint Cajetan roasted on a plinth. On a previous visit, Dev had pointed out a man crouched at its foot, frantically kissing each card in a pack and laying them on the ground.

"Saint Cajetan is the patron saint of gamblers," Dev had told her.

The man had replaced the cards reverentially in their pack and then prostrated himself at the base of the plinth. Saint Cajetan stared at the rocky hill in the distance, his loose fist raised in wonder.

Today, there were neither gamblers nor lovers. The sun was at its zenith over the barren patch of land. The whole scene felt like madness, sin, despair. The figure of the saint continued to stare at the rocky hill in the distance, his loose fist still raised in wonder.

She cycled back to the villa, her head pounding, sweat stinging her eyes. The cool of the house sent a light shiver over her body. Sitting on the verandah, Kamya was dressed in one of her fancier printed outfits, picking at her toes.

"Oh, hello," said Ania, "were you out somewhere?"

"Me? No. Was just doing a few laps and then had a shower."

Ania went into the bathroom and splashed cool water over her face and arms. She sat on the edge of the bath without drying herself, letting the water drip onto her dress and the floor. As she stood to leave, she noticed Kamya's bikini hanging on a rail. She knew she was acting like a fool but it still gave her a dart of pleasure, the comfort of vindication, to touch the bikini and find that it was bone dry.

THAT EVENING FLAVIA came to Ania's rescue again. As a local dignitary, she had been asked to judge the dance competition at the boys' seminary in the village, and she had accepted with great enthusiasm. Ania was delighted to be able to accompany her, especially once Kamya refused, saying that she had plans.

"Flavia, I feel I shouldn't ask, but are you a good dancer?" asked Ania.

"Please," said Flavia, stretching her leg and rotating her foot, "just look at that line. Also, I couldn't possibly say no. Father Brian regularly sends me pumpkins from their vegetable patch."

In front of the seminary, the statue of the Virgin was bathed in a clear blue light. With great ceremony, Father Brian showed them through a series of dimly lit passages to the central courtyard, where a judging table and rows of seats had been arranged opposite a dais. The vines on the walls gleamed under the full moon, and clumps of crossandra flamed around the edge of the archways. All around the building were boys and young men in shorts and T-shirts, cricket jerseys and hoodies, standing under archways, taking their places on the courtyard seats, fiddling with a laptop and speakers near the dais.

Father Brian was the first to speak but certainly not the last. The speeches and felicitations unspooled under the blue gaze of the Virgin. The young men listened with their heads bowed, as though they were in church. A row of trophies for the winners in each category stood on the judge's table, to be supplemented by generous checks from Flavia. Eventually, piercing shrieks of feedback from the mic forced the last priest to cut his speech short, and the competition began.

A sharp charge shot through the dancers lined up next to the dais. The audience felt it too: a reprieve, an unfastening as bodies stepped onstage. And the boys took a deep breath, one after the other, as they stepped into their performance: a salsa-inflected hustle, full of sass and brio; popping and locking through the whumps and glitches of a hip-hop track; a pelvic-thrusting number to a Hindi film song that dripped with innuendo; a jive that snapped and clicked and seemed to make the courtyard whirl; flips, jumps, and splits; the yearning sequences of a mujra; an undulating belly dance that ended in a heroic backbend.

Ania leaned across to Flavia and said: "It's like this is their real religion."

"Divinity does something to people's bodies. Music, singing, warm blood, and God," said Flavia.

At the end of the competition, Flavia jammed her reading glasses farther up her nose and diligently revisited the notes she had scribbled down. Ania walked around the courtyard, pretending not to notice the stares from the young men. She sat down on a stone ledge next to a boy who gave her a broad smile. He said his name was Moses, and he had been at the seminary for four years.

"Don't you miss your family or your other friends when you're here?" asked Ania.

"I do, ma'am, especially at night. We have entertainment like this but not very often. Usually it's prayers in the chapel, then dinner, and then an hour's study time. But after that, it's very quiet. For me."

He paused and glanced up at the sky, streaked now with midnight blue.

He spoke in a lower tone. "When we are all supposed to be in bed I come back to the corridor that leads to the dining room. Did you go there? Did you see the portrait of Christ there?"

Ania shook her head.

"I stand in front of the portrait and look. Every night. His face looks a little different. The eyes and the forehead. And the smile. It's amazing. But I promise you there is a small change every night. Then I come here into the courtyard and sit under that guava tree. The lights all go out, but there is one light that stays on up there, on the third floor. The small window at the end. I have tried to go into the room, but when I'm inside I can't find any small room with a window on that part of the floor. It's strange. So I just stay here and watch the light in the room. And when I can barely keep my eyes open, I quietly go back to bed."

He stopped speaking and looked at her, as though wanting to make sure she had understood.

She had.

"I think I'd come and sit here under the tree too," she said.

Ania shook his hand and returned to the judge's table. As she sat down she glanced back: he was still sitting on the ledge, looking up at the window on the third floor.

The prize announcements were made to a barrage of cheers and hoots, and the music started up again, boys rushing to the floor, returning to their earlier swing and swagger. Flavia shouted encouragement as she walked around the courtyard, a little shake of her hip, a fluttering of her hands. Father Brian leaned against a pillar, his eyes closed, a smile forming on his tired face.

Soon it was the last song of the evening, a slow Brazilian number, the man's voice trembling with a fragile beauty, gliding above the backing sounds of the orchestra, seeming to hesitate before disappearing through the archways and down the passages of the seminary. The young men paired off and danced with a complete lack of self-consciousness; in a few minutes it would all be over, their bodies seemed to say; where was the time to be bashful? They were too shy to ask Flavia and Ania to dance, so the two danced with each other, Ania towering above Flavia by a few inches, Flavia fluttering her eyelashes.

When Flavia dropped her off at the villa, Ania saw that Dev had finally arrived.

"You took your bloody time," said Ania as they hugged.

"Please don't say anything now," he murmured into her ear.

Kamya had returned too, and for the first time seemed ill at ease and irritable. She monopolized Dev for a while, asking him for insider updates about media interest in the story. When he had little to provide, she completely ignored him. She said she was going to bed and then rejoined them ten minutes later. She slapped at her arms, complaining about the mosquitoes.

"I still can't believe Flavia's idea of entertainment was to take you to a dance at a seminary. What did you do there? Try to make them break their vows?" asked Dev.

"Was that a dig at me?" asked Kamya. "The slutty seductress in town? I told you I wasn't there."

"I'm sorry; no, it was a joke," said Dev, his face creasing in confusion.

"A joke. I see. Of course it was," she said.

She went back into the house.

The kitchen lights were on, and they watched her move past the windows, linger at the table for a few seconds, her head lowered, and then disappear out of view.

"It was honestly only a joke," he said.

"She's just unbelievable. She's in *your* house. Ignore her, she's been really strange all day. Being snappy with me and Flavia, rushing out of the room to take calls. And then apparently she was with some guy at the cemetery."

"What guy?"

"I don't know. Even if there was nothing with that film director, there's definitely some kind of strange drama going on. She's been acting like a cat that got caught in the rain."

A warm breeze brought a waft from the night-blooming jasmine. Ania had found the same Brazilian song on the laptop at the house, and the voice of the singer from Bahia joined them for a reprise.

"The party with the young priests was wonderful. I wish you'd been able to see it."

"Are you being sarcastic?"

"No, you idiot."

"What was so wonderful?"

"They had such absolute faith in their calling, even though they're so young. And when it came to letting loose for an evening, they had absolute faith in that too. It made me want to believe."

"In God?"

"In something. It's the way they all just let themselves go as they danced, like nothing else mattered. Dev, this music, it's just too beautiful. Come on, we're going to dance too."

"No way. You know how terrible I am."

"It doesn't matter. I'll lead."

She put her arms around him, and they faltered around the lounger and onto the path that led to the house. He clasped her arms and then her shoulders and then her arms again.

"You see?" he said.

"Shut up and keep going."

Ribbons of light wavered across the pool. There was a glow on the white bougainvillea that foamed over the wall and the pale paving stones that led to the house. She felt a safety in his presence, that under the leaves and vines, they would find a soft trail along which to move, with a grace that they would eventually earn.

Debris was already strewn around their feet: the bunch of carnations that Father Brian had given Ania, a pack of cigarettes and a brass lighter, a glass tumbler with a fingerbreadth of melted ice, her wrap that lay on the grass like gossamer. By the time they woke the next morning, someone would have restored this world to order.

The music died down as the singer held a long note, and then it swelled again to meet his words of loneliness and yearning, which sounded so much more luxuriant and meaningful in Portuguese. Foliage moved above their heads, and there was a tiny shift in the shadows. They shuffled around on the grass for the rest of the song, Dev's hands finally resting on her hips, until the voice and the strings faded into nothing.

CHAPTER TWENTY-EIGHT

NIKHIL HAD LEFT the door open and Nina lay in bed, listening to the water beat down in the shower. Her neck and cheeks still felt raw and flushed, and she ran her hand over the place that he had vacated. When he turned the water off, she settled herself once again on her side of the bed. On her bedside table, along with the rings she had taken off, his watch glinted. He walked back into her bedroom naked, toweling his hair, clouds of steam drifting in behind him.

It was always a wonder to observe—that supreme lack of self-consciousness. She would not have said she was particularly self-conscious either. In her best days she had walked topless along the beach at Juan-les-Pins, with only a thin gold chain resting on her collarbones. But Nikhil's confidence was of an entirely different constitution. He flung his towel over a chair and, still naked, picked up his phone to scroll through his messages. He grinned and began to tap away, consumed by the cleverness of his response. And then, as if suddenly realizing where he was, he smiled at her and tossed the phone onto the bed. He walked to the window and then back toward the bathroom.

"What did we do with my underwear?" he asked.

He looked around the room as though, having conquered a dominion, he was now seeking the best spot to plant a flag.

He had leaped out of bed and into the shower moments after they had finished, saying he was late for an appointment. The thought struck her that he had felt a sudden revulsion. What was it that he had seen? Or smelled? The stale perspiration of someone trying to cling to their best days; the fusty smell of a dry scalp; the odor of some sour secretion that had leaked out of her body? She pulled the duvet up a little higher.

He was framed perfectly in the dressing table mirror, and she watched him as though a film was about to unfold, the mirror a distancing medium that permitted her intent contemplation. He pulled his boxer shorts up, snapped the waistband, and absently ran his hand over his crotch. He disappeared for a moment as he retrieved his trousers from a chair. There was a quick *swish* as he stepped into the chinos; he had to jiggle the slider until it moved to the top of the zipper; his tongue pressed against his lower lip as he pushed the prong through the belt notch. With a swift movement he scooped his T-shirt off the floor and shook out the creases. As he pulled it over his head, it began to fill out, the sleeves settling over his biceps, the thin fabric stretching over his chest. He leaned into the mirror and brushed his hair with his fingers, still oblivious of her gaze, eyes locked onto his own.

"Socks, socks," he muttered, looking under the chair, the desk, the dressing table.

"On this side," she said.

He scooted around and picked them up. Perching on the edge of the bed, he dusted off the soles of his feet with a balled-up sock and then pulled them both on. He headed to the mirror again and gave his hair one last caress. This time he caught her eye in the reflection and smiled.

"Sorry, it's not something I can get out of," he said.

"I love the way you imagine that I have nothing else to do but lie here luxuriating in the sheets," she said, "with or without you."

He let out a guffaw.

"This is what I love about you," he said. "The way you always cut to the chase."

He tied the laces on his sneakers, patted his pockets, and grabbed his phone.

"Away for the weekend," he said, planting a kiss on her shoulder. "See you next week?"

"If you're lucky," she said.

She waited for him to leave the flat and then turned to look at the watch that still lay on her bedside table. It wasn't her responsibility to remind him to take all his belongings. After all, she wasn't his mother.

"I HATE MY name," Dimple said to Ania.

"Everyone hates their name. It's like listening to your own voice in an interview and cringing. But things could be so much worse. My poor dental hygienist in New York is called Veraminta. Just imagine. Are you quite satisfied with your name, Dev?"

Dev shrugged and stirred his coffee at the patio table.

"You're in a mood," she said. "Don't worry, Nikhil's leaving in a few days, and then you won't have to run into him here."

"Who said anything about him?"

"It's bloody obvious. So tell me again, why is it that you find him so unbearable?"

"He's a fraud, totally bogus. And what's he still doing here?"

"That's so not specific. And he's not been here that long. Four months, it's a sabbatical or something."

"Yes, a sabbatical, of course it is. Have you ever tried talking to him about anything serious? About politics, for example?"

"But I don't talk about politics with anyone. Why would I talk about it with him?"

"I'm sure we've talked about politics."

"Probably very much against my will."

"Anyway, the point is he displays every ghastly diasporic trait. He thinks he knows India better than any of us. There are endless moronic facts he has learned about the mother country in New Jersey or wherever, and he tries to explain them to me."

"India-splaining," said Dimple, looking pleased with her contribution.

"It's New Hampshire, actually. Look, I'm sorry, I'm not going to agree with you just because you want me to. I've never seen that side of him. I've come to know him pretty well, and you have no idea what you're talking about," said Ania.

Dimple made her excuses, saying she had a meeting, and slipped away.

"You made her feel very uncomfortable with your judgmental haranguing. That's why she left," said Ania.

"*I* made her feel uncomfortable? It's not me that's using her for my own purposes, adopting her for some kind of mission civilisatrice."

"What the hell is that supposed to mean?"

"Look it up."

"Of course I know what it means. But how dare you imply that I'm trying to civilize her. That's completely offensive. You are *such* a pompous, patronizing, unbearable goat."

"Takes one to know one."

"Oh my God, did you just say 'takes one to know one'?"

"Well. You're the one being offensive, trying to stage-manage her life just so that she can fit in with your awful friends."

"Like you, you mean?"

"I'm surprised I even make the list." An odd look crept onto Dev's face, a look of great hesitation. He pushed his cup to one side and stood up to leave.

Ania continued to look up at him, as though she was trying to amass further evidence against him in her defense.

"Also, I'd love to know how you're able to feel so confident as a judge of character. I mean, your taste in close friends is hardly impeccable," she said.

"What close friends?"

"Have you any idea that your dear friend Kamya has been lying to you for weeks?"

"What?"

Ania stood up and leaned across the table.

"She was having an affair with that film director all along. She lied to you. All that ridiculous business about hiding out in Goa. He even came to see her there. I told you there was something weird going on. He's left his wife now and followed her to America. I'm sorry to say, but she used you."

"How do you know all this?"

"You're always accusing me of being a socialite. Well, socialites talk. We know things. It'll be in the press by the weekend."

"I don't know if I believe you."

He turned away from her, so she raised her voice.

"Believe what you want. Obviously, why would you take my word over the saintly Kamya's, Blessed Wordsmith, Our Lady of the Human Condition."

They stared at each other across the table. But a moment later, Dev's shoulders started to shake with laughter.

"None of this is funny," he said, sitting down again. But his voice was catching as he spoke. He was still laughing.

"I suppose it's sort of funny," she said, sitting down next to him, without a smile.

They stayed silent for a few moments.

"What was that song?" he asked.

"Which song?"

"The Brazilian song we danced to in Goa?"

"I can't remember the name of the singer now. Why?"

"I don't know. It was a good song."

"I thought you hated music and dancing."

"Mostly, I do."

The silence returned.

Ania glanced at Dev to see a trace of a smile still on his face, as though for some strange reason their quiet pleased him.

DIMPLE HAD STARTED to read new kinds of books, self-help books that provided insights into overcoming anxiety but also touched on spiritualism and philosophy. The advice they provided was not easy to understand, or even remember, but she persisted. She had always been a finisher. One philosopher said that if gods did exist they carried on with their work, uninterested in what mortals thought of them or even whether mortals existed. She felt sure that she had come close to mortals who had espoused the outlook of the gods.

Ankit had proposed, and she had accepted. He had not asked her directly, still struggling with a small lingering suspicion that she would prefer to disappear into the shimmer of the faraway world she had found. He later told Dimple that he had been ter-rified of watching reality play itself across her features if he had asked her in person.

Instead, he had sent her an audio file.

"There's a recording on it. I've sung a few songs for you, just to make you laugh when you're bored. But promise me you'll listen right to the end," he said, outside her apartment.

"Of course, I'll listen to the end."

"No, you really have to do it. Don't forget and turn it off halfway."

"Yes, fine."

He had got back into his van and reversed out of the parking spot. Sticking his head out of the window, he shouted, "Listen till the end."

There were choruses belted out in the way she loved; short

introductions to each number, as though he were a radio announcer from the '70s; the sound of his ringtone and a snatch of a conversation accidentally recorded as he tried to appease a supplier. And then the crucial final seconds, where he apologized for not asking her in person and then gabbled his plea—it would make him the happiest man in the world—all the while, a strange clanking noise in the background.

She pulled the earphones out of her ears and let them drop to the ground.

She had called her mother, but it had been difficult to gauge her reaction. There had hardly been one. But when she saw Ankit's mother and sisters a couple days later, they had been warm and demonstrative. She had reclaimed all her lost ground, and she was grateful, feeling it was more than she deserved.

She had not told Ania yet. But she would. She was waiting for an opportune moment.

THE COLONEL PARKED his car at the edge of the woodland and glanced at Nikhil. His head had fallen toward his chest, and there was a thin line of drool forming at the side of his mouth.

"We're here," said the colonel sharply.

Nikhil's head shot up, and he stared at the dense clumps of amaltas and bamboos, still partly shrouded by the early-morning fog.

He grunted and made a great play of opening the car door.

"It's not even light yet," he said.

"It is, although I suppose with a hangover it might be hard to tell."

The colonel had tried to remain warm and unobtrusive during

Nikhil's stay. But the young man had continued to stumble home in the early hours, spend the day in bed, remain unresponsive during the early evenings, and then spark into action the moment he heard from Ania or one of her friends, darting out of the door with a cheery wisecrack. The colonel would have liked to have had at least one or two interesting conversations, although he knew that he had no right to expect them.

He greeted the guard at the entrance post and waited for Nikhil to catch up.

Dileep had inherited the acres of woodland, once on the outskirts of the city but now surrounded by arterial roads and construction sites. No one in the Khurana family had made much use of the land. A few close friends were permitted to walk their dogs there or go for a morning run, but it was a favor bestowed only after great deliberation. Signs around the property warned that it was private land, and people tended to keep away. It was widely said that a number of forgotten Sufi saints had been buried nearby and that their spirits drifted through the forest, seeking out their devotees. And if that was not alarming enough, a woman who had hanged herself from a peepul tree in the heart of the woodland was known to appear without warning, staring with red-rimmed eyes through thorny branches.

"I've been so keen to catch a glimpse of the ghosts," said the colonel. "But nothing in all these days. Renu wouldn't be caught dead here. She really believes they roam through the forest."

Nikhil did not respond. They set off through the trees, the colonel setting a brisk pace.

"I wanted to have a word with you," he said.

Nikhil looked as though he was finding it difficult to keep up with the colonel, a fact that irritated him: a young man in his prime, not being able to manage a decent stride. He picked up his pace.

"It's not that I consider myself in any way, you know, in loco parentis. I mean, you have your parents for that. I suppose I'm telling you as an older friend who has seen the fast crowd you're running with these days. Of course it's fun, why wouldn't it be? But in life, one needs a focus."

Nikhil was silent, still lagging a pace behind.

"All I'm saying is that it is probably time to return to a normal life after the fun you've had. Sure, you wanted a break. You called it a sabbatical, didn't you? Isn't your firm wondering where you are?"

"What?"

"Your job in America."

"Yeah, they're cool. I'm going back soon anyway."

"You hadn't mentioned. When?"

"In a few days. I'm sorry, did I overstay my welcome?"

The colonel stopped and put a hand on Nikhil's shoulder.

"No, you must never think that. It really wasn't my intention to make you feel unwelcome. It's just that I've seen so many youngsters here lose focus and end up ruining their lives, so much potential wasted. That's all."

The colonel decided not to mention the rumors that he had heard about a liaison with Nina Varkey; an incomprehensible dalliance with a spiteful woman, which if true, would lead only to grief and trouble.

"You are our son too, and we wish you lived closer. It really has been a joy having you. But us old folks sometimes worry about the future in ways that you don't."

Nikhil seemed finally to have woken up. He gave the colonel a breezy hug and ended it with a few reassuring pats on the back.

"I know you're trying to help but trust me, everything's fine. Like you say, I just needed a break."

They resumed the walk, this time Nikhil setting the pace, striding down the path, on the verge of breaking into a run, with the colonel anxiously trying to regain his advantage.

CHAPTER TWENTY-NINE

IT HAD BEEN an intimate dinner, and by now almost all the guests had left Serena Bakshi's apartment. She had redecorated again, and the guests' various perfumes mingled in the foyer. Silence closed over the hallway and the stairs—and the soft night returned. The cushions on the sofas still bore the imprints of backs; someone had left behind a tortoiseshell lighter on the coffee table; someone else had forgotten a lace fan. It was almost the moment when a hostess could gratefully murmur that nearly everything had gone according to plan and sink into her favorite armchair. In the sitting room, however, Fahim and Mussoorie remained.

Ania spotted them through the doorway as she was returning from the bathroom, preparing to leave. She turned to a passing maid.

"Do you know where madam is?"

"I saw her in the kitchen. If you go straight down this corridor, then turn left."

In the kitchen, the rubbish had been bagged up, and the clean dishes rested on a draining board. Another maid was returning the unused wineglasses to their cupboards, examining each one for any chips or cracks.

"Serena, I've just popped in to say goodbye," said Ania.

"I'm so sorry, I thought I would get more of a chance to speak to you," said Serena. "I'll be out of here in a minute."

"I know how it is when you're hosting," said Ania.

Serena looked drawn and tired, her usual self-possession replaced by a strained restiveness.

"Well, I have you here now, and I'd love to be frank, if I may?"

"Of course."

"I'm not sure if the air needs to be cleared but I'm going to try to clear it anyway. I've always thought of you as a friend; your whole family has meant so much to me. And I know you will have heard these ridiculous rumors about me and your father."

"I've heard a few things," said Ania, sitting down at the table.

"Absolute lies. Just people spouting trash. I promise you, there's absolutely nothing between us. We're friends; I bounce ideas off him, we meet for a drink now and then, that's about it. Nothing more. You do believe me?"

"I believe you and, more to the point, I believe him. If there had been anything, I know he would have told me."

"You're absolutely right. He adores you. I'm so glad we've had this conversation. I must confess, it's the reason why I invited you tonight, even though I wasn't sure that you'd come."

"Well, thank you, Serena, it's sweet of you to be so concerned. I'll say goodbye now; it's so late."

Ania stood up.

"No, you can't go. Your friends are still here," said Serena, almost barring her way.

"Who? Those two? They're not friends of mine."

"But I met them at a wedding reception, and I'm sure they told me that they had been on vacation with you somewhere. Or at least, Mussoorie did. Maybe I misunderstood. But that's why I invited them, because I understood that you were all such good friends."

"I've known Fahim very casually, but I'd never met his wife before. And to be completely honest, she's really not someone I'd spend much time with. I couldn't think how you'd know them."

Serena grabbed Ania's arm.

"Oh my God, what a relief. All evening, I just couldn't understand how they were close to you. At first, I thought, well, she seems practically to live with the Somwari royals, how bad could she be? I should have known better. I only just remembered that we'd once arranged to do a photo shoot at their palace, but it was horrific because mice kept racing across those gorgeous teak floors. We had to leave. Absolutely in tears, all of us."

"How *awful*."

"Isn't it? And as for him, I know he did an important story about some war, and as you know, I always try to have a good mix of minorities at my soirees. Unfortunately, that violinist from Nagaland couldn't make it tonight. But, really, these two have just been intolerable. My God, the overfamiliarity. And now they won't leave."

Serena walked to the kitchen door, listened for a moment, and then returned.

"I'm sure they're still just sitting there."

"They're hardly going to leave without saying goodbye."

"I really wish they would."

"Why don't you just tell them you're really tired and have to wake up early in the morning?"

"I couldn't possibly. You know how much I hate confrontation. I think I'll just have to hide here for a bit."

"Stop being so ridiculous. Look, it's late and I'm leaving; I'm sure you'll find a way to deal with them."

Serena grabbed Ania's arm again.

"No, you *can't* leave me here with them. I've not been well. Please, Ania."

"I'll stay five more minutes. But only because you've had the sense not to have an affair with my father."

Serena let out a high-pitched laugh, which sounded as though it had been trapped inside her for hours.

"You go, I'll be right behind you. Give me a minute," she said.

Nests of candles flickered on the occasional tables as Ania walked down the long passage toward the sitting room. The thought crossed her mind that Serena was engaged in a pronounced bluff, resorting to the pretense of an intimate conversation to divert her from the truth. But she dismissed the suspicion in an instant. Her father was incapable of hiding any kind of affair from her. All these years she had watched him remain insensible to advances from all kinds of women, or brush off the bolder approaches, pretending not to notice their ruses as he politely answered their questions. And she was sure that he had done it all on her account, not wanting to risk their relationship by exposure to a new wife. She had never believed that he remained devoted to the memory of her mother; deceit and degradation could never inspire such fidelity. He had remained unattached for his daughter's sake. It was a sacrifice that suddenly felt unbearable, the weight of its sadness making her stop to lean against the wall. She couldn't cry: she had to prepare herself for some sort of unpleasantness in the next room. A few seconds went by. She returned to the sitting room.

Fahim and Mussoorie were on the sofa, his hand in hers, fingers locked together. Ania sat opposite them. Mussoorie reached for the lace fan and began to fan herself, even though the room was decidedly cool. Fahim looked at his glass of red wine.

"We've hardly had a chance to speak," said Mussoorie.

"No, Serena's so strict with the dinner seating that I didn't dare interfere."

"Of course not. She's such a darling though."

"One of the best. So, you're living in Delhi now?"

"I come and go, don't I?"

Fahim nodded at her.

"I'm not sure if you know, why would you, although maybe you would? I'm working on a biography of the royal family of Somwari so I spend a fair bit of time there."

"How wonderful. I've never been but I've heard it's magical."

"Completely. And the family are so delightful. They've been so kind to me. You really must come and visit us."

"That would be something."

"I'm serious; we really must arrange for you to come up there. The palace is just gorgeous, isn't it, darling, although we're having some restoration work done after the monsoons, so maybe toward Christmas would be better."

Ania nodded.

"Do you ride? The stables are really splendid. I have the most adorable dun called Ophelia. I love her to bits. But if you don't ride, that's fine, we could just spend time in the palace. There are lots of gorgeous nooks, the library is marvelous, and, well, there's some interesting art, shall we say."

She put the fan down and leaned forward.

"I heard that years ago the maharajah's mother took great exception to the nudes they had hanging in the palace and had local craftsmen paint saris over all the bare breasts. One of them was an Amrita Sher-Gil, can you imagine?"

"God, how tragic."

"Absolutely. But that's enough about us. Tell us about you, what are you up to these days?"

"Up to?"

"I know, how awful of me; that made it sound like you're up to no good. Although, who knows."

She laughed and picked up the fan again.

"So, are you seeing anyone at the moment?"

"Not at the moment."

"You know, I'm sure I know one or two men who would be perfect for you. We must have lunch one day before I disappear into the wilds again. What do you think?"

The housekeeper had dispatched a boy to collect the ashtrays from all the balconies. He walked into the room, expecting it to be empty, and then retreated in fright. They heard his footsteps as he ran down the passage.

Ania watched Fahim staring at the carpet, his face strained and worn. His gaze shifted to one side and came to rest on the coffee table. Ania felt a rush of shame at her previous exuberance. How had she thought that this shell of a man would be suitable for her vibrant friend? And how had he come to entertain his own delusions? It came back to her: the wetness of his mouth.

She checked herself. It was a ludicrous moment that had long passed. She felt that she almost had a duty to plow on.

"Fahim, are you still doing freelance work?" asked Ania.

"He's got some exciting plans," said Mussoorie in a lilting voice. "Have you told her?"

"There's some stuff brewing," he said. "I'm thinking of starting my own venture."

"What's a venture?"

"You know, a media start-up."

"You should speak to Dimple about that . . . ," she said, the words emerging from her mouth before she had a chance to stop them.

"She does PR for start-ups," she said, finishing the sentence.

"Of course, I remember," said Fahim. "How is she?"

"She's well," said Ania, "extremely happy."

She thought of the weekend spent at Altaf Masood's constituency home, the strangely joyous way in which they had all danced around each other. There had been gentle teasing as they had warmed their hands over braziers; there had been so much sweet tea. She felt another swell of sadness and stood up to leave.

"It really is so late," she said, "I must say goodbye to Serena."

She left the room and then returned a moment later to get her purse. She saw Mussoorie lean over to whisper in Fahim's ear, but he drew sharply away from her, his features hard with scorn. It was almost a look of revulsion.

They looked up in the next instant to see that Ania had

returned and noticed. She remained standing as they all listened to Serena's footsteps coming down the passage.

They waited for her. No one spoke. There was nothing to be done.

"WELL, TO EACH their own," said Dileep.

The Khuranas said this often, as a surface acknowledgment that matters of taste were, after all, so subjective. They didn't believe a word of it. Their judgments were the result of an instant but complete appraisal—and they knew they were always right. Nothing amused them more than what they considered to be clownish displays of wealth; nothing would stop them from lending their own refinement to the buffoons in question if they saw a solid advantage. The thought of owning a private plane filled Dileep with horror—the waste, the bother—but he knew the value of being seen disembarking from a Learjet at a secluded airstrip, a lone paparazzo lurking behind a hangar.

He disliked yachts, where he ran the danger of being confined for long periods of time with objectionable characters. He was also convinced that they were breeding grounds for virulent bacteria, which would only result in a boatful of passengers vomiting in the wood-paneled aisles. And he hated not being in full control of what arrived on his plate.

But there were important reasons why a short spell on an Australian zinc-mining tycoon's superyacht was desirable, connected to the way myths were made in the modern age. The Australian had many admirable qualities but, above all, he knew not to grub about for reciprocal favors the moment he had spent some money, and he was loyal to the people he considered his friends. Dileep had a sense that the Australian would go much further still.

The yacht had to anchor out of port as it was too large to dock in the marina. At the end of his stay Dileep said his goodbyes, delighted that he would soon be alone again on firm land. As he boarded the launch, Saint-Tropez was soaked in its own special twilight. He shifted in his seat to face the shore and lifted his face up to the wind. They sped past the thicket of sails and masts, and beyond them on the shore, the ochre roofs, the yellow dome of the clock tower, the splashes of woodland on the hills.

The launch docked at the hotel's private jetty, and he was shown to his suite by a hospitality executive in spotless Riviera white, her friendly inquiries perfectly timed. The room had drawn in the dusk, and the lamps cast shadows over the pale surfaces. After she had left, he reached deep into his case and pulled out the envelope he had collected from Mr. Nayak. He placed it on the desk and turned away, determined to put it out of his mind.

It was the hour when sand-flecked towels were trailed over terra-cotta floors and salt was washed off sun-warmed skin. From the terrace he could see the tumble of the hotel gardens, the stone steps that led to the beach, the sea streaked with gold. And somewhere in the distance, candles were being set on tables outside waterfront restaurants; women in boutiques peered at trays of diamond rings through the great fringe of their false eyelashes; day-trippers took pictures of the fancy boats, nursing their cocktails.

A young woman in a white bikini came running up the steps pursued by a man. He grabbed her arm and twirled her into an embrace. Her laugh was full and dirty as she wrapped her legs around his waist. He carried her up the rest of the steps, her legs gripping him tight, feet flexed, her hair falling over their faces. Dileep watched them and felt one of his rare pangs of desire.

He came back into the room, took off his clothes, and lay down on the bed to think of his wife. They had come to Saint-Tropez nearly thirty years ago, driving up into the hills in a convertible, as though they were in a film, believing that they deserved to be in a film. He had bought her a scarf as a joke, blue anchors on white silk, a parody of the kind of vacation they were supposed to have. And she had worn it in the same spirit, a jaunty knot between her collarbones.

They had stopped in a village for lunch, walking through a square where the farmers were selling sausages and cheese. At the end of a cobbled lane braced by medieval walls, they watched a woman put her shopping down on the pavement. She reached under her blouse, unhooked her bra, whipped it out, and dropped it into her basket. With a large handkerchief, her hand laboring under her blouse, eyes closed, she mopped her breasts and under her arms carefully, almost sensually. The look of relief on her face was captivating. They watched, not bothering to hide their fascination, both realizing that the sight had ignited something urgently carnal between them. They held hands and continued their exploration, their palms burning. In the mid-afternoon heat they found a cool stone courtyard where a waiter brought them stuffed artichoke hearts and clams cooked with saffron. She wet her finger in her mouth and drew a line through the fog on his wineglass.

His face was creased in concentration as he held on to the image, working his penis hard, frantic for the release that he seldom allowed himself. He saw his wife now on the steps, where the girl in the bikini had been, her skin sparkling with drops of seawater, ducking, twisting, escaping his grasp. And then he had both arms around her, his face lowered into her neck, the swell of her breasts. He tasted the salt on her skin, and when he looked up, they were both lying on a hospital bed, his arm caught in a tangle of tubes, as he continued to probe her unresponsive mouth with his tongue. She lay like a dead woman, her skin already losing its suppleness and warmth. He pressed on, sucking her lip, pushing his head into the crook of her neck. He lifted himself up and looked at her face—he could see that she was not breathing. He pulled open her eyelid, and the eye stared at him, cold and yellow. When his orgasm came, it was an acute pain that shot up through his stomach, like a vicious spasm after some sort of medical procedure.

The room was in darkness when he woke a couple hours later. He shivered and pulled the bedcover over his body. Night sounds drifted in through the open terrace door: a woman's high-pitched laugh, a short burst of jazz. He turned over onto his side. It was exactly as Serena had said. Mr. Nayak's words took form and significance long after he had spoken. And he was right: in this place where they had once experienced those perfectly formed moments, he felt closer to his wife than he had for years.

He forced himself out of bed and slid the contents of the envelope onto the desk. A bottle of powder, a copper amulet, a curl of burdock root. He placed a photograph of his wife facedown on the blotter and sprinkled the gray powder over it; as instructed, he left the amulet and the burdock root a few inches away, close to an open window. He turned off the lamps even though this had not been an instruction: it seemed the correct thing to do.

He pulled on a robe and sat in the armchair, prepared to wait. He was not a character in a cheap supernatural thriller. He was not a fool. It was clear to him that the curtains would not billow, the lamps would not flicker, the sound of footsteps would not trail through the suite. And yet, he expected something to happen. The thunder in his rib cage proved that.

Eventually Dileep fell asleep again, his chin lolling against his chest. When he started awake, his eyes took a while to adjust to the different types of darkness. He counted out a few breaths before telling himself he had been a complete idiot and turning on the desk lamp.

She was there. She sat on the edge of the bed, her hands placed in her lap, as though this were a difficult first meeting. On her face there was a look of profound sadness. Was it regret? Was it a plea for forgiveness? His tongue was thick in his mouth; his throat had seized up. There was nothing he could say out loud to her. His hand opened as though she might slip her hand into it. But she didn't move. He continued to look at her face in terror, searching her eyes for a clue.

ANIA HAD BELIEVED it to be a foregone conclusion. But so much time had gone by without Nikhil making a real play for her. Her occasional moments of self-doubt had been short-lived as she was far too fluent in this idiom—candid glances, infinitesimal pauses— to have misinterpreted his intentions. He was merely another example of the deteriorating male specimens all around her, too feeble to face the prospect of rejection. She had spent long enough supporting and encouraging others; the time had come to help herself.

She booked a suite at the Regent and sent him a message telling him to be ready for a small private party.

"How small?" he replied.

"Just the two of us."

"Awesome."

She tried to take his response in her stride.

When she walked into the hotel lobby, he was already there, pacing like an expectant father. A piano tinkled in the background and huge orchids glowed in the pale yellow light. When he hugged her, his face nestled near her ear.

"A private party, huh?" he said.

She smiled but stayed silent.

As they walked past the staircase that swept up to the mezzanine, he paused to read the details of a mining-industry event that was being held there.

"Hey, wait a minute, I've got an idea," he said. He grabbed her hand and led her up the stairs.

"Where are we going?"

"There's some sort of convention going on here. I just want to do something, mess their shit up."

"*Why?* What the hell is wrong with you?"

"It's no big deal! It'll be funny, just watch."

He shepherded her through the double doors toward the registration desk in the large hall.

"Good evening," he said to the woman behind the desk while scanning the rows of name badges. "That's me."

He pointed to a badge that read "Mansukh Gulabchand."

"Good evening, Mr. Gulabchand," said the woman, pushing a form toward him. "If you could please sign here. And your name please, ma'am?"

Ania's eyes darted over the names, all of which were male, as far as she could see.

"There you are," said Nikhil, picking up a badge that read "Lovely Walia."

"Welcome, Miss Walia, please sign here."

"Stay here and mingle," he said before she could protest again, "when you see me walking out, head down to the elevators as fast as you can."

She watched him skirt the room and head toward the bar, before suddenly veering off and infiltrating a group of men. A note of caution rang in her head, as clear as a bell. His lack of regard for consequences had always been part of his reckless charm; taking her on those sudden dashes into unfamiliar corners of Hong Kong, casually flouting rules and laws. They were both secure in the knowledge that in their world consequences could be delayed, mitigated, ignored. But this silly charade was a distraction from her plans. She felt provoked, even though Nikhil's eyes were on her at every moment, and when a waiter offered her a glass of wine, she drank as much of it as she could stomach in one go.

"Didn't we meet at the Minerals Expo in Canada?" asked a man standing next to her.

"Yes, I think we did," she said.

As the man continued to speak, her gaze darted around the room. There were guffaws that set out to make themselves heard at the other end of the hall, handshakes that were a test. She could no longer see Nikhil. And then he suddenly reappeared, throwing her a knowing look. His satchel bulged. She turned away from the

man while he was in mid-sentence and reached the hall doors at
the same time as Nikhil.

"A bottle of the finest cognac for my lady," he said.

She took his arm and said, "You really are insane."

They hurried down the staircase, a blur of maroon carpet and
brass stair rods, dodged past the members of a wedding party,
crossed the lobby, and made it into an elevator just as its doors
were closing. Her heart pounded with the ridiculous thrill of it,
and all recollection of her previous annoyance erased.

A breathlessness pressed upon her as the elevator rose through
the endless bulk of the hotel. She would not look at him. Earlier,
in the midst of that ridiculous escapade, he had constantly performed for her. Even as he stood on the other side of the room
there had been a tautness between them, a trance-like knowledge
that he would soon be her lover. She could sense that he was on
the cusp of falling in love with her; she closed her fist around that
instinct and kept it close; it made her impatient, restless, greedy.

He had barely kicked the door shut when she pressed herself
against his body, looking into his grateful eyes. His satchel dropped
to the carpet with a loud *thud*. For all they knew, the bottle could
have smashed, the cognac richly pooling in the thick pile.

There was almost a cruelty with which she took her pleasure, a
complete self-absorption that Ania saw as the reward for her pursuit. The bed was wide, its posts solid, like a great boat. There were
little gold threads on the ceiling. The silk on the headboard was
cool as it grazed against her arm. His face was pinched, almost as
though he was in pain. When he opened his eyes, his irises seemed
to engulf her. And then she stopped seeing or thinking.

Later, as she lay on her side, sated, her hands tucked between her thighs, a single violent shiver ran over the length of her body. The blackout curtains ensured that the room was in complete darkness. All she could hear was Nikhil's slow, steady breath.

And then her phone lit up, and she lifted her head to see that the call was from Renu. She declined the call, but the phone began to vibrate a few seconds later. Again, Renu. She glanced at Nikhil, still asleep, a childlike softness about his lips. It was an innocence, a vulnerability that filled her with a rush of tenderness. She slipped out of bed and padded to the bathroom with her phone, sliding the door shut, fumbling for the light switch.

"Bua, you've not stopped calling, is everything all right?" she asked as soon as Renu picked up.

"No, I'm awfully upset; it's all so horrible."

"What's happened?"

"Of course, I didn't believe it, but even the colonel has now confirmed that it's true."

"But what?"

"Nikhil has been having an affair with Nina, can you believe it? Nina Varkey. It's too dreadful to even talk about but I had to tell you. I still can't face the fact that it's true and not idle gossip. But it is true. Just awful. Are you still there?"

"Yes, I'm here."

"Isn't it *awful*? How could he? Of course she would do it. But him? How could he? Of all the people in the world. Was there really no one else? I mean, she's my age and he's your age. And more than that, it's *her*. Nina. It makes me sick to think about it."

"Are you really sure?"

"That's what I kept saying. But yes, it's definitely true. People have seen it with their own eyes. The colonel told me."

"I'm sorry, I can't really talk now. I have to go. I'll call you later. I will."

Ania shivered and turned away from the mirror. A sour taste filled her mouth. She pulled on one of the hotel robes that hung in the bathroom and turned toward the closed door. For a while, she stood motionless in front of the hard curve of the enormous bath, her feet feeling icy on the tiles. The room was a sickly white. She slid open the bathroom door as noiselessly as she could. Beyond the spill of light she could just about make out his sleeping form, the soft hump of the covers she had cast off, the paleness of the side where she had lain, the sheet now stone cold.

CHAPTER THIRTY

IN A CITY where Victorian façades were blasted out of sight, old timber bungalows razed and swept aside, Indo-Saracenic towers and pavilions torn down and sold for scrap, the restoration of a hundred-year-old opera house was a momentous event. The grand opening night of Mumbai's Royal Opera House succeeded in luring out patricians who rarely stepped into the vulgar glare of the new world. They were chauffeured out of their hidden driveways; they descended from their sea-facing art deco apartments; they leaned on their canes and confronted their doormen, demanding to know what had happened to the palms in the foyer.

It had taken years of painstaking work, as the opera house's girders threatened to collapse and balconies had begun to list. The building had to be shored up, floor by floor, the roof repaired, columns reconstructed. Architects and restoration specialists pored over old books and photographs. They studied every frame of a film that had been shot in the building forty years ago and questioned anyone who had any familiarity with the halls of the old theater. Console tables were sourced from a private collection in Gujarat.

Tiles and beveled glass of the correct vintage were brought in from dealers all over the country. The insides of the royal boxes were papered in shades of ivory and gold.

When the gates finally opened, polite society swept in to make up its mind. The opera house courtyard was golden with Mumbai's early-evening glow, an almost holy light that poured over the assembled company. A strong wind riffled through the leaves in the floral arrangements; it set upon perfect coiffures and raised goosebumps on pale, delicate skin; when it pressed against the stiff white tablecloth, there was a sound like paper tearing.

"Well, we're among friends here," announced Flavia da Costa.

Champagne glasses clinked in one corner of the courtyard. The group gave the impression of schoolchildren having just been released for summer vacation. Their laughter was heady, infectious, and not entirely innocent. They seemed to be trying to keep nightfall at bay, determined to revel in that golden moment, consumed by their own visibility.

Serena Bakshi heard a lowered voice behind her and took a couple steps back to listen to the conversation.

"Well, you know how it is with these royals. They've not been the same since the British left, moping about in their decrepit homes, devastated that a twenty-gun salute will never sound again in Nowhereabad. And they can never resist boasting to a white person that their grandfather fed Edwina Mountbatten her first Peshawari plum. As for this Mussoorie or whatever she's called, I'm sure she's only too keen to indulge them. And when she gets a day off from kissing their hem, she pushes her way into all sorts of decent people's events. It's intolerable."

"Which royal is it?"

"That spiteful old bag from Somwari."

"Oh dear."

"Isn't everyone *awful*?"

"Simply heinous."

A strong breeze had dislodged the label from a tray of canapés—the organic persimmon topped with Iranian caviar and a pickled onion—and it had fluttered across the cobblestones and attached itself to Silky Chhabra's heel.

"I'm still trying to get the banquet hall at the Regent for my female empowerment panel. It's a nightmare because the cleaners at the hotels have all gone on strike over their pay. How on earth are we supposed to uplift working-class women when it's so difficult for us to secure a decent conference venue?"

A pair of sapphire drop earrings trembled angrily in agreement.

At the far end of the courtyard, an elderly gentleman had been provided with a chair. His eyesight was deteriorating, but it was far more reliable than his hearing, which was irremediable, proffering at times nothing but a series of high-pitched squeaks, loud clinks, or a great whoosh of emptiness. He knew that he had been invited because he had been born the same year that the opera house had originally been inaugurated. It made for a good story— the organizers would be able to display their thoughtfulness at including a local resident, a senior deserving of concern—and he was glad of it.

He would not be able to hear the music, but he was looking forward to the spectacle of the show. The lovely young girl had given him a shawl in case the air-conditioning proved too much. It was the softest thing he had ever held; he felt as though he had plunged his arms into a pile of down. And she had assured him of a seat by the aisle after he'd told her about his bladder. He had a flutter of anxiety that they would forget and no one would come for him when it was time to go into the theater. He locked his hands together and counted backward from a hundred, an old technique that helped to calm his nerves.

The group in front of him moved away, and he had a clear view of the façade of the reconstructed building, its plasterwork now a pristine white, the late sun turning the louvered wooden shutters a honeyed brown. He remembered this wall as pocked and speckled, whipped by the salty sea winds, chipped away by each savage monsoon, fouled by the hundreds of pigeons that had made their home on the top-floor terraces.

Images flickered into his vision, as though projected on this new white wall. His mother put her hand on his jouncing knee as he watched the amazing Marathi actor Bal Gandharva appear onstage dressed as a woman with flowers in her hair. He saw himself as a middle-aged man, ignoring the musicians and peering upward as water dripped onto his shoulder through a hole in the ceiling. And he remembered the thrill of that scene on the giant screen, after the theater became a cinema, the couple lying with such abandon on the beach, the waves crashing over their bodies as they kissed. His head had filled with the roar of the surf then—and the sounds around him now, the chatter, the applause, the laughter of beautiful people, were filling his head with a similar roar.

"Mind if I butt in? Over there, they're ranking Meenu Lakdawalla's ex-husbands in order of net worth, but I can barely remember any of them."

"Do join us, we were discussing Europe."

"Oh, yes, what about it?"

"Well, it's not what it was, is it?"

"Absolutely agree. I never go now. Europe is just not my idea of a vacation. Trudging around some schloss, waiting in line with people in horrible raincoats, paying through one's nose for awful service. Give me the tropics, heat, jungles, adventure. I've just come back from Belize, and I feel five years younger. And so much fitter. When we're inside I'll let you feel my glutes."

The speeches had begun, but not everyone could be bothered to face the front and pretend to listen. Someone mentioned that Gandhi had once made a speech in the opera house, shortly after he had cabled the viceroy, insisting that Nehru be released from jail. But there was no response: no one was in the mood for a history lesson.

"Anita Malwani's not here."

"Obviously not, she's out on anticipatory bail."

"Oh dear God, what's she done now?"

"You know about her attempting to poison her husband?"

"Oh, yes, everyone knows."

"Apart from that, have you heard about the delightful little scam she had going? There's a horribly creepy jeweler on Lamington Road, but he does have the most fabulous pieces. Anita was a regular customer, and they had agreed that he would invoice her husband for at least fifty percent more than the actual price. She then stashed away the difference, with a cut for the jeweler. And Bobby being an absolute cretin didn't have a clue about it until some mix-up with the tax people, when it all came to light. So now, in addition to the poisoning business, the poor thing's been charged with criminal breach of trust or something and is confined to her home, no doubt shackled in the billiards room."

"Anita is, of course, ghastly, but I can't help feeling it's such a shame she was caught."

"Oh, I agree, it's completely tragic. It's not like Bobby would even miss that money. She phoned me the other day, you know, wanting some advice."

"And?"

"I told her that she should get a publicist and plant her side of the story in the *Mumbai Mirror* as soon as possible."

"Oh, but, darling, that's probably illegal if it's all going to court, and you know what Bobby is like about having his name in the papers. That's probably the worst possible advice you could have given her."

"Naturally."

They laughed like excited seals.

The opera house program directors had not found it difficult to settle on a star for the opening night performance: Niloufer, the only internationally celebrated soprano of Indian origin, was the obvious choice. She went by one name, although it was cattily suggested that this was because she had no idea who her father was. And even if this was true, it hardly mattered when critics and crowds in New York, Paris, and Vienna were in thrall to her gloriously rounded voice and magnificent presence. Special arrangements had to be made at the opera house for Niloufer's preparatory rituals to comply with the building's fire regulations. A stone basin had been placed on the external stairs at the back of the building to accommodate smoldering splinters of palo santo wood, whose fumes Niloufer inhaled to cleanse her spirit and preserve her energy. As she leaned over the smoke, coughing and spluttering in her kimono, the opera house staff exchanged nervous glances. But at the front of the building, the evening's performance was distant from the minds of many of the invited guests.

"Did you hear? Serena Bakshi's been ditched by her husband. This time for good."

"To be expected, of course. Can't really understand why he took up with her in the first place. I mean, I know it was all a long time ago, but running brothels and whatnot, it's just not the kind of thing one's family ought to be doing. I don't object on moral grounds, of course, people's sexual peccadilloes are entirely their own business. It's just that, as a métier, it's so *tawdry*."

"I don't really know Serena that well so I shouldn't comment."

"Oh please."

"I have been to a party at her brother's house in Kasauli though."

"And?"

"The garden was full of dahlias in the most vulgar colors."

It BEGAN AS a ripple of gossip, a tantalizing little wave that flowed into the general stream of slander and tattle outside the opera house. But the information had been verified and, unfortunately, it was true. Someone closely connected to Renu Khurana—her beloved husband's nephew, in fact, who had been doing the rounds—had been arrested in New York on charges of fraud, money laundering, and perjury. There might have been other infractions; it was difficult to remember. Americans had such

antiquated terminology for their crimes, all that felony and lar-
ceny, so much more suited to Elizabethan highwaymen than spirited Indian immigrants on Wall Street.

Discreet three-quarter turns were made to see whether any of
the Khuranas were at the event. A wonderful opportunity had
presented itself, to greet them warmly while searching for signs of
internal collapse. But no one from the family appeared to have
come to Mumbai, and any probing would have to be done in a
few days' time in Delhi.

Uncharacteristically, Nina had arrived on time. Her eyes were
bright, and her throaty laugh sounded often. She feigned great
admiration for a real estate tycoon's latest project, making him
increasingly nervous about his achievements. She flattered intem-
perately. She blew Silky Chhabra a kiss.

The news came to her in little snatches, solidifying slowly until
there was a jolt of recognition. Her heart hammered. Voices
crowded in. She took an old friend aside and made him repeat
what he knew.

"Ripped loads of people off apparently. Every cent that he
took, he invested in dodgy schemes, and now it's all just vanished.
The FBI had been onto him for a while, and they arrested him a
few days after he returned to America. He'll be out on bail, I
guess, unless they think he's a flight risk. I mean, he was here for
ages, wasn't he? Do you know him?"

"We've met."

"My parents know his mother. Oh well."

Nina excused herself but remained motionless. She had no
idea that Nikhil had returned to New York. She had assumed that
his current elusiveness was another game that these young men

liked to play. Even on her way to the opera house, she had imagined turning up at the opening with him, enjoying the picture of the scandal. She would take him by the hand and guide him through the crowd, all the faces that she had known for years. He would hand her a drink, and they would exchange deliberate looks.

She felt that she must have been spared. Perhaps he had gambled other people's money but hers had been saved, that last stockpile preserved out of a sense of loyalty and affection. It would be returned to her in due course. She would be safe.

But then the reality crashed over her again: her stomach churned, and an acid burn flared through her chest. He had provided her with information, so much information, documents with details of past returns and future projections, market conditions, regulatory frameworks, compliance mechanisms, matters that she had pretended to understand as she had no desire to display her ignorance in front of him. And he had taken her for every penny. She had borrowed as much as she could against the apartment, cashed in a life insurance policy, sold a few items of jewelry to turn it all into a round figure—the last of which had been her own greedy and specious suggestion—and transferred the whole amount to his account in New York. He had flung a few sweet smiles at a lonely, foolish old crone, and she had clasped them to her bony chest. He had violated her. And now he had ruined her.

She wondered if they all knew, whether there were lists of his victims being shared with a combination of pity and contempt. The chatter continued around her, but it seemed to emerge now with a hard, tinny edge, the laughter rising with an unruly eagerness. Nina knew she was flushing, that there might even be beads of sweat at her hairline. She looked for somewhere to put her drink down, and when she caught sight of a passing waiter, reached for his arm to stop him. It was only when she saw his expression that she realized she must have dug her fingers into his flesh. She put her drink on his tray and turned away.

She pushed past a couple and headed for the courtyard gates. Over the heads of guests, she could see that the swarm of photographers was still in place, bystanders thronging the pavement, the road choked with cars. Security guards had formed a cordon in front of the metal detectors. She approached a steward who told her that there was no other exit from the courtyard but that the congestion at the gates would subside once the evening's performance began.

She turned around. They were all there. Silky Chhabra was shrieking with delight, weighed down with emeralds, her teeth long and yellow. And behind her, Herman Van den Broeck was trying to catch Nina's eye, a shrewd and alert expression on his face. A mumble in Nina's ear made her move toward the opera house steps. More people hemmed her in. She felt the graze of a man's jacket on her arm and a warm gust against the back of her neck. Krish and Candy Mehra were weaving through the crowd, making their way toward her. The performance was not due to begin for a while, and all the doors to the building looked firmly shut, an usher positioned outside each one. She began to edge her way toward the far corner of the building. A foot dragged at the hem of her sari, and a woman in dark glasses said something unintelligible to her.

Around the corner, a few steps led up to a side entrance. She felt a desperate, dizzying need to remove herself from the crowd. If she managed to get into the building, she would be able to stand in a dark corner or passage until they all filed inside; then she would slip away. She walked quickly toward the side door, grabbing at the handrail and almost pulling herself up the steps. The usher in the doorway shook his head as she approached.

"I'm sorry, madam, we are preparing for the show. We are not allowed to have unauthorized personnel here. In another twenty minutes the main doors will open."

The last vestiges of her dignity hardened on Nina's face.

"If you value your job, you'll let me in now," she said.

"Madam, it is not allowed."

Nina clicked her fingers.

"I give you three seconds to decide."

Confusion flickered over his face as he weighed the threat. Nina had never looked more somber or purposeful. He stepped aside and she pushed open the door, knowing that he would probably phone a superior immediately. She staggered through a passage into the foyer, ablaze with lights and mirrors. Members of staff had their backs to her, deep in conversation. She ducked through a doorway into the theater, stepping into its consecrated hush. She stood deep in shadow, staring at the dull shine of the gilt, the whirl of scarlet opulence. Soon every seat would be occupied, the room filled with applause. A voice echoed behind her; she did not have much time.

Turning into the aisle, she walked past another usher, startling him and making him look round the room in bewilderment. She breezed past him. A moment later she recognized the precise look she had seen on his face when their eyes met: it was not one of fear but of pity, normally reserved for lunatics who raved in the street.

She saw some hurried movement in the distance, an oblong of

light as a door was opened and closed. Musicians were tuning up in the orchestra pit, and there was a blast from a clarinet, a warning. Security guards would soon grab her by the arms and escort her out. She would be paraded past the entire audience. For the first time that evening, complete silence would descend on the courtyard. Terror made the ground seem to shift, rearing up to meet her. She forced herself up the steps at the side of the stage and looked frantically around her in the wings. A spiral staircase led to the upper floors, but she would never make it to the top quickly enough in her sari and heels. Her breaths had begun to turn into gasps. A man called out, and there was a commotion at the foot of the stage. She had walked into a trap that she had set for herself.

She fled to the outer passage and realized that the row of three doors led to the artists' dressing rooms. She tried each one; the third was unlocked. Rushing into the room, she slammed and bolted the door and then stepped away as if it had the power to harm her. Footsteps thundered toward her followed by a crescendo of hammering on the door. There were shouts as the handle was shaken violently. She could barely find the strength but she pushed the sole chair in the room against the door. Then she tried to move the dressing table, but it would not budge. The knocking and shouting continued. Sooner or later they would smash their way into the room. She collapsed onto the sofa and buried her face in her arms. A few moments passed as the blood thundered in her head. She raised herself on her elbows and turned toward the mirror to see her face as it came apart.

CHAPTER THIRTY-ONE

DIMPLE HAD GONE so far as to rehearse her words in front of the mirror. She knew she had never been under any firm obligation to keep Ania informed about her marriage plans or to seek her opinion, but she found it difficult to escape the notion that her silence had been an act of deception. She had the confidence to realize that she knew some things better than Ania, but she still lacked the courage to be able to tell her.

She could not put it off any longer.

She had wanted to avoid a long evening of chat and possible awkwardness or recriminations. At first she had accused herself of cowardice and then persuaded herself that she was merely being practical. They planned to meet in front of the cinema at the mall, and then Dimple would reveal all to Ania over a quick drink after the film. There would be no time for a long and difficult conversation. She would tell Ania, breezily, confidently. All would be well. But the film times had changed, and at the cinema they discovered that they had missed the show. The evening gaped before them.

Ania led them out of the building and onto the terrace. They sat at a table by the fountains, watching the jets rise and fall in concert, changing color from silver to lilac to purple. Banners fluttered above their heads. Children raced around on skateboards, their parents hurriedly in pursuit. The sky was clinging to its final moments of deep blue before dusk.

Dimple had called Ania as soon as she had seen news of Nikhil's arrest, but the conversation had been brief. She was wary of bringing it up again, but it was preferable to the strain of revealing her own news.

"The whole thing with Nikhil, I still can't believe it happened. But maybe you don't want to talk about it. I understand a hundred percent," she said, her look as earnest as she felt.

"It happened, I guess. I still can't believe it either. I've never felt so stupid in my life."

Dimple put her hand over Ania's arm.

"But how were you supposed to know? He fooled everybody," she said.

"You know what, you were right. I don't think I want to talk about it."

And another silence fell. Dimple stole a glance at Ania and tried to find the words she had come to say. Her tongue felt thick in her mouth. She took a sip of her drink. Ania appeared not to have sensed her unease.

The sky was dark now and looked clear, the stars unusually bright, ablaze like distant fire balloons. Earlier that day Dimple had read the poem that was e-mailed to her by a poetry subscription website. She received one every day, and she read it repeatedly on her way to work, the meaning becoming clearer as the train pulled in at each station. That morning's poem had described the Brazilian custom of launching fire balloons into the sky to celebrate a festival. They were delicate objects whose paper chambers were flushed with light as they drifted over the mountains, at the mercy of the wind. An observer on the ground would mistake them for a star or a planet, beautiful in the night sky. But the poem revealed the truth: the fire balloons had no business being in the sky. A strong gust would turn the whole structure into a fireball, spewing smoke and ash, falling to the earth, the whole endeavor ending in destruction. The splendid planets and stars had their places in the dark sky. There could only be danger in floating toward them as a fire balloon in an unpredictable wind, no matter how bright the fire.

Dimple blurted it out. "I'm getting married."

"What?"

"Ankit proposed and I said yes."

"Oh my God."

Dimple searched Ania's face for whatever it would reveal: anger, heartache, disappointment. But Ania had stood up too quickly, and she couldn't see her expression.

Ania bent down to give her a hug. Dimple still could not see her face. Ania's arms held her tightly, and the warmth of her cheek came up against Dimple's ear. Dimple had put her arms around Ania too, and they stayed motionless, in their tight embrace.

Ania whispered in her ear, "That's great, Dee, that's really great."

It was far more than Dimple's mother had said.

Muffled sounds still reached them: the shouts of the children, the fountains gushing. Dimple told herself that she would not cry. And she didn't.

AFTER DIMPLE HAD left, Ania stayed seated for a long while. The fountains were more sedate now, and there was only an occasional spurt high into the air. When Dimple had told her, she had felt a surge of annoyance and betrayal at the fact that she had been told at the final hour, after a ring had been produced, when dates had already been considered. The long discussions with Dimple, the trips, the plans, the description of men's bodies and tastes and odors, the gasping laughter, seemed to belong to a distant, un-complicated time. Ania would never have believed it possible: Dimple on her way to marry Ankit, while she burned with her own humiliation by Nikhil.

She pictured him with Nina. It seemed unendurable that there were days, weeks, months ahead of her, when she would shudder at the thought, angry tears pricking at her eyes. It felt as though a huge tidal wave of shame had broken over her head. Everything decent and safe had been swept far out of reach. She felt an over-whelming desire to unburden herself to the one person who could sympathize. But it was too soon to tell Dev.

His words came bobbing to the surface again; he had called her friendship with Dimple a mission civilisatrice. She would have to prove him wrong. Even if this marriage wasn't what she would have chosen for her friend, at least she could act with what he would consider a kind of grace.

The stars had glowed like sparks of fire earlier in the evening but now they looked dull and indistinct, pale points about to be shrouded by the returning smog. She stirred what was left of her drink and pushed it away. The fountains had been turned off. Chairs were being lifted and upturned onto tables at the far end of the terrace. Ania stood up to leave. She was determined to be pleased for Dimple but, in that instant, she was glad to be alone.

CHAPTER THIRTY-TWO

Most people moved on quickly from news of Nikhil's downfall. The mechanics of his scam seemed so grubby and sordid: running an Indian call center that persuaded thousands of people to invest in unfamiliar financial products; charging credit cards without authorization; pilfering small amounts from middle managers and hairdressers and flight attendants. The particularly greedy and gullible had been stung for large sums. But the details of the fraud held little interest in the drawing rooms of South Delhi. There was none of the pizzazz and pyrotechnics of the great financial scandals of the day, embezzlements that brought down venerable institutions, scams that shamed Hollywood celebrities into admitting their lack of business acumen. Nikhil's name would not resonate in the swindlers' hall of fame; many of them could barely recall it by the end of the week.

Renu had refused all invitations and had been going out only when absolutely necessary. She would rush home, uncharacteristically urging the driver to speed through the side lanes or sneak up a one-way road. It felt as though all of Delhi was stuck in a ball of mucus at the base of her throat, and she could spit and spit and never expel it.

As she came home from the doctor's, she realized that it was a bereavement. The staff were sent home early. She thought it best to cancel the newspapers for a few more days.

She had absentmindedly been drinking cups of tea all day, taking a few sips and then leaving them to get cold. In the kitchen she made another cup, the loud stream of water from the kettle shocking. She laid the teaspoon in the sink, making the faintest *clack*.

She glanced into the sitting room. The colonel was still in the armchair, his back straight, hands on his knees, feet flat on the floor. It was how elderly men sat. She seemed to remember that she had seen her father in his armchair in the same position.

She took a sip of her tea and left it on the table. She settled into the sofa opposite him, and the minutes went by.

"I read about his victims," he said. "The report said one man had attempted suicide. Some of them worked all their lives and lost everything. There was a picture of a lady, a close-up, gray hair, glasses on a cord, I can't describe the expression in her eyes. She looks after her disabled husband, and now she has to try to return to work at the age of sixty. My age."

His eyes were deep in their sockets, his pallor ashen. He worried a button on his shirt, his fingers twisting at it, pushing it back and forth through its hole. In a moment he would pull it right off. Renu moved his hand gently away. He laid it flat on the table, watching its slight tremor.

"Somehow we have become monsters," he said.

———

FOR FAHIM, the fraud became an obsession. He bristled at the lack of fresh information, repeatedly finding that new reports regurgitated old facts. It was a matter of great satisfaction that someone from a charmed circle could meet such an ignominious fate. He clicked on image after image of Nikhil being led away in handcuffs; the photo where his head was covered in a blanket was particularly gratifying. He had never met Nikhil, but he knew all about his connection to the Khuranas. He imagined the family conferences in the Khurana reception rooms, Dileep's anger, Renu's anxiety, the way in which Ania would try to brush it off as nothing that concerned her.

But in the end he exhausted himself. His interest petered out just as suddenly as it had blazed. He had his own concerns: financial worries that would rear up even when he felt he had achieved a measure of calm; anxieties about his lack of appetite and weight loss, which only made him put off a visit to the doctor.

DILEEP THREW HIMSELF down on the mat and looked up at the ceiling. Sweat stung his eyes as he waited for his heartbeat to return to normal. His trainer had left the room, and the only sound was an occasional ghostly *click* from one of the machines. He was allowed a five-minute cooldown before he resumed the next stage of his regime. He tasted the salt in the dip above his lip, and it gave him a small jolt of satisfaction.

The news about Nikhil's fraud had not interested him much. He had been surprised to see the amateur nature of the scam and the gullibility of the poor wretches who were drawn into it. He knew Nikhil had been friendly with Ania and had been to the house a few times; so had any number of chancers. He was Renu's nephew, and it was for her and the colonel to manage whatever talk they heard. There would be no reputational damage to Dileep. Contrary to what some might have thought, it mattered as much as one of his gardeners cheating at cards on his day off.

Dileep's preoccupations lay elsewhere. His wife continued to appear before him, and through Mr. Nayak's mediation, he had finally recognized the full measure of her regret. He sensed her in a room now only as a benign presence. But there were new anxieties. It felt as though each time he met Mr. Nayak a niggling doubt would emerge, which in a couple days would turn into the beginning of a new obsession. Only Mr. Nayak could assist with unknotting the matter, since he was the one who had noticed it in the first place.

There were concerns about his health, his businesses, his friendships. And above everything, Mr. Nayak had indicated that there could be trouble after Dileep's death. In the past he had mocked the conservative outlook of men in his set, some of whom were younger than him: their obsessions with fathering sons, their anxieties about settling their daughters, the way they cowered before tradition. He reveled in the fact that he was more reflective and responsive to change, another mark of his essential juvenescence. Ania had never shown an inclination toward the Khurana enterprises, and he had believed it foolish to press the issue. Her future was secure, whatever she chose, and the soundness of their foundations and personnel meant that his businesses would succeed long after he had gone.

It was Mr. Nayak who mentioned his assets getting into the wrong hands and then refused to elaborate further. All his life Dileep had heard of this threat. Now he realized that he had reached an age when they had come to haunt him too: the wrong hands.

His increased reliance on Mr. Nayak had made him irritable and possessive. He felt a surge of annoyance when Mr. Nayak was unable to take his calls, and resented the time he spent on his other clients. Dileep had even distanced himself from Serena. Inevitably, they would discuss their experiences with Mr. Nayak, since it was a secret they shared and had become the dominant factor in their friendship. But Dileep no longer wished to share; he did not even want to be reminded of the fact that Serena was aware of this new intimacy in his life.

He decided to offer Mr. Nayak a generous retainer to act as his exclusive adviser.

"But that will not be fair to my other poor clients, isn't it? They all have needs and worries," said Mr. Nayak.

Dileep raised his bid. Mr. Nayak said he would think about it but no more was said. Dileep managed to refrain from contacting him for a few days, in order to demonstrate his pique. When he did call Mr. Nayak, it was to offer him even more money.

He had wondered whether to confide in Ania, but he knew that she would not be capable of understanding his dependence on Mr. Nayak. She would pity him or, worse, mock him. The closeness with his daughter—a camaraderie of equals—that he had depended on all his life could vanish in an instant. It was all that he had ever really had.

The trainer returned to the room and shook his head.

"You were supposed to be stretching, sir," he said.

"I was stretching," said Dileep with irritation.

"Okay, if you're done, sir, five minutes at the speed bag," he said.

Dileep put his gloves back on and took up his stance. His eyes narrowed. He jabbed at the bag, once, twice, and then tore into it with a ferocity that surprised even his trainer.

CHAPTER THIRTY-THREE

IT HAD BEEN one of the strangest and most unsettling fortnights of Ania's life. First, there had been the revelation from Dimple. A few days later in a café she had run straight into Fahim. They were both paralyzed in the doorway, equally uncomfortable, leaning away from each other: there was nowhere to duck or shrink away.

"It's been ages," said Ania.

"Yes, not since that party," he said.

"Always some party," she said.

Even to her ears, her laugh sounded forced.

"How's Mussoorie?" she asked.

"Really well. She's gone to England for a little while. But she'll be back soon."

"Oh, that's nice."

They moved into the street as nannies with strollers tried to maneuver their way around them. In the bright sunlight, Ania could see that his jacket sagged off his shoulders, and his cheeks had retreated so far that his face had taken on the dark stare of a skull.

"Anyway, you look well," she said.

"So do you. I'll let you know when Mussoorie's back. We could do something. Get together."

"Great, I look forward to that. Let me know."

"Definitely, definitely."

"So, lovely to see you, don't be a stranger."

"No, we should all do something."

"Definitely."

She had walked down the street, knowing that he was watching her, feeling those sunken eyes boring into her back. What she hadn't expected was to come out of the pharmacy a quarter of an hour later and find him standing in the same spot, hands jammed into his pockets, his fists agitating the fabric in a strange and precise rhythm.

Ania went home and did what she had done constantly over the last few days. She retraced her steps. The evening she had first met Nikhil, the conversations in hotel bars and on flights, the easy hours by the pool, the clues he might have inadvertently dropped, a calculating look perhaps, an imprudent brag or an unnecessary explanation of some aspect of his life. But there was nothing she could recall that could have alerted her. She had been blind, foolishly blind. She felt another hot surge of shame. But then she reminded herself of what had really happened: she had lost a little self-respect; many hundreds had lost everything.

On the ground below her window smoldered a cigarette that she had tossed out in anger at her loss of self-control. A thin wisp of smoke drifted into the faultless flower beds.

Once these matters were unearthed, it was common practice in Delhi to raise a beautifully threaded eyebrow and inquire in bafflement: "Didn't you know?"

Ania was able to admit that she did not know, that she would not have imagined it for a second, that many of her certainties were splintering and landing where she dared not look. The differences between genuine and false, decorous and improper, known and unknown, would have to be learned all over again.

There was certainly a grim kind of symmetry: she had taken great pleasure in telling Dev how wrong he had been to trust Kamya; she had been sure that he would waste no time in telling her that he had predicted Nikhil's despicable actions. But the day after the story broke, when Nikhil's name was on every news channel, Dev had given her a grave look and shaken his head. But he had said nothing more.

In the square of the window, flowers dipped and swayed. A wooden tray on the sill contained an assortment of mementoes whose significance had long been forgotten and now simply formed an attractive still life. A flat stone speckled blue, a piece of driftwood that might have been pilfered from Dev's house in Goa, a cork from the bottle of champagne that Dimple had brought on Ania's birthday, a signed photograph of Altaf Masood, cricketer-turned-politician. Propped up against the driftwood was a postcard from Saint-Tropez, an illustration of a woman getting into a boat, the tail of the scarf around her head fluttering in the breeze.

Ania sat cross-legged on the floor of her bedroom, bent over her laptop. She read for a third time the last paragraph that she had written. Some of it she recalled but most of it seemed alien, as if devoid of any connection to the rest of her novel and inserted there by some curious glitch in the software.

She scrolled to the end of the passage and held down the delete key, watching the blank page attack and devour her writing, word after word, line by line. It would have been easier to send the file to the trash but she wanted to put herself through the painful ritual of renunciation. She needed to bear witness to the sacrifice and experience the poignancy of the moment. On it went. She realized she had written far more than she'd thought. The cursor finally reached the first page. It annihilated her name and the title. There was nothing left. She put the laptop away and emerged onto the landing. Dina was speaking to someone at the front door. Ania wondered whether she should shed a few tears. Strangely, if there had been any sadness, it had passed and she was already beginning to feel a sense of relief.

Dev called up to her from the hallway, and she led him to the patio.

"Did you know? Dimple is getting married," she said.

"Really? Who to?"

"Do you remember Ankit? From that party ages ago?"

"Of course, she's marrying him?"

"He's a wonderful guy. Thoughtful and sweet."

"That's great, I'm really happy for her."

"Yes, me too. The wedding's quite soon. They can't bear to wait, I think. I'm sure they'll be brilliantly happy. I know exactly what I'm going to get them. And Dimple's going to need a lot of help with the organizing. The poor thing, her mum's completely useless in these matters."

They both stayed silent, and then she said, "It's going to be a wonderful wedding."

He put his hand on her arm but barely for a second.

It did come to pass as Ania thought it would, in some ways.

She would go to the wedding in a few months, bearing a lavish gift, giving Ankit a warm hug, throwing herself into the last drunken dance of the night, trying to hold back the tears as the final photographs were taken, unable to control the sense that something had been sundered, but determined that the friendship would not change, looking out at the silent city streets on her way home, the procession of streetlights bathing the world in amber, the music still echoing in her ears, her feet throbbing where her sandal straps had cut into them.

As she closed her eyes on the sweet melancholy of the night, she would have been horrified to learn that this was the last time she and Dimple would ever speak, and that they would, in fact, never see each other again. There would be good intentions and fond memories but nothing strong enough to overcome the inevitable drift and inertia. There would be no calculation, no subterfuge. It would be nobody's fault.

"Are you staying for dinner?" she asked Dev.

"I don't know. Your dad said he's nearly home, so I thought I'd say hello to him before I go."

"Okay. By the way, something I've been meaning to ask you for ages. I have this memory of lying on the grass, listening to you read to me. Something funny, we were both in stitches. And there were people playing tennis in the background. Did that really happen or did I dream it?"

"I remember that. It was in Landour, years ago. I was reading you the best bits of *Cold Comfort Farm*. We laughed so hard, we felt feverish and thought we had sunstroke. We went and sat in the pond, which looked beautiful but it was full of slime."

"Oh my God, yes, we did."

"What made you think of that?"

"I have no idea. It just sort of drifted into my head."

She reached out and touched his jacket.

"Look, your button's really loose. Do it up once more and it'll fall off," she said.

He put his fingers on the spot she had just touched, the seam firm against the soft wool. They both looked at the dangling button.

"Do you know where Sigmund is? Did you see him on your way in?" she asked.

"He's outside the kitchen door. Why?"

"I just need him. I'll see you if you're at dinner."

He watched her leave and then return with Sigmund nosing at her tracks, his face crumpled as though it had known only sorrow and adversity. He followed her up the stairs, and she pulled him gently into her room by the collar. The door shut, and the lock turned with a soft *click*.

He waited at the foot of the stairs, trying to make his mind up. A few seconds later he was outside her door. And it was a few seconds more before he knocked.

As SOON AS she opened the door, he stepped in and looked around as though searching for something.

"What have you lost?" she asked.

"Nothing, I just need to talk to you."

Sigmund lay on the floor and followed him warily with his eyes.

Dev walked to the desk, picked up a couple of books, and then put them down again. Moving to the French doors, he tried the handle, found that they were locked, and moved away again. He looked at a pair of sandals on an ottoman, lifted them up, seemed unsure how to proceed, and then put them down on the floor.

"I'm assuming you haven't come in here to tidy up. That would be totally out of character," she said.

"Sorry?" he said.

"Oh God, I know what this is about," she said, collapsing on the bed.

"What?"

"I don't know exactly, but I can guess. I've done something else, right? I've made some awful mistake and completely misread something or someone, well, maybe not completely but partially, but it's got a bit screwed up and you've come to tell me. Which, by the way, I do appreciate, although you might be surprised to hear that. But, could this please wait till tomorrow? It's just that at the moment I'm feeling, well, it doesn't matter what I'm feeling, but tomorrow, I promise, you can definitely tell me what I've done and what's happened and I promise you I will listen with total concentration and not say anything sarcastic and I'll try to fix it. Or not. If that would be better. Maybe not fixing would be the thing. We can totally discuss it. But not today, please? It's just that at the moment, I can't go through with it. I really can't. I'm so sorry. But tomorrow, for sure, come here after work? Or I could come to you? Whatever's easiest. Tomorrow we'll have that conversation. Would that be okay?"

He walked back to the desk and picked up another book.

"Why aren't you saying anything? You're beginning to freak me out. What have I done? Wait, don't tell me. Oh God, when did

everything become so difficult? Is it to do with Mimi Faujdar? Because, I swear, I haven't seen her for months. Not that I've been
avoiding her, it's just that we've both been busy. Is it to do with her?
Or someone else? No, actually, please don't tell me. I'll come over
tomorrow. I really will. We'll talk then. That'll be okay, won't it?"

He waved the book at her. She could see now that it was *Cold
Comfort Farm*.

"Is this the same copy that you had in Landour? When I read
to you that time on the grass? It looks old enough. Is it?" he asked.

"I think so. I don't know."

She propped herself up on her elbows and stared at him.

He walked toward the bed and then stopped. Opening the
book, he began to read from somewhere in the middle. His voice
filled the room. It was modulated and careful, almost cautious.
He did not look up from the page. She tried to remember what
had come before this point in the novel. But then gave up.

Sigmund closed his eyes, his breathing sounding deeper.

She looked at Dev as he read, every part of him becoming
more distinct. He had achieved a sort of solidity that made everything else seem a little insubstantial and watery. His lips moved
with great concentration. The gray flecks in his hair caught the
light. His free hand beat some mysterious rhythm against his
thigh. She felt ragged with delight.

Like the woman in the Vermeer painting, he too had dropped
out of time. But his absorption was different. It was as though he
was holding himself in abeyance, preparing for a much greater
task ahead.

He turned the page and read on. But he had turned more than
one page, and what he read no longer made sense. There was no

sign that he had noticed. He seemed suspended in this action, unable to transform its intimacy into anything else. It looked as though he would continue reading to the end of the book. She allowed him to keep going for a few seconds more.

Then she stood up and gently took the book from his hand.

AFTER DINNER WITH Ania and Dev, when he noticed that they were both unusually quiet and absorbed in their own thoughts, Dileep had a meeting with Mr. Nayak. He continued to plead with him to accept the retainer, offering him even more spectacular sums of money. He went from ingratiating to peevish to melancholic. The meeting drew to a close. For an instant, he saw on Mr. Nayak's face the deadly malice that the man could impel— but it was the briefest of moments and he immediately dispelled it from his mind. It was nothing, a tic, a trick of the light. Dileep would recall the moment only years later, in the dark foyer of the mansion on Prithviraj Road, when his dependence on Mr. Nayak was complete and his ruin was certain and imminent.

That night he went to bed reassured but then heaved and grimaced through one nightmare after another. In the early hours they coalesced into one terrible vision. When he opened his eyes, he was spent, immobilized like a patient after a lengthy bout of fever. The long juddering night had finally come to an end.

He managed to roll over onto his side and peered at the strange angles of the room. An empty carton of ice cream lay on the floor, trailing a dribble of congealed gloop. He remembered taking the carton from the fridge but did not remember bringing it upstairs and certainly did not remember eating all its contents. He forced himself out of bed and into the bathroom. Leaning over, he stuck two fingers down into the extremity of his throat. His retching sounded bestial and repulsive, even to him.

When he had finished, he staggered back and stopped at the door to his dressing room. On the table inside, there lay a slim black box. After three fittings, the shirt had finally arrived. He took the lid off the box and lifted the shirt out, holding it like an infant. He had spent many minutes deciding on every detail from the point collar and the soft front placket to the two-button cuff. The twill weave was of an oyster white. On the reverse side of the cuffs, faint silver lines streaked across the fabric like a spring shower, a detail that only his housekeeper and dry cleaner would ever see, but its existence gave him a great sense of gratification. The mother-of-pearl buttons glinted with a hint of lilac in the dim light. He ran his hand across the cool front of the shirt, before putting it back into its nest of tissue. He had reclaimed the day.

He opened the balcony door, and the curtain puffed with a little sigh. The sun dappled the tiles and had begun to warm the wooden balustrade. He put his hand on the back of one of the chairs, leaning on it with all his weight. The gardeners had already started sweeping leaves off the lawn, gathering them into neat piles. He heard the front door close and looked down on the driveway. Dev was leaving the house and walking toward his car. He must have spent the night. But it was too early in the morning for Dileep to puzzle out the reason. That would have to wait for later. The security guard closed the gate after Dev's car had left and returned to his booth to note down the time of departure.

Dileep began to feel much better. He thought of the plans he had made with Ania for the afternoon: they would watch a sentimental Hollywood film from the '30s or '40s in the screening room. He pretended to favor them more than he actually did, knowing how much Ania liked to curl up beside him, making arch comments, while he shushed her in mock annoyance. He played the part of an old romantic, and she seemed to be declaring that she did not believe in love, would never believe in it. These moments always appeared to foretell a happy and permanent companionship.

ON THE OTHER side of the house, Ania too had come out on her balcony. The tiles were cold against her bare feet, but a tender pulse warmed her. There was a delicacy about the morning: in the meek sunlight that touched the tops of the trees, in the hesitation of the birdsong, in the way she still wore the weight of Dev's arm across her stomach. He had left early but promised to be back in a few hours. His jacket still hung on the chair in her bedroom. They would spend the afternoon together, maybe even the evening.

She leaned forward, resting her elbows on the balustrade.

Stepping lightly across the dew-tipped grass was the pool boy, swinging a key on a cord, unable to stave off his morning yawns. He walked down the steps to the pool area and unlocked the cabana where the equipment was stored. At the edge of the pool he trailed the long-handled skimmer through the water in an elegant arc. He shook the collected leaves and twigs into a bucket and dipped the skimmer into the water again. A dark, speckled form floated past, and he scooped up the dead frog. He liked to stand as close to the edge as possible, toes curled against the pool's lip, leaning forward at a sharp angle, a tautness in his calf muscles, perfectly poised, reaching out as far as he could, the right kind of pull in his shoulders, almost like a dancer frozen for a brief instant. His sense of balance was superb, and he had never fallen in. He pulled a last frangipani petal toward him and looked at the water with evident satisfaction. It was a clear, placid blue.

ACKNOWLEDGMENTS

All my thanks to: Faiza S. Khan, Guy English, Madhu Jain, Georgina de Rochemont, Asad Lalljee, Felly Gomes, Aparna Jain, Mimi Wadia, Anushree Kaushal, Cibani Premkumar, Ranjana Sengupta, David Forrer, Helen Richard, Tara Singh Carlson, Juliet Mahony, Felicity Rubinstein, Sarah Lutyens, Rajni George, and Somak Ghoshal.